Dear Dad if you are
reading this I

love you!

Also by Derek Landy:

Derek Landy

HarperCollins *Children's Books*

First published in hardback in Great Britain by HarperCollins *Children's Books* 2011
HarperCollins *Children's Books* is a division of
HarperCollins*Publishers* Ltd
77-85 Fulham Palace Road, Hammersmith, London W6 8JB

Visit us on the web at www.harpercollins.co.uk

www.skulduggerypleasant.co.uk

Derek Landy blogs under duress at
www.dereklandy.blogspot.com

1

ISBN 978-0-00-732602-0

Typeset by Palimpsest Book Production Limited, Falkirk, Stirlingshire
Printed and bound in England by
Clays Ltd, St Ives plc

MIX
Paper from
responsible sources
FSC® C007454

This book is dedicated to my nieces.

Girls, none of you were born when Skulduggery Pleasant first appeared. But since you've arrived, no one in our family wants to talk about the *writer* any more. Now all they want to talk about are the damn *babies*. All of a sudden, no one wants to cuddle *me*, and for that I blame *you*.

But, I suppose you have your good points. It's because of you that Valkyrie has a little sister, after all. You're all mildly cute, reasonably adorable, and you make me laugh when you fall over.

So this book is dedicated to you, Rebecca and Emily, Sophie and Clara and

(insert names of any more nieces *or* nephews that might sprout up between now and when they're old enough to read this).

I know, beyond a shadow of a doubt, that I am your favourite uncle. And you probably prefer me to your parents, too.

(I've met your parents. I don't blame you. They're rubbish.)

PROLOGUE

The closing door made the candlelight dance, waltzing and flickering over the girl strapped to the table. She turned her head to him. Her face, like every other part of her, was decorated with small, pale scars, symbols painstakingly carved into her flesh over the course of the last few months. Her name was Melancholia St Clair. She was his secret. His experiment. His last, desperate grasp for power.

"It hurts," she said.

Vandameer Craven, Cleric First Class of the Necromancer Order, esteemed Scholar of Arcane Languages and feared opponent on the debating battlefield, nodded and patted her hand.

She had entered into this arrangement with the kind of zeal that only the truly greedy can muster, but recently her bouts of annoying self-pity were becoming more and more frequent. "I know, my dear, I know it does. But pain is nothing. Once our work is done, there will *be* no pain. You have suffered for all of us. You have suffered for all life in this world, in this *universe*."

"Please," she whimpered, "make it stop. I've changed my mind about this. Please. I don't want it any more."

"I understand," he said sadly. "I do. You're scared because you don't think you're strong enough. But I *know* you're strong enough. That's why I picked you, out of everyone. I believe in you, Melancholia. I have faith in your strength."

"I want to go home."

"You *are* home."

"Please…"

"Now now, my dear girl, there's no need for begging. The Surge is a beautiful, wondrous thing, and it should be cherished. You've taken your next step. You've become who you were always meant to be. We all go through it. Every sorcerer goes through it."

She gritted her teeth as a spasm of pain arched her spine, and then she gasped, "But it's not supposed to last so long. You said I'd be the most powerful sorcerer in the world. You didn't say anything about *this*."

Craven made the effort to look her in the eyes. He despised people who sweated, and the perspiration was rolling off her in heavy rivulets. It turned his stomach to look at her wet, dripping, scarred face. "With the power I promised you, you've just had to suffer a little more than the rest of us," he explained. "But all the work we've been doing, preparing you, it's going to be worth it. Trust me. The symbols I've etched into you are seizing the power of the Surge and they're keeping it, they're looping it around, letting it build, letting it grow stronger."

"Let me out."

"Just another day or so."

"Let me out!" she screeched, and shadows curled round her, rising and thrashing like tentacles.

He stepped forward quickly, gave her a smile. "But of course, my dear. You're absolutely right – the time has come."

Her eyes widened, and the shadows retreated. He doubted she was even aware of them. Strapped and bound as she was, she shouldn't have been able to wield any kind of power. For once, Craven's smile was genuine. This was a good sign.

"It's done?" she asked, her voice meek. "You're going to let me go?"

"Let you go?" he echoed, and gave a little laugh as he undid her straps. "You make it sound like I've been keeping you *prisoner*! Melancholia, I am your friend. I am your guide. I am the one person in the whole of the world that you can trust to always be honest with you."

"I... I know that, Cleric Craven," she said.

He took a handkerchief from his robes and used it to take hold of her wet, slippery arm in order to help her sit up. "We have to choose the right moment to tell the High Priest about you, but once we tell him what we've been doing down here for all this time, it's all going to change. Word will get out that you are the Death Bringer, and there will be many people vying for your favour. Trust none of them."

She nodded obediently.

"There will be some who won't understand," he continued, "even within the Necromancer Order itself. Whenever you feel unsure, or scared, or whenever you just want to talk – I'm here for you."

"I'm scared now," Melancholia said, her fingers closing around the skin of his wrist. It took all his self-control not to shiver with revulsion at her clammy touch.

He smiled reassuringly. "There's nothing to fear, not while you're with me. Rejoice, my dear. Very soon, you're going to save the world."

"Good and evil are so close as to be chained together in the soul."

Dr Jekyll and Mr Hyde (1941)

1

KENNY

enny Dunne wasn't an expert on cars. He knew enough, to be fair to him. He knew what wheels were. He knew how to open and close the doors. He even knew where to put the nozzle thing when the car needed petrol. He knew the basics, enough to get by, and nothing more. But even to a man like Kenny, smoke billowing from beneath the bonnet while you're driving is generally seen as a Bad Thing.

The car spluttered and coughed and retched, and Kenny's grip tightened on the steering wheel. "No," he said. "Please." The car belched and juddered in response, smoke filling his windscreen. Images flashed into his mind of the car suddenly exploding into a giant fireball, and he tore off his seatbelt and lunged out on to the sun-drenched street. Horns honked. Kenny jumped sideways to avoid a cursing cyclist who shot past him like a foul-tempered bullet. Dublin traffic on a Sunday morning wasn't that bad at all. Dublin traffic on a Sunday morning with a big game on was *terrible*. Irate drivers with county flags stuck to their cars glared at him as they were forced to change lanes.

Kenny smiled apologetically, then looked back at his car. It was not exploding. He reached in, grabbed his bag and turned off the ignition. The car wheezed and slipped gratefully into an early death. Kenny left it there in the street and hailed a taxi.

He was late. He couldn't believe he was late. He couldn't believe that he hadn't learned his lesson, even after all these years of being late to things. How many interviews had he messed up because of his inability to arrive on time? Actors, rock stars, politicians, business people, citizens both rich and famous and poor and unknown – he had been late to meet all of them. It was not a good quality in a journalist, he had to admit, especially when every newspaper was cutting back on staff. Print was dead, they were saying. Not as dead as Kenny was going to be if he didn't get the piece finished by the end of the month.

This story was juicy. It was glorious and bizarre and unique – the kind of thing that stood a chance of being picked up by other papers around the world, maybe even a few magazines. Whenever

Kenny entertained that possibility, his mouth watered. A solid pay day. Food in the fridge, no worrying about rent for a while. Maybe even a half-decent car, if he got really lucky.

He glanced at his watch. Fifteen minutes late. He bit his lip and tapped his fingers on his bag, willing the road ahead to miraculously clear. He didn't know how long his source would stick around, and if Kenny missed this chance, he doubted he'd get another. Tracking down Paul Lynch in the first place had not been easy, but then finding one homeless person in a city like Dublin was never going to be straightforward. And it wasn't like Lynch had a *phone* or anything.

The taxi crawled along to another set of traffic lights and Kenny almost whimpered.

It was probably unhealthy to pin so much hope on one article that hadn't even been commissioned, but there was really very little choice. Kenny needed a lucky break. He'd started off well, worked up to some high-profile interviews and articles, but then it all started to slide away from him. He could see it happening, but couldn't do anything to stop it. Now he was freelance, thrown the occasional job, but his editors left it up to him to go out and find the stories himself. And that's what he'd done.

When he'd first heard the rumours, years ago, he'd dismissed them. Of course he had. They were crazy. He wrote a few articles, noting the trend in the modern urban legend, but he'd never read more into it than that. But they persisted, these stories of strange people with strange powers doing strange things. Wonderful stuff, and not just the ravings of lunatics and paranoids and the disturbed. These stories were everywhere. They popped up occasionally on the Internet, then vanished just as fast. A few of the reports he'd followed up on had turned out to be hoaxes, with the person who reported the sighting now claiming to have no idea what he was talking about. He'd been close to forgetting the whole thing when he met Lynch. Lynch was Kenny's link. In all his years of casual investigation, Lynch was his one solid lead – as solid a lead as a muttering homeless man could be, anyway – and Kenny had a feeling he was ready to reveal everything he knew. Kenny had spoken to him three times already, and felt he was beginning to earn his trust.

Today was the day, he knew. If only he could get there in time.

The taxi stopped again and Kenny lost patience. He paid the driver, lurched out of the car, swung his bag over his shoulder and ran.

Twenty seconds of running and he was seriously regretting this move. He hadn't run in years. Good God, running was *hard*. And hot. Sweat formed on his brow. His lungs ached. He had shin splints.

He staggered to the next corner and hailed a taxi. It was the same taxi he'd just got out of.

"Didn't go too well for you, did it?" asked the driver smugly.

Kenny just gasped and panted in the back seat.

They finally reached the park and Kenny paid the driver, again, and hurried across the grass. There were people everywhere, stretched out in the May sunshine, laughing and chatting, walking and eating ice cream. Small dogs scampered after their owners. Music played. The pond glinted.

Kenny saw Paul Lynch, sitting in the shade away from everyone, and a smile broke across his face like a wave of cool water. He wiped the sweat from his brow and walked over, taking it slower, holding up a hand in greeting. Lynch didn't return the gesture. He just sat there, his back against the railing, shoulders slumped. He was probably in a bad mood.

If only he'd really *been* a psychic, then he'd have foreseen Kenny's late arrival and there wouldn't be a problem. Kenny's smile turned to a grin.

"Sorry," he said once he stepped into the shade. "The traffic, you know, and the car broke down, and I had to get a taxi."

Lynch didn't answer. He didn't even raise his head.

Kenny stood there awkwardly, then shrugged and sat down. "Glorious morning, isn't it? I swear, you can never tell how an Irish summer is going to turn out. Do you want an ice cream or something? I'd love an ice cream."

Again, no response. Lynch's eyes were closed.

"Paul?"

Kenny reached out and nudged his one solid lead. Nudged him again. Then he saw the blood that drenched Lynch's shirt, and he grabbed him and shook him. Lynch's head rolled back, revealing a throat with a long, smooth slit, like a red eye opening.

2

ME AND THE GIRL

Kenny sat in the interview room and tried not to fidget. He was mildly disappointed that there was no two-way mirror built into the wall, like he'd seen on cop shows. Maybe they only had two-way mirrors in America. In Ireland, the Guards probably didn't even have *one*-way mirrors.

The door to his right opened, and two people entered. The man was tall and thin, dressed in a dark blue suit of impeccable tailoring. He wore a hat like a 1940s private eye. He sat on the other side of the table and took the hat off. He had dark hair and high cheekbones. His eyes seemed to have trouble focusing. His skin looked waxy. He wore gloves.

His companion stood against the wall behind him. She was tall and pretty and dark-haired, but she couldn't have been more than sixteen years old. She was dressed in black trousers and a tight black jacket, zipped halfway up, made of some material Kenny didn't recognise. She didn't look at him.

"Hi." The man's smile was bright. He had good teeth.

"Hi," Kenny said.

The girl said nothing.

The man had a smooth voice, like velvet. "I'm Detective Inspector Me. Unusual name, I know. My family were incredibly narcissistic. I'm lucky I escaped with any degree of humility at all, to be honest, but then I've always managed to exceed expectations. You are Kenny Dunne, are you not?"

"I am."

"Just a few questions for you, Mr Dunne. Or Kenny. Can I call you Kenny? I feel we've become friends these past few seconds. Can I call you Kenny?"

"Sure," Kenny said, slightly baffled.

"Thank you. Thank you very much. It's important you feel comfortable around me, Kenny. It's important we build up a level of trust. That way I'll catch you completely unprepared when I suddenly accuse you of murder."

Kenny's eyebrows shot up. "What?"

"Oh dear," said Inspector Me. "That wasn't supposed to happen for another few minutes."

"I didn't kill Paul Lynch!"

"Could we go back to the nice feeling of trust we were building up?"

"Listen, I had arranged to meet him, I was going to interview him, but when I got there he was already dead."

"You'd be surprised how often we hear the 'he was already dead' defence in our line of work. Or maybe you wouldn't, I don't know. The point is, Kenny, it's not looking good for you. Maybe if you tell us everything you know, we can persuade our colleagues to go easy on you."

Kenny stared at the man, then looked over at the girl. "Who are you?"

She returned his look, raised an eyebrow, but didn't answer.

"She's here on work experience," said Inspector Me. "Don't you worry about her, Kenny. You just worry about yourself. What was your relationship with the corpse?"

"Uh," Kenny said, "I'm a journalist. He's someone I'd interviewed a few times."

"About what?"

"It's… nothing. He is, or he *was*, a conspiracy nut, kind of."

"Conspiracies? You mean like government cover-ups, that sort of thing?"

"No, not really. He was more…" Kenny sighed. "Listen, it's a long story."

"I don't have anywhere else to be," said Inspector Me, and glanced back at the girl. "Do you?"

"Yes, actually," she said. "I have a christening to get to."

"Oh," said Me. "Of course." He turned back to Kenny. "So maybe if you talk really fast, you can explain it to us."

Kenny took a moment, deciding on the best way to avoid sounding like a lunatic. "Right," he said. "For the past few years, I've been investigating some oddball stories. Nothing big, nothing major, but stories that get ignored because when you hear them, they sound insane. No newspaper is going to take this stuff seriously, so I can really only devote a small amount of time to them.

"It started when I did a piece on urban legends. You have all your usual stuff, modern myths and burgeoning folklore, some funny, some horrible, some creepy, everything you'd expect to hear. But I started hearing new ones."

"Like what?"

"Just rumours, snippets of stories. Someone saw a gunfight where people threw fire. Someone saw a man leap over a building, or a woman just disappear."

Inspector Me tilted his head. "So the modern urban legend is about superheroes?"

"That's what I was thinking, but now I'm not so sure. I've been hearing whispers about an entire subculture where this stuff goes on. Lynch said it's everywhere, if you know what to look for."

"I see. And did Lynch claim to be such a superhero?"

"Lynch? No. God, no. I mean, he wasn't well, obviously. He had visions, he said. That's what he called them, *visions*. He'd had them since he was a teenager. They scared the hell out of him. He was sent to psychiatrist after psychiatrist, given pill after pill, but nothing worked. He'd describe these visions to me and they seemed so vivid, so real. He couldn't hold down a job, couldn't maintain a relationship... He ended up homeless, drinking too much, muttering away to himself in doorways."

"And this," Inspector Me said, "was your source?"

"I know he sounds unreliable."

"Just a touch."

"But I stuck at it, listened to what he was saying. Eventually, I learned how to separate the ramblings from the... well, the facts, I suppose."

"What kinds of things did he see?" asked the girl.

Kenny frowned. He didn't really understand what gave a student on work experience the right to question him, but Inspector Me didn't object, so Kenny reluctantly answered. "He saw the apocalypse," he said. "He saw a few of them, to be honest. The first one concerned these Dark Gods, the Faceless Ones, whatever he called them. Someone banished them eons ago, nobody knows who, and they've been trying to get back ever since. When he was seventeen, Lynch had a vision in which they returned. He saw millions dead. Cities levelled. He saw the world break apart. He kept having these visions, and every time it would be some new aspect, some new viewpoint from which to watch the world end. He was convinced we were all going to die one night, a little under three years ago. He said these things, these god-creatures, would emerge through a glowing yellow door between realities. Of course no one would listen to him. And then the night came when the world was going to end… and it didn't. And the visions stopped."

"I love stories with a happy ending," Inspector Me said.

"It wasn't over, not for Lynch. More visions came to him. He predicted the Insanity Virus, you know."

"The last I heard it wasn't a virus," said the girl. "It was a hallucinogen. They got the guys who did it."

Kenny laughed. "You actually believe that?"

Inspector Me looked at him weirdly. "You don't?"

"It's all a little convenient, isn't it? As a Christmas prank, a radical group of anarchists drop a drug into the water supplies around the country – and then months later they come forward and admit to it? Anarchists, taking responsibility for their actions? That defeats the whole point of being an anarchist, doesn't it? Do you know when the trial is? Do you know which prison they're locked up in until it happens? Because I don't."

Inspector Me sat back. "This sounds awfully like a conspiracy theory, Kenny. What do *you* think happened?"

"I don't know, but Lynch said it wasn't anarchists that did this. He said it was little slices of darkness, flying around and infecting people."

To Kenny's surprise, neither the Inspector nor the girl smirked.

"Do you know how many people reported seeing strange things over those few days?" Kenny continued. "I've read dozens of reports. There was a nightclub in North County Dublin that was apparently swarmed by the things, but it wasn't even reported in the local paper."

"Sounds like a bunch of people hallucinating to me," said the girl.

"Lynch didn't think so. He had a vision of those things spreading out, infecting the world, making everyone do crazy things, kill each other, drop bombs..."

"All right then," said Me. "We have established that Lynch was psychologically disturbed, that he believed in a subculture of superheroes and evil gods. So why was he killed?"

Kenny blinked. "Uh, he was robbed, wasn't he?"

"Was he?"

"Wasn't he? That's what the... that's what the guy said, the Guard, the one who spoke to me. He said it looked like a mugging."

"I see."

Kenny frowned. "You think it's got something to do with his visions, don't you?"

"It's a possibility," said Me.

"Why were you meeting him this morning?" the girl asked.

"I'm sorry," said Kenny, "I don't mean to be rude, but why is she asking me questions? Why is she even here?"

"Work experience," said Me.

"You accused me of *murder*. Do you make a habit of bringing schoolgirls into interview rooms with murder suspects?"

Me waved a hand. "Oh, I was only joking about that. I don't *really* think you murdered anyone. Unless you did, in which case I reserve the right to say that I knew it all along. But she asks a good question, Kenny. Why were you meeting him?"

"For the past few months, he'd been having new visions, of shadows coming alive, of people dropping dead. His latest apocalypse."

"What did he say about it?"

"Why is this important?"

"Everything is important."

"But it's not like he identified anyone. It's not like he heard any names in his visions. He saw someone in a black robe, that's it."

"Male or female?"

"He couldn't say."

"Did he happen to mention the Passage at all?"

Kenny looked at him. There was something about the Inspector's face that wasn't quite right. As soon as Kenny noticed it, he looked away. His mother had taught him it was not polite to stare.

"He didn't use that word," Kenny said. "But I've heard it from others. How did you hear about it?"

"Who did you hear it from?" asked the girl.

"Others," Kenny said irritably. "Three or four people, who had overheard it in pubs or alleyways or whatever. It sounds like the Rapture, to be honest."

The girl frowned. "What's that?"

"The Rapture," Inspector Me said, "is a Christian belief in which God will collect the faithful and deliver them into Heaven. *'And the dead in Christ shall rise first: Then we which are alive and remain shall be raptured together with them in the clouds, to meet the Lord in the air.'* Those found unworthy will be left here on earth with the rest of the sinners."

"The Passage sounds like that sort of deal," Kenny said. "Mass salvation before the end of the world. Whether or not there's any kind of a god at work behind it, I don't know, but there usually is."

"Did Lynch give any kind of a time frame?" Me asked.

"His visions were getting stronger and more frequent," Kenny answered. "The way it worked in the past is that he'd have another six or seven days at this level of intensity, then the apocalypse wouldn't happen and he'd be able to relax again."

"Seven days," said Me.

"Or thereabouts, yeah. How did you hear about the Passage?"

"We're detectives," said Me. "We detect things."

"She's a detective as well, is she?"

"She's a detective-in-training."

"Look, this is all very, very weird. Why are you focusing on rumours and urban legends? You haven't even asked me any normal questions."

"Normal questions? Like what?"

"Like, I don't know, like if Lynch had any enemies."

"*Did* Lynch have any enemies?"

"Well, not that I know of, no."

"Then there really was no point in me asking that, was there? Unless you wanted to distract me. You didn't want to distract me, did you, Kenny?"

"No, that's not—"

"Are you playing a game with me, Kenny?"

"I don't know what you're—"

Inspector Me leaned forward. "Did you kill him?"

"No!"

"It'd be OK if you did."

Kenny recoiled, horrified. "How would *that* be OK?"

"Well," Me said, "maybe not *OK*, but understandable. Perhaps he said something that annoyed you. We've all been there, haven't we?" He looked back at the girl. "Haven't we?"

"I've been there," said the girl.

"We've all been there," said Me, looking at Kenny again. "We know how it goes. He says something that annoys you, you get angry, all of a sudden he's lying dead and you're wondering where *did* the time go."

"I didn't kill him! I didn't kill anyone!"

"Anyone? You mean there's more?"

"What?"

Me sat back, tapped his chin with a gloved hand. "You know what, Kenny? I believe you. You have an honest face. You have honest ears. So who do *you* think killed him?"

"I *had* thought it was just a mugging."

"And now?"

"Now… I don't know. Do you think someone killed him because of the Passage? Are there people out there who really believe in this stuff?"

"People are strange," said the girl, then started humming a few bars from the song.

"Did Lynch talk to anyone else about this?" Me asked. "Did he have any friends? Any family he still spoke to?"

"No, no one."

"So he only talked about his visions to you?"

Kenny hesitated.

"He's hesitating," said the girl.

"I see that," said Me.

"There's an old woman," Kenny said, "Bernadette something. Maguire, I think. She helps out at one of the shelters. She used to be a teacher, or something. She's retired now, lives in the country somewhere. He talked to her. She hasn't been around that much lately. I think she's just too old. The first time I'd seen her in months was a few weeks ago. She was talking to Lynch."

"You think he told her about his visions?"

"Yeah. I do."

"You think Bernadette Maguire killed him?"

"Uh... no. She's, like I said, she's old."

"Old people can kill people too."

"I know, but..."

"She could be a ninja."

"She's not a ninja, for God's sake. She's somebody's great-grandmother."

"I want you to think carefully about this, Kenny. Have you ever seen her with a sword?"

"What?"

"How about throwing stars?"

"This is ridiculous."

"Have you ever seen her *dressed up* as a ninja? That would have been my first clue."

The girl sucked in her cheeks so she wouldn't laugh out loud.

"What kind of cop are you?" Kenny asked, resolutely unamused.

"I am the kind that is determined to get to the bottom of this mystery," said Me.

The door opened, and a boy with blond hair poked his head in. Kenny was so startled by the way the boy's hair stood on end that he completely missed Inspector Me getting to his feet.

"Thank you for your co-operation," Me said, quickly following the girl out the door. "My colleague will be in to see you shortly." Out in the corridor, the girl held the boy's arm and reached for Inspector Me as he closed the door. It clicked shut, and all was suddenly quiet for a very brief moment.

The door opened again. A middle-aged man walked in, carrying a notebook. Inspector Me and his two teenage students were gone.

"Mr Dunne?" said the man. "My name is Detective Inspector Harris. Sorry to keep you waiting."

"Don't worry about it," Kenny said, a little doubtfully. "The other Inspector kept me busy."

Detective Inspector Harris smiled good-naturedly as he sat down. "Other Inspector?"

"The one who just left."

"Hmm? Who was that, then?"

"Detective Inspector Me."

"Detective Inspector You?"

"No, Me. That's his... He said that's his name. You just passed him. He was with a girl on work experience and a boy with spiky hair."

Harris blinked at him. "I didn't pass anyone, Mr Dunne, and I'm the only Detective Inspector on duty right now."

Kenny stared at him. "Then... then who the hell was I just speaking to?"

3

THE CHRISTENING

Valkyrie Cain cradled her little sister in her arms and hoped to God she'd get through the day without being splattered with regurgitated baby milk. She'd barely made it home from the police station in time to get changed, and one top had already been rendered unwearable before they'd even left the house. It had been a nice top, too. It had really gone with her jeans.

"Please," she whispered to little Alice, "do not throw up on me."

Alice watched her with big blue eyes, but wasn't promising anything.

Squinting slightly against the sun, Valkyrie glanced back into the church. Alice wasn't the only one who had just been christened today, so the place was full of chatting, laughing families with camcorders, saving every gurgle and wail. She may have been biased, but it was Valkyrie's sincere opinion that none of the other three babies were half as cute as her three-month-old sister. They just didn't measure up where it counted. It was sad, really. Those babies had already lost the cuteness war and they wouldn't even know it for years to come. A real tragedy.

She looked down at her sister. "You don't do much, do you? You're fairly limited, as far as most things go. Mum says I have to keep talking to you, to get you used to my voice. So, well, I suppose I'll keep talking. There are two of me, you know. There's me, the real me, and then there's my reflection. The reflection looks like me, and talks like me, and acts like me, but it isn't me. It steps out of my mirror and goes to school and does my homework and, yes, sometimes it babysits you. And I don't like that. I don't like leaving you in the care of something that has no emotions, but I'm a busy girl. Yes I am.

"When you're a bit older, we're going to read you stories about princesses and wizards and magic, and we're going to let you believe, for a few years, that some magic is real. And then, this is the sucky bit, we're going to tell you that most magic *isn't* real. We're going to tell you that people can't fly and they can't turn each other into toads and that there are no magical, mystical monsters. Between you and me, though, *that's* the big lie. There *is* magic, people *can* fly, there *are* monsters… I'm not sure about the turning each other into toads bit, though. But who'd want that anyway? That'd be gross."

Valkyrie started swaying the top half of her body slightly as she walked in a circle. "Who's a cutie? Who's a cutie? You are, that's who. You're a cutie. And who's sounding pretty dim-witted right now? That'd be me, wouldn't it? Yes, it would."

She looked down, saw the baby gazing up, and she laughed. "Oh God you're adorable. I'd ask you to stay like this for ever but, you know, that'd be a little awkward. Especially when you're old enough to go out on dates.

"We have a weird family, do you know that? You've probably already noticed. Mum's normal enough, in her own way. But when she gets talking to Dad, a different side to her comes out – an immensely silly side. He's a bad influence on her, that's what he is. Because our dad is an oddball. Mm-hmm. As odd as they come. Uncle Fergus is odd too, but not in a nice way. He's just mean all the time. It's a shame you never got to meet Gordon. You'd have liked Gordon. He was a cool uncle." She kissed the baby's cheek and kept her head down. "Want to know a secret?" she whispered. "Magic runs in our family. You might be magic. Someday you might be able to do all the things I can do. Someday you might have to take a new name, like I did. Or you might not. But I don't know if I want that for you. Being normal isn't so bad, once you've seen the other side. I know it wouldn't be fair if I kept this from you, but I don't want you getting hurt. Do you understand me? Something like that, it'd kill me."

The baby reached out, took a small handful of Valkyrie's hair.

"I'm glad we understand each other. For someone with such a small brain, you're very smart, you know that?"

Alice gurgled.

Valkyrie took her baby sister back inside the church, made her way over towards her folks. Her aunt emerged from the crowd, hair pulled back off her face, pinching it tight. It was not a good look.

"Hello Stephanie," Beryl said. "You're holding her wrong."

"She seems pretty comfortable," Valkyrie responded, making sure she said it politely.

Beryl reached out thin hands. "No no no, let me show you." But, as usual, Alice's spider-sense picked up the incoming threat and she turned her head, saw Beryl's suddenly smiling face and wailed. Beryl recoiled sharply, fingers twitching. When their aunt had retreated to an acceptable distance, Alice stopped wailing and glomped her gums on to a button on Valkyrie's top.

"She's been grumpy all day," Valkyrie lied, pleased with how things had turned out. Beryl made a noise in her throat, obviously unimpressed with her brand-new niece. Valkyrie jerked her head back slightly. "Mum and Dad are over there," she said. "They've been wanting to talk to you. Mum said earlier what a lovely dress you're wearing."

Beryl's eyebrows wriggled like two tiny tapeworms. "This?" she said. "But I've had this for years."

It was a beige dress that would have looked better on an eighty-year-old. *Any* eighty-year-old, man or woman.

"I think you've really grown into it," Valkyrie said.

"I always thought it was a little shapeless."

Valkyrie resisted the urge to say that was what she meant.

Beryl broke off the conversation as she usually did, without any warning whatsoever and with her husband trailing after her. Hilariously, Fergus nodded to the baby as he passed, as if Alice was going to nod back, but he reserved a look akin to a glare for Valkyrie. She hadn't a clue what *that* was about.

She watched Carol and Crystal walk towards her, and prepared herself for the onslaught to come. In the past, she would have been expecting poorly thought-out taunts and flatly executed jibes from her cousins at a time like this. These days, unfortunately, it was a whole lot worse.

"Hi Valkyrie," Carol whispered.

Crystal jabbed Carol with an elbow. "Don't call her that!"

Carol glared. "I whispered it. No one else could hear."

"You still shouldn't call her that! Call her Stephanie!"

A few more precious moments of life were sucked away from Valkyrie's grasp, never to be seen again.

"Fine," Carol said, not looking pleased. "Hello, Stephanie. How are you?"

"I'm doing good," Valkyrie replied, talking quickly in an effort to hijack the conversation and steer it towards calm and unexceptional waters. "How are you guys? How's college? Looking forward to the summer holidays? Crystal, I love your shoes. Your feet fit really well into them. Doesn't Alice look adorable?"

She turned slightly so that they could see the baby. They both murmured something about cuteness, and then it was as if Alice didn't even exist.

"We were thinking," Carol said, and both twins stepped closer so they wouldn't be overheard. "You know the way you said we were too short to learn magic? Well, we're not sure that we *are*. You started to learn magic when you were shorter than we are now, didn't you? And also, elves."

Valkyrie blinked. "I'm sorry?"

"Elves," said Crystal. "You know, with the pointy ears? They're pretty small, aren't they? I know in some movies they're regular-sized, but mostly elves are small, and *they* can do magic."

"Uh, elves aren't real," Valkyrie said.

Carol sighed at her sister. "*Told* you."

Crystal glared back, then looked again at Valkyrie. "Why aren't they real?"

"I'm not sure I can, uh, answer that."

Crystal looked confused. "What about goblins?"

"Oh," Valkyrie said. "Yeah, OK, goblins exist. Right, listen, it's not a height thing, it's a danger thing. The fact is it isn't safe. I've been beaten up more times than I can count. I've had bones broken and teeth broken and five months ago I was technically dead for half a day. I even had an autopsy done on me."

"What was that like?"

"Unsurprisingly unsettling."

Carol's eyes gleamed. "But you get to do magic, and save the world, and hang around with cool people."

"And have friends," Crystal added.

"And what do we get to do? We get to go to college and do exams and get spots and we don't get to have boyfriends."

Valkyrie attempted a smile. "I get spots too, you know. Everyone does. And you've both had plenty of boyfriends."

Crystal shook her head. "Not like Fletcher. He's nice."

"And I wouldn't call them boyfriends, either," mumbled Carol. "Stephanie, we just want what you have. We want to have fun and we want to have powers and do exciting things. We've been talking, and we've decided that we want you to teach us magic."

"I really don't think that's a good idea."

"And we really do."

"Even if I wanted to, I couldn't. I just don't have the time. Tanith is still out there, and she's got a Remnant inside her, and she's with Billy-Ray Sanguine and she knows much too much about my life and my family. I need to find her and get her some help, and I've also got to stop the end of the world and… It's just not safe to start showing you things."

"Just a few tricks," Crystal pressed.

"They're not called tricks," said Valkyrie.

"Illusions, then."

"They're not illusions."

"Spells?"

Valkyrie hesitated. "OK, you can call them tricks."

"Just show us a few small ones," said Carol, "like flying."

"Flying is not one of the small ones."

"Can you fly yet?"

"No, I can't. Skulduggery's the only one who can."

"Maybe *he'll* teach us."

Valkyrie couldn't help it, she had to smile. "I doubt that very much."

The twins suddenly started fixing their hair, and Valkyrie knew that Fletcher had arrived.

"Hello, ladies," he said to them while his left arm wrapped round Valkyrie's waist.

"Hi, Fletcher," the twins said in unison.

"Having a good christening?" he asked. "I've never been to one and I have to admit, it seems kind of... well, boring. But in a nice way."

"I found it really boring too," Carol said before Crystal had a chance. "And I didn't understand most of what the priest was saying."

"I wasn't even listening," Crystal said. "It was something about babies, I think. I really like your hair today. You have it sticking up really nicely."

"Don't encourage him," Valkyrie groaned. Fletcher laughed, and gave her a quick kiss.

"Unfortunately," he said, "we have to go for just a moment."

"We do?" Valkyrie asked. He nodded to her, all serious. "Ah," she said. "OK. Yeah. Guys, we have to go."

Carol's eyes widened. "Is there trouble? Are we in danger?"

"Is the world ending?" Crystal asked. The twins looked up at the church ceiling, like they were expecting to see it crack and fall in on top of them.

"Don't worry about it," Valkyrie said with a chuckle. She headed over to her parents, Fletcher beside her. "They *don't* have to worry about it, do they?"

He shrugged. "I'm sure they'll be OK for another few days."

"Did you find Bernadette Maguire's house?"

"Skulduggery's there right now, waiting for me to return with you."

She grinned at him. "Was it a nice drive?"

"It took two hours," he grumbled. "And he wouldn't let me speak. Do you know what it's like to be driving for two hours and not be able to speak?"

"No. What's it like?"

"It's boring."

She nodded. "I could probably have guessed that."

They reached her parents, and Valkyrie's mum lit up when Valkyrie passed her Alice.

"Here she is," her mum said, cooing at the baby, "my special girl."

"Oh, cheers," Valkyrie said, rolling her eyes.

Her mum laughed. "Hello, Fletcher, when did you get here?"

"I just arrived," he said. "Sorry. The bus service on a Sunday is awful."

"You should have called us – Desmond could have picked you up."

"No, I couldn't have," Valkyrie's dad said, stepping into earshot. "Sorry, Fletcher, but I had important fatherly duties to take care of, which included eating breakfast, showering and finding my trousers. Of those three, I only managed two. Without looking down, can you guess which one I missed?"

Valkyrie's mother sighed. "Des, it's too early in the day for your nonsense. Fletcher, will you be joining us for the post-christening lunch?"

"Yes, I will," Fletcher smiled back. "I just have to borrow Stephanie for a moment."

"Take our daughter," Valkyrie's dad said, waving his hand airily. "We have another one now."

Valkyrie laughed, leading Fletcher through the crowd. They left the church and walked round the corner. When they were sure they weren't being watched, Fletcher turned to her, kissed her, and the moment their lips touched, they teleported. The church and the grass and the sunshine vanished, replaced by a cottage being lashed by rain.

Valkyrie broke off the kiss instantly and leaped sideways to the Bentley, which was under the cover of a tree. Fletcher joined her.

"The sun is splitting the stones in Haggard," she said, glaring. "Don't you think staying dry will be kind of important for when we teleport back?"

"You make a good point," Fletcher conceded. "See, there's a reason why you're the girl and I'm the boy. You think about things, while I…"

"Don't?"

"Exactly," he said happily.

Skulduggery walked towards them from the cottage, his gloved hand raised to divert the rain around him. His suit was impeccable, his hat cocked just right. His face was sallow-skinned, but as he neared he tapped the two symbols etched into his collarbones, and his features flowed away, revealing the skull beneath. "Sorry to pull you away," he said to Valkyrie.

She shrugged. "I was there for the christening itself. Once that's done with, it's just a family get-together, and Christmas is enough for me. Is the old lady home?"

"I knocked on windows and doors, but there's no answer," he said. "We'll have to let ourselves in." Fletcher held out his hands, but Skulduggery shook his head. "Relying on teleportation is making us lazy, so we're going to do this the old-fashioned way. Valkyrie, would you mind keeping the rain off?"

He turned, started walking back to the cottage. Valkyrie hurried after him, raising her arms, moving the air into a shield.

"You should really get used to manipulating water instead of relying on air all the time," he told her. "One of these days you're going to wish you'd practised more. There's very little point in being an Elemental sorcerer if you only use two elements."

"But air and fire are the handiest," she said, pretending to whine. "Manipulating moisture just doesn't grab me that way. And as for earth..." She trailed off.

They reached the front door and Skulduggery knelt, working

the lock pick. Fletcher stood behind Valkyrie, trying to avoid the raindrops that got through her defence.

"And yet," Skulduggery said, "your Necromancy lessons are continuing without interruption, are they not?"

"Well, yeah, but I *need* more lessons in Necromancy because Solomon isn't as good a teacher as you are." He looked at her and she grinned, then shrugged. "Besides, most of the training I do with you these days is combat. I'll get the Elemental stuff back on track, I promise."

Skulduggery grunted. Ever since Tanith Low had been lost to a Remnant, he had changed what he'd been teaching Valkyrie. There was no way she'd be able to match Tanith's speed and agility, so going up against her using pure martial arts would end in disaster. The new stuff she'd been learning was ugly, brutal and effective – combatives, not martial arts. It had taken Valkyrie a while to adjust, but the threat of Tanith's return had spurred her on. A rematch was inevitable, she knew, so when she did go up against Tanith again, she was making damn sure that it wasn't going to be on Tanith's terms.

The lock clicked, and Skulduggery stood up and opened the door, then poked his head in. "Hello? Mrs Maguire? Anyone home?" He waited. No answer. He stepped inside, Valkyrie following. His hair suddenly in danger of getting wet, Fletcher hopped in after her. Aside from the steady rhythm of the rain, the cottage was quiet. It was orderly, and smelled of old person. Valkyrie took another step and the ring on her right hand grew colder.

"Someone's dead in here," she whispered.

Stepping slowly and carefully, they entered the living room, where small porcelain figurines lined every surface and an old woman sat in an armchair, very dead.

Skulduggery took out his gun.

"Wait a second," Fletcher said, his eyes widening. "Look at her. This was natural causes. She was old. Old people die. That's what old people do."

Skulduggery shook his head. "There was someone else here."

He motioned them to stay put, and left the room. Fletcher looked at Valkyrie searchingly, but all she could do was shrug. After a few moments, Skulduggery came back in and put his gun away.

"How do you know there was someone else here?" she asked.

He nodded behind him as he took a small bag of rainbow dust from his pocket. "Notice the figurines. Horrible little things, aren't they? Little cherubs, cheap and tasteless. See how they're so lovingly arranged, evenly spaced, all looking outwards? Now look at the ones beside you."

Valkyrie looked down. Fat little figurines, holding harps and little bows and arrows, were positioned haphazardly along the edge of the cabinet. "They fell," she said, "and someone put them back in a hurry. Someone who didn't care enough to face them all in the same direction."

Skulduggery broke up the lumps in the powder. He took a pinch and threw it into the air. It fell gently in a small cloud, changing colour as it did so. "Adept magic was used," he murmured. "Hard to tell what sort. But it was recent."

"How recent?" Valkyrie asked.

Skulduggery put the bag away. "The last ten minutes."

Fletcher glanced over his shoulder. "So the attacker could still be in the area?"

Skulduggery took out his gun again. "Always a possibility."

Valkyrie patted Fletcher's arm. "Don't worry," she said. "If the bad man comes, I'll protect you."

"If the bad man comes," Fletcher responded, "I'll bravely give out a high-pitched scream to distract him. I may even bravely faint, to give him a false sense of security. That will be your signal to strike."

"We make a great team."

"Just don't forget to stand in front of me the whole time," he said, and then yelled. Valkyrie jumped and Skulduggery whirled, and Fletcher pointed at the window. "Outside!" he blurted. "Bad man! Outside!"

Skulduggery charged, thrust his hand against the air and the window exploded outwards. He jumped through, Valkyrie and Fletcher right behind him. The rain pelted them, made the ground muddy. A bald man in black slipped on the trail that led into the woods, fell to his hands and knees. He cast a quick glance behind him. He had a long nose and a ridiculous goatee beard that ended in wispy trails far below his chin. He fumbled with something they couldn't see, and then sprang up. He slipped and slid, but kept on running, leaving a wooden box open on the ground behind him.

"Back," Skulduggery said. "Back inside the house. Move!"

Valkyrie went first, vaulted through the broken window, landing just as Fletcher teleported in. Skulduggery came last, flattening himself against the wall.

"Hide," he whispered.

They ducked down.

The rain battered the cottage. Valkyrie risked a look up at Skulduggery.

"What is it?" she whispered.

"It's a box," he whispered back.

"What kind of box?"

"A wooden one."

She gave him a look. "OK, I'll try this. Why are we hiding from a box?"

"We're not. We're hiding from what's *inside* the box."

"What's in the box?"

"Is it a head?" Fletcher asked.

"It's the Jitter Girls."

He peeked out. Valkyrie raised herself up slightly so she could see over the windowsill. The wooden box sat there on the trail in the mud and the rain.

"Who are the Jitter Girls?" she asked.

"Triplets," Skulduggery said. "Born in 1931. When they were six years old, something tried to get into this world through them."

"*Through* them?"

"It planted seeds in their minds, changed them mentally and physically. It dragged them just out of step with our reality, tried to make them a conduit through which it could emerge."

"What are we talking about here?" Fletcher asked. "A Faceless One?"

"No," Skulduggery said, "I don't think so. This was something else. Their parents panicked. Doctors couldn't help. Remember, this was Ireland in the 1930s, cut off and isolated from a world that was advancing around it. Everyone thought the children were possessed by the devil. They tried exorcism after exorcism, but the girls just got worse. Then I was called."

"Could you help?" Valkyrie asked. She took another peek. The box was still just a box.

"They were too far gone," Skulduggery said. "They spent a

year in agony, twisting and squealing while strapped to their beds in the asylum."

"Good God."

"Their parents came in every single day. They'd sing to them. Nursery rhymes and old Irish songs. There was nothing I could do. The thing, whatever it was that was using them, I think it realised its plan wasn't going to work. So it retreated. It went away, left them alone. They died soon after."

"That's terrible."

"It is."

"And so how are they in that box out there?"

Skulduggery shrugged. "They came back, didn't they? Any poor soul tortured like that isn't going to rest easy. They have too much pain to deal with by themselves, so they need to spread it around. That's what I think, anyway. The truth is nobody knows why they came back, or why they started killing people. But that's what happened."

"And they're in the box because…?"

"Everyone needs a home."

"I see. I'm not altogether sure, though, why we're hiding from them. If they can fit into that small box, how dangerous can they be?"

"It looks like you're going to see for yourself," Skulduggery said, his voice dropping back to a whisper.

Valkyrie peeked.

Impossibly, a pale hand emerged from the box. It trembled slightly as it lengthened, and it was an arm now, that curled. The hand gripped the edge of the box.

She ducked down.

"What's happening?" Fletcher asked.

"They're climbing out," Valkyrie said dumbly.

"If they're as dangerous as you say they are," Fletcher said to Skulduggery, "then let's go. Let's get out of here."

"They need to be contained," Skulduggery said. "That's why the killer brought them, to cover his escape. We can't leave – there's no telling what they'd do if they were allowed to roam free."

Valkyrie took another look. At first, she thought there was something wrong with her eyes. A girl climbed out of the box. A little blonde six-year-old, wearing a white dress with a bow, moving like bad animation. She was stiff, jerky, missing out the smooth motion between the lifting of the foot and the placing it down as she walked. There was no other word for it. She *jittered*.

Behind her, another pale hand emerged.

"How do we fight them?" asked Valkyrie softly.

"I don't know," Skulduggery said. "Fletcher. Go see China. She must have *something* in her books about fighting these things."

Fletcher shook his head. "I'm not leaving."

"It wasn't a request."

"Then come with me," Fletcher said. "Valkyrie, at least. I'm not leaving her here."

Valkyrie turned to him. "Yes you are. Go. Be quick."

He grabbed her. "I'm not—"

She took his hand off her. "We don't have time to argue. Do it. Go."

He stared at her, torn, then narrowed his eyes. "I'll be right back."

"I'll be waiting."

He didn't even kiss her – he just vanished.

Valkyrie turned back to the window. "Hell," she breathed.

All three Jitter Girls were out, and all three were walking towards the cottage.

4

CRAVEN

raven walked into the High Priest's office with his head bowed.

"Late again, Cleric?" said Auron Tenebrae, High Priest of the Order, Patriarch of this Temple and a man with a gaze so withering the sun itself dared not show its face when he was in one of his moods. Or so the legend went. "This is the third time this week. If our little meetings are too much of an imposition for you, please let it be known and we will surely reschedule around your most arbitrary of whims."

Craven bowed again. "My deepest apologies, Your Eminence.

I have no excuse for my tardiness, other than I work without cease for the good of the Order."

"And I'm sure we appreciate it," Tenebrae said, already sounding bored.

Craven bowed so low his back hurt. He hated the High Priest, hated the distaste that flowed from him daily. A constant stream of snide remarks over the years, collecting in a vast reservoir inside Craven's mind that he was never going to forget, and was certainly never going to forgive. No matter the flattery he offered, the compliments, the fawning, all he got in return was this river of barely concealed contempt. The worst of it was that Tenebrae made no effort to confine this contempt to moments when they were alone. Standing at the High Priest's shoulder was Nathanial Quiver, Cleric First Class of the Necromancer Order, stringent Keeper of the Law and a man who seemingly possessed no facial muscles that would enable him to smile. Any such muscles, Quiver probably thought, would be put to better use on a good frown.

"Cleric Wreath," Tenebrae said, "you may continue."

And the last of Craven's supposed peers, the last to witness this constant belittling – Solomon Wreath. Cleric First Class of the Necromancer Order, infamous Field Operative and notorious trouble-maker, standing there in his tailor-made black suit while the rest of them wore proper Necromancer robes.

Craven had a special place of hatred reserved for Solomon Wreath, down deep in his heart.

"I believe Valkyrie is about to make a breakthrough," Wreath said, and Craven's eyes widened in alarm. "She's becoming more proficient at Necromancy with every lesson. She's taking giant steps now, progressing faster and faster. If she continues like this, I'm confident that she will choose Necromancy over Elemental magic when it's time for the Surge."

"I see," said Tenebrae. "And how has Pleasant reacted to this?"

Wreath allowed himself a smile. "They've argued about it enough, so he's not saying anything for the moment. He trusts her to find her own way, and so do I. It's just that I think *her* way will be *our* way."

"And you think she's safe out there, with Lord Vile on the loose?"

Wreath hesitated. "I think she's as safe with Skulduggery Pleasant as she'd be anywhere. Besides, Vile hasn't been seen since he attacked Pleasant in the Sanctuary. He may well have vowed to kill the Death Bringer, but for all we know, he won't be returning."

Craven coughed lightly, and waited till they were looking at him. "Forgive me," he said, "but I fail to see how any of this is a noteworthy development. We do not *all* believe that Valkyrie Cain will be the Death Bringer, Cleric Wreath. Some of us, in this room, believe she's just another unexceptional girl."

"Unexceptional?" Wreath echoed. "This girl is but a few months away from her seventeenth birthday and already she has saved the world and killed a god. What have *you* done?"

Tenebrae chuckled and Craven bristled. "What I mean to say is that while she may have the makings of a fine sorcerer, I have yet to be convinced that she will ever have the power to become the Death Bringer and initiate the Passage. And even if she *does* have that potential, she is, as you say, not even seventeen. She won't experience the Surge for another three or four years. You want us to wait four years to see if she *might* be strong enough?"

"You have an alternative to waiting?" Wreath asked. "Did someone invent a time machine while I wasn't looking?"

"Your sarcasm notwithstanding, I think it would be a mistake to put too much faith in a girl so heavily under the influence of Skulduggery Pleasant. Besides which, we have plenty of our own candidates. Take my protégée, for example. I believe that Melancholia St Clair has been showing signs of definite—"

"Melancholia?" Tenebrae interrupted. "You're still insisting on her? Cleric, I haven't seen anything special about that girl at all. The only extraordinary quality she seems to possess is the ability to look extraordinarily annoyed whenever I see her. Which hasn't been for quite some months now."

"Begging your pardon, High Priest, but I have been spending a lot of time as her personal tutor, and I think she could be the one."

Tenebrae sat back in his chair. "You're tutoring her?"

"Yes, High Priest."

"But I thought you wanted her to *excel*," Tenebrae said, laughing while Wreath smirked. Craven's face burned, but he managed a grateful smile nonetheless.

"Waste your time however you want," Tenebrae said, waving his hand. "But right now, the Cain girl seems to be the one viable possibility we have. No other Temple around the world has any candidates of worth. All eyes are resting on us. Cleric Wreath, I hope she doesn't let us down."

"As do I, Your Eminence," Wreath said, nodding instead of bowing. Tenebrae didn't seem to mind.

Craven stormed into the depths of the Temple, replaying the conversation in his head, substituting the things he had said with the things he wished he had said. They were so much better, all the caustic witticisms that occurred to him afterwards. They made him sound strong and smart and in control. In his imagination, he never blushed.

He reached the heavy wooden door, and spent a few moments calming himself. Tenebrae's days were numbered, as were Wreath's. Quiver, he wasn't so sure of. Quiver never mocked him. Quiver never mocked anyone.

He entered the room, and Melancholia raised her head.

"I'm tired," she said. She spent half her time tired. The other half was spent pacing the floor, practically crackling with energy. It was either one or the other – extremely powerful or extremely weak. Craven had wanted another few days to run more tests, to find the source of the instability and purge it, but his patience had run out.

"It's time," he said. "I'm presenting you to the High Priest. Clean that sweat from your face and follow me."

"I don't feel well," she said, almost whimpered.

"*I don't care!*" he roared, and grabbed Melancholia's arm, yanking her to her feet. "They will *not* laugh at me again! No one will *ever* laugh at me again! We will wipe the smiles from their smug faces and they will worship you and obey *me*!"

She looked at him fearfully, with tears in her eyes, and he caught his anger and quelled it. He couldn't afford to lose her. He couldn't afford to lose the trust he had spent so long building up while he was carving those symbols into her flesh and listening to her scream.

"Don't be afraid," he said softly. "I'll be with you. No one will hurt you while I'm with you. You're a very special girl, and I love you as I would my own daughter."

Melancholia nodded bravely, and he gave her a gentle smile as he led her to the door. What he'd said was quite true – he did love her like a daughter. He had a daughter, somewhere in the world, and he absolutely and without reservation despised her.

5

THE JITTER GIRLS

alkyrie and Skulduggery backed away from the window.

The first Jitter Girl approached in that awful, messed-up, stop-motion way, moving slowly, her face blank. She reached the wall and vanished, and was suddenly inside the cottage with them.

Skulduggery's hand closed around Valkyrie's wrist. "Don't move," he whispered. "Don't look at her."

Fighting the urge to run, Valkyrie stayed where she was and kept her eyes down. The Jitter Girl flickered into her peripheral vision. Her heart thundered in her chest like hoof beats. The Jitter

Girl paused, maybe to examine the porcelain figures on the sideboard. Valkyrie's hair was wet. Her jeans were damp and her top was sticking to her. She was aware of all of this as she stood perfectly still. One of the Jitter Girl's sisters moved slowly by the window.

The Jitter Girl passed behind Valkyrie, out of her line of sight. Valkyrie had never wanted to turn round so much in her life. Goosebumps rippled her flesh.

There was a mirror on the wall. Valkyrie could see Skulduggery and herself reflected on the edge of the glass. Her mouth was dry. In the mirror, she saw a pale hand slowly reaching for her own.

Skulduggery grabbed her, twisted her away, the air rushing as they hurtled through the broken window without finesse. They landed in the mud and scrambled up, a Jitter Girl on either side. The Girls grew as they came forward. Every flash made them bigger, made them older, made their hair paler and wilder. Their faces changed, from pretty and blank to contorted and tortured. Lines appeared on smooth skin. Mouths opened, lips cracked and white teeth became yellow, became brown, became blackened, and still they came forward.

Skulduggery's gun went off, again and again, the bullets passing through the flickering creatures. Valkyrie hurled fire, threw shadows, but the Jitter Girls, all three of them now, advanced impervious.

Skulduggery was yanked from Valkyrie's side. One of them had him, her fingers pressing into his clothes, sliding between his ribs. He screamed.

Valkyrie lunged for him, but slipped, splashing down in mud and muck, her hair in her eyes, calling his name. And then one of them was right in front of her, standing over her, her hand pressed against Valkyrie's forehead, pressed into her skin. Valkyrie screamed as the fingers melted into her skull, poked through her brain. White daggers of blinding light seared across her mind. Her body seized up and her jaw locked. She couldn't move, couldn't speak, couldn't think. Images played in darkness as the little girl-monster wriggled her fingers. Images and memories, sensations and emotions, mixing up, matching up, latching on to each other, splitting off from each other, and still the little girl-monster played, curious, sifting through the insides of Valkyrie's mind like she was looking for something, searching for someone, and she found it, found it waiting, found it watching. Found it ready.

Valkyrie went away, and Darquesse wrapped her hand around the little girl-monster's wrist and she crushed it as she pulled the fingers from her mind.

Darquesse stood, still holding on to the wrist. The Jitter Girl screeched and contorted and jittered, but her arm remained in Darquesse's grip. Darquesse watched her, fascinated. She poured magic out through her fingers and the little girl-monster returned to her normal size and screamed. It was like no human scream. It was like no animal scream. It was the scream of a creature who had never felt the need to scream before. It was new, and raw, a freshly born thing of exquisite agony and sudden, overwhelming fear.

Darquesse dropped her. Another was coming, jittering across the mud, eager to play, and there was so much magic in Darquesse's veins, broiling and coiling and boiling inside her, that she just had to share it. The power leaped from her hand in a twisting, turning stream, crossed the distance between them and washed over the Jitter Girl, taking her off her feet. Unable to escape the flow, the little girl-monster squirmed and kicked and writhed in the mud, and Darquesse increased the intensity until she became bored of the screeches.

She turned to the last little girl-monster, who held her gaze for a moment before releasing Skulduggery. He fell, gasping. The Jitter Girl returned to her normal size and shape, regarding Darquesse with those wonderfully blank eyes, then moved to the box. Her sisters dragged themselves, in that flickering manner, to join her, and one by one they climbed back inside. Once all three were in, the top of the box closed over.

Darquesse turned back. Skulduggery Pleasant got to his feet, his exquisite suit covered in muck. His hat was in the mud somewhere, and the rain ran off his gleaming head.

"Hello," he said. "I've been waiting for you."

Darquesse smiled, walking towards him.

"You're very impressive," he continued. "That's a kind of magic I don't think I've ever seen, and I've seen every kind of magic. You are quite the curiosity, aren't you?"

Darquesse could have turned his bones to splinters where he stood.

"Is she in there?" Skulduggery asked. "Valkyrie? Can she hear me?"

Darquesse said nothing.

Skulduggery's head tilted. "Are you going to let her come back? That's her body you're wearing. That's her face you're using. You can't keep her sleeping for ever. It isn't your time yet. This is still Valkyrie's time. She gets to walk around. She gets to live. Not you."

She could see his consciousness. It formed a shell around his skeleton, a shell of multicoloured lights. It sparkled prettily. This shell was how he thought. This shell was how he felt. When he had pulled himself back together, all those hundreds of years ago, he recreated himself in a form that only she could see. She reached out and gently dug her fingers into the shell of light. Skulduggery gasped and went rigid. She turned her hand, twisting his consciousness, feeling and understanding how she could tear through it or pull it away, shred it to pieces or turn it to vapour.

What she held, buzzing, between her fingertips, was life itself. It was a wonderful thing, a glorious thing. She released him and he staggered back, but she was already forgetting he was there.

She rose off the ground, into the rain-filled air, floating high above the cottage. She could see across the countryside from here, to the city in the distance. She wondered how easy it would be to turn the whole city to dust. Probably not that hard. Not if she focused.

Somebody rose up to meet her.

"I want Valkyrie back," Skulduggery said. "Give her back right now. I'm not going to ask again."

Darquesse smiled at him. She liked him, she really did. He was unique. She didn't want to kill him. Not yet. Not when there were still ways for him to amuse her.

Darquesse went away, and when Valkyrie blinked her wet hair was in her face and she was falling to the earth.

"Bloody hell!" she hollered.

Skulduggery swooped down, caught her, held her close as he descended.

"No need to shout," he told her.

She clutched him tightly. "What's happening? How'd we get here?"

"You don't remember?"

"How I got into the bloody sky? No, I don't bloody..." She trailed off. "Oh, wait. I do. It was her."

"Indeed it was."

She sagged in his arms. "Great," she mumbled.

They touched down. Valkyrie swayed on her feet a moment then nodded, and they walked over to the wooden box.

"So that's it, then?" she asked, a headache starting up behind her eyes. "She can just come and go whenever she likes? Every time things get too dangerous, am I just going to Hulk out, change into the person who's going to kill the world?"

"I don't think it's quite so simple," Skulduggery responded. "From what I could see, the Jitter Girl literally had her hand inside your head. That would shake *anything* loose. And I know you don't want to hear it, but Darquesse did save us."

Valkyrie folded her arms, shivering. "You're right. I don't want to hear it."

"*You* saved us, then. Does that sound better?"

Valkyrie glared at him through the rain. "I had nothing to do with it."

"Yes, you did. You *are* Darquesse, Valkyrie. Darquesse isn't a different person, no matter how many times we talk about her like she is. At its simplest level, Darquesse is a state of mind."

"I'm sorry?"

"She's you, without your conscience, or your feelings. She's you without your humanity."

"You're saying she's a mood swing?"

He shrugged. "Or maybe you are *her* mood swing."

"Don't even joke about that."

Skulduggery picked up the wooden box and they started back towards the cottage. "I'm not joking. The fact is we have no way of knowing if the person who we *think* we are is at the core of our being. Are you a decent girl with the potential to someday become an evil monster, or are you an evil monster that thinks it's a decent girl?"

"Wouldn't I *know* which one I was?"

"Good God, no. The lies we tell other people are nothing to the lies we tell ourselves."

"You have an amazing ability to depress me sometimes, you know that?"

"I try my best." Skulduggery gestured, and his mud-soaked hat rose into his hand. He gazed at it forlornly. "How are you feeling?"

"Headachy. But fine. Bad man got away."

"Yes, he did."

"He killed Paul Lynch and now the little old lady Lynch confided in. Somebody doesn't want us to know anything about the Passage. You think he was a Necromancer?"

"Even though dressing in black is in no way an indication – yes, I quite do."

She nodded. "Me too. Plus, he had a ridiculous beard. I should probably ask Solomon about him."

"I should probably help."

"No hitting."

"A small amount of hitting."

Fletcher lunged out of thin air before them, his eyes wide, fists clenched, ready to fight. He looked at them, spun round, spun back again.

"Where are they?" he asked.

"Back in the box," Valkyrie told him. "Did you find out anything?"

"China wasn't at the library," he said, the rain flattening down his hair. "Nobody there could help me. How did you beat them?"

"With unimaginable skill," Skulduggery said. "Valkyrie, I've got a two-hour drive back to Dublin where dry clothes await me."

She nodded. "I'll be ready."

He walked to the Bentley. Fletcher turned to Valkyrie, hands loosely holding her arms. "I didn't want to leave," he said quietly.

She smiled. "I know."

"You should have come with me."

"Let's not ruin a nice moment by arguing, OK?" She kissed him.

He sighed, and instead of rain on her face there was sunshine, and instead of being outside a small cottage with a broken window they were behind a tree in her back garden. "Much better," she murmured. Dripping wet and covered in mud, she took Fletcher's hand and they stepped out from behind the tree.

Her parents, cousins, aunts and uncles, friends and neighbours, people she'd known all her life and people she'd never met stood around the barbecue pit and stared, their chatter dying away.

"Uh," said Valkyrie.

6

CHINA'S SECRET

n Monday morning, China Sorrows walked the weed-strewn gap that led to the Church of the Faceless. She entered without knocking, found the head of this little chapel on his knees with his eyes closed, praying. A small man who greatly resembled a weasel – Prave, his name was. She didn't know his first name and she didn't care. She'd been here only once before, and by the time she left she had blood on her hands and a gun to dispose of.

"Curiosity," she said, and Prave's bulbous eyes snapped open and he jumped to his feet. "That's what brought me here. Who, I wondered, would be audacious enough to summon *me* to a squalid little house of worthless worship such as this? Surely, I told myself, it can't be this man Prave, this snivelling little toad-person with a penchant for bad suits and terrible shirts."

"What… what's wrong with my shirt?" he burbled in a Yorkshire accent, his voice a nasal whine that triggered a primal urge within China's psyche to hit something.

"It's orange," she told him. "It can't be him, I thought. The man has no backbone to brag about, no spine to speak of. Who, then? Who is pulling the strings of the weasel-faced toad-person? So it is curiosity that brings me here, Mr Prave. Unveil your hidden master or risk me growing bored. I do terrible things when I grow bored."

Prave stared at her with those round, wet eyes of his, and China heard slow, measured footsteps in the other room – high heels on wood. China knew who it was instantly.

Eliza Scorn walked through, dressed in black trousers and a jacket. She had left her long red hair to fall round her face, framing those cheekbones, those lips. Many men had fallen in love with Eliza Scorn, and then instantly forgotten her when China walked into the room. That was only the start of the animosity between them.

"China," Scorn said, smiling.

"Eliza. What a surprise."

"Please. I bet you've known I was back for months, haven't you?"

"I may have heard talk."

"And you didn't try to get in touch? We could have met up, talked about the old days, traded gossip. Who's alive, who's dead, who's about to die, that kind of thing."

"My apologies, Eliza. I've been very busy."

"Of course, of course, with the library. I must call round, see how it looks. How have you been? You're still as beautiful as ever."

"As are you, my dear. I love your shoes."

"Aren't they delightful? I saw them and just had to have them. Their previous owner wasn't too keen to let them go, but I can be very persuasive when I want to be."

"Is that her blood on the left one?"

"And no amount of scrubbing will get it out, either. I hear you are still a treacherous heathen, then? Your back is still turned to the Dark Gods?"

"Both firmly and resolutely. I met some of them, a few years ago. Not very nice, to heathen and disciple alike."

Scorn shrugged. "If the Faceless Ones deemed those disciples to be unworthy, so be it. We'll just have to make sure that the rest of us are worthy of their love the next time they return."

"The next time? Oh, my dear Eliza, you're not going to carry on with this, are you? The Faceless Ones had their chance. They returned, and they were sent away again. It's time to move on. Time to take up another hobby, like crocheting, or serial-killing."

"Nonsense. Their return, however brief, was a signal that it can be done. We just need better organisation."

"And you are going to provide that?"

"Naturally. The Church of the Faceless is going to have to expand, of course. We can't be seen to be congregating in run-down old chapels like this. We need to appeal to a higher level of patron. Which is where you come in."

"Now this should be fascinating."

"We need your resources to get us started. Not just money, although we'll be taking that too, but your contacts. The people you know, China. They are what we want. They can get us what we need. It's going to be glorious, let me tell you."

"Eliza, I don't wish to be rude, but… actually, no, I don't really care. Eliza, I came here today to find out who would have the audacity to summon *me* anywhere. If it had just been that weasel-faced gentleman cowering in the corner, he would be begging for forgiveness right about now. But as it's you, seeing as how we are such good friends, I will simply depart. It was lovely seeing you again."

"Prave," Scorn said, "why don't you step forward like a good little weasel, and tell China what you told me?"

Prave stepped up, coughed, brushed the dust from his knees. "A year and a half ago," he said nervously, "you had just left here. I watched you go."

There was a part of China that immediately tensed, but all she did was brush a strand of hair back over her ear, and wait patiently.

"You met Remus Crux outside," Prave continued. "You were talking. He looked, he looked agitated and… I went out and hid behind the wall. I heard what he said, before you shot him."

"Do you remember what Crux said?" Scorn asked China. "I bet you do. He said that you handed Skulduggery Pleasant's wife and child over to Nefarian Serpine. He said that you led them to their deaths."

China looked at them both, and nodded slowly. "I see," she said.

Scorn smiled again. "Look at her face, Prave. Isn't it a beautiful face? Isn't it the most beautiful face you ever did see? But beauty is so deceptive. Looking at her now, you'd never guess that she was calculating the most efficient way of killing us, would you? There's not a hint of that in those startlingly pale blue eyes. If we didn't know better, we'd still be gazing at her, falling in love all over again, and she could walk right up and stab us through the heart, and we'd never see it coming. All because of that beautiful face.

"But we do know better, don't we, Prave? We know better because I know China. I've known her a long, long time. We were inseparable once. We did everything together. We were so close we could practically read each other's minds."

"Can you read my mind now?" China asked.

Scorn laughed. "I don't even need to, dear China, and I know you don't need to read mine. Blackmail is such an ugly, ungainly word, but these are ugly and ungainly times in which we live. You will do as I say, *exactly* as I say, or I will tell the Skeleton Detective your terrible, terrible secret. Do you agree to my terms?"

"I really can't see that I have any other choice, now do I?"

"No, you really don't."

"Then I agree to your terms," said China. "I'm usually the one doing the blackmailing, so at the very least it will be interesting to experience it from the other side."

"I'm glad you're taking this so well."

"Oh, dear Eliza, we are professionals, are we not? To allow something like this to get personal would be an unforgivable lapse of character. By the way, I was lying earlier. Those shoes are horrible on you."

Scorn laughed, and shook her head. "Oh, China. I have missed you."

"And I have missed you, Eliza. But don't worry. Next time, my aim will be better."

Scorn clapped her hands. "Delightful! Delightful!" With her hands clasped over her chest, she walked from the room. "We'll be in touch, my love! And you'll remember the way it used to be – Scorn and Sorrows, together again! The world will tremble!"

China watched her go, then turned and left the church without even glancing at Prave. The moment she stepped into the open air, her eyes narrowed and her jaw clenched.

China spent the next few hours sitting in her apartment, running through scenarios in her head. Her only option seemed to be to kill Eliza Scorn, but even this had its problems. For one thing, someone as resourceful as Scorn would certainly have found a way to release the incriminating information in the event of her untimely demise. For another, the actual physical act of killing her would not be easy. Scorn was a formidable adversary, and not one China would be confident of taking down on her own. The main problem in all of this was that China had a lot to lose, while Scorn had virtually nothing. This automatically put China in the weaker position. And if there was one thing China hated, it was a weak position.

Someone knocked on the door and China looked up, waved at the symbol carved into the doorframe. A section of the door turned translucent from her side, and she saw Valkyrie exchanging a few words with Skulduggery before he went into the library and she turned back, continuing to wait. Neither seemed particularly furious, so China deemed it safe to open the door.

"Hello, my dear," she said, greeting Valkyrie with the warmest smile she was capable of. "Come in, come in. Let us talk of important things before Skulduggery disturbs us. You look as beautiful as ever."

Valkyrie smiled in response and walked in, wearing her usual black. "You should have seen me yesterday," she said. "Myself and Fletcher turned up at my sister's christening dripping with mud."

"Irish weather is not kind to teleportation. How did you manage to explain it?"

"Sprinkler system, flower beds, a lost dog – it wasn't easy, but eventually we bombarded everyone with enough conflicting details that they figured it was easier to just let us get away with it."

"Ah, the curse of maintaining a secret identity," China said.

Valkyrie sat at the elaborately carved eighteenth-century table – what was commonly referred to as an antique, even though China was much older. "We went up against the Jitter Girls," Valkyrie said.

China's eyebrow rose fractionally. "How did you escape?"

"Skulduggery and I managed to get them back in the box."

"My word, that *is* impressive."

"We're trying to identify the man who released them."

"I am sorry, Valkyrie, I can't help you. The last I heard of the Jitter Girls, they'd been seen in New Zealand, but this was maybe ten years ago. I have no idea who would have had access to them since then. Of course, when I said we should talk of important things, that is not quite what I had in mind."

Valkyrie laughed softly, and crossed her legs. "You want to know about Fletcher."

"But of course. Some people watch television for their vicarious thrills. All I need do is talk to you. How *is* Fletcher these days? Apart from muddy?"

"He's grand."

"Still annoying you?"

"Sometimes."

"And how is this mysterious *other* person?"

Valkyrie's head dropped. "I wish I hadn't told you about that."

"Oh, come now, you've barely told me anything. Today is the day when you reveal all, though. I can feel it. Do I know this person? Boy or girl?"

"Boy," she said, then frowned. "Well, I don't know if you'd call him a boy. Male. Definitely male. I don't know what I'm... When I say there's someone else, I don't mean it's someone I'm going to dump Fletcher *for*, but... Doesn't the fact that there *is* someone else mean something? Doesn't it mean that my feelings for Fletcher aren't as strong as..."

"As his feelings for you?"

"Well, yeah."

"But that was always going to be the case, was it not? That he would feel more deeply for you than you did for him?" China sat down. "I'm enjoying this immensely, by the way."

Valkyrie looked quizzical. "Enjoying what?"

"I've never had any children," China said, "and I haven't had a friend in centuries. To me, talking like this is wonderful. So tell me the truth now – have you committed the cardinal sin?"

"Uh, that depends," Valkyrie said warily. "What's the cardinal sin?"

"Have you told Fletcher you loved him?"

"Oh," Valkyrie said, sagging again. "Yes."

"Oh my."

"It was ages ago, but... I didn't mean it like that. Not really. But I said it, and he took it to mean that I'm *in* love with him. I haven't mentioned it since. I just... I don't know."

"Are you playing with Fletcher's heart, my dear?"

"I'm trying not to."

"And this other man?"

"I've no interest in a relationship with *him*, either," said Valkyrie.

"Either?"

"Sorry?"

"You said you have no interest in a relationship with him, *either*. Implying that you have no interest in a relationship with him *or* Fletcher."

Valkyrie looked startled. "I... That's not what I meant."

"Is your relationship with Fletcher coming to an end?"

There was silence, and then, "I didn't mean it like that. I just meant… Oh, God, I don't know. I like having Fletcher. He's warm, and nice, and safe."

"All good qualities," China assured her, "in a puppy. You need someone smart, and strong, and capable. Someone assured. You need someone to challenge you. You need someone better than you. That's what love is, you know. Love is finding someone better than you are, and holding on for dear life."

"It sounds hard."

"The good things in life always are. But you're not looking for love, are you? Of course you're not. What girl your age is? You want fun. You want someone… amazing. Yes?"

"Yes."

"How long have you been going out with Fletcher?"

"A year and a half, maybe."

"If you care for him, and I know you care for him, you won't want to hurt him. But time passes and feelings deepen. And that's when the real hurt will set in. Are you taking him to the Ball?"

Valkyrie blinked. "The what?"

"The Requiem Ball, dear."

"Oh. Um, I don't know. Am I even going? Skulduggery didn't say anything."

"Of course you're going. You've saved the world, haven't you?"

"Well, yeah, but the Requiem Ball is to commemorate the end of the war with Mevolent, and I had nothing to do with *that*."

"Do you really think you'd be allowed to miss it because of a trifling matter of *details*? If you don't go this year, you'll have to wait another ten years for it to come around again, and that would never do. Oh, you'll love it. The women dress in the most beautiful gowns, the men wear tuxedos and we dance the night away. It is quite the social highlight of the decade."

"When you say 'dance'," Valkyrie said, "you don't mean the way you'd dance at a nightclub, do you? Because that's the only kind of dancing I know how to do."

"It's nothing extravagant," China assured her. "A waltz or two. A tango. A minuet. Even a quadrille, if we're feeling debauched. We're going to have to get you into a gloriously decadent dress, I think, with gloriously decadent shoes that will make you even taller than you are now."

Skulduggery knocked on the door, and China let him in. He was, as ever, impeccably dressed. "We were just talking about the Requiem Ball," she said. "I assume the two of you are going?"

"Naturally," Skulduggery replied, removing his hat.

"We are?" Valkyrie asked, clearly surprised. "You didn't tell me."

"Did I not? How unlike me. Still, I simply couldn't deprive you of your chance to see me in a tuxedo. I wear it well, as you can imagine. Besides, it would be rude not to invite you. Technically, you own the venue where it's being held."

"I what?"

"It used to be held in a mansion owned by the late Corrival Deuce," China said, "but your dear uncle Gordon has offered us the use of his house instead. Or *your* house. Whichever it is."

"Ah," said Valkyrie. "Well, it's certainly big enough. I mean, it's got rooms I never go into. Will I have to do anything? Like stand at the door and welcome people, or…?"

"Nothing like that," Skulduggery said, sounding amused. "You'll be treated as just another very important guest. There'll be nothing for you to worry about. And if all the smiling and small talk proves too much for you, you can always disappear into Gordon's study and read one of his books until everyone leaves."

Finally, Valkyrie smiled. "OK. OK, yeah, I can do that."

Skulduggery turned to China. "Back to business, though. Has Valkyrie spoken to you about what we're after?"

"You mean the person who set the Jitter Girls on you? I'm afraid I was of no assistance in the matter. I do, however, have other news you may not have heard. I was waiting for you to join us before I divulged."

"Please," Skulduggery said, "divulge."

China gave the information a respectable pause. "The Necromancers have their Death Bringer."

Valkyrie looked up sharply. "They what?"

"Who?" asked Skulduggery.

"Nothing has been announced yet," China said, holding up her hands, "so nothing has been confirmed, but apparently one of the fledgling Necromancers has recently experienced the Surge. It must have unlocked some hitherto unknown reserves of power, because every Temple around the world is celebrating in typical Necromancer fashion. Very quietly, of course, with barely any smiles."

Skulduggery looked at Valkyrie. "Do you have any idea who the Death Bringer could be?"

"Well, the only one I know of who was waiting for the Surge was Melancholia, but—"

"That's her," China said. "That's her name. Melancholia St Clair."

Valkyrie shook her head. "She's the Death Bringer? Wow. I mean… wow. Didn't see that coming. It's nice to be let off the hook and all, but… You're sure?"

"That's the rumour going around."

"When did you hear?" Skulduggery asked.

"This morning. I was going to call to let you know, but I was a little… preoccupied."

"We should go," Skulduggery said. "We need to report this to the Elders."

China smiled. "It must be such a relief, after all this time, to have two of your best friends on the Council."

"It's a nice change," Skulduggery admitted, "but really, I mostly go to mock the robes they wear. China, thank you very much. Valkyrie?"

Valkyrie nodded, Skulduggery put his hat back on and they left, shutting the door behind them.

Silence settled in the apartment once again, and China frowned. She usually liked silence, liked the solitude that accompanied it. But not recently. Recently, the solitude was starting to feel rather like loneliness, and that was not a feeling she was accustomed to.

She stood by the window until she saw Skulduggery and Valkyrie walk to the Bentley. She felt an irrational urge to rush after them, to continue their conversation, to help them formulate plans and strategies. But she didn't. That wasn't who she was. China didn't join people. People joined *her*. That was the simple, inalienable fact of her existence, and she'd been around for too long to change it now. How much of this sudden fear of being alone was due to the threat posed by Eliza Scorn, China didn't know. But the fact was, if she allowed the situation to worsen, she could very well lose the friendship of the two most important people in her life.

And then those same two people could very well come after her with murder on their minds.

7

THE DEATH BRINGER

Wreath watched her, while the others fawned. She sat like she was delicate, as if a sudden move might snap her in two. She was pale, sickly. Her blond hair was limp, her face a network of small, raised scars. She was still the tall, skinny girl she'd always been, but there was something different about her, even Wreath had to admit that. There was something in the way she looked at the people around her. No longer the student, no longer the girl who opened doors and fetched the High Priest's meals. She was special. She was important. She was the most important person who would ever live.

Craven was loving it, of course. Over the past few months he had taken a personal interest in Melancholia's studies, which was distinctly unusual for a man who despised helping anyone other than himself. But here he was, shaking his head in an attempt to appear modest, the man who had recognised the potential and nursed the Death Bringer through her Surge. Wreath had hoped that *he* would have been the one to do that, to guide Valkyrie when she needed guidance the most. It was not to be, however. The honour had never been meant for him. But why, oh *why*, had it gone to someone like Craven?

"Here sits our saviour," Cleric Quiver said from Wreath's elbow. Wreath hadn't even heard him approach.

"I suppose she does," Wreath said. "I have to hand it to Craven, though – he saw something in Melancholia that I completely missed. I had always viewed her as somewhat... unexceptional."

"As had I," Quiver responded. "I fully expected young Valkyrie to be the one."

Wreath raised an eyebrow. "You never told me that."

"It's not my job to tell you things, Cleric Wreath."

"Has anyone ever told you that you're a hard man to like?"

"My mother may have said something along those lines."

"That doesn't surprise me in the slightest."

"Not to put a dampener on the occasion, but does the Death Bringer appear... *weak* to you?"

"She looks tired," said Wreath, nodding. "She looks drained. From what I've heard, it was an unusually long Surge. What do you think those scars are for?"

"Cleric Craven says they are protection sigils, to guard her from her own power."

"Do you believe him?"

The ghost of a shrug was all Quiver offered. "Our tests have shown extreme spikes and drops in her power level," he said. "It is quite conceivable that she could hurt herself if careless. You don't believe him, I take it?"

"I don't know, to be honest. I don't even know if it matters. If she gets the job done, who am I to complain? Have your tests told you when she'll be strong enough to initiate the Passage?"

"Every spike is stronger than the one preceding it. If she continues in this fashion, a few days. Maybe a week."

"With our dear friend Cleric Craven holding her hand every step of the way," Wreath said, allowing the distaste to creep into his voice. "Are you ready for the world to be a better place?"

"I never really liked this world all that much to begin with, so any change would be an improvement. And you? You've always seemed to like things the way they are."

"I got used to it," Wreath admitted. "But I've lived my entire life waiting for the Passage – I'm not going to bemoan the fact that we're finally about to get it. You know, I think this is the most we've ever talked, you and I. Why is that, do you think?"

Quiver shrugged. "Until this point, I confess that I was never sure if I liked you. Now I just don't care any more."

Wreath smiled.

8

FRIENDS IN HIGH PLACES

Roarhaven stood like a dirty inkblot on a nice clean page. A small town, barely even that, beside a dark and stagnant lake, it was hemmed in on two sides by steep banks of brown grasses. It had its main street and its offshoots, its houses and bars and grim-windowed shops. Sorcerers lived in this town, but only the truly bitter, the genuinely resentful. The outside world was a world gone wrong, a world of ignorant mortals with their squabbling ways. In the bars of Roarhaven, of which there were two, the citizens were known to whisper of some future time when the mortals would fall and the sorcerers rise. And when the drink gave them the courage, these whispers would grow louder, turn to muttered oaths punctuated by fists pounding on tabletops.

Change, they said, was coming.

Roarhaven, Valkyrie knew, was many things. One thing it was not, by any stretch of the imagination, was a tourist town. So when the Bentley passed a rental car stopped outside what passed for the town's corner shop, Valkyrie frowned.

"Pull over," she said.

Skulduggery looked at her as they slowed. "Here?"

"I've seen how this place treats strangers. I just want to make sure we're not going to need Geoffrey Scrutinous to come in and smooth things over."

The Bentley stopped and Valkyrie got out. Skulduggery continued on to the Sanctuary as she walked back to the rental car. A woman sat in the passenger seat. Three kids were squashed in behind. American accents.

She smiled at the woman, got a curt nod back, and then she entered the shop. A few newspapers on the racks. No magazines. Some food, confectioneries, stationery, a fridge with cartons of milk and ham slices, and a broad American man arguing over the counter with the tight-lipped shopkeeper.

Valkyrie smiled as she walked up. "Is there a problem?" she asked.

"This man won't leave me alone," said the shopkeeper.

The American frowned at him. "I'm trying to buy something."

The shopkeeper ignored him. "He just won't leave."

The American turned to Valkyrie. "We came into this store—"

"It's not a store," interrupted the shopkeeper, "it's a shop."

"Fine," the American growled. "We came into this *shop* ten minutes ago. My kids picked out what they wanted, brought them up to the counter to pay. This jerk stood there, right where he is now, looking up at the ceiling while we tried to get his attention."

"I was ignoring them," said the shopkeeper. "I had heard that if you ignore them, they go away. This one did not go away."

"You're damn right I'm not going away. I'm a customer and you will serve me."

The shopkeeper sneered. "We don't serve *your* kind here."

"You don't serve Americans?"

"I don't serve mortals."

The American raised his eyebrows at Valkyrie. "And then he starts with this nonsense."

Valkyrie looked at the shopkeeper. "Wouldn't it be easier at this stage to just let him buy the stuff and leave?"

The shopkeeper shook his head. "You do that for one of them, you'll have to do it for all of them."

"For all of who? There isn't anyone else waiting out there."

"They'll hear about it, though."

"Hear about it?" the American said. "Hear about this little

shop in the middle of nowhere where I actually bought something? First of all, I don't even know where we are! Far as I can tell, it's not on any of our maps. I can find that dirty lake out there, but there's not supposed to be any freaky little town beside it."

"If you didn't know there was anything here," the shopkeeper said, "then how did you find us?"

"We're sightseeing."

"Sightseeing," the shopkeeper said, "or spying?"

"Spying? On you? Why the hell would we spy on you? You're a lunatic with a crummy little store who seems to have a pathological need to *not* sell anything to his customers."

"I'm sorry," said the shopkeeper, "I can't understand your ridiculous accent."

"*My* accent?"

"It is quite silly."

"So you can't understand me?"

"Not a word."

"Then how did you understand *that*?"

"I didn't."

"You didn't understand what I just said?"

"That's right."

"You understood *that*, though."

"Not at all."

The American glowered. "I swear to God, I will reach across this counter and I will punch you right in the mouth."

"Uh," Valkyrie said, "I think we should all calm down a little. Sir, as you may have guessed, this isn't the friendliest town in the world. You go to any other town in the area, I can guarantee that you will be greeted with the biggest smiles you've ever seen. But they do things differently here."

"We just stopped off for some soda for my kids. And I'm not leaving until this guy takes my money and gives me my change."

"Please," Valkyrie said to the shopkeeper, "take his money."

The shopkeeper lowered his eyes to the money on the counter. His lip curling distastefully, he placed a finger on the note and dragged it to the till.

"You're a piece of work, you know that?" the American asked.

The shopkeeper ignored him, and spilled a few coins on to the counter. With a sigh, he looked up. "Happy?"

The American stuffed the change in his pocket then picked up the drinks. "I heard the Irish were especially friendly."

"That was before anyone ever came here," the shopkeeper told him. "Now we're exactly as friendly as everyone else."

The American narrowed his eyes, but managed to restrain himself from slipping further into the argument. "I'm going to walk out of here. Someone as rude as you, you're not worth my time."

The shopkeeper didn't respond. He had gone back to looking up at the ceiling.

Valkyrie escorted the American to his car. "I'm really sorry about that," she said. "I've been visiting this town for almost a year now, and they still don't like talking to me, either."

Skulduggery walked over, a bright smile on his fake face. "Hello there!" he cried. "Everything OK?"

The American frowned suspiciously, but Valkyrie nodded to him. "Just the shopkeeper being rude again, that's all."

"Ah," Skulduggery said, "yes. Very rude man, that shopkeeper. All's well, though? No harm done? Excellent." He crouched at the car window and looked in. "What a lovely family you have. What a charming family. They're all lovely. Except for that one." His finger jabbed the glass. "That one's a bit ugly."

The American stepped towards him. "What? What did you say?"

"Oh, don't worry, I'm sure his personality makes up for his face."

Valkyrie jumped between them, keeping the American back. "He didn't mean it," she said quickly. "My friend is not right in the head. He just says things. Bad things. I'm really very sorry. You should probably go."

"Not before this creep gives my kid an apology."

"Oh, God," Valkyrie muttered.

"Have I offended you?" Skulduggery asked. "Oh, dear. I really am sorry."

"Don't apologise to *me*," the American snarled. "Apologise to my son."

"Which one? The ugly one?"

"Whichever one you were talking about."

"It was the ugly one," Skulduggery confirmed.

"Stop calling my kid ugly!"

Valkyrie elbowed Skulduggery in the ribs. "Apologise this instant," she said through gritted teeth.

"Of course," Skulduggery said, and leaned down to the window. "I'm very sorry!" he said loudly so they could hear. "Sometimes I say things and I'm not aware that I'm saying them until it's too late. It's entirely my fault. My sincerest apologies for any offence caused." He straightened up.

The American finally dragged his eyes off Skulduggery. "This," he said, "is the nastiest town I've ever been to."

"I couldn't agree with you more," Valkyrie said.

He glared at Skulduggery one final time, then got into the rental car and drove off.

"What," Valkyrie said, "was that?"

Skulduggery tilted his head. "What was what?"

"You called his kid ugly!"

"Did I?"

"It just happened twenty seconds ago!"

"Oh. I didn't notice, to be honest. My mind was elsewhere. I'm sure I was joking, though. And I'm sure he knew I was joking. It's all fine. It *was* an ugly kid, though. Did you see it? It's like it had two half-finished faces pushed together. Still, all that's in the past. I do hope they come back. They seemed nice. Come along."

He walked towards the Sanctuary. Valkyrie hurried to catch up.

"Are you feeling OK?" she asked.

"Me?"

"You."

"I suppose I'm feeling a little discombobulated. A little out of sorts. But I'm fine. I'll be fine. Why are we here?"

She frowned. "We're meeting with the Elders about Melancholia."

He snapped his fingers. "Yes! Excellent. Good. So we are. Marvellous."

The Bentley was parked outside an ugly building of concrete and granite. The Sanctuary was round and flat and low, and squatted beside the stagnant lake like someone had dropped it from a great height. It had one main entrance and three hidden exits. No windows. No paint. No frills. Inside it was just as frugal, stone walls and curving corridors flowing in a concentric pattern to the middle. Cleavers stood guard and sorcerers and officials went about their business. No matter the weather outside, it was always cold in the Sanctuary.

The Administrator met them when they entered. "Detectives Pleasant and Cain, the Council is waiting for you."

Skulduggery nodded. "Lead the way, Tipstaff."

Tipstaff nodded politely. They followed him on a bisecting route through the ever-decreasing circles of corridors, straight to the Round Room at the building's core.

Pictures of dead Elders lined the walls, salvaged from the gloom by small spotlights. Three large chairs, like thrones, were placed in the middle of the room, and on those thrones sat the Elders. Ghastly Bespoke sat to the left, the light playing on the ridges of the scars that covered his entire head. In the middle sat Grand Mage Erskine Ravel, a handsome man with beautiful eyes and the slyest smile Valkyrie had ever seen, and on the right sat Madame Mist, a Child of the Spider, who looked at them through her veil. Out of all three Elders, she was the only one who didn't seem to mind the robes they had to wear.

"Skulduggery Pleasant and Valkyrie Cain seek an audience with the Council," Tipstaff announced, bowing before them. "Does the Council acquiesce?"

Ghastly sighed. "Is this really necessary?"

Tipstaff looked up. "Protocol must be followed, Elder Bespoke."

"But they're our friends."

"That may be so, yet rules exist to guard us from chaos. This is a new Sanctuary, and protocol must be established and followed."

"So we sit up here on these bloody thrones," Ravel said, "and they stand down there? We can't walk around or, I don't know, grab a coffee while we talk?"

"If you want coffee, I'll be more than happy to bring you some, Grand Mage."

"I don't want coffee," Ravel grumbled. "Fine. OK. We'll follow the rules. Skulduggery, Valkyrie, sorry about this."

"No need to apologise," Skulduggery said. "The whole situation is highly amusing, believe me. I like your robes, by the way."

"I tried to redesign them," Ghastly muttered, "but apparently, that's not allowed, either."

Tipstaff said nothing.

Madame Mist didn't move an inch as she spoke. "Now that the quaint small talk has been dispensed with, perhaps the detectives could tell us what they came to see us about – something to do with Melancholia St Clair, no doubt."

Skulduggery hesitated. "You've heard, then."

"We have," said Ravel. "What do we know about her?"

"She's a few years older than me," Valkyrie said. "Not much more than a low-level student. She's spent her life in the Temple, reading the books and practising how to sound really pretentious when she talks. I don't think anyone expected her to suddenly become so powerful. Wreath didn't. Tenebrae didn't."

Ghastly moved in his seat, trying to get comfortable. "Is she trouble?"

"She's nothing but a Necromancer," Mist said in her soft voice. "All this talk of the Death Bringer is a waste of our time. Darquesse is the true danger. We should be focusing our energies on finding and killing her before she has a chance to strike."

"The Necromancers should not be dismissed so casually," Skulduggery said as Valkyrie looked away.

"I agree," Ghastly nodded. "If Valkyrie had turned out to be the Death Bringer, we could have kept a close eye on things. That would have been ideal. But now that there's an actual Necromancer in that position, we lose that advantage."

Mist sighed. "The Necromancers are selfish cowards. They haven't posed a threat to anyone in hundreds of years and I doubt they're going to start now."

"I hate to say it," said Ravel, "but Elder Mist is right. It's hard to take them seriously when they've barely poked a head out of their Temples in so long. Maybe if we knew a little more about this Passage thing...?"

"The Necromancers are working to keep us in the dark," Skulduggery said. "Two people with vital information have so far been killed. That in itself tells me they're planning something big."

Ghastly frowned. "You told me once that the Passage is

something that will break through the barrier between life and death."

"Yes."

"So what does that actually *mean*?"

"To be honest, Ghastly, I haven't a bull's notion."

"Elder Bespoke should be addressed by his title," Tipstaff said.

"Of course," Skulduggery said. "To be honest, Your Highness, I haven't a bull's notion. The Necromancers believe life is a continuous stream of energy, flowing from life into death and around again into life. It's all very vague and unsatisfying. They want to save the world, which is nice of them, but as of yet, they haven't told us what they want to save the world *from*."

"Well," Ravel said, "maybe we'll get lucky and Lord Vile will make an appearance, kill the Death Bringer like he said he would, take care of this whole thing before it becomes a problem and then walk off into the sunset."

"I think it would be a mistake to count on Lord Vile to do anything other than murder a whole lot of people," Skulduggery said.

"Agreed," said Ghastly.

"Detective Pleasant," Madame Mist said, "it is a well-known fact that you don't like the Necromancer Order. That you take particular exception to their activities – especially since Solomon Wreath began training your protégée."

"That would be an accurate summation, yes."

"You don't feel that your attitude could be tainting your objectivity?"

"When it comes to the Necromancers," Skulduggery said, "I'm not objective in the slightest. That doesn't mean I'm wrong. Our next move should be a visit to the Temple, where we can ask Solomon Wreath about this unknown agent who keeps killing the people we want to talk to."

"So you're requesting that more Sanctuary resources be made available to you, should you need them?" Ravel asked.

Skulduggery shrugged. "Yes I am, Your Almighty Holiness. What's the point of having friends in high places if you can't use them to settle old grudges?"

Ghastly looked at Ravel. "We need to find out what they're up to."

"This is a waste of our time," said Mist.

Ravel shook his head. "I'm willing to go along with Skulduggery on this one. It might turn out to be nothing, but we need to find out what this Passage is, and we need to stop people dying." He sat back in his throne, raising an eyebrow. "Hear that, Skulduggery? The Elders have spoken. That is the sound of the system working *for* you."

Skulduggery tipped his hat to them. "I'm not going to lie to you, I could get used to this."

9

FRIENDS IN LOW PLACES

Valkyrie's boots crunched on old graveyard gravel on their way to the crypt. Skulduggery didn't even have his façade up – there was no one around on this bright evening to see them anyway. By this stage, Valkyrie knew the cemetery well, which was an odd boast for a sixteen-year-old to make, she was aware.

Skulduggery knocked heavily on the crypt door. Thirty seconds later, it opened, and a pale face regarded them with casual indifference. Valkyrie recognised him. His name was Oblivion, or Obliviate, or something. Or maybe Oblivious. No, she doubted it was Oblivious. Although…

"Yes?" said Oblivious. "What?"

"This is why I like Necromancers," Skulduggery said. "You're all so *cheerful* all the time. We'd like to speak with Cleric Wreath, please."

"Cleric Wreath is busy," Oblivious said lazily, and started to close the door.

Skulduggery jammed it with his foot. "I'm sure he'd love to see us, though. Look, she's his favourite student."

Oblivious observed Valkyrie then sighed. "We already have a Death Bringer, thank you. We don't need another one."

"He's expecting us," Valkyrie said. "He said to come right over, he's got exciting news. He said we could walk right in, actually."

"Your name isn't on the list," Oblivious responded.

"Well, maybe not on *your* list," Valkyrie laughed.

"Are you implying that there is more than one list?"

"I don't know," Valkyrie said mysteriously. "Am I?"

Oblivious frowned. "I'm not sure what you're—"

"Super!" Skulduggery exclaimed, and Oblivious yelped as Skulduggery shoved the door open and barged through. Valkyrie hurried down the narrow steps after him.

"I didn't give you permission!" Oblivious raged. "Guards! Guards! We have intruders!"

Two Necromancers appeared at the bottom of the stairs. Skulduggery waved to them. "We're not really intruding," he called down. "This is all a big misunderstanding."

"Stop right there!" shouted one of them.

Skulduggery held his hand to an ear he didn't have. "What's that?"

"Stop!"

"Keep going?"

"*Stop!*"

"OK, we'll keep going."

The Necromancer guards backed off as Skulduggery and Valkyrie reached the bottom of the stairs.

"Is Solomon in?" Skulduggery asked. "We'd like to give him a present that Valkyrie got for the Death Bringer. It's a small gift, just to say congratulations, the best woman won, et cetera et cetera. Valkyrie, show them the gift."

Valkyrie smiled at them, searched through the pockets of her jacket and came out with a half-empty packet of Skittles.

Oblivious came charging down the stairs. "You do not have permission to be here! You are trespassing!"

"Only a little bit," Skulduggery said. "We'll wait here for Wreath, if you wouldn't mind calling him."

Oblivious jabbed a finger into Skulduggery's chest. "I demand that you leave!"

"But that would defeat the whole purpose of coming here."

"We can do this the easy way," Oblivious snarled, "or the hard way."

"What's the easy way?"

"You leave *immediately*."

"And what's the hard way?"

"We *make* you leave."

Skulduggery's head tilted. "What's the easy way again?"

"Let them through," said a voice from behind the guards. Solomon Wreath walked towards them, dressed in a black suit with a black shirt, cane in hand.

"But they're trespassing," Oblivious protested weakly.

Wreath waved a hand. "Only a little bit."

"But our orders are from the High Priest himself. Now that we have the Death Bringer, we can't allow any outsiders into the Temple, for her safety."

"Then they'll stay here in the Antechamber. They're practically already outside." Wreath's good humour faded for a moment. "Now go away."

The guards dispersed, and Oblivious swallowed thickly and backed off.

"Sorry about that," Wreath said, turning to them.

"Quite all right," Skulduggery responded.

Wreath smiled. "I wasn't talking to you. Valkyrie, I wanted to speak to you before this, I really did, but things have been hectic here, and—"

"Don't worry about it," she said, shrugging. "Melancholia gets to save the world. That's cool. Saves me from having to do it, right?"

"Still, I should have been the one to tell you. No one was more surprised than I when Craven brought her forward as the Death Bringer. But we've run some preliminary tests on her powers and they exceed anything we've ever seen, so she certainly qualifies. I'm not sure how it happened, it defies explanation, but... well. It happened."

"Really, Solomon, it's OK. You're not going to ask for the ring back though, are you?"

Wreath smiled. "No. Just because you're not the Death Bringer doesn't mean you won't make a powerful Necromancer."

"But if this Passage thing happens, and I'm not trying to mock your beliefs or anything, won't we be living in a paradise?"

"Am I to take it that you don't yet believe the world is about to change?"

"Sorry. It's just kind of hard to imagine. Again, it's your belief and I don't want to offend you..."

Wreath smiled. "You could never offend me."

"I bet *I* could," said Skulduggery. "Solomon, we want to talk to you about a friend of yours we ran into yesterday. Absolutely charming fellow – bald, he was, with a terrible goatee. He set the Jitter Girls on us while he made his escape."

"That's dreadful," Wreath said. "But I'm afraid it doesn't ring any bells. Anything else? Any other distinguishing marks or specific traits?"

"He was killing an old woman because she knew something about the Passage, and a few days earlier he'd killed a homeless man for the same reason," Skulduggery said. "Is that specific enough for you?"

"That all sounds terrible," Wreath said. "And yet, again, no bells are ringing."

"Solomon," Valkyrie said, "come on. He was a Necromancer. He was one of you."

"That doesn't mean I know anything about what he was doing."

"But you *do* know him, yes?"

He looked at her. "Bald, with a goatee? I might."

"The people he killed were of no threat to anyone. Paul Lynch was a Sensitive with a history of mental health problems. The only person who was ever going to listen to him was the old lady who was killed next."

Wreath nodded. "It does seem quite… excessive."

"What's the bald man's name?" Valkyrie asked.

Wreath sighed. "Dragonclaw."

She frowned. "Seriously?"

"Seriously."

"That's a ridiculous name."

"We are quite aware of how ridiculous it is, thank you. He's used for black ops, but not very often. He tends to... go too far. Using the Jitter Girls as a delaying tactic is a perfect example of this."

"And you know nothing about it?" Skulduggery asked.

"Not a thing," Wreath said. "I've been busy lately, in case you haven't noticed. I *was* ready to take Valkyrie to the next stage of her training – but now it seems as if Melancholia will be taking up everyone's time. Joy of joys."

Valkyrie heard the main door open again as someone else entered the Temple. She heard footsteps coming down the stairs.

"So when might we get to experience this wonderful and world-changing Passage?" Skulduggery asked.

"Soon enough," Wreath said. "Don't you worry about it."

"We heard we had until Sunday. Would that be about right?"

Wreath did an impressive job of keeping the frown off his face. "Where did you hear that?"

"So it *is* Sunday, then."

Wreath scowled. "Maybe. By our calculations, Sunday would seem to be the best time to attempt it. Whether or not things work out the way we'd like remains to be seen."

"On Sunday the world changes."

"On Sunday the world is *saved*."

"Yes," Skulduggery said, "well, we'll see about that."

They turned, saw Dragonclaw coming down the steps. He caught sight of them and froze.

"Some people here to see you," Wreath called lazily, and Dragonclaw spun on the step and ran back the way he had come.

Skulduggery bolted after him, Valkyrie at his heels. They ran up the steps and burst out into the open air to see Dragonclaw sprinting for the gate. He had a dagger in his hand, and with it he drew in the lengthening shadows and flicked them behind him. Skulduggery went right, Valkyrie went left, and the shadows passed harmlessly between them. Dragonclaw waved the dagger in a circle, surrounding himself with darkness, and vanished.

Skulduggery didn't stop running. "He can't shadow-walk far," he said. "He's still in the area."

A car sped by on the road outside the cemetery, Dragonclaw at the wheel.

They ran for the Bentley. Valkyrie had barely buckled her seatbelt when Skulduggery jammed his foot on the accelerator and they shot forward. They got to the end of the road and turned, taking the corner so tight it was like the Bentley was on rails. Dragonclaw's car, a black Hyundai, appeared through the windscreen. It overtook a van and swerved dangerously. The Bentley was gaining fast.

The Hyundai left the road, spinning its wheels as it slid sideways, and then took off down a narrow lane, careening from wall to wall. Skulduggery braked, changed gears, swung smoothly into the lane in pursuit. The walls whipped by on either side and

Valkyrie cringed, expecting the wing mirrors to be snapped off. Skulduggery, of course, would never allow that to happen.

Dragonclaw wasn't as skilful. The Hyundai hit a broken pallet that had been discarded in a pile of rubbish and it jumped slightly, its left side screeching against the wall. He pulled away too sharply and hit the right wall, jamming the Hyundai the width of the lane. As the Bentley braked, Valkyrie could see Dragonclaw clambering over the seat and tumbling out of the car on the far side.

She got out, Skulduggery already moving for the Hyundai. They both used the air to jump the ruined car, but when they landed on the other side, Dragonclaw was gone. Valkyrie started to run, but Skulduggery reached out, grabbed her arm.

"He must have known we'd go to the Temple," Skulduggery said. She realised he had his gun in his hand. "He must have taken into account the chance that we'd find him."

Valkyrie frowned. "You think this is a trap?"

"I don't know," he said, "but I try not to underestimate my opponents, no matter how ridiculous their beards."

A man walked into the lane from the other end. Valkyrie tensed. He walked towards them slowly, taking his time. Wary of distractions, Valkyrie splayed her left hand, doing her best to read the air. If someone dropped from the buildings above, hopefully she'd notice the disruption to the air currents before they landed on her head.

The man walked closer. He wore a frayed coat and old, ill-fitting clothes. He was unshaven, and needed a haircut. He was holding something – a photograph. When he was twenty paces away, he stopped, examined the photo, then looked up.

"Skulduggery Pleasant and Valkyrie Cain," he said. His accent was thick, Eastern European, and he sounded bored. "I've been paid to kill you." He put the photograph away.

"Interesting," Skulduggery said. "Does it make any difference, the fact that I'm pointing a gun at you?"

The man shrugged.

"He doesn't seem worried," Valkyrie murmured.

"That's never a good sign," Skulduggery murmured back. He spoke louder. "We have no quarrel with you. We just want the man who hired you – we want Dragonclaw."

"It doesn't matter if you have a quarrel with me or not," the man replied, raising his hand. "I'm going to kill you both."

"Happy to disappoint," Skulduggery said, and pulled the trigger.

The bullet hit the man in the neck, opening up a wound from which burst dazzling yellow light. He clamped a hand over the wound, shutting off the glare, and when he removed it, the bullet hole had sealed.

"You're a Warlock," Skulduggery said. "I thought your kind were extinct."

For the first time, the man smiled. "Almost. Not quite. We're growing stronger every day."

"What are you doing here? You're a mercenary now, is that it? Being paid to kill people?"

"This is a special favour," the Warlock replied. "When it is over, when I am told my services are no longer required, I will return home."

"What are you getting out of this? What is Dragonclaw doing for you in return? Or maybe it's not Dragonclaw. Maybe it's the Necromancers as a whole. What do they want?"

"I can't see the point of telling you, seeing as how you will be dead soon."

"What do you know of the Passage?" Skulduggery asked.

The Warlock shook his head. "I don't know what that is, and we have talked enough."

His hand bubbled and boiled, and when he thrust it forward, his palm burst open and a stream of yellow light erupted from beneath. It hit Valkyrie's left shoulder and she spun, cursing, her shoulder tingling then going numb, and by the time she found her balance again, her whole arm was dead.

Skulduggery had used those few seconds to launch himself at the Warlock. His hat flew off as he slammed his forehead into the man's face, followed it with three sharp elbows and then clubbed the man with the butt of his gun. The Warlock

111

reached out, taking hold of him and launching him through the air.

Valkyrie whipped her good hand at the Warlock, and a trail of shadows sought the man out. They slashed across his face, tearing skin. More light burst from the wounds. Valkyrie whipped her hand back, pouring her magic into the next strike, aiming to take the man's head from his body. But her opponent ducked, moving fast, and another beam of light escaped from the jagged hole in his palm. Valkyrie jerked away, the light narrowly missing her, and the man was upon her, fingers closing around her throat. The Warlock hauled her up, slammed her against the wall with one hand. His other hand, the hand with the hole in it, was inches from Valkyrie's face.

It began to bubble again.

10

THE WARLOCK

Skulduggery slammed into the Warlock just as the yellow light exploded. The beam missed Valkyrie and she fell awkwardly, aware of Skulduggery and the Warlock tumbling away from her. Skulduggery was the first up, made to grab the Warlock, but the Warlock kept ducking and dodging, giving himself room, not letting Skulduggery latch on to him. And then his hand opened up again and that light burst out, catching Skulduggery full in the chest. Skulduggery crumpled to the ground.

The Warlock straightened up, held his hand out towards Valkyrie. She swept her arm up and a sudden wind took her off her feet as the yellow light exploded, lancing the space where she had just been standing. She spun through the air, hit the ground and tumbled, finally rolling to her feet. The Warlock wasn't looking so calm any more. He cradled his wounded hand close to his chest, flexing the fingers. He was pale, his jaw clenched. Using that kind of magic was taking its toll.

Valkyrie's left arm was tingling now as feeling returned to it. She'd probably only get one chance at ending this fight, and she had to seize it. She broke into a sprint, barrelling right at the Warlock. She saw the man's other hand too late, saw how the skin bubbled, and though she tried to twist out of the way, she wasn't fast enough. The yellow light filled her vision and she lost all bearing.

She wasn't running any more, she knew that. She wasn't doing anything any more. She blinked, saw the sky above. She was lying on her back. Her body was numb. Unresponsive.

She heard footsteps. The Warlock. Walking slowly. Dragging his feet. Getting closer. He came into view. His hair clung tight to his scalp. He was sweating. He held his hands away from his body, the fingers curled painfully. He looked weak. He looked drained. He looked hungry.

With much effort, the Warlock straddled Valkyrie, sitting on her belly, a bent knee on either side. The wounds on his hands were trying to close, but they were too great. The Warlock didn't move for the longest time. He was gathering his strength. Valkyrie tried to move, but she couldn't. She tried to speak, but she couldn't do that, either.

The Warlock licked his dry lips, pulled them back off his teeth. He did that a few more times, and every time he did it, his mouth widened. His jaw clicked and cracked. His teeth darkened. He was getting ready to eat.

In her mind, Valkyrie screamed and raged. She kicked and punched and fought. In her mind, she reached up and raked the eyes of the Warlock, gouging them from their sockets. She clawed the Warlock's face, leaving bloody furrows in the skin.

But her body did none of that. Her body lay where it was. The Warlock was going to eat through her flesh to her soul, and by the looks of it, Valkyrie was going to be alive when it all happened.

She felt something. A tingle in her right boot. Her big toe. She could feel her big toe. She wriggled it, tried to get the feeling to spread.

A finger now. The middle finger on her left hand. Tingling and buzzing. Pins and needles. Lovely pins and lovely needles.

She could feel the Warlock's weight now. Her hip buzzed, the buzzing travelling slowly across her waist. The Warlock knew none of this. The Warlock just sat there, licking his lips and widening his mouth. The teeth looked bigger, darker, stronger. They looked like teeth that could tear through bone and gristle.

Valkyrie's own lips were burning as sensation flooded back into them. Her nose was itchy.

The Warlock's mouth stopped widening. The process was complete. The Warlock was going to eat, before feeling returned to Valkyrie's arms and legs. The Warlock bent down, the huge mouth wide open, and Valkyrie sat up and crunched her head into his nose. He gagged, dropped back a little, shaking his head, eyes closed, too stunned to react properly. She did it again, the pain exploding through her skull, and this time the Warlock toppled backwards. She shifted her hips to the side, managed to get to her knees, tried to run but collapsed. The Warlock roared in pain and anger. His hand closed around her ankle and he pulled her to him.

Skulduggery grabbed him from behind, wrapping him up in a sleeper hold and hauling him to his feet. The Warlock's huge mouth snapped and snarled.

Valkyrie fumbled clumsily for the handcuffs she kept on her belt. Moving unsteadily, she fell against the Warlock. He tried to bite her, but she swayed away from him, grabbed an arm and clicked the handcuff around his wrist.

The Warlock gasped as his magic was bound. His mouth shrank. Skulduggery threw him against the wall and stomped on his knee. The Warlock howled in pain as Skulduggery cuffed the other hand.

Valkyrie's knees gave out, but Skulduggery grabbed her, stopped her from falling.

"I'm all tingly," Valkyrie said.

"I have that effect," Skulduggery responded.

"You won't stop us," the Warlock snarled from the ground. "My brothers and sisters will be coming for you."

"Lots of people are coming for us," Skulduggery told him. "We're very unpopular in certain circles. Evil circles, you know. But your brothers and sisters are very far away, and it's going to take a while for them to even hear about this, so they don't really concern us right now. The only thing we care about is finding Dragonclaw. If you can help us do that, we'd be willing to make a deal."

"You cannot bargain," the Warlock said. "It is too late for that. Too late for you. I will be avenged."

Valkyrie raised an eyebrow. "We hit you a few times. Is there really a need to be avenged for a few slaps?"

The Warlock managed a smile. "Look out for us," he said. "We're coming."

He contorted in pain, eyes screwed tightly shut. When he opened them, yellow light spilled out.

"Uh-oh," Skulduggery said. He scooped Valkyrie into his arms and they flew, the wind in her hair, landing behind the Hyundai as more light burst from the Warlock's screaming mouth. Skulduggery pulled Valkyrie down behind cover and there was an explosion of blinding yellow light – and then nothing.

Valkyrie blinked rapidly, trying to get her vision back. She felt Skulduggery stand up, and she did the same. "What happened?" she asked.

"He's dead," Skulduggery answered. "Some kind of Warlock self-destruct thing. It must have been triggered the moment his powers were bound."

Her sight was returning to her, and she looked over at where the Warlock had lain. Now there were only his empty clothes.

Skulduggery called the Sanctuary, then searched through the Warlock's clothes while they waited for back-up to arrive.

"Nothing," he said. "No receipts, no ticket stubs, no clues."

"Warlocks, eh?" Valkyrie said, watching him.

"Warlocks are dark sorcerers on a dark path. They eat the souls of their enemies to absorb their strength. I haven't gone up against them in… a long time. I didn't think there were any left." Skulduggery picked up his hat and put it on. "During the war, Mevolent tried to form an alliance with them. He sent a squad of his best people to open negotiations, and they were never heard from again."

"And yet we just took down one of them," Valkyrie said. "They don't seem to be that tough. Apart from the nearly killing us bit. Do you think there'll be more?"

"Eventually. Not for a while. If we're lucky. This is the second time Dragonclaw has got away from us, though. First the Jitter Girls, now a Warlock. He really is breaking all the rules." Skulduggery looked up. "Still, maybe this will convince the Elders to take the Necromancer threat seriously."

Valkyrie frowned. "You don't think they do already?"

"Not really, no. Neither does anyone else. All the Sanctuaries around the world are either too busy with their own problems or they're preparing to battle this oh-so-mysterious Darquesse. If the Death Bringer *was* seen as a threat, we'd have teams from twenty different Sanctuaries storming the Temple as we speak."

"Maybe that means the Passage won't be a bad thing, then. Maybe it *will* save the world."

Skulduggery shook his head. "Paul Lynch had a vision of something that got him killed. This ridiculous Dragonclaw person isn't covering up that trail for the fun of it."

"Then maybe the other Sanctuaries are just hoping that Lord Vile carries out his threat and kills the Death Bringer."

"Very likely," Skulduggery said.

Valkyrie hesitated. "Do you think he'll come after me, like he told you he would?"

"That was before," Skulduggery said. "That was when everyone thought that *you* were going to be the Death Bringer. Now that we actually have one confirmed, all his attention will be focused on her."

"Lucky, lucky Melancholia. You're sure about this, though?"

"I'm sure. Killing you won't help Lord Vile achieve his aim."

"Do you have any idea why he's so keen to stop the Passage from happening?"

"I don't," Skulduggery murmured. "It must be important, though, to bring him back like this. I thought he was gone for good."

"Guess he just doesn't want to live in a perfect world."

A van pulled up at the mouth of the lane. Sanctuary sorcerers got out, nodded to them as they began cordoning off the area.

"You don't think the problem here is us, do you?" Valkyrie asked. "I mean, maybe we're so used to being the ones who save the world that we can't see it when someone else is about to do the same. Solomon keeps saying that the Passage is going to *help* people."

"True," Skulduggery said. "But if you asked Serpine why he wanted to bring the Faceless Ones back, he'd have told you the same thing. It all depends on what *people* you're talking about helping. That's the wonderful thing about just about every religion on the planet – they're all so incredibly selfish."

"You are a cynical man, Mr Pleasant."

"We live in cynical times, Miss Cain."

*

120

He dropped her off at the pier, and she watched him drive away before turning to the shadows. "I know you're there," she said.

He emerged, his footsteps silent. He was tall and slender, his hair black and his skin pale. He had died as a nineteen-year-old, and it was in this form that he was frozen. He would never grow old. He would never fade. His face would never lose its beauty.

"I've been waiting for you," Caelan said, his voice barely audible over the gentle lapping of the waves.

"Couldn't you have found a safer place to wait?" she asked, hooking her thumbs into her pockets. "People like you really shouldn't be hanging around the waterfront, you know. If you swallow any sea spray, your throat's going to close up and you'll die."

"And would you be sad?"

"Sure I would. I once lost a gerbil. I'd imagine the pain would be similar."

He moved closer to her. "So I'm your pet, am I?"

"Of course. You're my vampire."

He was right in front of her now, and he leaned in and they kissed. "And are you my human?" he whispered.

"So long as you're OK about sharing me, sure," she said, and they kissed again.

His hand went to her face. "I don't like sharing things."

"And I don't like being called a thing, but life isn't fair."

"You should be mine alone."

She gave him a smile. "Have you taken your serum tonight? Because you're sounding awfully territorial."

He stepped back. "The serum is not to be joked about. Without it, I would tear off my skin and devour you."

"Sounds tempting, doesn't it? But I can't tonight, dear, I'm on babysitting duty, which I'm actually quite looking forward to, and then it's bedtime."

"Then I will remain beside you while you sleep."

"My folks would love that," Valkyrie said with a chuckle. He didn't smile. "You're *not* going to watch me sleep."

"I have made up my mind."

She looked at him. "Eh, what?"

"I don't know what I'd do if something happened to you, Valkyrie. But you needn't worry. From this moment on, you are mine to protect."

"I'm a little stuck for words here," she said. "I'm just trying to get my head around it, trying to find the right way to… OK, yeah, I have it now. Caelan, cop on to yourself."

He blinked his beautiful eyes. "I'm… I'm only doing this because I care so much. I'm here to protect you."

"See, that's where the problem is stemming from. I don't need you to protect me. I'm not saying I don't need protection. My God, the amount of trouble I get into, I could use all the help I can get. But my protection comes from people like Skulduggery, and Ghastly, and China – you know, people who are powerful enough to protect me from the things I can't protect myself from."

"You… think I'm weak?"

"I think you're grand. And I acknowledge the fact that you're a vampire – that's very impressive. But let's face it, your real power kicks in when you turn and, unfortunately, when you turn, you tend to forget who's a friend and who's a foe, so that's not a whole lot of use to any of us."

"I would never hurt you."

"Aw, that's sweet, but, really, you'd never get that chance. Caelan, you're not my protector, you're not my guardian angel and you're not my boyfriend."

His perfect jaw tightened. "But I love you."

"Here we go."

"When will you admit that you're in love with me too?"

"I swear, talking to you is like talking to a really good-looking and mildly stupid brick wall. Look, I like you, OK? I do. I know I shouldn't, I know it's a cliché to fall for the bad boy…"

Caelan frowned. "I'm a bad boy?"

"But it happened," she continued, ignoring him, "and that's it. I think you're cute. You could probably ease up on the brooding and self-loathing, though – that stopped being attractive a while ago. But I mean, on the whole, I like you, and you like me—"

"I love you."

"Yeah, well…"

"You make my heart want to beat."

"That's nice and creepy. But I'm with Fletcher."

"You've been with him for a while now. It doesn't stop you coming to me."

"Yeah, and that makes me feel so much better about it all. I'm cheating on my boyfriend, who is really nice and sweet and hot, and I'm cheating on him because, let's face it, I'm really not a good person. I'm a cheating girlfriend."

"Then never see him again and your conscience will be clear," he said, taking her hand in his.

She frowned at him. "But I *want* to see him again."

"If you wanted him, you wouldn't be with me."

"It is possible to want more than one person at the same time, you know."

"I only want you."

"And you should really get out more." Valkyrie disentangled herself from him. "Also, all these proclamations of your undying love for me are getting kind of… It's a bit much, to be honest. Just hold back a little."

"But my love for you is eternal."

"That's exactly the kind of thing I'm talking about."

"I need you. I need to be around you. I'm dead, Valkyrie. I'm dead, but when you're here, I feel alive. Memories are stirred of a pulse, of breath in my lungs, of life in my heart. The more I'm with you, the more I need. My passion burns..."

She made a face. "I don't need to know about your burning passion."

"It burns for you, Valkyrie. I'm on fire. My mind is in flames."

"Couldn't we just be each other's bit on the side?"

"You love me. I see it in your eyes."

"I think you're mistaking confusion for love."

"I love you with everything that is me."

"Remember when you were the strong, silent type? Could we go back to that?"

"It's too late to go back. You've reawakened the old Caelan. Because of you, I remember who I used to be. Because of you, I can push the monster down."

"And that is very much appreciated."

"Before you, my life was in darkness. It was hollow and empty and cold. But you shone a light through the darkness. You led me home."

"Yeah, I'm great. Could we stop talking now?"

"But I want to talk. I want to talk for ever."

"I think you *are*..."

"You, Valkyrie, are my sweet agony."

She held up a hand. "OK, I'm really going to have to stop you there. You say one more thing that sounds like it's ripped from the pages of a really bad gothic romance and I'm out of here, are we clear? You'll have talked yourself out of ten minutes with me. Is that what you want?"

Caelan shook his head.

"Good doggy. And never call me your sweet agony ever again."

11

ALONE AT LAST

Melancholia listened patiently while the woman explained what all the charts meant. Two other Necromancers stood by the door, and Cleric Craven hovered nearby, as was his new habit. He seemed reluctant to let Melancholia out of his sight for more than a few minutes at a time.

"The good news," the woman said, "is that we have established a pattern. If our calculations are correct, you should start to feel strong again sometime in the next twenty minutes, and this strength should stay with you for anywhere between three and four hours."

The woman had an annoying tendency to wait for some indication that Melancholia had heard and understood, so Melancholia gave her a nod. "Four hours," she echoed.

"You may experience some dizziness and some fatigue during those four hours, and if you do, don't worry about it. It should pass within moments." The woman's name was Adrienna Shade. She was powerful, and intelligent, and had risen quickly through the Necromancer ranks. There had been rumours that she was to be made a Cleric, a virtually unheard of promotion for one so young. Melancholia used to admire her. But that was before Craven's experiment, before the Surge. Now Adrienna Shade meant nothing to her. Melancholia glanced around the room. None of these people meant anything to her.

"But in four hours' time," Shade continued, "you'll grow weak again. Very weak. We'll have IV drips and oxygen standing by in case you sink to dangerous levels. Whatever happens, we'll be ready for it."

Melancholia doubted that very much, but she smiled and thanked her nonetheless, and Shade put away her charts and instruments, and left the chamber.

"Cleric Craven," Melancholia said, "is it OK for me to be alone for the next few hours?"

He frowned. "We need to conduct more tests, Melancholia."

"But this is a lot to take in, and I think it would really help me if I had the night to myself. I'll submit to all the tests in the morning, I promise."

Craven sighed irritably. He had a tendency to get irritated very easily. "Yes, very well. The night, then. Tomorrow, tests."

"Thank you, Cleric," Melancholia said, and bowed her head. She knew Craven responded well to things like that.

The Cleric walked from the room, ushering the guards out before him. The door closed, and Melancholia allowed herself a smile. Twenty minutes, and she'd feel that power again. Twenty minutes, and she could have herself a little fun.

12

BUMP IN THE NIGHT

lice woke at a little before midnight, and Valkyrie muted the TV before scooping her out of her bed. Her parents were out. Valkyrie didn't mind. It had been a long day and all she wanted to do was relax at home with her little sister.

"Hello," Valkyrie said. "You're awake, then. Did you have a good sleep? Are you rested?"

The baby looked at her and said nothing. Valkyrie took one of the bottles from the side table, teased it down to Alice's mouth until she started feeding. Her phone rang.

It was Fletcher. "Are your folks still out?"

"Yep. Me and the kid are downstairs. Want to come over?"

"Be right there," he said, and hung up.

She looked at Alice. "Your sister is a bad person," she whispered. "Two-timing is not an admirable quality in anyone."

Fletcher appeared beside her. He peered at the baby.

"Can it do any tricks yet?" he asked.

"I'm still working on it. Want to hold her?"

"God, no," Fletcher said, laughing. "I'd drop it."

"It's not an it, it's my sister. Go on, hold her. You won't make a mess of it, I swear. Only an idiot could drop a baby."

"You always say I *am* an idiot."

"But you're a special *kind* of idiot. Here."

She passed Alice into his arms, and he stood there, rigid, a look of intense concentration on his face.

"I've got to support the head, right?" he asked. "And the rest of the body, obviously, but mostly the head. The head's the important bit. Am I doing it right?"

"You're doing fine."

"Do you think it likes me?"

"Honestly, I think she has more taste than that. The baby's like me – she tolerates you." She gave him the bottle, waited until Alice was feeding again, then stepped back. "Want a cup of coffee?"

"I'd better not, I'm holding a baby."

"Suit yourself." Valkyrie went to the kitchen, dumped a spoonful of coffee into a mug while she waited for the water to boil. She looked up at the window, tried to peer through the blackness on the other side, but all she could see was her own face staring back at her.

Fletcher walked in on stiff legs. "Haven't dropped it yet."

"You're a natural," Valkyrie said, smiling and turning away from the window.

"Do you think so?"

"Oh, yeah. All you need is to wipe that petrified look off your face and you'll be inundated with babysitting jobs."

"In that case, I think I'll *keep* this petrified look, thank you very much."

She poured the boiling water into the mug and gave it a few quick stirs, but just as she was about to take a sip, they heard a noise coming from upstairs.

They froze. Fletcher looked at her.

"I thought we were alone," he said softly.

"We were," Valkyrie replied. She put down the mug. "Stay here."

Fletcher shook his head, holding Alice out to her. "*You* stay here. I can teleport up and back again before whoever it is even blinks."

"It's my house. I'm in charge. I'm going up. If it's trouble, take the baby to the twins, then get back here immediately and help."

"Valkyrie, for God's sake—"

"We're not arguing about this."

She walked past him, out of the kitchen and into the hall. The lights were on upstairs. It was brightly lit and warm and welcoming. She climbed the stairs. Shadows curled around her right hand.

Another sound, coming from her room. The first thought that entered her mind was that Tanith had lied when she'd said she'd leave Valkyrie's family alone. Valkyrie hesitated, then shouldered the door open and barged in.

The reflection turned to her.

Relief flooded through Valkyrie's veins, followed by puzzlement, and then anger. "What are you doing out?"

"I'm sorry?" the reflection said.

"You're out of the mirror. How the hell are you out of the mirror?"

"You didn't put me back in."

"Yes, I did."

"No. You didn't. You told me to get into the mirror, but you didn't touch the glass."

Valkyrie frowned. "I did. I did touch it."

The reflection shook its head. "You must have forgotten."

"I didn't *forget*, for God's sake. It was two hours ago. I climbed through the window, you got in the mirror, I touched the glass and absorbed your memories. I remember everything you did today."

Now it was the reflection's turn to frown, a perfect simulation of a puzzled expression. "I'm afraid you're mistaken."

"Oh for God's sake… I let you out of the mirror this morning, you went downstairs and Alice was crying—"

"That was yesterday."

Valkyrie stopped. "What?"

"You're remembering yesterday. Alice was fine this morning. You came back two hours ago, I got in the mirror but you left the room before you touched the glass, that's all. You just forgot."

"But I *remember* touching the…"

"Do you? Do you *actually* remember? Or do you just assume you did it because it's what you *always* do?"

Downstairs, the baby started crying.

"She probably needs her bottle," the reflection said, and walked past Valkyrie, out of the room. Valkyrie watched it go, still frowning. She looked at the mirror, piecing together the events of the last two hours. She'd climbed through the window and the reflection had been doing their homework for school the next day. Valkyrie had told it to step into the mirror, and she'd changed her clothes, fixed her hair and… and…

She was *sure* that she'd touched the mirror. She was *sure* that the reflection's memories had flooded her mind. She was almost certain of it. It was possible, of course it was, that she was getting mixed up. It was an easy mistake to make, after all. It was like locking the front door before bed, then lying in bed minutes later and wondering if you'd *actually* locked the door or you'd just thought about it.

Valkyrie went downstairs. Keeping track of two sets of memories had been tricky at first, but she was an expert at it by now – two parallel tracks of experiences, happening at the same time, sometimes even in the same space. It had taken the longest time to get used to sorting through conversations that she'd had with herself. Viewing a conversation from both sides had been brain-meltingly unsettling. And even though there were some flaws in the process, some gaps in the reflection's memories that she couldn't access, she had always felt that she had a handle on it all. Until just now.

Valkyrie walked into the living room. The reflection had Alice in its arms, and it was smiling gently as the baby guzzled from the bottle. Fletcher stood nearby.

"Sorry," he said. "She kept batting the bottle away and then started crying."

"Don't worry about it," Valkyrie said, keeping her eyes on the reflection. "So you've been in the mirror for the past few hours?"

"Yes," the reflection said.

"And then what? You got bored? Decided to go for a walk?"

"I don't get bored. There was homework that needed to be finished. I finished it."

"Right. But, see, I'm sure I touched that mirror."

"You didn't. I'm sorry if I startled you. Fletcher, could you hand me a tissue?"

Fletcher snagged a tissue from the box on the mantelpiece and gave it to the reflection. The reflection used it to wipe milk from the baby's chin, and then went back to feeding. "You can continue your conversation, if you like. Forget I'm even here."

Fletcher started grinning, and Valkyrie turned her frown on him. "What's so amusing?"

"Nothing," he said. "Nothing. Well... OK, I was just thinking... And don't get mad, because this is just a thought that entered my head, so it's not my fault, it's the thought's fault, but... If you found me with your reflection one day, would that technically be cheating?"

Valkyrie's frown turned to a glare, and Fletcher backed away, laughing. "It was a thought! It was a question I had to ask! I mean, come on, you've thought about it yourself, haven't you?"

"No," she said coldly, "I haven't."

"Yes, she has," the reflection said, and Fletcher burst out laughing. The reflection laughed along with him.

"I knew it!" Fletcher cried. "I knew it!"

Valkyrie narrowed her eyes. "What are you doing?"

The reflection smiled at her. "I'm simulating appropriate human responses. Fletcher found the truth amusing and I joined him in laughing at your embarrassment."

"I'm not embarrassed."

"Yes, you are."

"It's fine," Fletcher said, "forget I ever said anything. I have the real Valkyrie anyway – why would I ever need a substitute?"

Fletcher went to wrap an arm around Valkyrie, but she moved away from him, keeping her eyes on the reflection. "Give me my sister." The reflection walked over, did as Valkyrie ordered. "Now go upstairs. Get into the mirror. Stay there."

"Of course," the reflection said, and its gaze dropped to the baby for a split-second. As it walked out, it smiled at Fletcher. "Goodnight," it said.

Fletcher waved, then frowned. "Goodnight," he said, unsure. They listened to it climb the stairs. "It's never done that before. It's never said goodnight."

"What the hell were you doing? You were encouraging it. You were playing with it."

"I was just having a laugh..."

"And *it* was having a laugh too. It was laughing at *me*. You don't find anything about that slightly weird? It's not supposed to do that."

"Well, I don't know, it's not supposed to do a lot of things, is it? The programming is a little off. There's a malfunction somewhere. So what? It does its job. It imitates you to perfection. And it got Alice to stop crying the moment it took her. So it acts weird every now and then, so you forget to touch the glass every once in a while, so what? It's not the end of the world, and you've got other things to worry about. Like the end of the world."

Valkyrie sighed. "Yeah, maybe."

"Here. We have an evening to ourselves. An ordinary, average evening, where we can be a normal boyfriend and girlfriend, babysitting and snuggling on the couch. I can pop over to Milan for a pizza from that great place under the arch, I can get that ice cream you love from that place in San Francisco... It'll be a nice, quiet night in. That sound good to you?"

"Yeah. Yeah, it sounds nice. I'm starving, actually. Get the pizza."

"And the ice cream?"

"And the ice cream."

He smiled, and vanished. Valkyrie laid Alice in her cot, made sure she was comfortable, and went upstairs to her bedroom. The reflection was in the mirror. Valkyrie tapped the glass firmly, and the memories transferred as the girl in the mirror changed to reflect her own image. The memories settled as she stood there. The reflection had been right. She had simply forgotten to touch the glass earlier on. She saw herself change her clothes, fix her hair and then just walk out of the room. She replayed the memory again, while it was still fresh in her mind, before the details faded and it was just another mix of sensations. She watched herself change her clothes, fix her hair and…

She was *sure* she had approached the mirror. She was *sure* she had touched the glass. But the reflection's memory made it clear that she had just turned and walked out. She hadn't even *glanced* at the mirror.

That was that. Mystery solved. She'd made a mistake and that's all there was to it.

The reflection had kept things from her before – there had been gaps, moments that were missing. There was nothing missing here, though. There was no sign of tampering – nothing obvious anyway. Unless the reflection had discovered a new way of editing its memories, a new way to seamlessly cover over the gaps, then it had been telling the truth. Valkyrie tapped the glass again. "It looks like I owe you an apology."

The reflection leaned forward till its head passed through the mirror. "No need. I am incapable of being offended."

Valkyrie frowned. "Yeah. Yeah, I knew that. I know that."

"Then why did you apologise?"

"I'm… not sure."

"Do you want me to finish your homework?"

"Yeah. Good. You do that."

The reflection nodded, stepped out of the mirror and sat at the desk. Unsettled, with no clear reason why, Valkyrie went back downstairs. Halfway down, someone knocked on the front door. Valkyrie crossed the hall, opened the door, looked out into darkness.

Melancholia stood where the garden path met the pavement. Her hood was down, the breeze playing with her hair, a smile playing on her lips.

"Hello, Valkyrie," she said, then held her arms out to either side and said, "Surprise."

13

SHADOWKNIVES

Valkyrie felt something cold twist in her gut. "What are you doing here?" she asked, her voice brittle and sharp. "This is my *home*."

"I know it is," Melancholia answered. "I've heard Cleric Wreath mention the pier in Haggard so many times that it was really no trouble finding you. So this is where you live, then. How... mundane."

Melancholia smiled as she approached. The hem of her robes flowed over the ground like a river of shadows. "What's wrong? Nothing to say? You usually have lots to say. Are you feeling all right? Are you sick? Are you ill? You don't look ill. Are you putting a brave face on it? You have nothing to prove to me, you know. I respect you for who you are. And who are you again? Oh yes, that's right. Absolutely nobody."

"Whatever you want," Valkyrie said, struggling to keep her anger down, "it can wait, OK? My baby sister's inside."

Melancholia's smile grew wider, and now Valkyrie could see the multitude of symbols that scarred her face. "You have a sister? I didn't know that. Do you think she'll grow up to be as ordinary as you, perhaps? How does it feel, to suddenly go from being the saviour of the world back to being some insignificant little schoolgirl?"

"I'm not going to tell you again. Get away from my house."

"You do not order me around, little schoolgirl. I am the Death Bringer, and you'll always be a silly little child playing grown-up games. I used to be like you, in a way. I used to be scared. I didn't understand what was going on. But then this happened, and all this power came to me, and it all became so, so clear."

Valkyrie shook her head. "What did Craven *do* to you?"

"What did he do? He did nothing. He released the power I had inside."

"No. He changed you. Look at yourself, for God's sake."

"Cleric Craven recognised my potential."

"He tortured you."

"You don't know what you're talking about. Nor would I expect you to. It's funny, seeing you stand there, all scared. I'm used to seeing you in your special black clothes that protect you from harm, always with a smirk on your face. You're not smirking, Valkyrie. I distinctly remember a smirk when you told me that I would have to start worshipping you. Isn't that what you said? But you're not the Death Bringer. You don't get to save the world. I do. And so *you* should really start worshipping *me.*"

"Leave," Valkyrie snarled, then stepped back inside the house, slamming the door. She turned as the shadows in the hallway lengthened and met in the middle of the floor, swirling, thickening, growing. Melancholia emerged from the maelstrom.

"My power is practically limitless," Melancholia said softly. "I'd describe the sensation to you, but words would not be sufficient. To understand what it's like to be a god, you'd really have to *be* a god. Like me."

"Get out of my house."

"I could destroy you and no one would be able to do anything about it. I would tear you from your family. Your friends would be powerless to stop me. The Skeleton Detective? I'd make him watch."

Valkyrie said nothing.

"What's this? No comeback at *all?* Silence? I'm starting to think that you *are* scared of me. I bet your heart is beating much, much faster, isn't it? I bet your mouth is dry."

"What do you want?"

"I want you to admit that you're scared of me."

"And then you'll leave? Fine, I admit it. I'm scared of you. I'm terrified of you. Now leave."

Melancholia smiled. "I don't think you're being genuine. Maybe if I say hello to your little sister, maybe *then* you'd show some genuine fear."

"Take one step and I swear I'll kill you."

Melancholia laughed. Valkyrie heard the back door open and saw Caelan blurring towards them, fangs bared, but the shadows were already curling around her and suddenly Melancholia was taking her shadow-walking. Valkyrie cursed, the shadows went away and she went stumbling to the grass. She looked up to the Martello tower beside her. They were on the cliffs overlooking the beach. But that was impossible. Shadow-walking was strictly short-range teleportation.

"No other Necromancer could shadow-walk this far," Melancholia murmured, obviously thinking the same thing. She looked back to the twinkling lights of the town. "How far was that? A kilometre? Two?"

At least they weren't in the house any more, or anywhere near Alice. Valkyrie got to her feet, and Melancholia remembered she was there.

"A vampire?" she said. "In your house? Was it coming for me or for you? Ah, I don't suppose it matters. Unless it's feasting on your little sister as we speak. Now that *would* be amusing."

"Why are you here?" Valkyrie asked. "Why are you out alone? Lord Vile is still on the loose, in case you've forgotten."

Melancholia sighed. "Lord Vile is overrated. Cleric Craven told me that he's really not as powerful as all the stories say."

"Craven? You'd put your trust in Craven?"

"At least he isn't running scared like your skeleton friend. And he has faith. He knows that if Vile does show up, and I doubt that he will, it won't be a fair fight. I'll crush that armour of his with him still inside. What's left of him will ooze out of the eyeholes in his mask."

"And you came all this way to tell me that?"

"I came all this way to tell you that when I save the world, I'm not going to be saving you. You're not on my list."

"I'll get by fine without you, don't worry about it."

Melancholia laughed. "You're so tough, aren't you? With all your fighting moves and your Elemental magic and your dainty little ring. I don't *need* an object in which to store my Necromancy. My power is stored inside me. I *am* my own weapon."

"Is there a point to any of this?"

"Yes, actually. There is. You're not on my list."

A fist of shadows crunched into Valkyrie's chest and lifted her off her feet.

"And if you're not on my list," Melancholia continued breezily, "then you don't get saved."

Valkyrie struggled to get to her hands and knees. The shot had knocked the wind out of her. "Seriously?" she managed to say. "We're going to fight?"

"Who said anything about fighting?" Melancholia asked. "I'm going to slash you to ribbons and you're going to take it. I'd hardly call that a fight."

Melancholia frowned, almost to herself, and for a moment she seemed to sway, like she was going to collapse. She suddenly looked drained. She looked exhausted.

Valkyrie stood slowly, warily, looking out for the trap. A moan drifted from Melancholia's lips, and Valkyrie realised it wasn't an act – Melancholia really was hurting.

And then, just as suddenly as the weakness had hit, it left her, and Melancholia straightened up. The darkness turned sharp and whipped across Valkyrie's right arm. Blood sprang into the air and she cried out. Melancholia raised an eyebrow and something sliced Valkyrie's back, opening up her skin as easily as it opened her T-shirt. Valkyrie stumbled, cursed, raised her hand, but the shadows wrapped around her wrist. They tightened and she screamed, the shadows cutting into her flesh like piano wire. The ring flew from her finger into Melancholia's hand.

"A gaudy trinket," Melancholia said, examining it, "containing an insignificant amount of power. Cleric Wreath had faith in you on the basis of *this*? How disappointing."

Valkyrie pretended to stagger, closing the distance between them, and then she lunged, but Melancholia twisted the darkness into a claw that ripped into her belly. Valkyrie doubled over, gasping at the white-hot pain. Another claw slashed her face. She spun, fell, blood running down her neck. Her face was ruined, cut open like a freshly ploughed field. Shadows snagged her wrists and ankles, holding her in mid-air, her body locked tight.

"All the little jibes," Melancholia said. "All the little taunts."

Knives of darkness cut into Valkyrie's skin and she screamed.

"Don't worry," Melancholia said, "I'm not going to kill you. I'm just going to cut you all over. When I'm done, there won't be an inch of you that doesn't have my mark on it. And even if you get to a doctor and they heal you right up and make all the scars disappear, you'll know that some scars are deeper than that. You'll know they're there, and every moment of every day, you will regret all those little jibes and taunts. Providing you don't bleed to death while I'm having my fun."

"Don't," Valkyrie said. Blood dripped from her torn lips.

"Are you begging? Is the mighty and fearless Valkyrie Cain begging me for mercy?"

"Don't," was all Valkyrie could manage.

Melancholia sent the shadowknives upwards and they cut through Valkyrie's T-shirt, making furrows in her flesh, changing the pitch of her screams.

14

THE CALL

Valkyrie awoke, lying face down on the grass. She turned her head slightly, tried to blink, but her eyelids were slashed. There were objects in front of her. It took her a while to register what they were. Her phone, and her ring. She moved a hand. It wasn't easy. Some of her muscles had been severed.

With trembling, blood-caked fingers, she speed-dialled a number.

"Hey," Fletcher said when he answered. "They've got the pizza almost ready. It smells delicious."

"Fletcher," she said softly. "Help."

15

THE DOCTOR IS IN

Ghastly braked beside the Bentley and jumped out of his van, hurrying up to Skulduggery as he stalked through the Sanctuary doors. "I just heard," he said. "Any idea what happened?"

"None," said Skulduggery, not slowing down. "She called Fletcher, said she was on the cliffs. She lost consciousness as soon as he arrived."

Sanctuary officials dodged out of their way, flattening themselves against the corridor walls.

"She'll be OK," Ghastly told his friend. "We have a new doctor.

Apparently he's brilliant on a level with Kenspeckle Grouse. Madame Mist brought him in."

"Fletcher said she's cut deep. Kenspeckle would take care not to leave scars."

"I'm sure it'll be fine."

Fletcher paced outside the operating theatre. His head snapped up when he saw them. "She's still in there," he said. He was pale. His voice shook.

Skulduggery barged through the doors, Ghastly and Fletcher behind him. Ghastly froze. Valkyrie lay on the table, eyes closed, covered in a blood-drenched surgical sheet. Above her stooped a creature dressed in a smock, with arms and legs longer than Ghastly's whole body. Its eyes were small and yellow, the lids punctured with black thread where they had once been sewn shut. Its mouth had received similar treatment, and its nose had been cut off. There was a scab there now that refused to fully heal.

"What the hell is going on?" Skulduggery snarled, his gun suddenly in his hand.

"Kill me if you must," Doctor Nye said in its high voice, "but if you do so, your friend will bleed to death. Make up your mind. I have a lot on my plate tonight."

"What's wrong?" asked Fletcher. "Who is that?"

"Step away from her," Ghastly commanded. "We'll get another doctor in here."

"Another doctor would not be able to save her life," Nye responded, sounding bored. "These are wounds inflicted with abandon. No method, no design, no finesse. But they are severe, and they are many, and organs have been sliced and arteries nicked. I have completed my examination and I know exactly how to proceed. If you call in another doctor, they would need to start over. By that time, she would be dead."

"You can save her?" Skulduggery asked.

"Undoubtedly. And if I am allowed to get back to work immediately, there won't even be any scarring."

Skulduggery looked at Ghastly, then nodded.

"Get back to work, Doctor," Ghastly said. "Skulduggery, I'm sure you'll want to stay, to make sure he behaves."

"I'm not going anywhere," Skulduggery said. He didn't put his gun away.

"Me neither," said Fletcher.

Ghastly left, anger quickening his step. He found Madame Mist in her chambers.

"Nye?" he said, barging in. "You have Doctor Nye working here? Are you out of your mind? Nye is a monster!"

Mist observed him from behind her veil. "Just because the Doctor is a being without specification does not make it a monster."

"Without specification? You mean because it isn't male or female? You mean because it isn't strictly human? No, that's not what I'm talking about. It's a monster because it conducts medical experiments on its captives!"

"That's all in the past."

"Nye is a war criminal!"

"Who has been punished for the crimes it committed. Elder Bespoke, I was tasked with equipping this Sanctuary with the very best medical staff available. Kenspeckle Grouse is dead. Doctor Nye was next on the list."

"And you didn't think to run it by us first? You didn't think we'd object?"

"When you say we, are you referring also to the Grand Mage? Because I *did* confer with him, and he agreed that this facility would benefit from Nye's expertise."

Ghastly frowned. "Ravel agreed to this?"

"Yes. If you have a problem, maybe you should take it up with him."

"Yeah," Ghastly said, "maybe I should."

Ghastly walked the corridors, his pace slower now. Ravel was like him – he was a soldier. He'd fought in the war, fought against Mevolent, and he'd had friends who were captured. They'd all heard the stories, about the torture and the sick experiments. They'd all heard of the doctor with the long arms and legs and the scabrous nose. Everyone had heard of Doctor Nye.

"Ghastly," Ravel said, looking up from his desk, "is Valkyrie OK?"

"She's hurt," Ghastly replied, "but she should pull through. She's in the Medical Bay now. That's what I wanted to talk to you about."

"Ah," Ravel said, sitting back. It was three in the morning and he was looking tired. "Nye."

"How could you agree to this? That thing killed some of our best friends."

"Sorcerers live a long time, Ghastly – how long are we going to hold grudges for things we did in wartime?"

"Fighting on the battlefield is one thing. Torturing prisoners to death is quite another."

"Do you know what Nye has been doing for the past hundred years? It's been working alone, secluded, cut off, doing research on the human soul."

"It wants to torture that too?"

"No, it wants to find it. Ghastly, can you imagine what that could mean? The soul is our essence – it's the strongest, most pure part of ourselves. The link between the soul and our true names has been discussed but never proven – but think what we could achieve if we harnessed that power. Think what we could become if we allowed ourselves to be the best we could possibly *be*."

"Erskine, all due respect, but what on earth are you talking about? If Nye did find the soul, what would it do then? Poke it? With what? It's a *soul*, not a plate of jelly. The soul should be left where it is – it causes enough problems without us adding to them. Angry souls can become ghosts, powerful souls can become Gists and evil souls can become Remnants. It's a dark and dangerous business, and we should leave it alone."

"We didn't recruit Nye so he could find the soul, Ghastly. I'm just telling you what he's been doing for the past century. He hasn't been hurting anyone, he hasn't been torturing anyone. He has repented."

"I find that very hard to believe."

"He's the best there is, damn it, and you know it. Do you think I like having him here? He's creepy as hell and if you think I don't remember the things he did to our friends, you're nuts. But with Kenspeckle gone, with Vile on the loose and with Darquesse coming our way, we need to put our issues aside and surround ourselves with the best people for the job."

"Even if that includes a known sadist and murderer?"

Ravel closed his eyes, and sat back in his chair. "I didn't think it would be like this. I really didn't. I thought every decision I'd have to make would be how many operatives to send on a rescue mission. I don't know how Meritorious did it." He opened his eyes. "Is Valkyrie conscious?"

"No. That's probably a good thing."

"Do we know what happened to her? Who did this?"

"I don't need Skulduggery's skills to recognise Necromancy when I see it."

"Speaking of Skulduggery," Ravel said slowly, "does he need to be contained?"

"Contained?"

"Don't play innocent. You know what he's like. Once she wakes up, he'll be going after every Necromancer in the country."

"Maybe we should let him."

"We're in charge now, Ghastly. We don't have that luxury. This has to be done right."

"Leave it with me. I'll make sure he understands."

"And listen," Ravel said, "I know this goes against every fibre in your body, but Doctor Nye is the best man-woman-whatever for the job. It *will* save Valkyrie's life."

"Yeah, I know, it's just… Things got complicated around here awfully fast, didn't they?"

"Yes, they did. But we're in charge now, my friend. We've got to be the ones to make the hard decisions. It's inevitable that people are going to start hating us, sooner or later."

"They can form a queue behind me, then."

Ravel smiled sadly. "Yeah. Let me know when she regains consciousness, OK? Oh, any news on Tanith?"

Ghastly hesitated. "She was in Berlin last week. With Sanguine. They almost got her. But no. No real news."

"You'll find her."

"Yeah," Ghastly said, and left.

He went back to talk to Madame Mist, who had a surprisingly good grasp of Sanctuary law and procedures. Once he had been sufficiently briefed, he walked back to the Medical Ward. Skulduggery was sitting outside the Operating Theatre, his head down, his hat on the chair beside him. His skull gleamed under the light. He looked up as Ghastly approached.

"Nye predicts a full recovery," Skulduggery said, his velvet voice sounding disturbingly hollow. "She'll wake in an hour or two. There's a nurse in there with her now."

"Where's Fletcher?"

"I sent him home. He seemed traumatised."

"Seeing your girlfriend slashed to ribbons will probably do that to you," Ghastly said. "And how are you?"

"Meaning?"

"She was almost killed."

"I am aware. You're waiting to see if I'll get angry."

"I already know you're angry. You're sitting very still and you're talking very quietly. You're getting ready to kill someone."

"I just need a name."

"You know the name. A Necromancer did that to Valkyrie,

and there's only one out there who'd be motivated enough to do it."

Skulduggery's head tilted. "You're going to tell me that I can't go after her?"

"Not at all. I'm telling you that if you do go after her, she'll kill you. She's the Death Bringer."

Skulduggery picked up his hat, and stood. "I'll take my chances."

"No you won't," said Ghastly, standing in front of him. "You think your brief encounter with Vile five months ago has prepared you? That was nothing. I went up against him during the war. I saw him slaughter dozens of sorcerers, including my mother – a woman, you'll remember, who had proved herself to be very hard to kill. He killed her with barely a wave of his hand."

Skulduggery was silent for a moment. "Melancholia is not Lord Vile."

"If she's the Death Bringer, their power levels will be similar. Skulduggery, you know as well as I do, if Melancholia had wanted to kill Valkyrie, Valkyrie would be dead. But she didn't. She just wanted to inflict some pain. And she won't get away with it. I've spoken with Erskine and Mist, and they agree. An attack on one Sanctuary agent is an attack on the Sanctuary as a whole. Melancholia has just handed us the excuse we needed to take that Temple apart."

"Then give me an army, and I'll take it apart and drag her out."

"We have to do this right. Before we go in, we issue a warrant for her arrest."

"She's not going to give herself up," Skulduggery said.

"No, but we have to give her the chance. Maybe High Priest Tenebrae will see it as an opportunity to bring his Order in from the cold. Maybe he'll co-operate."

"I doubt it."

"I doubt it too. So if she doesn't turn herself in within twenty-four hours, then yes, we go after her, and you get all the back-up you need."

"If Melancholia resists?"

Ghastly looked at him. "Then you do what needs to be done."

16

FULL RECOVERY

octor Nye had a smile like splitting skin. "Welcome back," it said, "to the land of the living."

Valkyrie jerked against the restraints tying her to the bed. Nye waved its hand.

"Do not exert yourself. You are still quite weak. The restraints, I assure you, are for your own good."

"Where am I?" she snapped.

"In the Sanctuary. You are quite safe. The woman who did this to you is long gone."

"It's not her I'm worried about."

Nye chuckled. "Oh. Of course. You remember our little… encounter. But that's all in the past, is it not? Any indiscretions I may have perpetrated against you I have made up for, yes? I replaced your organs, sewed you back together and you walked from my facility as a living, breathing person once again. Forgive and forget."

"You tried to dissect me."

"I *did* dissect you. I just didn't dissect you *enough.*"

"Let me out of here."

"I am worried that you may injure yourself."

"Let me out of here or I swear to God—"

"What do you swear? Do you swear to tell the Elders about me – about what I did? But then, of course, you would have to explain to them why you had come to me. You would have to explain that you had discovered your true name, and you wanted it sealed so that no one could control you against your will."

"There's nothing wrong with what I did."

"You were talking, you know. As I dissected you, you were talking to yourself. Muttering. I believe, at times, hallucinating. You said a name. When you said it, it meant nothing to me. Why should it? I was leading a secluded existence. But after you'd gone, I heard that name again. Darquesse. The one who kills us all."

Valkyrie stopped struggling.

"I don't know what you have to do with Darquesse, but if you tell the Elders about the extent of the experiments I was conducting, I shall be forced to tell them that you are involved in this somehow, and I'm sure they'd start asking all sorts of awkward questions."

Nye smiled again, and suddenly hurtled backwards, knocking over a tray of instruments. Valkyrie turned her head, saw Skulduggery and Ghastly marching in. Skulduggery had his hand splayed, using the air to pin Nye against the wall. He glanced at her as he passed, his eye sockets moving fractionally in her direction, and then he continued towards Nye as Ghastly undid the restraints around Valkyrie's wrists.

Nye grunted, its frail body struggling uselessly like a daddy-long-legs trapped in a web. With his other hand, Skulduggery took out his gun, pressed it against Nye's forehead. Nye stopped struggling.

"Skulduggery," Ghastly said, alarmed. "What are you doing?"

"I told myself if I ever got the chance to end this miserable excuse for a life, I wouldn't hesitate. Now that I have no more use for it…"

"Don't. Skulduggery, do not pull that trigger. What Nye did during the war was unforgivable, but we have other concerns now."

Skulduggery's voice was cold. "I don't care what he did during the war. I'm thinking about something much more recent."

Ghastly approached, walking slowly. "What are you talking

about? Doctor Nye has been locked away in its laboratory for the last hundred years."

Skulduggery looked back at him, and didn't say anything. There was nothing to say. Nye was right. Any accusations on their part would raise questions about Valkyrie, and that was a truth they weren't prepared to share with anyone.

"Skulduggery," Valkyrie said, holding the surgical sheet around her as she slid off the bed. "It's OK. Nye fixed me. I'm OK."

For a moment, she doubted her words would be enough, but then Skulduggery lowered the gun, and stopped pressing against the air.

Nye stood, towering above them all, outrage showing on its face. "This… This is deplorable. Madame Mist personally granted me amnesty for past misdeeds, and she assured me that I would not be held accountable for merely following orders. Elder Bespoke, I hope you will discipline Detective Pleasant for his unacceptable actions."

"Shut up, Nye," Ghastly said. "I'm this close to putting a bullet in you myself. Where's your assistant? He was supposed to stay with Valkyrie at all times."

"The man was an imbecile," Nye replied stiffly. "I told him to go away and never let me see him again. If I had known it was so important to you, I would have had him stay."

"It's not important to me, Doctor," Ghastly said. "It's essential.

It's essential both for my peace of mind and for your well-being that you have an assistant with you at all times. You are not to be left alone with any patient. Do you understand me? Do you understand *those* orders?"

"Yes," Nye said. "Of course."

On the drive to Skulduggery's house, Valkyrie took off the black ring and examined it thoughtfully.

"Want me to open the window so you can throw it out?" Skulduggery asked.

She smiled. "No, but thanks for offering. Melancholia took this off me, you know. Just whipped it off my finger and *bam*, I had no Necromancer magic to call on."

Skulduggery nodded. "That's the problem with Necromancy. It's powerful magic, absolutely it is, but it's so unstable it needs to be housed in something to make sure it can be controlled. Power that unstable… it's a terrifying prospect, if one were in the habit of being terrified."

"Is Necromancy the only discipline that has to do that?"

"Not the only one, but the main one. There are very few others. It's called Inhabiting."

Valkyrie nodded. "Solomon told me about it. He said a perfect example was Lord Vile's armour. When Baron Vengeous wore it, it still had all of Vile's power. Maybe that's what happening now.

Maybe Vile *isn't* back – maybe someone is just wearing his armour and using his magic and pretending to be him."

"I don't think so," Skulduggery said. "He spoke to me. It was him. It's impossible, but… it was him."

She put the ring back on. "Have you found any trace of him since?"

He turned his head slightly. "How do you know I've been looking?"

"Little things," she said. "You've been taking more of an interest in odd little crimes that don't make any sense, you've been asking certain kinds of questions that aren't really relevant to whatever case we'd be working on… You're trying to find someone."

"My my," said Skulduggery. "What dashing mentor has been teaching *you* to be a detective? Oh, that's right, it's me."

Valkyrie laughed. "So? Any trace?"

"None," he said. "He killed Tesseract, I hit him, he exploded in shadow and no one's seen him since."

"He might be dead," she said hopefully.

"I don't hit *that* hard."

She shrugged. "It might be his ghost."

"Actually," Skulduggery said, "I've been thinking the same thing."

"What? Seriously?"

"Yes, indeed. Look at what we've got. Armour that is brimming with power. All it needs, let's face it, is the will to get up and move around. All it needs is intent."

"So you think Vile's ghost found his old armour and now it's living inside it?"

"That's one possible explanation. His ghost or… I don't know."

"So inside the armour would be, like, nothing?"

Skulduggery hesitated. "It's a theory. One of many. But right now, it's the only one that fits."

"Then what was Vile doing at the Sanctuary?"

"Our beloved former Grand Mage Guild had the armour stored in boxes that were then shipped to Roarhaven. My fight with Tesseract must have disturbed it, or…"

He went quiet, and she frowned at him. "Is there something about Vile, or about what he said to you, or… Is there something you're not telling me?"

Skulduggery laughed. "Oh Valkyrie, my loyal and trustworthy combat accessory. Of *course* there's something I'm not telling you. That's what makes me fun."

Valkyrie stood in Skulduggery's hat room and looked at her hand. It wasn't shaking. She turned it, frowning, trying to spot a hidden tremble. Nothing. She knew this wasn't right. She'd been attacked and almost killed, endured pain and agony on a scale most people would never experience, and yet she didn't seem to be suffering from any psychological side-effects whatsoever.

She remembered the attack vividly. It was seared into her memory. She wasn't repressing anything, as far as she could tell. She wasn't numb. She wasn't traumatised. Then what was wrong with her? Why wasn't she in shock? Or maybe this *was* shock. No, she'd been in shock before. She knew the signs. This thing she was experiencing now was... normality.

Her body had been half ripped to shreds the previous night, and now she was fine with it. It was like there was something cool in her centre, keeping the panic down, gently guiding her past the horror. She could almost hear the voice in her mind.

Calm, it said. *Keep calm. You're still alive, aren't you?*

She turned to the full-length mirror that Skulduggery kept in here, just so he could check the overall effect of whatever hat he was wearing. Hugely vain and narcissistic, but endearingly so. Her clothes – freshly washed – were so ripped and torn they barely stayed on. Valkyrie parted a long slash in her T-shirt and traced a finger along her side. *Still alive.* She leaned in and examined her face. "The scars are almost gone," she said loudly.

"That's good," Skulduggery responded from the other room.

So many hats in here. She took one, a black one, and tried it on. It looked pretty good on her, she had to admit. She liked the way it came down low over one eye. It gave her a rakish quality.

Calm. She put the hat back on the stand and walked into the main living room. Skulduggery stood among the ruins of what had once been a sofa. Valkyrie raised an eyebrow.

"I was trying to make up the sofa bed so you could get some rest," he explained, and pointed to the second sofa across the room. "Unfortunately, it would appear that *that* is the sofa bed, and this, apparently, is just a sofa."

"Not any more it's not."

"Well, yes, now it's a dead sofa. It put up a valiant struggle, however."

"I'm sure its family would be proud." She wrapped herself in a blanket and collapsed into an armchair.

"I kill a sofa for you and you go and sit in a chair?" Skulduggery asked. "I don't think you appreciate the sacrifice that has been made for you."

"I don't need a bed right now. I just need to nap for a few hours, then the scars will be completely gone and I can go home and collapse into my own bed."

"So you'll be OK here on your own?"

"I'll be fine. Go off and issue that arrest warrant. But don't kill anyone. I want the chance to beat the hell out of Melancholia for what she did – but I don't want her dead. Not yet anyway. You're going to be calm about this, aren't you?"

"Exceedingly."

"You promise?"

"I cross the place where my heart used to be and hope to be even more deader than I am now."

"Well, OK then." Valkyrie looked away for a moment. "Why didn't Darquesse come out?"

"Sorry?"

She shrugged at him. "Melancholia nearly killed me. I was kind of expecting Darquesse to take over and, you know…"

"Relying on Darquesse to save you would probably be a bad habit to get into," Skulduggery said.

"I know," she responded quickly, "and I wasn't. But still… it'd help if I knew the rules. Do I Hulk out when I'm in danger, or does it have to be like when the Jitter Girl actually had her fingers in my brain, or…?"

"I don't know, Valkyrie. Maybe you subconsciously knew that Melancholia didn't actually intend to kill you. Maybe Darquesse only emerges as a last resort in order to keep you alive. Or maybe it's a whim. I don't know."

Valkyrie nodded. "She weakened, you know."

Skulduggery tilted his head. "Melancholia?"

"Right before she inflicted the serious damage, she weakened. She almost fainted, I think. There's something wrong with her. I didn't stand a chance once she got her strength back, but if I'd gone after her in that moment, when she was weak, I could have battered her around the place, I know I could have."

"Interesting," Skulduggery said.

"What does it mean? Is it anything useful?"

"I'm sure it is," he said. "Get some rest, OK? And maybe you should call Fletcher. You've been through a traumatic experience."

"I'm used to them."

"I'm sure Fletcher's worried about you."

"Since when do you care if he's worried? I called him from the Sanctuary, told him I'm fine. I'm fine, he's fine. You're the only one who's worried."

"I care too much, that's always been my problem. Well, if you're absolutely positive you don't need company, and you don't need me to tell you a story before you go to sleep…"

"Actually," she said, "maybe a small one."

"Oh?"

"Having little Alice around got me thinking. You never did tell me why you abandoned your family crest."

His head tilted. "Did I not? Are you sure? I'm sure I mentioned it. Possibly when we were fighting something huge and horrible. I think I shouted it to you, but you may have been too busy being thrown against a wall. Still, the important thing is that I told you, so let's cherish that moment and move on."

"Or you could just tell me again."

"Oh, Valkyrie, you know how much I hate repeating myself."

"Yet you've told me the story of how you saved that orphanage, like, a hundred times."

"That's because it's an exciting story, with twists and turns, and it paints me in an impressive light."

"So the story of why you abandoned your family crest paints you in a negative light?"

"Essentially."

"Hey, if you really don't want to tell me, that's OK, I understand."

"Excellent." He walked towards the door.

She frowned. "So?"

He stopped. "So what?"

"So tell me."

"You… said you understood…"

"Don't you know anything? That was me, lying. Whenever someone says you don't have to tell them, you have to tell them. That's a rule. It's how communication works."

"It seems to be a flawed system."

"Tell me why you abandoned your crest, and I'll tell you one of my secrets."

"You have no secrets."

"I have loads."

"You have none. Let's see, your given name is Stephanie Edgley. Your true name is Darquesse, and apparently you're destined to extinguish all life on the planet. Oh, and you're seeing a vampire behind your boyfriend's back."

Valkyrie's eyes widened. "You… you know about that, then?"

"Of course I do."

"You're not mad?"

"I think it's a huge mistake that will end extraordinarily badly – but if that's the only way you'll learn, so be it."

"I can't believe you're not mad."

"I comfort myself with the thought that I may have to kill Caelan at some stage."

"Oh. Then just tell me why you abandoned the crest, for God's sake. If ever I have a big secret from this moment on that I wouldn't normally tell you, I'll tell you. Deal?"

Skulduggery sighed, walked over to the remains of the sofa and sat on the arm. "I abandoned my family crest because I hadn't lived up to the high standards as set by my parents and my brothers and sisters."

"You had brothers and sisters?"

"Of course."

"What were their names?"

"What does it matter? They're all dead now. I'm the only one left, the only one to carry that crest down through the years. They were good, honourable, decent people. When they were alive, the crest meant something."

"But you're good and honourable and decent too."

He took off his hat, brushed imaginary lint from the brim. "Unfortunately, in war, you let some of those qualities slip. When I feel I have regained the right to reclaim that crest, I'll reclaim it."

"I don't know, I think you overreact."

"Do you, now?"

"I know people do terrible things in war, but I can't imagine *you* doing something so bad that it changes your opinion on who you *are*. You're being too hard on yourself."

"That's always been a flaw of mine."

"Were you the oldest?"

"Second oldest. I had an older brother."

"Wow… the great Skulduggery Pleasant had a big brother. What was he like?"

Skulduggery's chin tilted to the right. "He was bigger than me, stronger than me, he liked to think he was smarter than me. He protected us, looked out for us. He was everything an older sibling should be. He was everything that you're going to be to your sister."

"I hope so. It's weird, isn't it? You meet someone and you become friends and you grow to love them, and that's the way it works. That's how things go. But then a baby is born, and you don't have that long period of getting to know them, of figuring out if you like them as a person… you just love them. Like, it's instant. You hold the baby in your arms and you feel so much real, overwhelming love, like you would do anything to protect it. *Bam*, just like that, your whole life is different. This baby, this little person that you don't even know, is now more important to you than anything else."

"It does come as quite a surprise," Skulduggery murmured, and stood up.

"Oh," she said. "Sorry. I was talking about a little sister, not… not a child of your own… I don't know what I'm talking about."

Skulduggery shook his head. "Nonsense. You described it perfectly. Pure, unconditional love. It's a wonderful thing. You'll experience it again when you have a child of your own."

"Whoa!" said Valkyrie, jumping to her feet, the blanket falling around her. "Whoa! Stop right there! We're not even going to talk about that! We're not even going to mention the possibility!"

"It unnerves you, then?"

"It freaks me out is what it does! I think I still have a few years left of, you know, playing the field before I find someone I want to settle down with. We're talking a few centuries, you know?"

"So you're not planning on rushing into anything?"

"Not if I can help it."

"Does Fletcher know this?"

She laughed. "He'd better."

"And Caelan?"

"I make sure to tell him every time I see him."

Skulduggery put his hat on. "That's my girl."

17

THE ZOMBIE KING AND CO

Vaurien Scapegrace, the Killer Supreme, the Zombie King, lay in a freezer, his legs curled up to his chest. He felt the freezer move slightly and he muttered dark things under his breath. The refrigerated truck he'd been using as a mobile base had broken down, so he'd sent that idiot Thrasher to get another one. But Thrasher couldn't find a refrigerated truck. The only thing he could find that even remotely met Scapegrace's requirements was a Percy Penguin Ice-cream Van.

Thrasher had tried to convince Scapegrace, when faced with

his wrath, that an ice-cream van was ideal – it was innocent, it was unexpected, no one would ever imagine it housed a terrifying zombie. Scapegrace fumed. Innocent was not the same as discreet. His mobile base had a smiling plastic penguin on its roof, and it couldn't go faster than forty kilometres an hour. They couldn't even find a way to switch off that damn Popeye music that jingled and jangled on a constant loop. It was driving Scapegrace mad. What was worse, every time they stopped in traffic, he could hear people run up and tap on the window.

They were moving through yet another small town. Scapegrace hated small towns. He felt the van slow, and heard the kids immediately swarm out on to the road, waving money and shouting their orders. Scapegrace stayed where he was, safe in the frosty confines of the freezer, trying to think of things that would soothe his impatience. He thought of tranquil lakes, of birds singing, of plucking out Thrasher's eyes, and eventually, he reached a place within himself that had some degree of balance.

He heard Thrasher's voice, the one thing guaranteed to ruin the Zen of even the most placid monk, and opened the freezer lid. He could hear people battering on the window above him.

"What did you say?" he called out.

"I'm just wondering," Thrasher answered from the driver's seat, "if maybe we should serve some ice cream."

"Why on earth would we want to do that?"

"To be inconspicuous. They're all around us. If we give them ice cream, they'll go away, and we won't arouse suspicion."

Scapegrace struggled to control his temper. Tranquil lakes. Birds singing. Eye-plucking. Calm.

"Thrasher," he called out, "we have no ice cream. *I'm* in the freezer, Thrasher. Did you forget that?"

"Well, what about the machine?"

"The ice-cream-making machine?"

"Yes."

"Do you know how to work it?"

"You just, you just put the cone under the nozzle and you pull the thing and the ice cream swirls out and you stick a chocolate flake in it."

"It's that easy?"

"Yes."

"Should I get out of the freezer and do it?"

"If you want."

"You're an idiot, Thrasher. I have bits falling off me and I have a burnt head. I'd say that would arouse a little suspicion, wouldn't you?"

"Oh… yes. Well, I could do it, if you want to drive. I always wanted to work in an ice-cream van, ever since I was a little boy."

"Is that right?"

"Oh, yes. My mother would take me to the beach and I loved

hearing the *tinkle tinkle* of the ice-cream van as it made its way across the—"

"Shut up!"

Thrasher shut up.

"We're not serving ice cream, do you hear me? We're not! Tell these people to go away! We're closed!"

"I tried that, sir. They don't really listen."

Scapegrace glowered. "Are there children out there?"

"Um, yes sir, they're all children."

"Run a few down."

"Sir?"

"Drive over a few of the little brats. That'll scare 'em off."

"I… I don't think I can do that, sir."

"You're not developing a conscience on me now, are you, Thrasher?"

"No sir!"

"You're still an evil zombie, aren't you?"

"Oh yes sir, evil to the core!"

"Then why can't you drive over a few children?"

"I just don't think we're capable of going that *fast*, sir. With this traffic, plus the fact that they do seem to be an unusually spry bunch…"

"Fine," Scapegrace said angrily. "I'll take care of it."

He pushed the lid all the way open and repositioned himself, then reached up and opened the window. Voices flooded the van, and hands poked through, waving money. Scapegrace pulled a face before plunging his head out of the window, and all the little kids screamed in terror and ran off, hands waving in the air. Scapegrace broke down, laughing hysterically, and fell back into the freezer, clutching his sides.

Thrasher glanced back, and Scapegrace heard him force a laugh. "That's very good, sir, very funny."

An hour later, Scapegrace felt the van slow again, and eventually stop. A few moments passed, then Thrasher appeared over the freezer.

"We're here," he said, sliding open the lid. "At least I think we're here. We're definitely somewhere."

Scapegrace clambered out, slapping Thrasher's hands away when he went to help him. Once out, he went to the front of the van.

They were in Dublin's docklands, outside an old warehouse. There was a girl out there with blue hair. She was looking at the warehouse door, same as Scapegrace, but hadn't once turned round to look at the van with the giant penguin on top. Thrasher joined him.

"Who is she?" Thrasher asked.

"How am I supposed to know?" Scapegrace scowled. "All I can see is the back of her blue head."

"Do you think she's crazy?"

"Why would she be crazy?"

Thrasher shrugged.

Scapegrace got out of the van, Thrasher close behind him. They approached the crazy girl with the blue hair.

"The doctor isn't here," she said without looking at them. "The whole place is empty. It smells of disinfectant and oranges."

"Nye? Is that who you're talking about? Doctor Nye?"

The crazy girl nodded, and looked at him. His face had been burnt off by Valkyrie Cain, and being a zombie meant that it had never even tried to heal itself. The crazy girl didn't even bat an eyelid. "My name's Clarabelle," she said. "What's yours?"

"You don't need to know his name," Thrasher snarled. "You don't need to know anything!"

"Cool." The crazy girl didn't appear too bothered.

"Where has he gone?" Scapegrace asked.

"Where has who gone?"

"Doctor Nye."

"Doctor Nye isn't a he. Doctor Nye is an *it*. I found a note that said it's got a job in the Sanctuary. Can you imagine that? Doctor Nye, working in the Sanctuary. Weirder things have happened, I suppose. Like Belgium."

Scapegrace frowned. "What about Belgium?"

"That's pretty weird, isn't it? If Belgium happened, why should

I be surprised that Doctor Nye is working for the Sanctuary? It's all relative, isn't it? It all depends on where you're standing. And where you've stood."

Wherever Scapegrace was standing in relation to the crazy girl, he was pretty sure he was lost.

"I came here looking for a job," she answered, even though no one had asked. "I had to leave my old job. I killed my boss. I didn't mean to do it, and it wasn't actually me who did it, but I still killed him. So now I need a new job. I dyed my hair. Do you like it?"

"I know you," Scapegrace said.

"Do you?"

"You worked for the old man. Professor Grouse."

"I did. I don't any more. I don't like to talk about it. He took care of me. He thought I needed taking care of. I let him think that. I think he needed to think that. He needed to take care of someone, so I let him take care of me. I don't like to talk about it. You're a zombie."

"He is the Zombie King!" Thrasher announced with too much enthusiasm.

"That's cool," said Clarabelle with the crazy blue hair. "And who are you?"

Thrasher faltered. "Me?"

"If he's the Zombie King, who are you? The Zombie Queen?"

"He's not the Zombie Queen," Scapegrace said quickly.

"The Zombie Prince, then?"

"He's Thrasher. That's all he is. Just Thrasher. I'm Vaurien Scapegrace."

Clarabelle nodded. "The Killer Supreme."

Scapegrace stared. "You've heard of me?"

"Of course. Do you like my hair?"

"It's very blue," said Thrasher.

"I dyed it and cut it. I think it was an attempt to leave that part of my life behind me, to start anew. I'm sure that's what it was. It's not just a fashion thing. Is blue hair in this year?"

Scapegrace frowned. "Is it in any year?"

"Is it not?" Clarabelle asked, looking genuinely worried.

"I don't know," Scapegrace confessed. "I don't know much about fashion. You've heard of me, then? The Killer Supreme?"

"Yes. You're a feared assassin."

"But he hasn't actually killed anyone," Thrasher said.

"I killed *you*," Scapegrace snapped. "That not enough for you? I killed the others too, made *them* into zombies."

"But we all came back to life," Thrasher pointed out, "so it can't really be counted, can it?"

Scapegrace towered over him. "It can be counted and it will be counted."

"Sorry, Master," Thrasher whimpered.

"Why do you want to see Doctor Nye?" Clarabelle asked.

"I think it can return me to full life," Scapegrace said, "and end this accursed affliction."

"What accursed affliction?"

"Uh, this. Being a zombie."

"Oh. That's a shame. I think zombies are kind of cute."

"Seriously?"

"I may be thinking about bunnies. Which one has the fluffy little tail, zombies or bunnies?"

"Bunnies."

"Then it's bunnies I'm thinking of. Do you want to go with me to see Doctor Nye? I'm going to ask it to give me a job, and you can ask it to give you life, and your friend can ask it to give him a brain."

"I already have a brain," Thrasher said defensively.

"I mean a better one."

"I like the brain I have."

"Shut up," Scapegrace said. He turned back to Clarabelle. "Do you know where this Sanctuary is? I heard they have a new one."

"They do," said Clarabelle. "It's in a far-off place, away from the prying eyes of the mortal world. Wicklow, I think."

"Then let's go to Wicklow," Scapegrace said. "Do you have a car?"

"I don't know how to drive."

"Don't worry, Clarabelle. You can ride in our van."

She looked over her shoulder. "It's got a giant penguin on it."

"Yes, it does."

"We should call it the Penguin-Mobile."

"OK."

"Or Fred."

"Penguin-Mobile is fine."

She nodded. "All right then."

18

THE ARREST WARRANT

In the otherwise silent Temple, raised voices darted through the narrow corridors like unwelcome guests. Craven followed them back to their source and barged through into the Antechamber.

"What the hell is going on?" he thundered, and watched with extreme satisfaction as the crowd of Necromancers parted for him, suddenly quiet and subservient. In that crowd he saw the faces of men and women he had argued with over the years, people he had despised, who had despised him, who had called him petty and sycophantic and weak. Now they bowed, they practically *prostrated themselves*, in his presence. Never had Craven felt so powerful.

As the crowd parted, he saw the others. Sanctuary agents, Skulduggery Pleasant standing in front, a piece of paper in his gloved hand. The Necromancers had been blocking their entry into the main Temple.

"This is private property," Craven said. He didn't sneer. He didn't snarl. He didn't hide behind the biggest Necromancer and issue threats. He was beyond all that now.

"This is a warrant for the arrest of Melancholia St Clair," Pleasant responded. "Either bring her out to us, or we'll go in after her."

"On what charge are you arresting her, Detective?"

"Assault on a Sanctuary agent."

Craven chuckled. "The Death Bringer, our great and glorious saviour, has not left the Temple since her Surge. Maybe you would be better off putting your energies into finding Lord Vile, instead of making up false allegations."

"She assaulted Valkyrie Cain."

"What are you talking about?"

"She went to her house while her little baby sister slept inside. You didn't know about that, did you? That your little saviour had sneaked out for a bit?"

Craven didn't allow his surprise to register on his face. "Miss Cain was attacked? How dreadful. I do hope there's no permanent damage. Is there?"

"If there was, Craven, you and your friends here would already be dead." There was something in Pleasant's voice that assured Craven that what he was saying was true. "In the meantime, we're going to have to take Melancholia in for questioning."

"I'm afraid that won't be possible."

"Hand her over."

"We all know what's going on here. This is religious persecution."

"Glorifying death is not a religion, it's a sickness."

"You are offending me."

"Look at the face I don't have, Craven, and tell me if it looks like I care. She broke the law. If you harbour her, you're breaking it too."

"So does that mean you're going to arrest me, Detective? You're going to arrest all of us? I hate to point out the obvious, but there are more of us than there are of you." At his words, the Necromancers started moving, encircling the Sanctuary agents. "I think it might be best for everyone if you just turned round and went away. Don't you think so, Detective?"

"If you try to stop us from carrying out our official duty, the full force of the Sanctuary will come raining down on this Temple."

"Well now, that certainly seems intimidating. Until, of course, you take into account that within this self-same Temple, we happen to have the Death Bringer, who would be the most powerful sorcerer the world has ever seen. So, factoring that in, your little threat doesn't really mean a whole lot, now does it? To be honest, there isn't anything *you* can do to stop *us* from doing anything *we* want to do. I don't wish to worry you, or any of the brave agents and operatives behind you, but we could kill you all right here and right now, and we'd get away with it."

Pleasant tilted his head slightly. "That's where your mind is going, is it?"

"That's the thought that has just entered my head, yes."

"Kill us. Kill the next group of agents who come. Kill the next."

"There is a pleasing simplicity to it, isn't there?"

"We'll be back, Craven. And there'll be more of us."

Craven shook his head. "Too late for that, I'm afraid. My mind is made up. These are your final moments."

"Is that so? You're going to give the order, then?"

"It's been a pleasure talking to you. Necromancers—"

Pleasant's hand blurred, and suddenly he was holding a gun, pointing it straight at Craven. "If you issue that order to attack, and if these Necromancers do manage to defeat us – which I doubt – then you won't get to see any of that. I'll put a bullet in your brain from right here, where I'm standing. You'll be dead before you hit the ground. Certainly, you'll be dead before any of your friends even move towards me. So you'll never know if they beat us or not. And you'll never know if we come back here with an army, and drag your Death Bringer away in shackles. You'll never know any of that. So go ahead, Craven. Give the order. Sacrifice yourself for the well-being of your Death Bringer. Be a martyr."

Craven hadn't realised it before, but he was thirsty. There was nothing in the world he wanted more right at that moment than a glass of water.

"We're going to walk out of here," Pleasant continued. "We're going to do it slowly. Your friends can back up against the walls. It'll probably be safer for them if they do so, because if even one Necromancer stands between us and the door, we're going to kill every last one of you. But you'll be first, Craven. You keep that in mind. You'll be first."

"Let them go," said Craven, his voice a croak.

Pleasant's gun didn't waver as he backed away, and Craven didn't move. Even if he'd wanted to, his body seemed locked in position.

The Sanctuary agents walked backwards to the stairs and he watched them climb. Pleasant stayed where he was until the doors above him opened. Daylight flooded the staircase, illuminating him as he stood there. His gun glinted. Beneath his hat, his skull was in the deepest, darkest shadow.

"Good boy," he said. He spoke quietly, but his voice easily carried across to Craven. "We're going to be keeping an eye on things here, to make sure you don't take Melancholia off on a nice holiday before we have a chance to speak with her. I'm sure you understand."

Craven said nothing, and Pleasant climbed the steps. A moment after he was gone, the doors slammed shut, cutting off the sunlight.

19

GODS AND MONSTERS

The cops hadn't been any use. Lynch's death was reported on the news as a mere robbery. No one cared if another homeless person died. Just another piece of rubbish swept into the gutter of the city. Who was there to mourn for someone like that?

Kenny would have liked to mourn, but in truth he was too excited. His run-in with the tall man who'd called himself Detective Inspector Me and the teenage girl had convinced him that something bigger was going on. Suddenly this article on modern urban legends had started to spiral into territories he would never have anticipated. What did the tall man and the teenage girl have to do with Lynch's murder? Had they killed him? His stomach churned with happy nerves. This was a *story* now. A proper *story*.

If his car hadn't died on him, he would have tried to find Bernadette Maguire's cottage and asked her what exactly Lynch had told her. There was the faint possibility that her life was in danger now that Lynch was dead, but he doubted it. Such things only happened in movies, unfortunately.

Which meant that Kenny now had only one lead left to him – and that was the tattooist he'd heard about.

It was a glorious Tuesday afternoon in Temple Bar. Kenny walked up cobbled streets until he found the brightly coloured building. Music played above. He climbed the wooden stairs, passing the photographs of tattoos and piercings and other works of body art. He had never been tempted to get a tattoo himself. It all seemed like a little too much pain.

There was a skinny man in a Thin Lizzy T-shirt, his arms inked, a ring in his lips and his head shaved. He turned down the music when he saw Kenny. Damien Dempsey was playing – 'Negative Vibes'.

"Are you Finbar?" Kenny asked.

"I am indeed," said the skinny man. "Are you looking for a tattoo?"

Kenny hesitated, then smiled. "Actually, no."

"A piercing, then? No need to be embarrassed. Just tell me what you want pierced and we'll pierce it. I'll pierce anything, me."

"Actually, I was hoping we could just talk."

"Oh," Finbar said. "Oh, right. Well, I'm flattered, I am, but before you go getting your hopes up, I have to tell you – I'm married."

"Uh, that's not what I meant."

"My wife's in the other room, if you want to meet her. I'd call her in, but she's not really speaking to me right now. Don't know why. She was in a cult, you see, and she had to shave all her hair off. She left eventually, like, and came back to me, and we're a family again, but her head's having a little bit of trouble re-growing all that hair. She says I'm unsympathetic. I say she looks like a tufty bowling ball. Maybe if you see her, you can decide who's right."

"I wouldn't really be comfortable doing that."

"Ah, fair enough, I suppose."

"I heard you're a psychic."

Finbar's laugh was delayed by a split second. "Not me, mate. But there's a Mystic Meg up the street there, she does a bit of tarot, that sort of thing. She's good, you know, if you believe in it."

"I don't want my palm read. You see the future."

"Who's been filling your head with this nonsense?"

"It's the word on the street."

"And what street would that be? No, not me. Sorry."

"What do you know of the Passage?"

Finbar didn't move away. He stood there, his tongue pressed against his lip ring. "Who did you say you were?"

"My name's Kenny Dunne. I'm a journalist."

"And why would a journalist be asking about stupid things like the Passage?"

"So you *do* know about it."

"Don't know anything that could help *you*, sorry. You'd probably better go."

"I can pay."

"Then you have more money than sense, mate. Keep it, spend it on something worthwhile. Like a taxi."

"They say you're a psychic who saw something so horrible that you haven't been able to see any visions since."

"In that case I wouldn't be any help to you, would I? But you don't know what you're talking about, and I haven't a clue where you're coming up with this stuff. I'm a busy man. I need you to leave."

Kenny indicated the empty room. "*This* is busy?"

"Tuesday takes a while to get going."

"Finbar, you know what's going on, don't you? I've been hearing about the end of the world, ancient gods, super powers, strange people who can do amazing things… I'm pretty sure I've even met some of them. A tall man in a suit. A dark-haired girl. You know these people?"

"They don't ring any bells."

"I'm going to find out, sooner or later. You can help make sure I get the facts right."

"I don't know any facts."

"Come on. I know you're not a stupid man."

"I'm quite stupid. Ask anyone."

"Finbar, are there superheroes living among us?"

Finbar snorted with laughter, and Kenny started to feel a little thick. "Superheroes? In tights and capes, flying around? If there *were* superheroes, Mr Journalist, don't you think they'd be in New York or somewhere like that? There's really not that many tall buildings for Spider-Man to swing from in Dublin, you know? He'd have maybe two swings and then he'd just hang there looking disappointed."

"These people don't wear tights and capes, Finbar."

"So they're naked superheroes? That's grand for now, but when the good weather is over they're going to regret it."

"They look like us. They dress like us. But they're not like us. They're different."

"You," Finbar said, "are sounding very racist right now."

"I'm going to find the truth, with or without you. Either way, you'll be seeing a lot of me in the next few weeks and months. I'm going to follow you wherever you go."

"I don't go anywhere."

"I'm going to trail your friends."

"I don't have any."

"I'm going to photograph every single person to enter and leave this tattoo parlour."

Finbar rolled his eyes. "And they'll hate that, because people who get dragons drawn on their backs are normally so shy about other people noticing them."

"It doesn't have to be this way, Finbar."

That tongue, pressing against the lip ring. "I can't help you," he said at last. "But I know someone who might be able to. His name's Geoffrey."

"What does Geoffrey do?"

"You can ask him yourself, if he meets with you. Three o'clock today, outside Bruxelles on Harry Street."

"How do I know he'll be there?"

"I'll give him a call. If he wants to meet you, he'll be there."

"If he doesn't show up, I'm coming back."

"Well, if you come back, I might not open the door."

"The door's always open."

"Then I'll get the lock fixed," Finbar retorted. Kenny waited to see if Finbar had anything to add, but he obviously didn't, so he left him alone.

Kenny had lunch in Milano's, then walked up to Grafton Street. He wasn't going to be late – not this time. He got there at half two and sat outside in the sunshine. At a little before three, a small man in khakis wandered up. He had a gentle face, beads in his beard, and hair the colour and approximate texture of wheat. He had many bracelets on his wrists and rings on his fingers.

He joined Kenny at his table.

"You're Geoffrey?" Kenny asked.

"Indeed I am," said the man. "And you must be Mr Journalist."

"Kenny Dunne, hi, pleased to meet you."

"The pleasure is all mine."

"I really want to thank you for meeting with me. I've been having a hard time getting anyone to talk about this stuff."

"I can't really blame them," Geoffrey said with a chuckle. "This kind of talk gets people killed."

Kenny frowned. "You're talking about Paul Lynch?"

"I'm sorry, I don't know who that is."

"He was a homeless man. He said he had visions of the apocalypse."

"Which one?"

"Sorry?"

"Which apocalypse? There are a few."

"Uh... there was one where these old gods came back..."

"The Faceless Ones, yes. What about the Remnants? Did he foresee that? Last Christmas?"

"The Insanity Virus thing? With all those slices of darkness? They're called Remnants?"

"Don't worry about them, they're all locked away, safe and sound. Did he foresee the Death Bringer?"

"Who's the Death Bringer?"

"The Death Bringer's the one who is going to initiate the Passage."

Kenny took out his notebook, started scribbling. "Death Bringer. One word or two?"

"Either. I've always preferred two. What about Darquesse?"

"I'm sorry, I don't know what that is."

"He didn't foresee Darquesse? Oh that's interesting." Geoffrey sat back, finger tapping the beads in his beard.

"After every apocalypse passed without actually happening," Kenny said, "he'd get a new set of visions."

"Ah, well, that explains it. He foresaw them one at a time. As each one was averted he'd see the next one. It's a pity he didn't see Darquesse, we've been trying to find out more about her."

"So it's all real?" Kenny asked. "All of it? The visions, the gods, the superheroes?"

Geoffrey chuckled. "Superheroes? They're not superheroes, Mr Journalist. They're sorcerers."

"Sorcerers, like... with magic?"

"Like with magic, yes."

"So, the tall man and the teenage girl... they're sorcerers too?"

"Oh," Geoffrey said, smiling. "You mean Skulduggery Pleasant and Valkyrie Cain. Those two, they're the good guys. We're all alive today because of them."

"They saved the world?"

"They've saved the world a few times, indeed they have."

"This is amazing."

"Yes, it is. You don't believe any of it, though."

Kenny smiled, and shrugged. "Well, I'm, I suppose I'm sceptical, but if *you* believe it, there must be something to it, right?"

"But I'm a crackpot," Geoffrey said, smiling broadly. "Finbar's a crackpot. Everyone you've spoken to about this is a crackpot. You can see that, can't you?"

Kenny frowned. "You're all nuts?"

"Sadly, yes. You're going to go home today and you're going to look at all your notes and research and you're going to realise that it's all just nonsense."

"Nonsense?"

"To be honest, you'll be happy. You were never really interested in this stuff in the first place. The fact is, you found it kind of boring."

Kenny nodded. "It's pretty dull, all right."

"The idea of people with strange powers is just ridiculous, isn't it?"

"It is, actually. It belongs in a comic book."

"That's exactly where it belongs."

"I've been wasting my time," Kenny said. "God, I've just been wasting my time…"

Geoffrey nodded, and didn't disagree.

Kenny gave him a smile. "Listen, hey, sorry for being such a bother," he said. "I really have to go, actually. I've got a story due tomorrow, and I need to work on it."

"Of course," Geoffrey said. "Don't let me delay you."

Kenny shook his hand and got up, started walking. He put his notebook away, glanced back to make sure Geoffrey wasn't wandering after him. The last thing he needed was a crackpot like that following him home.

When he got back to his apartment, Kenny started packing all that nonsense away. He couldn't believe he had wasted so much of his time on this, couldn't believe he had actually got excited about the possibilities. What possibilities? A group of nutcases who all subscribed to the same delusion? He would have burnt everything, shoved it in the bin, but that wasn't his way. He never discarded his notes – not until the article was done. Everything was useful. He might not write a world-shattering exposé on a secret subculture of superheroes, but he could use what he'd learned if he was ever tasked to write about the homeless in Dublin, or the plight of the psychologically disturbed. Nothing, he knew, was ever wasted. Not really.

He flicked through his notes. The Remnants. Darquesse. The Death Bringer – one word or two – the Passage. The tall man and the teenage girl: Skulduggery Pleasant and Valkyrie Cain. They were real, even if the identities they had given him were not. But that was to be expected, after all. Fragments of reality can be glimpsed through even the most fractured of window.

He read back over it, battling the tide of boredom that swept over him. It didn't stop him reading, of course. He was a journalist. Research was what he did, and oftentimes research was mind-numbingly boring, just like this was.

He didn't know *why* it was boring, though. He couldn't put his finger on it. It didn't *sound* boring. Super powers and the apocalypse and saving the world. But Geoffrey had known. For all his lunacy, he'd hit the nail right on the head with that one, and the moment he'd uttered those words, Kenny had felt it. The boredom. The dullness. It just seeped in, robbing him of his enthusiasm.

Kenny frowned. Before Geoffrey had told him that this was all boring, Kenny had found it fascinating. He remembered that distinctly. But then it was like a switch had been flicked inside him, and all his interest had faded away. He sat on the arm of the chair, brow furrowed. How had that happened? How could it have happened?

He remembered Geoffrey's face. Smiling. Avuncular. A bit of an oddball, granted. A crackpot, even, as he himself had said. His voice was nice. It wasn't as smooth as the tall man's, but it had a quality that got inside your head. It was a warm voice. Comforting. It made you want to trust him. It made you want to believe him.

Kenny's notes dropped from his hand, scattered across the floor. His eyes were wide. His mouth was half open.

He'd been hypnotised.

He didn't know how Geoffrey had done it, but he'd convinced him with a few short words that he didn't think what he thought, that he didn't believe what he believed.

"Good God," he said to his empty apartment.

All of a sudden his enthusiasm came back to him, his interest roaring inside him like a furnace in his chest. Finbar had sent him to meet with Geoffrey so that Geoffrey could work his hoodoo on him, make him walk away from what might have been the biggest story of his career.

Kenny grinned. *You're gonna have to do better than that.*

20

RIDING OUT

China gripped the reins and pulled, straining against the horse's resistance. He was a wilful one, all right. Every turn they made, he tried to shake her loose. Every ditch they jumped, he threatened to throw her into. She'd been fighting him since she swung into the saddle. Her arms ached and her legs burned. Her jodhpurs were splattered with mud and her shirt stuck to her back. Her hands were raw from the reins.

God, she loved him.

A creature of fierce strength and beauty, and one that made her work to get him to do what she wanted. A challenge.

She used to ride out all the time when she was younger, but as her friends fell away or died, or she betrayed them or they betrayed her, it had become a solitary pursuit – and for a while, she preferred it that way. Just her and the horse and the open countryside, the hoof beats that thudded through her body, clods of grass and mud kicked up behind them. No talk, no flattery, no professions of love.

But people change, and she was as vulnerable to this phenomenon as anyone. Decades of solitude had hardened her, but isolation without end was a dangerous thing. Suddenly she didn't want to be alone on these afternoons.

Valkyrie would enjoy this, she knew. China had heard her talk of when she rode out as a young girl, before she met Skulduggery – just a beginner, but with a natural's love for it. Maybe one of these days, as soon as Valkyrie got a break from saving the world, China would invite her to the stables. She even had the perfect horse picked out – strong and fast with a hint of mischief. The perfect way to get reacquainted with the saddle.

Providing, of course, that China found a way to settle this Eliza Scorn business. It required not just a single strike against Scorn, or even a strike against Scorn and Prave together, but multiple strikes against multiple targets at the same time. The biggest problem with that, and this was truly the hold that Scorn had on her, was that China didn't know who these targets might be.

There may have been none, of course, Scorn may have been

bluffing, but China doubted it. In order to build up the Church of the Faceless, Scorn would need a lot more than China's resources. She had to have benefactors, secret backers and interested parties. She wouldn't have told them what China had done in her misspent youth, but she would have worked out a way to get that information to them if something bad happened to her. Which meant that China needed to find out who these mysterious benefactors were, and take them all down at the same time.

China slowed, pulling the reins firmly until the tired horse complied. She took the trail down to the river, and the creature splashed in gratefully, the fast-moving water cooling his muscles and rising past China's boots, but she didn't mind. She patted his neck, told him how good he was, how he was the best horse to be kept in these stables in twenty years.

When they were done, she guided him up on to the bank, and walked back to the yard. She had a small army there tending to the horses, all unmarried men and women. These were talented people who did their jobs well – she didn't want them leaving their wives and husbands and families just because they'd fallen in love with her. It was easier to deal with love-struck sorcerers, who at least knew her reputation – but mortals didn't stand a chance. At her instruction, all workers were to vacate the yard whenever she was in it unless explicitly asked to stay.

That afternoon, the yard was empty. She dismounted, led the horse into the stable. She undid the saddle, swung it up on to the edge of the door. The horse nuzzled her neck and China smiled. She forked in some fresh hay and stepped out, and there was a man behind her. China swung back her elbow, caught him on the jaw. He staggered and she turned, swept his feet from under him. He hit the floor, went to roll away, then stopped, and held up his hands.

"China," Jaron Gallow said, "I'm not here to fight you."

China raised an eyebrow. "Good. That will make this so much easier."

"I'm here to help."

"Help what?"

"Help you." He rubbed his jaw, and looked up at her. "I know Eliza is back in town. I know she's been hanging around with that Prave idiot. I've been watching them. I saw you visiting."

"Everyone's spying on everyone else," China said. "It warms my heart, it truly does."

"Can I stand up?"

"Of course you can. There's no guarantee I won't put you back down again, but you can at least try."

He narrowed his eyes then stood, moving slowly. He was dark-haired and graceful, though thinner than she remembered. His face was gaunt. She watched him, noticing his right hand for the first time. It was gloved.

"The last I saw of you," she said, "you were chopping that arm off to avoid being used as a vessel for the Faceless Ones. Did it grow back?"

"This? No, this isn't mine. It belonged to a donor."

"Willing or otherwise?"

"Otherwise."

"What do you want, Jaron?"

"I can only imagine what Eliza Scorn has over you. That's why she called you, right? To force you to do something? It must be pretty substantial, whatever it is."

"I can't tell if you're circling a point or just boring me on purpose."

"I know what their plans are. I know they want to build up the Church of the Faceless all around the world. I'm pretty sure that Eliza views herself as some kind of Pope figure, thinks she can lead the faithful into a world where the strong are rewarded and the weak are discarded."

"The same kind of world *you're* looking for," China reminded him.

He shook his head. "Not any more. People change, China. You know that better than anyone. You led the Diablerie before me, you taught me everything I know. You were a zealot, through and through. And now look at you. Is it so hard to believe that I could have gone through the same transformation? That day, at the farm, when we opened the portal and the Faceless Ones came back… I saw them for what they really were. They're not gods. They're *things*. Creatures. Monsters. As powerful as gods, perhaps, but they certainly don't deserve to be worshipped."

"Blasphemy," China said with a smile.

"Indeed it is. I've lost my faith, China. There is no hope of a beautiful world if they return, and that's been the big lie, right from the start. The idea that we disciples would be spared, that we'd be welcomed while everyone else perished… Ridiculous. Those things don't care about us."

"All right," China said. "So you've had a change of heart. You have seen the light and you have turned away from wickedness. That's all wonderful. But why should I be at all interested?"

"I'm here to stop them."

"Eliza?"

"Eliza, Prave, any and everyone else. I'm here to shut down the Church of the Faceless, but I need your help to do it. I've already wandered in from the wilderness and rejoined them. It'll be like the good old days. They're not going to trust you, but they do trust me."

"So you have infiltrated their ranks – now what?"

"Eliza wants to build the Church's strength. In order to do that, she's going to need a comprehensive plan of how strong, or weak, the Church is right now, right at this moment. She'll have names, locations, funds, resources… She'll have the identities of spies and informants loyal to the Faceless Ones. She's already told me of a list of people who are going to help her build the Church back up. Twelve names on it, she said, all powerful sorcerers, most in positions of influence and authority, and unlike you, they won't need to be blackmailed into helping. From what she's told me, some of these people sit on certain Councils around the world."

China kept her smile to herself. "Everything we would need, in other words, to completely dismantle the whole thing."

"Exactly. Once we have that information, we won't need Eliza any more. We can either share it with your friends in the Sanctuary, or take care of things ourselves."

"Travelling the world," China said, "killing everyone on that list. How romantic."

"It's the only way to be sure. These people, what they want… it's all too dangerous. We have to erase them from the face of the planet, to make sure it never happens."

"So dramatic."

"Has it ever been any different when it comes to the Faceless Ones?"

"I suppose not. That's why I was drawn in at such a young age. Now, Jaron, all that sounds very thrilling, and very wonderful, and I'm sure it would be a thoroughly diverting adventure – but why on earth should I trust you?"

"What would I have to gain by lying?"

"I sincerely don't know, but Eliza is a cunning lady, and she always has been."

"You think I'm working for her?"

China smiled. "It is crossing my mind even as we speak."

"You're just going to have to believe me."

"And that, my dear, is where this whole proposal falls flat. I don't believe *anyone*, let alone someone who once tried to kill me."

"I tried to kill you twice."

"Really?"

"That time in Naples? The fire?"

China laughed. "That was you? That fire scorched my favourite shawl."

"And it killed eighty-three people."

"But the *shawl* was exquisite. Still, I suppose I can't blame you. I would have done the same."

"You might not be able to trust me, China, but I know I can trust you. You want Eliza gone, you want the Church of the Faceless gone. I'm your only chance to make that happen."

She didn't really have much in the way of other options, so China gave him a smile.

21

THE LOVE OF A VAMPIRE

Valkyrie woke. It was getting dark outside, and as usual, it was cold in Skulduggery's house. Her clothes, ripped to shreds as they were, didn't exactly help. She stood and stretched, eased a crick out of her neck and went to the mirror, checking for scars. As much as she hated to admit it, Nye had done an excellent job. She was tired but feeling good, confident that a night in her own bed was all she needed to make a full recovery.

She called for a taxi, went out to meet it and sat in the back. If she had called Fletcher, she'd be home already, but she would have also had to listen to him disapprove of the many injuries she sustained over the course of any given month. She just wasn't in the mood for him, not this evening.

The taxi dropped her in Haggard and she cut through the park. She could almost have predicted who would step out in front of her.

"I failed you," Caelan said.

"Hi Chuckles," she responded. She didn't stop walking.

"I should have been faster," he said from beside her. "I should have torn that Necromancer's throat out. But she took you away before I... I will not fail you again."

"Don't worry about it. What're you doing in town?"

"I'm here for you."

"Did you drive? Get the bus? Do vampires get buses?"

He stepped in front of her. "You make jokes," he said. "But I see nothing to laugh at. The Death Bringer, Lord Vile, the end of the world... none of that would be as bad as losing you."

"I'm sorry? No more smooches is worse than the world ending? Seriously? You really want to stand behind that statement? You don't think it's a teensy bit melodramatic?"

"Without our love, Valkyrie, there is no world left to save."

"And that statement actually makes less sense than the one before it. Caelan, you've got to cop on to yourself. I've read *Wuthering Heights*, OK? I know the whole gloomy-tortured-romantic figure thing. Everyone knows it. It's not as romantic as you'd think. Where's the fun? Where's the laughter? I couldn't be with anyone I couldn't have a bit of craic with. I know you hate him but for God's sake, at least Fletcher is fun to be around."

Caelan's face shifted, becoming cold. "Do you love him more than you love me?"

"I never said the word love. I said the word fun."

"We have fun."

"We have a certain kind of fun, yes, but we don't laugh. When was the last time we laughed together?"

"You laugh with Fletcher?"

"All the time."

"Then the boy has his uses. When you need to laugh at something, you have him to laugh at. When you need to be fulfilled, you have me."

"You're really not getting this."

He took her hand in his and knelt before her. "Marry me," he said.

Valkyrie looked at him. He was serious. She had never used the word *dude* in a serious conversation before. She didn't think this qualified. "Dude, I'm sixteen."

"I love you."

"That doesn't make me any older. Stand up."

"Not until you say yes."

"You're going to shuffle around on your knees for the rest of your life? Stand up, for God's sake." She waited until he did as she asked. "Did you seriously propose to me? Have you not heard anything I've been saying these past few months? This is ridiculous. This is beyond ridiculous."

"Be my wife."

"Shut the hell up. What did I tell you? What did I tell you about coming on too strong? Do you not think a marriage proposal falls into that category?"

"We are destined for each other."

"No we're not. Caelan, I've made it quite bloody clear. I've been with you because you're really good-looking and you're dangerous. That's attractive to me. That's a good combination. But they are the only reasons we were together. It's not love."

"It's fate."

"It's not fate either, you idiot. Why do you like me?"

"I love you."

"Then why do you love me? Give me five good reasons why you love me."

"Because you're beautiful."

"You're absolutely right there, but that's got nothing to do with me, that's genetics. Four more, sunshine."

"You're intelligent. You are the light in my darkness."

"Intelligent, that's reason number two. Light in the darkness? That's not a reason, that's a bad song lyric."

"You're full of life. I look at you and I'm reminded of the glory of humanity, how they seize life and let it fill them to the brim."

"I remind you of the glory of humanity. OK, that's reason number three. Two more."

Caelan smiled. "There are more reasons why I love you than there are stars in the night sky."

"In that case you won't have any problem coming up with two more."

He hesitated.

"You don't love me," she told him. "You think you do. You like the idea of it. But the fact of the matter is that you're a hundred and something years old and I'm sixteen. I'm a teenager. Do you not see anything wrong with that?"

"If I repulse you…"

"You don't repulse me, Caelan, because you look like a hot nineteen-year-old. But every time you say something, I'm reminded of the fact that you're really just an old man. And… OK, I've never actually said that out loud before and it's really kind of disgusting."

"For people like us, age doesn't matter."

"For people like *you*, the old men, age doesn't matter. For people like *me*, the teenage girls, it suddenly becomes very icky."

"I'm trying to make you understand, Valkyrie, that love

transcends the meaningless. If I love you, I won't let anything stand in my way. If you love me—"

"Which I don't."

"—then *you* won't let anything stand in *your* way. Marry me, and we'll be together for ever."

"No."

"You can only hide from your feelings for so long."

"And you can only hide from reality for so long. I'm not going to marry you, Caelan. Right now, I'm going home."

"I will accompany you."

"No, you will not."

"The Death Bringer might return."

"You really need to relax. I've got my phone worked out so that all I have to do is tap a little button and Fletcher and Skulduggery come teleporting in. She won't be back, though. She's had her fun."

"You don't need them. I am the only one you need. I am your guardian angel."

"I'm giving you the night off, OK? Go out. Have fun. Meet a girl. Don't obsess over her too much. I promise you, you'll be much more cheerful in the morning."

"You are the only one for me."

"I'm walking away now."

"Say you love me!" he called after her, and she rolled her eyes.

22

THE CHURCH OF THE FACELESS

Scorn kept her waiting, but it was a beautiful morning outside so China didn't mind. It was an obvious little game, designed to teach her who was in charge. A little clumsy, and somewhat disappointing to see that dear old Eliza would resort to it, but it was an inoffensive tactic. According to Gallow, today was the day that he would be revealed to China. She wasn't sure yet if she believed him, but she definitely didn't trust him. He had told her to act suitably surprised when he appeared. China hadn't made any promises.

She became aware of Prave glaring at her from across the church, and arched an eyebrow. "Can I help you?"

"I'm not in love with you," he snarled.

"How dreadful for me."

He gripped the sweeping brush like he was strangling it. "You think everyone falls in love with you. Well, you're wrong. They are weak-minded fools. That's not me."

"Obviously."

"The only love in my heart is for the Faceless Ones, and you will not take that from me."

"Perish the very thought, Mr…" She paused. "Whatever your name is."

"Prave," he blurted.

"Mr Prave, excellent."

"I have worshipped the Dark Gods since I was a boy. My parents were loyal to them. My father fought alongside Mevolent himself."

"That's nice."

"He wasn't a traitor. Not like you!"

"And what was your father's name?"

"Benzel Travestine. He was at Mevolent's side when they destroyed the Sanctuary in Marseilles."

"I doubt it. I've never heard of your father, and I was in Marseilles when the Sanctuary fell. It was my Diablerie that opened the doors to allow Mevolent entry. Your father wasn't there, I'm afraid."

Prave stared at her. "You're lying."

"I could name each and every sorcerer who toppled that Sanctuary. I won't, because you're truly not worth the effort, but I could. It seems your father was exaggerating his importance, Mr Prave."

"My father was a hero!"

"To his weak-minded son, I'm sure he was."

Prave hurled the sweeping brush away and stormed over, fists clenched. China turned her head to him and sighed. He stopped a hand's breadth away, face red and snarling, like he was forcing himself not to commit incredible acts of violence.

"You," China said, "are a very impressive man."

"*Do not mock me!*" he screeched.

China smiled. "Walk back over there, pick up the sweeping brush and continue cleaning. Or go for a nice walk and think about all the lies your father told you. I really don't care what you do, so long as you stop breathing on me. It's really not as soothing as you might think."

Prave's bulging eyes bulged even further, which was a feat in itself. "I should kill you right here."

"You know," China said, "there was a time when nobody dared threaten me. I just wouldn't stand for it. The amount of people

I killed, of bodies I twisted and bones I snapped, all because they had allowed their anger to momentarily overwhelm their good sense. I regret it all now, of course. I was out of control. I was indulging the darkness inside me far too often. I was not, Mr Prave, a very nice person. But I have changed. I have allowed the years to mellow me. Now I find joy in simple pleasures. A good book. A fine wine. Good company. All of these things make me smile. They make me happy.

"But every once in a while, I get the urge. You know what I'm talking about, don't you? The urge for destruction. The urge to hurt, maim, kill. It's quite a thing, to experience that urge, to let it wash over you, to give in to it. It's addictive. It's all-consuming. You lose yourself to it. It's quite, quite wonderful. I can feel it, even as I speak, tapping around the edges of my mind, trying to prise me open, slip its fingers in. And it would be so easy to let it happen. But we're all like that, aren't we? We're all barbarians at our core. We're all savage, murderous beasts. I know I am. I'm sure you are. The only difference between us, Mr Prave, is how loudly we roar. I know I roar very loudly indeed. How about you? Do you think you can match me?"

Prave had grown quite pale. His fists were no longer clenched and he was no longer gritting his teeth. He took a step back, then another one. He hesitated, then slowly turned and went back to his sweeping brush.

China shrugged, and Scorn appeared at the door.

"China," she said. "So sorry to have kept you waiting."

"Not at all," China smiled. "Mr Prave here was entertaining me. I do so like how you've kept him around."

Scorn shrugged. "Ah, well, I made the mistake of feeding him, you see, and now he just won't go away."

China heard Prave muttering under his breath.

"But I didn't ask you here to help me insult the help, as fun as that may be. I have a surprise for you."

"Let me guess," China said. "You've changed your mind and you're going to put all this nonsense behind you."

"Not even close," said Scorn. "Do you want another try? I bet you won't guess what it is."

"You're going to tell Skulduggery Pleasant what you're planning to do and let him shoot you in the head."

"Wrong again, I'm afraid. Do you want one more try?"

"I'd love one more try."

"Then go ahead, China. Guess what the surprise is."

China paused, tapped her chin thoughtfully and smiled. "I know. Is it, by any chance, Jaron Gallow with a brand-new arm?"

Oh, she wished she had a camera to capture the look on Eliza Scorn's face. Gallow emerged from the doorway behind, suddenly unsure, suddenly paranoid that he'd been betrayed, that he was walking into a trap. There was a sudden fear in his eyes that was almost impossible to fake, and now China did believe him.

"How did you know?" Scorn asked. Almost snarled, in fact.

"Please," China said dismissively. "I know what he had for breakfast this morning. I know what he's been doing since he got back to Europe. I was only wondering how long it would take you to reveal him."

A smile appeared on Scorn's lips. "You always were impossible to surprise. Jaron here has just returned to the fold. I hope there's no bad blood between you."

"What's in the past is in the past," China said. "I'm going to end up killing every one of you for all this, and one more name added to the list won't make much difference."

Gallow looked at her, then at Scorn. "I thought you said she was under control."

"She is," Scorn said. "She just likes to say these things to pretend she's still in charge. But as long as I keep her secret, China will do what she's told. For instance, I told her to come back with information about all this Necromancer fuss I've been hearing about. China?"

Everyone else was standing, so China sat on a pew and crossed her legs. She looked at Scorn without tilting her chin, pleased with the way she had changed the dynamic of the room. "Melancholia St Clair is the latest Necromancer to be handed the title 'Death Bringer'," she said. "Unlike the others, however, it seems that this girl will actually strive to fulfil her duties."

"And what are her duties?" asked Gallow.

"To usher in the Passage, and to save the world. If your next question is to ask me about the Passage, you can save your breath. It is something of a mystery, even to those who trade in mysteries. Suffice to say, the end result is a supposedly better world where the living and the dead exist side by side."

"Ridiculous," Scorn said. "That would completely negate death. It would reduce it to a mere concept."

"And, possibly, make the world a better place."

Scorn shook her head. "The world is how the Faceless Ones left it, and that is how it shall stay. If it looks like the Necromancers have a chance of success, we may have to act against them."

"But that's what the Sanctuary is doing," Prave said, hurrying over. "Shouldn't we stay out of it? We'd just get in the way."

Scorn didn't even look at him, but Gallow did, and Prave shrank back. "I don't know you," Gallow said. "I've just met you. Already I want to hurt you."

"You, uh, you actually do know me," Prave said. "We met twice, actually. It was only for a few minutes, though, so you probably don't remember."

"I don't," Gallow said. "At all. Even remotely. And I'm glad. Remembering you would annoy me. It would mean you somehow managed to take up space in my head, and I reserve space in my head for people who interest me or, at the very least, have something worthwhile to offer. Now shut up, and don't say anything else."

Prave gaped at him. "How... how dare you. I rescued the Church of the Faceless from collapse. I built it back up to—"

"You built it back up to *this?*" Gallow didn't have to gesture to his surroundings to make his point. "You're a weak, miserable little man, with no concept of what it will take to bring back the Dark Gods. We *could* leave this Death Bringer business to the Sanctuary, but that would mean entrusting the Sanctuary with all of our future plans. Is that what you want?"

Scorn turned her head, smiled at Prave. "Maybe you could make us all some tea."

Prave blinked his bulbous eyes. "Tea?"

"A nice big pot, there's a good man."

"But... but I'm in this! I'm involved in... in this whole thing. I'm one of the *leaders!*"

Scorn raised an eyebrow. "You? Oh, my word, no. No, Prave, you are not one of the leaders. There is only one leader here, and that is me. Gallow is my second, China is our reluctant sponsor and untrustworthy ally, and you're the one who makes the tea. So, Prave, enough of this silly talk and the giving of your inconsequential opinions. Be a dear, and go and make the tea."

Prave closed his mouth, his wet lips pressing together like slippery eels, then turned abruptly and left the room. His ears, which were substantial, burned so red they practically left a heat trail behind him.

Scorn nodded to China. "Continue."

"Melancholia attacked Valkyrie Cain, and the Sanctuary have seized upon the chance to issue an arrest warrant."

"They're getting ready to strike," Scorn murmured.

"What about Lord Vile?" Gallow asked. "I haven't been so out of the loop that I didn't hear of his return."

"His *supposed* return," Scorn said. "But has he been seen since he battled Skulduggery Pleasant?"

Gallow looked at her. "You think his return is a lie?"

"Perhaps. What could spook the Necromancers more than a rumour that Lord Vile is out to get them?"

"But if he has returned, and he does seek to destroy the Death Bringer, then maybe we can convince him to come back to our side."

Scorn looked at him. "And how do you propose we do that? Are you going to use your longstanding friendship with him to delay his killing stroke while you make your case? Oh, no, that's right. You don't *have* a longstanding friendship with him, do you? No one does. We may have fought alongside him during the war, but that was a long time ago. We don't know where his loyalties lie."

"We know it's not with the Necromancers," Gallow said. "That's something, at least."

"China," Scorn said, "what do you think?"

"I think approaching Lord Vile is a wonderful idea," China answered, smiling. "I think the pair of you should go and talk to him. I'm sure he'd love that."

"If I didn't know any better, I'd swear you were trying to get me killed before I have a chance to upstage you at the Requiem Ball."

"You're attending?"

"Why, yes. And why shouldn't I? We're celebrating the end of the war, aren't we?"

"Indeed we are," said China. "But I doubt there will be many guests there who fought on the losing side."

Scorn shrugged. "Winning side, losing side, it's all a matter of degree. And then there's you, of course. You don't *have* a side, do you? You abandoned your side. Turned your back on your—"

"If you're going to describe what a traitor I am, I feel I have to tell you that I've heard it all before, and if you're finished with me, I have a library to get back to."

"Finished with you?" Scorn laughed. "China, my darling, I haven't even *started.*"

She met Gallow later that night, under the moon and the stars.

"That list of twelve people," she said, "the important and

influential sorcerers Eliza was talking about. They're going to be at the Requiem Ball."

Gallow frowned. "You're sure? She'd meet with them right under everyone's noses? It's far too dangerous."

"Not for Eliza. It's the perfect excuse to talk to them. We're going to need that list if we want to shut this down before it starts."

Gallow smiled. "You want to assassinate them, don't you?"

She shrugged her left shoulder. "It is one option."

"The first person we'll have to take care of is Scorn herself. Once we have the list, we won't need her any more."

"No," said China. "We take them all out at the same time."

"That may not be possible."

"Let me worry about that. Once they're dead, the Church will crumble, once and for all." She looked at Gallow. "Do you think you can retrieve it without her knowing?"

"It shouldn't be a problem. You think you can organise the assassination of Scorn and twelve others?"

China smiled. "It shouldn't be a problem."

23

THE HOMECOMING

They'd been on the road for a little under twenty-four hours when the Penguin-Mobile stopped, and Clarabelle tapped on the glass. "We're here," she said.

Scapegrace slid open the freezer and got out. He watched Clarabelle stretch, envying the yawn that accompanied the movement. He was dead. He didn't get tired any more. He missed it.

It was another gorgeous day outside. Grumbling, he put on a coat and pulled up the hood to hide his head. Clarabelle left the van first, and Scapegrace pushed Thrasher aside so he could go next. He stepped on to a pavement. It was awfully familiar. He looked around.

"We're in Roarhaven," he said.

Clarabelle nodded. "This is where the new Sanctuary is."

He stared at her. "But I know Roarhaven. I lived here for years. I know how to get to Roarhaven. We didn't have to spend twenty-four hours driving around waiting for you to remember where the Sanctuary was. You could have just said Roarhaven and I'd have known. We could have been here in an hour."

"It's not about the destination. It's about the journey."

"It's a little about the destination," Thrasher said quietly.

"And besides," Clarabelle said, "we got to see the sights, didn't we?"

"I was stuck in a freezer," Scapegrace reminded her.

"This is my home now," Clarabelle said, ignoring them. "Or it will be, if I get the job. It's a lovely town, isn't it?"

Scapegrace hesitated. "Do you really think so?"

"No, I don't," she admitted. "I liked where I was living in Dublin more. I had a nice flat, and I had a gerbil. His name was Theodore."

"That's a nice name," said Thrasher.

"I don't think he liked it. Roarhaven, though, it isn't a gerbil kind of place."

"I don't suppose it is," Scapegrace said.

"The people aren't very nice."

"They don't trust outsiders."

"I don't think Theodore would have fitted in. Before I left, I released him into the wild."

Thrasher frowned. "You released your gerbil into the wild?"

"Yes. Back into his natural habitat. It was only fair. Now he can live out the rest of his life, hunting his prey and raising a family."

"What, uh, what would a gerbil's prey *be*?"

"Nuts, mostly."

Thrasher frowned. "And how would he hunt nuts?"

Clarabelle shrugged. "He'd probably lie in wait or something. I don't know. But he's out there now, living his life, and I'm here, in Roarhaven, trying to start a new one. I'm going to ask for a job now." She started walking towards the Sanctuary. Scapegrace hesitated, then followed after her. Thrasher scurried along behind.

"If you get a job," Scapegrace said, "maybe you could ask Doctor Nye to bring me back to life, as a favour."

"Doctor Nye doesn't do favours," Clarabelle said. "Doctor Nye is not that kind of boss."

"You don't know what kind of boss it is. You said earlier you'd never met it."

"I'm only guessing. I'm guessing it'll say no. It'll have to, or I'll get it into my head to ask it for favours every day, and then where will we be? You'll have to ask it yourself."

"But why would it say yes to me?"

"Maybe it's kind."

"You mentioned something about it being a war criminal."

"Yes, I don't think it's kind."

"If it is such a horrible creature," Thrasher said from behind them, "then why do you want to work for it, Clarabelle? You seem really nice."

"Thank you, Thrasher," Clarabelle said. "You're nice too. I hope Doctor Nye doesn't give you a new brain. I hope it just washes the one you already have."

Thrasher smiled, and Scapegrace hit him and turned back to Clarabelle. "The problem," he said, "is that we don't have anything to bargain with. We don't have money, we don't have property. We have no skills to speak of. So what's the point of even going to see it? It's only going to say no. It's only going to laugh at us and say no. Why should I go and see someone who is only going to laugh at me? Everyone laughs at me. The people in this town laughed at me for years, and that was even before I was a zombie."

Clarabelle turned to face him. "I'm not laughing at you."

"I'm not laughing, either," Thrasher said.

"Shut up, Thrasher." Scapegrace looked at Clarabelle. "I... I'm sorry. Being back here, suddenly all my old insecurities come to the surface again. I wasn't always the confident person you see before you. I had... doubts. I wasn't the Killer Supreme. I wasn't the Zombie King. I was just... Scapegrace."

"Well," Clarabelle said, "I think Scapegrace is a great guy."

"Do you believe in me?"

Clarabelle frowned. "I'm not sure. I've hallucinated before. That's how I met my first boyfriend."

"No, not do you believe I exist. I'm asking, do you believe in *me*? As a person? As a… a being? It'd be nice to hear that, to hear that someone believes in me."

"I believe in you, Vaurien."

"Thank you."

"I believe in lots of silly things."

"Oh."

"That doesn't mean they're not important."

"Right."

"I believe you can do whatever you put your mind to."

"Really?"

"I don't know what I'm saying any more." She resumed her march towards the Sanctuary.

There was a man leaving just as they came to the door. He frowned at them. "Can I help you?"

"No," Clarabelle said cheerily, and breezed by. Scapegrace and Thrasher kept their heads down and shuffled after her.

A man and a woman emerged from a doorway, deep in conversation. They seemed to recognise Clarabelle, and she asked them for directions and then they continued on, with Clarabelle singing 'We're Off to See the Wizard'. She led them through swinging doors into an Operating Room, where a spider-like being was dissecting a corpse.

"Doctor Nye," Clarabelle said.

The spider-like being turned to them. "Zombies," it said, mildly surprised. "And a blue-haired girl."

"My name is Clarabelle. I'm here looking for a job."

"A job?"

"Yes. I have no medical or scientific training to speak of, and no inclination to learn, and I pick things up fairly slowly because of my short attention span."

Nye blinked its yellow eyes. "But…?"

"But what?"

"I'm waiting for you to list your good qualities now."

Clarabelle blinked back at him. "Those *were* my good qualities."

"Clarabelle… Clarabelle… You worked as Kenspeckle Grouse's assistant, did you not?"

"One of them. He fired all the others."

"But not you?"

"He fired me on the second day, but I kept coming in. I had nowhere else to go."

"And then you killed him."

"Yes."

"A Remnant squirmed inside you, and you killed Kenspeckle Grouse."

"Yes."

Nye grinned. "You're hired. But I have to warn you, if you try to kill me, I will dissect you and sing along to your screams."

"Can I have Mondays off?"

"You may. Who are your friends?"

Scapegrace cleared his throat. "My name is Vaurien Scapegrace, Doctor. I have sought you out to cure me."

"To cure you of what?"

"Of this accursed affliction."

"I cannot cure stupidity."

Scapegrace frowned. "I meant being a zombie."

"And why should I do this?"

"Because… it's a challenge worthy of your skills?"

"I don't like challenges," Nye said dismissively. "Do you have money? I like money."

"I don't have an awful lot."

"Do you have any?"

Scapegrace hesitated. "No."

"Do you have any skills, then? Could you be of use to me?"

"I honestly don't see how."

"Me neither. It looks like you're destined to remain a zombie until your brain rots in your skull. Which, judging by the rate of your decomposition, should be in a year or so."

Scapegrace stared. "A year? I only have a year left?"

"If you stay out of the sun."

"But... but that's terrible!"

Nye shrugged. "It's not so bad for me."

Scapegrace stumbled out of the Sanctuary, aghast, and Thrasher ran out after him, an idiot. Clarabelle was staying because Clarabelle had a job now, and details needed to be ironed out and suchlike. But Scapegrace had just been handed a death sentence for the already dead. He stopped by the water's edge and looked out across the dark lake.

"What does it all mean?" he asked aloud.

Thrasher looked up at him, and didn't answer.

"What is a life?" Scapegrace continued. "Is life merely living? Is it having a heartbeat? Or is life the effect you have on others? Is it the effect you have on the world around you? If so, what have I done with mine? How have I wasted it?"

Thrasher shook his head sadly.

"I was never that great a sorcerer," Scapegrace said. "I can admit it now. My magic was never that powerful. But I thought my skills and my talents would make up for it. Even when I realised that I had no skills or talents to speak of, that still didn't stop me.

I was the Killer Supreme, and then I became the Zombie King. That, I thought, was a life worth having."

Thrasher nodded in agreement.

"But now… now look at me. I barely have a face. Bits fall off me all the time. I have to keep them in jars in the ice-cream van. And I'm going to rot away to nothing within a year."

"You still have me," Thrasher said kindly.

Scapegrace shoved him in the lake, then marched back towards the town. "Unless I take action. Unless I seize the day! Nye won't return me to life until I make it worth his while? Then I will make it worth his while!"

Thrasher splashed about.

Scapegrace avoided the main street, went instead down one of the alleys between buildings until he came to a pub. The doors were chained shut, fastened by a rusted old padlock. He smashed the padlock with a rock and walked in. The place was dark and dusty. Thrasher scurried in wetly behind him.

"This will be my base of operations," Scapegrace said grandly. "From here I will build my power, make my plans and convince Doctor Nye to return me to life. I have a year to do it, and by God, do it I shall!"

Thrasher applauded. Scapegrace pointed to a bar stool beside him.

"Sit there and don't annoy me."

Thrasher hopped up on to the bar stool.

"Vaurien," said a voice from behind.

Scapegrace turned. A man walked in, tall but thick around the middle. His hair was silver, and he had a stern look in his eye.

"McGill," Scapegrace said.

Taciturn McGill walked right up to him. "Why are you here?"

"How are you?" Scapegrace smiled. "How have you been? You're looking well. Better than me, anyway. But that's not hard. I'm a zombie now. How are you?"

"Why are you here, Vaurien?"

"I, um…"

"Can I take it that you won't be staying?"

"This bar is mine," Scapegrace said, losing the smile.

McGill shook his head. "You lost this establishment to Deadfall ten years ago."

"That was a gentleman's agreement, that was. I lost that bet and I handed everything over, and I left without kicking up a fuss."

"I recall some crying."

"My point is, legal ownership never transferred. Technically, this place has always been mine. Now that Deadfall is dead, there's nothing to stop me from picking up where I left off."

"Actually," McGill said, "there's plenty to stop you. We don't want you back, Vaurien."

Scapegrace blinked. "What do you mean? Roarhaven is my home."

"It *was* your home. But even back then, we didn't want you here."

"I have close ties to the community."

"You owe me money."

"That's one of my ties."

"It's not a lot of money, though. It certainly isn't enough for me to let you stay while you repay me."

"I've done great things for this town!" Scapegrace protested. "I was here when it all started! I brought the Torment in, for God's sake! Taciturn, please. I've got nowhere else to go. Look at me. I'm a zombie."

"We don't like zombies here."

"You don't like *anything* here! I'm looking for a cure. I think Doctor Nye can cure me. It works at the Sanctuary—"

"I know who Doctor Nye is."

"It can help me, McGill. Once I'm human again, I'll leave. I will. You'll never see me again. But for now, let me stay. Let me have my bar back. I won't cause any trouble, I promise. I know that if *you* say it's OK, then everyone else will say it's OK too."

"That's not how things work."

"What are you talking about? Of course it is."

"Not any more. There are things you don't know about, Vaurien."

"What things? The people of this town will still do what you tell them, right?"

"The Torment changed all that. He started talking, himself and his friends. They started telling people about their big ideas... You think it's an accident the Sanctuary was relocated here? You think that wasn't part of their plan?"

"Part of whose plan?"

McGill sighed. "Listen, Vaurien, I've known you a long time."

"We're friends."

"We're not friends, but I've still known you a long time. If you stay here for a few weeks, I don't think anyone will object too loudly."

"Thank you, Taciturn. And I swear, we'll only be here a few months. A year, tops."

"Weeks, Vaurien."

"Right. Yes."

"Try not to annoy anyone, and try to, y'know, stay away from people. Nobody likes zombies."

Scapegrace chuckled. "I know the feeling."

"You *are* a zombie."

"Yes, but I was talking about Thrasher."

"Who's Thrasher?"

Thrasher sat forward. "Hello."

McGill jerked away. "Ahh! How'd he do that? I didn't even see him there! Is he some kind of ninja?"

"No," Scapegrace said sadly. "He just fades into the background really well. You have my word, McGill, we will not get into trouble. Thank you."

"Yeah," McGill said, and stood up. "Don't make me regret this."

"Of course I won't," Scapegrace said, crossing his fingers behind his back. He must have crossed them too hard, though, because one of them came loose and fell to the floor. He waited until McGill had walked out before picking it up, then trudged away to find some ice.

24

THE TEMPLE SIEGE

At a little past noon, the first truck pulled up to the gates of the cemetery. The rear doors opened and Cleavers slipped out quietly. They moved in easy formation through the rows of graves to the crypt that acted as the entrance to the Necromancer Temple. One of them twisted the hemispheres of a cloaking sphere, and a bubble of energy rippled outwards. Once the bubble had expanded to the outskirts of the graveyard, the second truck arrived. More Cleavers disembarked and took up positions around the perimeter.

Wreath and Tenebrae watched the Cleavers, viewing it all on

a large screen broken into squares. Each of these squares was a different camera angle. The cameras wouldn't last long, but at least they gave an indication of what the Necromancers were up against. From what Wreath could see, they were up against a lot.

Men and women joined the Cleavers, sorcerers of both Elemental and Adept magic. Sanctuary agents, operatives and detectives. These people didn't wear uniforms and didn't carry badges. Some of them were armed, some of them weren't. All had power coursing through their veins.

Seven minutes after the first Cleaver had stepped off the first truck, Wreath watched Valkyrie Cain follow Skulduggery Pleasant up the cracked path to the crypt. They stopped under a camera, looked right up into it.

"My name is Skulduggery Pleasant," the skeleton said, his voice coming loud and clear through the speakers. "I have with me a warrant for the arrest of Melancholia St Clair, to be charged with the assault of a Sanctuary operative and detained by us until trial. If this door is not opened immediately, we will be forced to break it down."

Pleasant waited a full five seconds, then nodded. Wreath's gaze flickered to another feed, as a battering ram was brought up, held by two Cleavers, who swung it into the crypt door in a heavy rhythm.

The screens went blank. So much for technology.

"The doors won't hold for ever," Wreath said, as Quiver and Craven came in behind them.

"What about their Teleporter?" Tenebrae asked.

Wreath shook his head. "Fletcher Renn can only teleport to places he's been or can see. He's never even seen inside the Temple."

Tenebrae sat back in his chair. "Reinforcements?"

"A dozen of our brothers and sisters are on their way from London," Wreath said. "But whether they'll make it in time, I don't know."

Tenebrae looked at Quiver. "Our escape routes?"

"Available," Quiver said in his steady, measured tone, "for the moment. Sanctuary operatives are covering over half of them – more than we thought they knew about – but there are still plenty we could use to evacuate key personnel."

"Speaking of key personnel," Tenebrae said, turning to Craven, "how is she? Is she well enough to be moved?"

Craven took a deep breath, and for a long moment he didn't speak. Just before Tenebrae opened his mouth to demand a response, Craven nodded. "She could make it if she had to, but I'd really rather keep her stationary. Her power ebbs and flows. If we can keep them out for five hours, maybe six, she should be back to full strength. Then we won't need to run anywhere."

Wreath frowned at him. "Six hours? We'll be lucky if they don't burst in here halfway through this *conversation*. The Temple is not a fort."

"But it *is* well protected," Craven said, hands clasped and looking off somewhere beyond Wreath's elbow. It was a new habit Craven had picked up, and Wreath didn't like it. It made Craven look like a holy man. "Once the barricades are in place, we could collapse the tunnels and seal ourselves in."

"We don't *want* to seal ourselves in," Tenebrae said gruffly. "We want an escape route."

"I understand, High Priest, but as I have said, once Melancholia regains her strength, we won't *need* to run."

"That, Cleric Craven, is your *opinion*."

"Indeed it is, Your Eminence. And with all humility, may I remind you that it was I who guided Melancholia to the brink of the Passage. Without meaning to overstep my bounds, one might think I was entitled to a little faith in return."

"I think," Tenebrae growled, "that you have indeed overstepped your bounds."

Craven bowed his head. "My apologies, High Priest."

With Craven's head still bowed, Tenebrae looked at Wreath.

"If we collapse the tunnels," Wreath said reluctantly, "we could hold them off for twelve hours at the most. The barricades would need to be reinforced. We'd need to move people around. But make no mistake, we *would* be sealing ourselves in. If Melancholia doesn't regain her strength, it could be disastrous."

"The Death Bringer will be strong when we need her," Craven said solemnly.

Tenebrae's jaw clenched. "Cleric Wreath, see to it."

"Of course, Your Eminence."

Wreath left the room, a plan of his own forming. He ignored the barricades for the moment and went deeper into the Temple.

Despite the alarming turn of events, there was still protocol to be followed, still rules to obey and pay heed to. Wreath was a senior Cleric with the ear of the High Priest, but even he had to slow down and wait like everyone else if he wanted to see the Director of Storage. It was a mundane title that suggested pedantry and a multitude of lists, but the reality was much different. The Director of Storage was the person who oversaw and controlled equipment and food supplies, and as such, he acted within a bubble of his own authority. Wreath was kept waiting almost ten minutes before he was told that the Director would see him now.

Cleric Bertrand Solus didn't bother to raise his eyes from the papers on his desk as Wreath walked in. He was a busy man. There was only one chair in the office, and Solus was sitting on it.

"Yes?" Solus said, his pen scratching ink on to parchment. Why these people couldn't invest in a computer was beyond Wreath's understanding.

"Sanctuary agents have us surrounded," Wreath said.

"I am aware of the situation."

"To keep them out until the Death Bringer regains her strength, we need to collapse the auxiliary tunnels and barricade the main door."

"As I said, I am aware."

"But there is one tunnel that we do not know the location of."

Finally, Solus's pen stopped scratching, and he raised his eyes.

"You have your own tunnel," Wreath continued. "You use it to bring in supplies you don't want anyone to know about. I've never had a problem with this. You do your job well, and if sometimes you feel that you are best served by secrecy, who am I to say different?"

"Why are you here?" Solus asked.

"I don't want to collapse your tunnel. I want to use it. If things go bad, I want as many personnel as possible to get to safety. The Sanctuary agents know about some of our tunnels, but not all. I doubt they have any idea about a tunnel so secret that it doesn't even exist in any official capacity."

"It's not wide," said Solus, "and it's long. If the Temple is breached, you could use it to evacuate perhaps ten or twelve people at a time. Any more, and it would be discovered."

"Twelve people at a time, then," Wreath said. "The first of which shall be the Death Bringer, the White Cleaver and ten senior Clerics. Yourself included, of course. Where is the entrance?"

Solus regarded him with cautious, wary eyes. "The small storage room below us," he said. "The tunnel is two miles long. It emerges into a small warehouse the Temple owns through three different subsidiaries. There are vehicles in the warehouse, enough to take a substantial number to a safe house."

"Thank you very much for your co-operation, Cleric," Wreath said. "If you'll excuse me, I have much to arrange."

Solus waved him away, his pen already scratching as Wreath left his office.

25

THE VIVID DEAD

The world felt different to her now, ever since the Surge. It even looked different: paler, more vague. Less real. The people looked different too. She could see, for the first time, how glassy and unfocused their eyes were, how translucent their skin. She thought, if she concentrated hard enough, that she'd be able to see through them, to the underneath, to the blood and the veins and bones. She wondered if that would reassure her that all this was real. She doubted it.

The White Cleaver was at the door. He stood like a statue, his scythe held in one hand. He was real to her. He was solid. He was as different to a zombie as humans were to apes, but he was still a dead thing. And as such, she didn't even have to look at him to know he was there. She could feel him. She didn't know how, she couldn't explain it, but while everyone else had become vague and distant, he was the one clear thing she could latch on to for comfort.

The other man in the room, another guard, was so insubstantial he was almost a ghost. She'd spoken to him a few times, and before the Surge he had appeared perfectly normal. But she was seeing things differently now. She reached out with her mind, trying to sense him in the same way she sensed the White Cleaver. She could feel her awareness expanding around her, moving out in all directions like a bubble. She felt emptiness, and the emptiness made her uneasy, tied a knot in her stomach. But still she expanded her awareness, searching for the man. He made a sound, his body stiffening, and he became real to her so suddenly that she pulled back in shock. The bubble of her awareness retracted and the man toppled. She knew he was dead, she could feel it before he hit the floor, and she pulled his death into her, absorbing it, letting it make her stronger.

The White Cleaver turned his head slightly to look at the dead Necromancer, but made no move other than that. Melancholia stared at the dead man, marvelling at how vivid he seemed now that he was dead. She reached out, touched his leg. He was so solid, she almost laughed. She wasn't alone. So long as there were dead people around her, she wasn't going to drown in a sea of uncertainty. Her heart felt lighter than it had all day.

26

TERMINAL TWO

Skulduggery's phone rang, and Valkyrie stepped away while he answered it. Cleavers and sorcerers were gathered in groups around the cemetery – the largest group stationed at the crypt that housed the Temple door. She wondered for a moment if Wreath was down there, and felt a stab of guilt that her side was taking action against his side. Then she thought about Melancholia, and all feelings of guilt evaporated.

Skulduggery put his phone away. "A man answering Bison Dragonclaw's description was spotted in Terminal Two at the airport a few minutes ago."

Valkyrie made a face. "His first name is *Bison*?"

"He must be there to meet their reinforcements," Skulduggery continued. "It stands to reason that the other Necromancer Temples around the world would send people over to help the Death Bringer. We'll have to take care of this ourselves."

"We will?"

"Unless you want to stay here. I feel I have to warn you, though, we're probably not going to find a way past their barricades for another few hours."

"You're bored, aren't you?"

"I need constant distraction. Shall we go?"

"Uh, aren't you going to delegate responsibility or something? If you're not here, who's in charge?"

Skulduggery looked around, and pointed to a sorcerer at the far side of the cemetery. "He is."

"Who is he?"

"Don't know. He looks like leadership material though, doesn't he?"

"Does he?"

"He's wearing a hat."

"And that means he's a leader?"

"Leaders wear hats. It's to keep the rain off while we make important decisions. He'll do fine."

"Shouldn't you tell him that he's in charge?"

"And spoil the surprise?" Skulduggery asked, and started towards the Bentley without waiting for an answer.

Valkyrie sighed and followed.

They left the Bentley on the second floor of the Terminal Two car park, and walked to the Arrivals Area. Skulduggery's façade had a small beard. It went well with the face.

They caught sight of Dragonclaw almost immediately. Dressed in black, thin, bald, with that ridiculously wispy goatee. He had his back to them, waiting with everyone else as passengers poured in. They moved up behind him, waited for a big cheer to go up somewhere to their left, and moved.

"Bison," Skulduggery said as he gripped his elbow. "What a silly name for a skinny man."

Dragonclaw's free hand went to his belt, but Valkyrie grabbed his wrist with both hands and stepped close to him.

"No public displays of magic, please," she said with a smile.

Skulduggery leaned in. "If you draw attention to your predicament, it will be most unfortunate. Not for us, but definitely for you. For you, there will be a lot of pain involved, and crying and squawking and horrible sounds like breaking bones. You're not a fan of pain, are you, Bison? Of course you're not. You're a reasonable fellow, after all. Let's take a little walk, shall we? Away from the nice people."

Still gripping each arm, they walked him from the crowd, looking like an exceedingly odd family during a really awkward reunion.

"You'll regret this," Dragonclaw snarled. "You'll regret standing against us. I'll *make* you regret it."

"You're in a bad mood," Skulduggery said. "I understand. I do. You're saying things you don't really mean. It's OK."

"I'll kill you both."

"Hurtful things said in the heat of the moment. We're not going to hold it against you, Bison. We're all friends here."

Valkyrie nodded. "We love you, Bison."

"We do," Skulduggery agreed. "You're our favourite Necromancer. You're the cuddly one."

"Shut up," Dragonclaw said. "Both of you just *shut up*."

They paused to allow a large group of large people to pass by, and then, from nowhere, there was a flash of yellow jacket.

"Excuse me," Dragonclaw said loudly, and the cop stopped, and looked at them.

"Can I help you?" he asked.

Valkyrie turned Dragonclaw's wrist painfully, and she felt Skulduggery apply pressure on his side. Dragonclaw yelped in pain and the cop's eyes widened.

"We're looking for the toilets," Skulduggery said quickly. "Our friend here isn't the best at holding it in, and sometimes he needs a little assistance."

The cop nodded in understanding. "Of course, yes. The toilets are right over there. See them?"

"There they are!" Valkyrie said brightly. "Thank you so much! It would have been a mess!"

Dragonclaw hissed in pain as they hurried him away.

"Try anything like that again," Skulduggery told him, "and you'll be talking to us with two broken arms. Whimper if you understand."

Dragonclaw whimpered.

They got to the toilets. Valkyrie grabbed an Out of Order sign from a nearby cart and propped it up at the entrance. Skulduggery threw Dragonclaw against the wall and searched him while Valkyrie checked that each of the stalls was empty. Skulduggery pulled Dragonclaw's knife from his belt, then took a scrap of paper from Dragonclaw's pocket and passed it to Valkyrie. On it was a time and a number.

"The flight he's waiting on has already landed," he said. They both looked at Dragonclaw. "How many are coming?"

Dragonclaw rubbed his arm, and sneered. "I don't know what you're talking about."

Skulduggery shook his head. "I would love to have a battle of wits with you, Bison, but I doubt it'd be a fair fight."

"Shut your face."

"Exactly my point. So if you think we're going to trade banter or get into wordplay or anything like that, I'm afraid I have to disappoint you. Instead, we're going to be very simple and very direct, because we obviously don't have a lot of time. How many are coming? And before you try another sneer, please understand that I will inflict pain if you fail to answer."

"Save yourself the bother," Valkyrie said. "You're going to tell us anyway, and you know you are. So why get hurt? Why not skip to the end?"

Dragonclaw looked at both of them for a long time before shaking his head. "No. I'm not a traitor."

"Yes, you are," Valkyrie said. "You just don't know it yet."

Dragonclaw stood up straight, chin stuck out defiantly towards Skulduggery. "If you're going to hit me, hit me. I haven't got all—"

Valkyrie rapped her knuckles right on his chin. Dragonclaw's eyes bulged and his knees quivered, then he fell backwards to the wall and slid down to the floor. Skulduggery looked at her and she shrugged.

"You'd have knocked his teeth out or something," she said. "All I did was give him a little brain-shake." She looked down. "Bison. Bison, can you hear me? How many are coming?"

"I'll never tell…"

"The plane landed ten minutes ago," Skulduggery said to her. "If we're lucky, they're only just starting to disembark. You need to get to them before they clear Customs."

Valkyrie's eyebrows shot up. "What? Me? Alone?"

"I need to ask Bison some questions about getting into the Temple. You'll be fine."

"How am I supposed to get by the security section? I don't have a ticket."

Skulduggery cocked his head. "Valkyrie, you've got magical powers. If you can't get through airport security, then I have failed in whatever capacity I have as a mentor."

She glowered. "Fine. What do I do when I find them?"

"You need to delay them for a few hours, at least."

"And how do I do *that*?"

"They'll be very serious people wearing black. It won't take much for the police to stop them for a chat. Go on now."

Still glowering, Valkyrie left the toilets and walked to the Departure gates. The queue wasn't very long. She followed an old couple and a businessman through the cordoned-off section. The businessman was obviously in a hurry, and the old couple weren't moving fast enough for his taste. He muttered and sighed and cursed under his breath, loud enough for them to hear. Valkyrie didn't like him. His passport and ticket were in his jacket pocket. She gripped the air and pulled it back, the ticket slipping into her hand.

The old couple showed their tickets to the woman at the desk and passed through. Valkyrie took the opportunity to wave the businessman's ticket to the woman while the businessman cursed loudly as he searched his pockets. The woman nodded to her and Valkyrie smiled, left the ill-tempered man to his bluster and frustration, and approached the metal detectors. Even if she'd been hiding a dozen guns on her person, the clothes would have shielded them all. She walked through and strode on.

She passed through the Duty Free shops, resisting the sudden urge to check out the sunglasses on offer. On the other side of the glass wall travellers walked in the opposite direction, having just arrived. That's where Valkyrie needed to be. There were a few Staff Only doors she could have tried to sneak through, but she didn't know where they led, and she didn't have the luxury of trial and error. The only way she was guaranteed to get where she needed to be was to get out on to the tarmac, and then come back in through an Arrivals door.

She reached the Departure gates. Three flights were boarding. She went to the huge windows that looked out on to the tarmac. Only one of those flights didn't have a walkway that connected to the door of the aircraft. She joined that crowd as they showed their passports and filtered through. She smiled at a man and he let her in front of him, then she waved her hand slightly and all the papers on the flight attendant's desk fluttered into the air. The attendant grabbed at them as Valkyrie slipped by unnoticed. She took the steps down, following the passengers out of the building.

Another attendant directed them to the pedestrian pathway that led to the plane. She was wearing a nice hat. Valkyrie waved her hand, less gently this time, and the hat flew off the attendant's head. Valkyrie turned sharply, heading for the door further on.

A man in uniform frowned at her. "Are you supposed to be here?"

"Yes," she smiled. "I got delayed."

She went to walk by him, but he stepped in her path. "Are you sure? What flight did you come in on?"

"Heathrow," she said. "I don't know the number of the plane, sorry. It was a big one, though. The plane, not the number. Though the number was pretty big too."

He held up a hand. "Could you hold on a minute? I'm going to have to call someone."

"Sure." She beamed a smile at him as he took his radio from his belt. "I bet your job's fun."

"Pardon me?"

"Being around airplanes and everything, meeting exotic people. Having a radio in a holster. I bet it's really fun. Did you have to do any special training for it?"

"Uh, yes. Excuse me, I have to call this in."

"Sure. My name's Valerie, by the way."

"I'm going to call my boss, all right?"

"Why? Did you do something wrong?"

"What? No, it's not for me. It's for you."

Valkyrie's face fell. "What did I do?"

"You shouldn't be here."

"But the plane landed here."

"I mean, you shouldn't be *here*, you shouldn't be standing here. You should be further on."

"Oh," she said, and laughed. "Sorry. God, I'm so dumb."

"We'll get it sorted out, don't worry." His radio clicked and he spoke into it. "Anthony, it's Sean. I'm down here with – hey." Valkyrie walked by him and he caught up with her. "Where are you going?"

She blinked at him. "You said I shouldn't be here."

"Yeah, but—"

"I'm just going to where I should be."

"Just hold on a second."

"Am I in trouble?"

"No, you're not, but—"

"Are you going to arrest me?"

"Arrest you? No."

"I just got lost. I got off the plane and there were so many people. Please don't arrest me."

"Listen to me. I'm not going to arrest you, OK? I'm not a cop."

"Are you sure?"

"Am I sure I'm not a cop? Yes, I'm sure."

"You might be undercover."

"I still think I'd know if I were a cop, though. I work for the airline. I'm not a Guard. I just work here."

"OK," she said, and breathed out. "Sorry. I panic sometimes."

"It's fine. Were you travelling alone?"

"No, there were other people on the plane."

"I mean, are you travelling with someone? A friend or family member?"

"Oh. No. Just me. Where do I collect my bag?"

"At the Luggage Section. Do you know where that is?"

"Is it up those stairs?"

"It is. First you come to Passport Control, then you pick up your luggage, and then you exit Customs."

Valkyrie smiled. "Thank you. You've been really helpful."

He nodded. "Sure. Just… try not to get delayed again, OK?"

"I'll do my best!" she laughed, and skipped up the stairs.

She moved onwards without encountering anybody else. Passport Control was quiet. Directly opposite her, across the open floor, was a glass wall, and beyond that she could see a crowd of people who had just passed through. Among the bright shirts and colourful dresses and blue jeans there were people in black, some in jackets, some in coats, some carrying bags and some not, walking apart so as not to attract attention. Necromancers. She peered round the door, to her right, where two cops were sitting in booths, chatting across to each other as they waited for the next influx of travellers. Valkyrie darted to the empty booth closest to her, using the air to rise over the barricade. She dropped gently to the other side and ran, crouched over. She sneaked behind the booths where the cops were sitting, and out into the corridor. Now she sprinted after the crowd of passengers.

She caught up with the ones lagging behind, the ones for whom this long walk was just proving too much. They puffed and wheezed with red faces, fat droplets of sweat running down their cheeks, travel cases trundling along behind like sulky children. She ran under the sign that pointed to the Luggage Retrieval area. She doubted the Necromancers would have any bags to collect. They weren't here for a holiday, after all.

She barged through a small group of people, got to the top of the stairs and leaped. People around her cried out in alarm, but she didn't have time to waste. She waited until the last moment to cushion her landing, hit the ground and rolled. She ignored the disapproving headshakes, immediately catching sight of the Necromancers on the far side of the baggage belts. She took off, using the air to nudge people from her path. She jumped on to a conveyer belt that wasn't moving, slid across the highest point and jumped down the other side. An airport official stepped into her path and she jammed her hand against his chest. His cheeks bulged and he stumbled back as she vaulted on to the next conveyer belt. This one was moving, full of luggage. She almost tripped, but made it to the centre and scrambled over to the other side, leaped off and into a crowd of startled civilians. The Necromancers hadn't noticed the commotion. She ran to intercept them as they headed for the Exit, coming to a sharp halt in front of the Necromancer leading the march.

The Necromancers stopped, each one of them suspicious. Valkyrie held up a hand while she doubled over.

"Sorry," she gasped. "Let me... get my breath... back."

They didn't try to move around her. Their eyes were on the ring on her finger.

"You have instructions?" the lead Necromancer asked.

She breathed deeply, in through the nose, out through the mouth, and straightened. "Yes," she said. "You're... not needed. You're to... go home."

"High Priest Tenebrae sent a *student* to tell us this?"

She nodded, and shrugged.

"What's happened? Is the Death Bringer OK?"

"False alarm," she said. "Wasn't the Death Bringer. Just a girl... looking for attention. You're to go home at once and... sorry for the inconvenience. Naturally, we'll refund your air fare."

A female Necromancer frowned at her. "Who instructs you in the Temple?"

"I'm not really in the Temple that much," Valkyrie said, her breathing under control now. "Solomon Wreath is my mentor."

"Oh," the woman said. "Well, that would explain the lack of formality."

"Even so," said the lead Necromancer, "Cleric Wreath ought to know better than to send a student with information like this. If the High Priest wishes us to return to London, he can send someone of higher rank to tell us."

They went to walk by her, but Valkyrie jumped in front of them again. "Actually, no," she said, "he was quite insistent. Everyone's busy. Sanctuary agents are everywhere and they're putting pressure on and all the Clerics have their hands full and—"

The lead Necromancer glared at her. "Step aside, girl."

Out of the corner of her eye, she saw the airport official she had shoved. He was jogging over, flanked by two cops.

"Fine," she said to the lead Necromancer. "I'm not a Necromancer. My name's Valkyrie Cain. I work with Skulduggery Pleasant. And I'm here to tell you that we're about to drag the Death Bringer into custody and there's not a damn thing you can do about it."

The Necromancers stared, and almost as one they reached for her, anger flashing across their faces. Then the cops were there, standing between them.

"That's her!" the official said. "That's the girl who hit me!"

"I'm sorry," Valkyrie said to the cops, looking as frightened as she could. "I lagged behind. They don't like it when I lag behind."

The cops frowned at her, then turned to the Necromancers.

"Is she with you?" the first cop asked.

The lead Necromancer scowled. "No. I've never seen her before. You can keep her."

He went to walk on, but the cops blocked his way.

"Just hold on a minute there, until we get this sorted out. She's dressed the same as you."

"So?"

"It's a little odd, isn't it?"

"Not for us."

"It's like a uniform," Valkyrie said, making her voice shake. "They make us wear black. It's for the church."

The second cop looked back at her. "Everyone here is part of a church?"

She nodded. "We call it a church, yes. Other people call it a cult. I shouldn't be talking to you. They don't like it when I talk to outsiders. They're afraid I'll tell people about their plans."

The cops turned to the Necromancers, and the airport official backed away.

"I'm afraid I'm going to have to ask you to come with us," the first cop said. "Just to answer a few questions."

"That won't be possible," the lead Necromancer said. "We have somewhere to be."

"I'm afraid I have to insist."

The lead Necromancer ignored him, turning his eyes to Valkyrie. "Are you sure you want to do this? In front of all these people? In front of security cameras? Because we'll do it. The world is about to change – we could start that change right here and now."

"That sounded like a threat," the second cop said.

"I wasn't talking to you."

"Yeah," the cop said, "but I was talking to you."

Valkyrie hadn't even noticed the movement in the crowds of people, but suddenly there were four more cops surrounding the Necromancers, done up in tactical gear and carrying automatic weapons. The Necromancers stiffened. Unlike Elementals and other Adepts, the Necromancers kept most of their magic in objects. But right now, their weapons were in their bags and pockets, and any move to get them would result in extreme violence.

Valkyrie backed away as the cops issued orders. The Necromancers glared at her, and she smiled back, slipping away through the crowd that had formed around them. She hurried for the doors, emerging into the Arrivals Area as more cops ran through to help their comrades. She rejoined Skulduggery and a handcuffed Dragonclaw, and they walked quickly for the exit.

"You handled it?" Skulduggery asked.

"I did. I could have used your help."

"Nonsense. You're more than capable of doing these things yourself. Were there many Necromancers?"

"Twelve or so. If they're not escorted directly on to a flight home, I'd say, at the very least, they're not going to be let near their weapons for another few hours."

"By which point we should have broken into the Temple. Well done, Valkyrie. You are good."

"Yes, I am. What about Bison here? Did he have anything interesting to say?"

"Indeed he did," Skulduggery said, his false mouth smiling. "He knows of a top-secret supply tunnel that leads right into the depths of the Temple, and he's going to take us there, aren't you, Bison?"

Dragonclaw sagged.

"How sweet," Valkyrie said. "You've made a friend."

27

INTO THE TEMPLE

The warehouse was dark. Three jeeps and two trucks were parked under a thick layer of dust. Dragonclaw led them to the centre of the floor, and stopped.

"You'd better not be lying to us," Skulduggery said, his gun out.

"I swear," Dragonclaw responded. "Director Solus used to have me guard it when supplies were brought in through here. Only a few people know about it."

He stepped on a pebble, put all his weight on it, and the floor beside him opened up, revealing steps leading down. Skulduggery motioned for him to go first, and they followed him into a long stone corridor lit by bare bulbs.

"This leads directly to the Temple?" Skulduggery asked.

Dragonclaw nodded. "There's a door with a lever at the other end. It opens up into a room nobody ever uses. It's how Solus transports all his best stuff."

"No passwords needed? Nothing like that?"

"No. You just pull the lever."

"Good to know," Skulduggery said, then smacked him with the gun. Dragonclaw spun and fell to the ground, unconscious.

Valkyrie glared. "You could have warned me."

"Of what?" Skulduggery asked, his arm encircling her waist. They lifted off the ground, started moving down the corridor.

"That you were going to hit him. It'd be nice to be told these things."

"Did it give you a fright?"

They were picking up speed now and Valkyrie's hair was being blown off her face.

"A little one, yeah," she said. "You were standing there all normal and then you hit him. I jumped."

"I do apologise."

"Just a little warning, that's all I ask."

"In my defence, if I had told you that I intended to hit him, he probably would have overheard the conversation."

"Then we should come up with a code or something."

The bulbs were blurring into one long stream of light above them.

"We already have a code," Skulduggery said. "It's *be brave*."

Valkyrie scowled at him. "*Be brave* is nothing. *Be brave* is you telling me to trust you, you have a plan, when we're surrounded by enemies. *Be brave* tells me nothing other than you're about to do something stupid. We should have another code for when you're about to hit someone."

"Very well. How about *the sparrow flies south for winter?*"

"Seriously?"

"What's wrong with it? It's a classic."

"And how would you work that into the conversation?"

"With my usual aplomb."

"So if that had been our code, and Dragonclaw had just told you that all we have to do is pull the lever, how would you have worked *the sparrow flies south for winter* into the conversation?"

"I would have said *OK, Bison, so you're sure we only need to pull a lever?* And he would have said *yes*, and I'd have said *excellent, thank you. Did you know, by the way, that the sparrow flies south for winter?* And then I'd have punched him."

"I'm going to do my best to ignore the ridiculous things you say from now on," Valkyrie decided. "What are we going to do when we get into the Temple, anyway? Are we going to fight our way through the Necromancers on our own?"

"No, we're going to find a way to let our friends in, and we'll let *them* fight while we stand by and look smug."

"I like that plan."

"It has its moments."

They slowed as they neared the end of the corridor, touched down on to solid ground and Valkyrie reluctantly stepped away. She loved the sensation of flying, but it did make walking seem absurdly clumsy.

Skulduggery pulled the small iron lever set into the wall, and the bulbs went out as the door swung open. They crept out into darkness. It was colder here – it was always cold in the Temple.

"We should be on the main level," Skulduggery whispered, "but I'd say we're half a kilometre from the Antechamber." Valkyrie's eyes were adjusting to the gloom as Skulduggery searched through stacks of boxes and supplies. He made an amused sound, and threw something to her. "We're going to need to fit in."

It was a robe. She put it on. The sleeves were gigantic, and swallowed her arms. She pushed them back to her elbows and then pulled up the hood. It wasn't as easy as it looked, getting the hood to sit just right. It kept falling down over her face. Finally, she got it to where it would stay up, and turned to Skulduggery. He stood there, the black robe flowing around him, his skull barely visible beneath the hood.

"Good God," she breathed. "You look like the Grim Reaper."

"I'll take that as a compliment."

"It wasn't meant as one."

"I'm taking it anyway. You're a regular visitor here – any advice on how we should proceed?"

She shrugged. "If anyone stops us, as long as we mumble something pretentious about the glory of death, we should be fine."

"Excellent."

They left the storage room, moving quickly but quietly. Valkyrie's heart sped up when two Necromancers hurried by, but they were too busy panicking about the Sanctuary forces outside to notice them. Occasionally she would recognise something and nudge Skulduggery to alter their course, but for the most part she hadn't a clue where they were. On all of her trips through the Temple, she hadn't really been paying attention. Wreath had been the one to lead the way and she'd been happy enough to follow along, continuing whatever conversation they were having without bothering to acquaint herself with her surroundings. She was regretting that now.

"Hey!" said a voice behind them. "You!"

They stopped. Valkyrie glanced at Skulduggery and they turned. A Necromancer stalked over to them, his hood down off his head. It was that man, Oblivious or something, the one who hadn't wanted to let them in days ago.

"Where do you think you're going?" he ranted. "We have our

orders! You think they don't apply to you? You think just because our enemies are massing at the gates, we should abandon our posts? Is that what you think?"

"Uh," Skulduggery said, "the stream of death carries us where it may."

"That may be true," Oblivious said curtly, "but we are still bound by the oaths we swore. Or have you forgotten them?"

Skulduggery shook his head beneath his hood. "My duty is to death, but death's duty is to itself. As of life, as of death, as of the stream between…"

Oblivious frowned. "What?"

"In the stream of life, we are but paddlers."

"I'm not sure I… who are you? Let me see your face."

Skulduggery looked round, made sure no one else was coming. "The sparrow flies south for winter," he said, and punched Oblivious right on the chin. He looked up at Valkyrie as he dragged the unconscious Necromancer into the nearest room. "See? It's a perfect code."

"We're paddling in the stream of life?"

Skulduggery came back out, shutting the door behind him. "I'm not very good at being pretentious. It's one of my few flaws. But there's no denying – that code worked."

"And you slipped it into the conversation *seamlessly*."

They carried on, managing to avoid the panicking Necromancers.

Finally, Skulduggery took Valkyrie's arm, pulled her into a dark corner, and nodded ahead.

"If I'm right," he said, "the door mechanism is in there. If the door isn't unlocked in the correct way, an alarm will sound, the door won't open, and everyone will come running. So you're going to have to stay here. If I were you, I'd find somewhere to hide. This may take a while."

She raised an eyebrow at him.

"You realise," he said, "that you're wearing a hood and I can't see your face, so if you're glaring at me, or scowling, or raising an eyebrow, I have no way of knowing. You realise that, right?"

"Why," said Valkyrie, "do I have to stay here?"

"Because what I'm going to do is extremely dangerous."

"So is *everything* you drag me into."

"Your point being?"

"What is up with everyone? *Fletcher* wants to protect me, *Caelan* wants to protect me, now *you*. For God's sake, I can handle what's thrown at me, all right? I don't need to be kept safe all the bloody time."

"I see," Skulduggery said. "Well, you make a very good point and I can't argue with your logic. Except I'm not trying to protect you. If I try to open the door and I fail, then I'm going to need someone else to do it once they've killed me. You see?"

"Oh," said Valkyrie. "Oh right."

"Now, if I fail, the odds are that you'll fail too. And if they can kill me, they can most *certainly* kill you, in an undoubtedly horrible manner. But by then I'll be past caring."

"So… you really *aren't* trying to protect me."

Skulduggery placed a hand on her shoulder. "Not even remotely," he said warmly.

He moved off. Valkyrie waited a moment, then backed away, turned and hurried in the opposite direction. She rounded a corner and immediately stepped back. Solomon Wreath passed without looking at her. She chewed her lip.

And followed.

She kept her head down as they walked the corridors. He disappeared through a door and she quickened her pace, following him in. A hand grabbed her, tore the hood from her head and shoved her further into the room. She hit the wall and spun, Wreath's cane stopping right before it met her face. His eyes widened.

"Valkyrie," he said, surprised.

"Hi Solomon," she responded. "You said if ever I needed a chat…"

He lowered the cane and stepped back, closed the door before anyone saw. "How did you get in?"

"Dragonclaw," she said.

Wreath sighed. "Oh, him. I assume Skulduggery is with you?"

"He's around here somewhere."

"Then things are probably going to get very loud very soon."

"More than likely."

"In that case," Wreath said, "now that we have a minute, I'd just like to say that I'm sorry for what happened. If I had known, if I had even *suspected*, that Melancholia might go after you, I would have—"

"You would have what?" Valkyrie asked. "Grounded her? What could you have done? Everyone's saying she's more powerful than anyone alive today. If she wants to slice me half to death, she's going to slice me half to death, and there's nothing anyone can do about it."

Wreath shook his head. "This isn't how it should be."

"You're right. She should be on a leash."

"No, I mean she shouldn't have this power. It should have been you. At least it would have come naturally to you."

"What do you mean?"

Wreath rubbed his face. He suddenly looked very tired. "Craven did something to her. He's been studying the languages of magic for years. He can't be as expert in the art as China Sorrows, but he'll be good, nonetheless. You've seen the scars on her face, right? They're all over her body. He says they're to protect her, but I think he carved those symbols into her skin to heighten her power during the Surge."

"Is that possible?"

"In theory. Of course it's highly dangerous, and extraordinarily unstable. If that is indeed what he did, he stood a higher chance of killing her than succeeding."

"But you think he *did* succeed."

"Yes I do. It doesn't matter, of course. All the Death Bringer is, all it ever *has* been, is a Necromancer with a certain degree of power. No matter how she got there, Melancholia does seem to have reached that level."

"She said something while she was kicking my ass. She said, if you're not on my list, you don't get saved."

"I doubt she was making any sense at all. With that much power reverberating inside her head, I think we can expect her to babble every now and then."

"What is the Passage?"

"I'm sorry, Valkyrie, there are things we don't share with—"

"Solomon, for God's sake. You never give a straight answer to that, yet it's supposed to be a wonderful thing where the world is saved and made a better place. Why do you need to keep any of that a secret?"

"Because some people aren't going to understand."

"What people? People who like being miserable? I'm sure they'll get over it. What's she going to do? What happens in the Passage?"

"The walls are broken down—"

"Between life and death, yes, I know. That much you've told me. The energy of the dead will live alongside us, and we will evolve to meet it. That's what you said. I haven't a clue what that *means*, but that's what you said. We're going to evolve, are we?"

"In a manner of speaking."

"Solomon, you have the Death Bringer. Whatever is going to happen is going to happen. So why not just tell me? Should I be worried? How much will the world change? Will everyone know about it? Will my family suddenly know that magic exists? Will people still have jobs? Will we still live in houses? Will people still be people?"

"It will be better, that's all you need to know."

"No, Solomon, it isn't. The fact is it's a pretty scary prospect. It's made even scarier by the fact that not even your average Necromancer knows what's going to happen. Only you guys. Only the High Priests and the High Clerics. Only the people who run the Temples. Why don't you tell the others? What is so awful that you have to hide it from your own people?"

Wreath looked at her. "How much is a better world worth to you?"

"What do you mean?"

"I mean, what would you sacrifice? Look at this world. Look at it. From the moment mankind took its first awkward step, it's been a long road to disaster. We hate each other. We fear each

277

other. We're going to kill each other. One of these days, someone's going to go too far, and every single one of us will die."

"What do you care? You're a Necromancer. Life flows into death and flows back into life, right? That's what you believe."

"That is what we believe, yes. But it's not what we want."

Valkyrie frowned. "What?"

"Our souls, our life force, flow through that never-ending stream – but not our minds. Not our memories. When I die, my essence will move on, but this man you see before you, this mind, this personality, this being, will be gone. I'll become something else. Someone else. But it won't be me."

"You're… you're *scared* of death?"

"We all are."

"But you're Necromancers! You *embrace* death!"

"We study Necromancy because we're trying to *defeat* death. That's what this is all about, Valkyrie. This is all it's ever been about."

"So what does this mean? You want Melancholia to break down the walls between life and death so that you'll never have to die? What was all that about evolution? We will evolve to meet the dead, or whatever it was."

"Society will evolve. It'll have to. Evolve or perish. We figure it's worth the risk."

"Solomon, what the hell is going on? What does the Passage mean?"

"The energy stream that flows through this world, this reality, it links up with the next reality, and the next, and it loops around again. It's a natural force and a natural system."

"OK. So?"

"So we want to stop it. We want those alive today to remain alive for ever."

"So no one dies? What about new life? What about babies being born?"

"No life leaves. No life enters."

Valkyrie stared at him, and immediately thought of Alice. "You can't do that. Are you insane? You can't do that."

"Society will adapt to the new way of living."

"No more babies? Solomon, come on! That's nuts! It's a biological need!"

"Having children is a biological need only because we are mortal – even sorcerers. We die. And we know we're going to die, and so we have children, to continue our bloodline, to continue our legacy, to try to ensure our own immortality. But when we *are* immortal, we won't have that need to procreate."

"That's… my God, Solomon, please tell me that you know this isn't right."

He sighed. "This is the kind of reaction we feared."

"People aren't going to accept this. The whole world will be after you."

"No. Not the whole world. Half the world."

"What?"

"In order to stop death, we have to block the flow. We have to dam the energy stream."

"And how are you going to do that?"

"We need a massive influx of souls."

"You mean you're going to need a lot of people to suddenly die."

"Yes. Their life forces will block the stream, overload it, cutting it off for ever."

"How many? How many people?"

Wreath shook his head. "I wish you hadn't asked me these things."

"How many people, Solomon?"

"It would have been so much better if you hadn't asked me."

"She's going to kill them? That's what the Death Bringer does?" Valkyrie pushed Wreath, her palm against his chest. "She kills all these people? That's the Passage?" She pushed him again. "How many people? How many? For God's sake, just tell me how many people she's going to have to kill!"

She pushed him again, but this time he caught her wrist, and raised his eyes to look at her. "Three billion ought to do it."

Valkyrie broke free, spun, sprinted for the door. A wave of shadows crashed into her and sent her to the wall. The shock rattled her body, but when she fell, she managed to keep her feet under her. She pushed at the air and Wreath snapped his cane, deflecting her aim. A tendril of shadow came from nowhere, wrapped around her throat, yanked her back. She staggered, used her ring to cut the tendril, and then the cane came for her face and met her jaw. She was on the ground then, trying to focus, trying to look up as Wreath's boot came swinging in, and she went spinning into darkness.

28

A VILE HISTORY

Valkyrie woke in a large room with no furniture to find Skulduggery crouching down and peering at her. She groaned. Her face hurt. Her head pounded. Her hands were shackled behind her.

"Wreath," she croaked.

"I know," said Skulduggery. "What did I tell you about wandering off? Why don't you ever do anything I say? If I didn't know any better, I would swear that you feel a compulsion to disobey authority figures."

"That can't be what it is," she said.

"Well, that's what it seems like."

"But I don't view you as an authority figure."

"Oh, not this again."

Valkyrie sat up. Slowly. "Are you going to lecture me all day, or are you going to get these shackles off me?"

"I'm inclined to lecture you."

She sighed, turned her back to him, waited for him to start picking the lock.

"Uh," he said, "exactly what do you think is going on right now?"

She frowned over her shoulder at him. "What do you mean? Skulduggery, I've got a headache. Wreath kicked me in the face. He kicked me. In the face. It hurts. So get these shackles off me, and we'll go find him, and I'll kick *him* in the face. Then *you* kick him in the face. Then I'll do it again. We'll take turns. It'll be fun."

"It would be fun," Skulduggery nodded. "I like kicking Wreath in the face. I haven't had a chance to do it nearly as much as I'd like."

"See? So, come on, stop delaying."

"I wish I could."

Valkyrie shook her head, and managed to get to her feet. Skulduggery stood beside her.

"So what are you doing?" she asked. "Teaching me a lesson? Is that what this is?"

"Indeed it is," he said brightly.

"OK, lesson learned. I shouldn't wander off. Got it."

Skulduggery's head nodded happily. "Excellent."

"Now get these shackles off me."

"I can't."

"Why can't you?"

Skulduggery turned, showing her the shackles that bound his own wrists.

Her eyes widened. "*You* got captured *too?*"

"It's the only way you'll learn."

"You got captured on *purpose?*"

"Don't be silly. When I triggered the alarm, I did my level best to run away, but I couldn't find *you*, so..."

"Ah," she said. "Sorry."

"Oh, it's fine," he shrugged. "I managed to punch some Necromancers, which is always fun. What was less fun was when they started punching me back. And then the White Cleaver arrived and joined in. It was, if I do say so, an epic battle, but I was heavily outnumbered. It's a pity you slept through it."

"I was unconscious."

"You were asleep."

"Don't annoy me, OK? I have a headache. How are we going to get out of here?"

"Oh, escape is easy once you have the right plan."

"*Do* we have the right plan?"

"Not yet."

"Do we have *any* plan?"

"Not yet."

"Typical. Still, silver lining. Wreath told me what the Passage is."

"Oh?"

"They're going to kill three billion people to stop the other three billion from ever dying."

Skulduggery hesitated. "That… I'll be honest, that doesn't sound too great for the first three billion."

"Can they do it? Is it possible?"

"Theoretically, yes," Skulduggery said. "I doubt they have much in the way of hard facts to support this theory, but who needs facts when you have faith?"

"So they could be killing three billion and it'd have no effect whatsoever on the lifespan of the others?"

"Very possibly. Of course, I think we can both agree that killing three billion people *anyway*, no matter what the supposed benefits might actually be, would still be a *bad thing to do*."

"Oh," Valkyrie said with a nod, "we are very much agreed on that one."

"But you're right – silver lining. At least we know what their ultimate goal is. Now we can work to foil it."

The door opened behind them, and High Priest Tenebrae stepped in. They stopped talking, and observed him as he smiled. "Ah," he said, "the awkward silence." He closed the door behind him. "How are you, Valkyrie? Things have changed greatly since the last time we spoke, have they not? It's all very unfortunate."

"I don't know how you could have thought that I would ever have been the Death Bringer," she said. "Did you honestly believe I'd be willing to kill billions of people for a *theory*?"

"The Passage isn't a theory, dear girl. It is an inevitability. We know it's a lot to accept – we know you don't understand. That's why we sent Dragonclaw to keep it a secret for as long as possible. But now that it's out in the open, now that we can have a conversation about it, yes, actually, we *did* think you would have been willing to kill billions of people – given enough time, of course. If you had chosen Necromancy over Elemental magic, which was a distinct possibility, this would have been the first schism to form between yourself and your skeletal mentor here. And once we had our hooks in you, really got them in there, you would have been ours. And you would have understood. We would have slowly opened your eyes to the truth and the glory of the Passage."

"I still wouldn't have killed those people."

"Well, that's rather a moot point at this stage, isn't it? Because now we have Melancholia. She wouldn't have been my first choice,

I admit, but she is dedicated, and she is passionate. These qualities count for something."

"She's unstable," Skulduggery said. "You can't even keep her under control, for God's sake."

"She's young," Tenebrae shrugged. "Impetuous. Yes, she went after Valkyrie the first chance she got, but that was nothing more than childish spite. Nothing to worry about, not really. We were all young once, weren't we, Skulduggery? Remember the adventures we got into when we were young men?"

Valkyrie frowned. "You knew each other?"

"He didn't tell you? We used to be friends."

"Friends is such a strong and misleading word," Skulduggery said.

Tenebrae smiled. "Acquaintances, then. In the early days of the war, before the Necromancer Order withdrew from the conflict, we fought side by side. Didn't we, Skulduggery?"

"If by side by side you mean I was always in front, then yes, Auron, we did. Not that it has any bearing on what is going on today."

"Really? I would have thought that you of all people would know the effect the past has on the present. But then, you've lied to yourself about so many things, why should this be any different?"

"Now this," Skulduggery said, "should be interesting."

Tenebrae looked at Valkyrie. "He's quite an angry man, isn't he? It's why his enemies are so scared of him, I suppose. I would even venture so far as to say it's why you're still alive. Don't misunderstand me, Valkyrie – you are becoming a capable sorcerer and a formidable opponent in your own right. But there are plenty of people out there who would love to kill you, and could do so relatively easily. The idea, however, that to kill you would incur the wrath of the Skeleton Detective is, in my opinion, the only reason you still draw breath. I hope you're not offended."

Valkyrie looked back at him, and didn't say anything.

"But there is a common misconception that must be addressed here and now," Tenebrae continued. "The legend of Skulduggery Pleasant is that his wife and child were murdered and he returned, fuelled by rage and a need for vengeance. A nice legend. Romantic, intimidating, ticks all the boxes that a legend should tick. Naturally, the only ingredient missing is the truth."

"Please," Skulduggery said, "enlighten us."

"You were always an angry man," Tenebrae said. "When you were alive, you just hid it better, hid it from your loving wife and your loving child. But I saw it, on the battlefield. That's when you allowed it to surface. That's when you allowed the real you to appear."

"I must tell you, Auron, that amateur psychoanalysts do not impress me."

"I wouldn't expect them to, but I have proof. I had a theory and I tested it, and my suspicions were confirmed. Valkyrie, Solomon Wreath told me that when you were fighting the Faceless Ones, you used his cane. Is that correct?"

"Yes," Valkyrie said. "He told me to."

"Of course he did. If he hadn't given you permission, the moment you tried to use it the power inside would have killed you. You took that cane and you used that Necromancer power, instinctively and without training, and he saw in you a great potential. The same potential I saw in Skulduggery, all those years ago."

Skulduggery tilted his head. "What are you talking about?"

"Remember Prussia? This was a few months after you were married. Mevolent's people had raided the Necromancer Temple where I was studying. I was one of the only survivors, and we linked up with you and your team and tracked the raiding party across the mountains."

"I remember," Skulduggery said. "It took us three weeks to catch up with them. Morwenna Crow was with us."

"That's right. My dear Morwenna, the only Necromancer to serve on the Council of Elders. Yes, she was a fellow survivor."

"I spent most of the time talking to her. I don't think you and I exchanged more than five words."

Tenebrae nodded. "One of the closest friendships I've ever had."

"You're a sad little man."

Tenebrae laughed. "Regardless, we tracked the raiding party and we caught up with them. We waited, and we attacked. In the battle, I was injured. You were injured. All of us were injured, but we kept fighting. I had dropped the dagger that housed my power. I was bleeding, tired, the dagger was just out of reach, and there, lumbering towards me, was the biggest ogre I'd ever seen. Twelve foot tall, green skin, dressed in stitched leathers with tusks as big as my arm."

"He was half that size," Skulduggery said. "And he didn't have tusks, he just had really bad teeth. Also, he wasn't an ogre. His name was Jeremy."

"You really know how to spoil a good story," Tenebrae said. "I was on my back, looking up, so he appeared to be a twelve-foot-tall ogre. One thing you cannot argue with is the size of the axe he was swinging."

"It was a big axe," Skulduggery conceded.

"Bigger than any I had ever seen."

"Oh for God's sake…"

"And just before that axe split my skull and found my brains, Valkyrie, Skulduggery staggered into view. He fell, reached out, grabbed my dagger, and sent fifty spears of darkness into the ogre's chest."

Skulduggery said nothing.

"I hadn't given him permission," Tenebrae said. "That power should have torn him apart. But he controlled those shadows, instinctively and without training, and when Jeremy the ogre was dead, Skulduggery dropped the dagger and went looking for the next enemy to kill."

Tenebrae looked at Skulduggery. "From that moment, I knew you were special. I knew I would need to keep an eye on you. A few years later, we Necromancers retreated to our Temples and fortified our positions. We decided to let the rest of the world fight among themselves. But not everyone respected our neutrality. Nefarian Serpine, in particular, seemed disinclined to leave us alone. He surrounded the Temple I was in, threatened us with utter destruction unless we shared some of our secrets. The High Priest chose me to be the one to venture out and teach Serpine what he wanted to know."

"The red right hand," Valkyrie said.

Tenebrae gave the slightest of nods. "Agonising death inflicted by merely pointing at your victim, providing he was within range. Serpine had heard about it and he wanted it. I taught him. During our lessons, we talked. He made clear his hatred of you, Skulduggery. He said you were the reason he was doing this. To be frank, I couldn't allow that. You had such potential. I couldn't allow this religious fanatic to kill you, so I altered what I was teaching. I added a little something. If ever this Necromancer power was used against *you* specifically, it wouldn't be the end. Your soul, your being, would be for ever tied to your body. If I had known he was going to burn your corpse and reduce you to a mere skeleton, I probably would have taken that into consideration."

Skulduggery's voice was empty. "*You* brought me back?"

"No. I merely allowed for the opportunity. You brought yourself back, Skulduggery. Through sheer force of will, your soul regained its consciousness. From there, your body acted as if it were whole again, allowing you to talk, to move, to feel pain."

"You. You did this. I'm alive today because of you."

"Yes. Doesn't that make you smile? Knowing you owe me everything?"

Skulduggery sagged.

"What's wrong?" Tenebrae asked. "Were you expecting something more? Did you fool yourself into detecting a divine hand in your resurrection? Did you believe your life to have some special purpose? Sorry to disappoint you, but your life had no special purpose other than the one I had planned for you. Which, as it turned out, was a waste of everyone's time.

"I didn't tell anyone, of course. You were my little secret. I continued to keep an eye on you. I watched you fight on, letting your anger consume you. It was a fascinating exercise, knowing there could really only be one outcome. All I had to do was wait. I knew you were coming."

"OK, stop," said Valkyrie. "What the hell are you talking about? What outcome? What were you waiting for?"

"For the knock on the door," Tenebrae said. "Necromancy killed him, Necromancy brought him back. His loved ones were dead, his life was war. His life was death. With every year that passed, he was losing more and more of the person he thought he was. With every year, he was becoming somebody else. And then he knocked on the door of a Necromancer Temple, and I knew he had come home."

The warmth drained from Valkyrie's face. "No."

"He abandoned his old life. He wore armour to disguise his old form. He took a new name to kill his old self."

"No," Valkyrie said. "No, don't."

"Skulduggery Pleasant walked off the battlefield, and Lord Vile walked into my Temple."

Omg!
I never would have guessed!

29

WHO KNOWS WHAT DARKNESS

Valkyrie looked at Skulduggery. "He's lying," she said. "I now he's lying. Tell me. Skulduggery, tell me he's lying."

"He can't," Tenebrae said.

"Shut up!" Valkyrie screamed. "Shut up! Say one more goddamn word and I'll kill you, I swear to Jesus! Skulduggery, look at me. Look at me!"

Skulduggery raised his head, looked at her with his hollow eye sockets. "I'm sorry," he said.

Valkyrie found herself walking backwards. "What are you talking about? What are you saying? What are you talking about? Skulduggery, he's lying. He's lying. Tell him he's lying, for God's sake. You're not Lord Vile. You *fought* Lord Vile."

"The real Lord Vile," Tenebrae said, "and I mean the fully powered Lord Vile, would have obliterated him. That thing he fought was mere… intention. It was simply the armour. Inside, it was empty."

"Yeah," Valkyrie snarled. "We thought of that. Vile's ghost. That's what it is. Vile's ghost is controlling it."

Tenebrae folded his hands in the sleeves of his robe. "Vile doesn't have a ghost. He's not dead. Skulduggery is the one controlling it."

"No, I think you'll find that he isn't."

"Not consciously," Tenebrae said. "Not willingly. But Lord Vile is a part of him, a part of his subconscious. Evidently, that particular part of his subconscious has… broken away from the rest."

"What you're talking about is ridiculous."

"No, Valkyrie, actually it's not. Our dear friend Skulduggery is, and let's be honest here, a little bit insane. He spent ten months being tortured by the Faceless Ones, didn't he? When you rescued him, was he the same well-adjusted gent you knew and loved?"

Valkyrie hesitated.

"He cracked. Don't you see? They drove him insane. And while he seems to have recovered for the most part, he's different, isn't he? You rescued him, he came back, and all of a sudden we're all talking about the Death Bringer. This is not good news for our dear friend. After all, we Necromancers called *him* the Death Bringer when he was Lord Vile, didn't we? But he turned his back on all that. And now that he's home, and we're saying that *you*, his precious little Valkyrie, might turn out to be the Death Bringer, well… It's all too much. Events conspire to bring him close to his empty old armour and all that power reawakens. His armour gains sentience, stands up. He has no more control over it than you or I have control over a stray thought."

"But Lord Vile was… Lord Vile is *evil*."

Tenebrae shrugged. "Who knows what darkness lurks in the hearts of men?"

"But he joined Mevolent. That means Skulduggery and Serpine were on the *same side*."

"No one was more surprised about that than I, believe me. But the more I thought about it, the more I understood. Don't make the mistake of thinking that Lord Vile is merely Skulduggery with a mask on. They're two different people. Skulduggery's anger and violence had overwhelmed him, and there was nowhere left to turn. So, he blinked, and was gone, and in his place stood Vile. Vile came to us, he absorbed our teachings, his power grew at an

again!

exponential rate, and he quickly became our most powerful Necromancer.

"Only he abandoned us. We didn't even get a chance to tell him about the Passage, but it didn't matter. He didn't want to save the world. He wanted to destroy it. And the quickest way to get what he wanted was to leave us, and join Mevolent."

"Serpine killed his family."

"Serpine killed *Skulduggery's* family. Vile didn't care. To Vile, Serpine was just another instrument to use, like Baron Vengeous, or Mevolent himself."

Valkyrie knelt by Skulduggery. "I know he's lying. He's trying to trick me. I know you're not Lord Vile. Lord Vile is a mass murderer. Explain this to me. Skulduggery, please, just explain it. Make it make sense."

He looked at her. She could see through his eye sockets, to the flickering shadows that played on the inside of his skull. He turned his head, the shadows moved, and he looked at Tenebrae.

"You brought me back," he said. "That's it. That's all there is to it. The great mystery I've never been able to solve. The great question. And you, you are the answer."

"You sound disappointed."

"I thought there would be more to it. Instead, I'm, I'm the result of a Necromancer *trick*."

"If it makes you feel any better, it wasn't *easy* to trick Nefarian

Serpine. I wasn't even sure it would work – something like that had never been tried before." cool!.

Skulduggery walked towards Tenebrae. "You didn't tell anyone. All these years, you didn't tell anyone."

"Why would I? What would it achieve? If your friends knew your secret, they'd have found a way to kill you long ago. And then my wonderful work would have been undone. I liked the fact you were walking around, saving the world in your own little way. It must be like what a proud parent feels."

"How do I stop it?"

"Stop what? Vile? I'm afraid I don't know. These developments are quite unexpected. Your subconscious is your own. Maybe if you wish really, really hard."

Valkyrie looked at Skulduggery. "It's true?" she asked, her voice hollow.

Skulduggery turned. "Yes. I told you it was Vile's ghost that was giving the armour purpose. In a way, that's true, once you accept that Vile's ghost is my subconscious. The armour is imitating me. Or it's imitating how I *used* to be, at any rate."

"You're Lord Vile."

"Yes. Sorry, I should have told you."

"You killed Ghastly's mother."

"Among others, yes. He doesn't know, obviously."

"Stop talking like that!" she roared. "Stop talking so normal!"

"What would you prefer? Sobbing? Wailing? Maybe some more silence? Regret never won a war, Valkyrie, and 'sorry' isn't a big enough word for what I'm feeling. I've spent my life since then trying to make up for it, but I'll *never* make up for it. The things I did were unspeakably evil, but for those few years, I didn't care."

"You… you told me you did terrible things."

"I did." skulduggery!

"I didn't think they'd be so…"

"I know. We can talk about this later." He turned back to Tenebrae. "If my subconscious is controlling the armour, and the armour wants to kill your Death Bringer, then why haven't you killed me?"

"Well," Tenebrae said, "let's face it, I might be wrong. The armour might be operating completely independently of you – it might have gained a higher degree of sentience. In that case, killing you would deprive me of a valuable asset in taking it down. The second reason and, quite honestly, the most pertinent, is that I don't know *how* to kill you. If I try, a bungled attempt on your life might redirect the armour against *me*. And I have no intention of dying before the Passage is brought about. Not when I'm this close."

"So you've been hoping that Melancholia brings about the Passage before Vile gets to her? That's your whole strategy? You've been *hoping*?"

"The centuries have changed all of us, Skulduggery. As Cleric Wreath delights in pointing out, we Necromancers are used to sitting back and not actually doing anything. We're a very lazy lot, now that I think about it."

"No," Skulduggery said, "you've waited too long for this lunatic scheme of yours to come true. You wouldn't leave anything to chance."

"Oh, don't worry, I'm not," Tenebrae said. "Melancholia is the Death Bringer. She is the only Necromancer to ever reach that level of power. You left before you reached it, and the Lord Vile that's walking around right now isn't even *you*. It's an echo of you, not fully charged. If you were in the armour, yes, I'd be worried. But you're not. So if Vile attacks Melancholia, she will destroy it. Or him. What are we calling Vile – an *it* or a *him*? Ah, I suppose it doesn't matter. The important thing is that you two stay locked up here until all this is over. I hope I've given you enough to talk about. I do hate those awkward silences."

Tenebrae turned, and the door closed as he walked away. Skulduggery looked at Valkyrie. "You have a right to be upset," he said.

"Oh do I?"

"I should have told you. I know you understand why I didn't, but I should have."

"You let me go through this Darquesse thing, with all the guilt and the fear and knowing the things that I'm going to do, and you didn't say anything."

"What did you want me to say? *Look at me. I was Lord Vile, but now I'm OK?* It would have made things worse. You would have looked at the things I did in that armour and you'd have assumed that in order to pass through and emerge on the other side, you'd have to do the same. But you don't. That's the thing. Violence and hatred and bloodshed became my reasons for existing. I stopped caring about anything else. I didn't care who my enemy was, as long as I had an enemy. I was falling, and I didn't know how to stop."

Valkyrie put her back to the wall, slid down to a sitting position. Her legs wouldn't take her weight. "You murdered all those people. How many? Do you even know?"

"I don't. I lost count. Everyone lost count. I was like you. Necromancy came far too easily to me."

"You're one of those sorcerers you told me about. The Elementals who can switch to being an Adept."

"It's rare, but it's possible."

"But... Skulduggery, you're the good guy."

"I'm sorry I didn't tell you. I'm sorry you found out this way."

"What do we do now?"

"Well, we escape. I'm not sure how yet, but—"

"No," said Valkyrie. "What do *we* do now? We're partners. You're my best friend. I love you. You were my... I looked up to you. What am I supposed to do now?"

He turned away. "You need to find yourself a new hero."

why does she need a new hero?.

30

TENEBRAE

He had to admit, that had been fun.

Tenebrae wasn't a sadistic man, but the look on Valkyrie Cain's face and the pain in Skulduggery Pleasant's voice were just… delicious. He had been carrying that secret around with him for centuries, had come close to spilling it a few times before this. But he was glad he hadn't. It was like an itch that you put off scratching – when you eventually did scratch, it was so much more satisfying.

His mood didn't last, however. When he got to his office, Vandameer Craven wasn't waiting for him as he had instructed.

Enough was enough. Tenebrae was sick of Craven and the

ridiculous serenity that seemed to have washed over him overnight. He was sick of everyone treating the spineless worm like he was some kind of holy man with the ear of the messiah. Craven was still a Cleric, and Tenebrae was still the High Priest, and the natural order of things *would* be restored.

So Tenebrae sat behind his desk, his temper boiling the longer he was made to wait. When his door finally opened, he had to force himself not to jump up and throttle the man.

"Cleric Craven," he said, "so good of you to grace me with your presence."

"My apologies," Craven said, bowing. "Our younger Necromancers are understandably nervous. They needed someone to reassure them that it was all going to be OK."

Tenebrae frowned. "And that someone was you, I take it?"

Craven smiled. "I go where I am needed."

"Take me to her," Tenebrae said, standing up.

Craven raised an eyebrow. "Your Eminence?"

"Take me to the Death Bringer, Cleric. It's time I spoke with her."

"Ah, unfortunately, I cannot. She is to remain undisturbed."

"I am the High Priest, Cleric Craven. You do not say no to *me.*"

Something flickered in the Cleric's eyes, something Tenebrae had never seen in those eyes before, and then it was gone. "Of course. Once again, my deepest apologies. I will take you to her at once."

Tenebrae stalked out of the room. Craven followed him through the corridor, struggling to match Tenebrae's long stride. The satisfaction Tenebrae derived from robbing Craven of his newly acquired dignity was a petty kind of satisfaction, but it was satisfaction nonetheless, and it made the corners of his mouth want to lift in a smile.

Things got even better when they reached the bowels of the Temple. Tenebrae gestured to Craven to lead the way to whichever chamber held Melancholia, but if the Cleric thought this would mean that he could dictate the walking pace, he was sadly mistaken. Tenebrae walked so quickly that Craven had to virtually scamper ahead of him lest Tenebrae tread on the hem of his robe. More than once, Tenebrae managed to stand on the trailing material, and Craven's head would jerk back with a strangled gag.

Finally, they came to a door, and the childish fun and games were over. Craven opened the door wide and Tenebrae swept by him. Melancholia St Clair lay in a hole in the ground, filled to the brim with mud. Her robes lay beside her. Her eyes opened to watch the two men enter. If she was surprised, it didn't register on her face. She remained where she was.

"Melancholia," Cleric Craven admonished. "The High Priest has entered the room."

"I can see that," Melancholia said. "Surely you don't expect me to stand?"

"That will not be necessary," Tenebrae said.

"Valkyrie Cain is here, isn't she?" Melancholia asked. "And Skulduggery Pleasant."

"Yes," Tenebrae said. "How did you know?"

"I can feel them," she said. "I can feel their energy. They are not happy, are they? She is angry, and scared, and hurt."

"I would say that she is, yes."

Melancholia smiled. "Glorious."

"How are you feeling, my child?"

She looked at him. "I'm tired."

"Are you hurt? This is a healing mud you are in, is it not?"

"It's regenerative," Craven said quickly. "It fills her with energy and—"

"I know what regenerative means," Tenebrae interrupted. "And I was asking the girl."

Melancholia closed her eyes and let her head loll back gently. "The girl has a name."

Tenebrae paused. "What was that?"

Her eyes were still closed. "I said, the girl has a name. Melancholia. Death Bringer. You can use either one. But you can't call me 'the girl'."

"I am the High Priest of this Temple, young lady. I can call you whatever I choose."

One eye opened, and she squinted up at him.

"I asked if you were hurt," Tenebrae continued. "I expect an answer."

The girl sighed. "Sometimes I burn. It's not nice. It hurts. The mud makes it feel better."

"Burn? Why do you burn?"

"Because of my scars."

"Ah yes, the scars. I've been meaning to ask about those."

Craven stepped forward. "I can explain to you—"

"I want her to do it. Melancholia?"

"He carved symbols on to me," Melancholia said. "It took months. It was painful. But it needed to be done. I was the Death Bringer, and I needed my power. It's all worth it now. Every moment I spent screaming. It's worth it."

"Then it's true," Tenebrae said, turning to Craven. "You carved her up to loop the Surge, didn't you? That's why she needs to recharge constantly."

"I did what had to be done," Craven said primly.

Tenebrae grabbed him, shoved him back against the wall. "You arrogant *fool*. That level of power isn't natural for her. There's no telling *what* will happen."

A fit of anger overcame the Cleric, and he struggled to break Tenebrae's grasp. Were he so inclined, Tenebrae would have found such a display of impotent fury fascinating. As it was, all he felt was disgust. He released his hold, wiping his hands on his robe as Craven stumbled away from him.

"I did what had to be done!" Craven shouted. "I did what you didn't have the imagination to do!"

"She can't be relied upon," Tenebrae said. "There's no telling when she'll be back to full strength. There's no telling if she ever will. She is not the Death Bringer!"

Something came at him, something dark and terrible, and it hit him and Tenebrae spun head over heels through the air. He crunched into the wall and dropped to the stone floor. Agony raced from his shoulder across his chest. A collarbone was broken. Maybe a rib. Hissing in pain, he looked over at Melancholia, standing there, the mud dripping off her.

"I *am* the Death Bringer," she said calmly. "I'm the one you've all been waiting for."

His vision dimmed suddenly. "No," he whispered, and then his life was dragged from his body.

31

FUEL

Bison Dragonclaw laid out his torture instruments on the table. Knives, saws, pliers, hammers, neatly arranged one by one. Valkyrie watched him.

When he was done, he hauled Skulduggery to his feet and shoved him against the wall, then went over to Valkyrie, did the same to her.

"You're not so tough now, are you?" he asked, his smile revealing small teeth behind that wispy goatee. "I bet you're really regretting the way you treated me. Now it's my turn. Now I get to inflict some pain."

She didn't answer him. She barely heard him.

"We've not finished treating you badly," Skulduggery said. "The moment we escape from these shackles, we're going to do it all over again."

"Even if escape were possible," Dragonclaw replied, "you'd be too late. The Death Bringer is about to change the world."

"You hope."

"It is a scientific inevitability."

"There's no such thing."

Dragonclaw stopped what he was doing, and looked round. "There is no such thing as a scientific inevitability?"

"Nope."

"And what about, for instance, gravity? If I drop an apple, it will not fall?"

"Not necessarily."

"You are ridiculous."

"Just because an apple falls one hundred times out of a hundred does not mean it will fall on the one hundred and first."

"I thought you were supposed to be a rational man."

"I am a rational man, but haven't you heard? I'm also insane. It gives me a unique perspective on things."

"Here is what I am going to do," Dragonclaw said. "I'm going to pull you apart."

"Your High Priest doesn't want me harmed."

"He doesn't want you *dead*. He was quite agreeable to my harming you."

"If you separate my bones from each other, my consciousness could dissipate."

"Don't worry, I'll leave most of you intact. The torso and the head, probably. Maybe I'll remove the jawbone. It might stop you talking."

"I wouldn't like to bet on it."

"Once you are incapacitated, I will then take apart your young apprentice."

"I'm not his apprentice," Valkyrie muttered.

"She's my combat accessory," Skulduggery nodded. "But you won't get a chance to do any of that, I'm afraid. We're going to get free in the next few minutes and then you're really going to wish you had a few guards here for protection."

"I see," Dragonclaw said. "And do you mind telling me *how* you plan to get free?"

"I'm picking the lock on these shackles as we speak."

"Those locks can't be picked."

"So says the prevailing wisdom."

"And you know better, I suppose?"

"That is the usual state of things."

"And what are you picking the lock with, may I ask? A toothpick? A hairpin?"

"The top of your pen, actually."

Dragonclaw laughed. "I don't have a pen."

"Not any more, that's true. But you had one in the pocket of your robes, don't you remember?"

Dragonclaw's laugh faded. He searched his robes. "You're lying. I didn't have a pen."

"The metal clip on the lid is the perfect size," Skulduggery continued, clearly enjoying the look on Dragonclaw's face. Behind his back, his arms were moving ever so slightly. "I should be out of these in forty seconds or so, and then I'm going to hurt you."

"You're lying," Dragonclaw said. "Even if I did have a pen in my pocket, you couldn't have taken it from me."

"But that's not strictly true, is it? When you pushed me against this wall, you got a little too close."

"You couldn't have taken it. There's no way—"

"Could you stop talking for a moment? This is a tricky bit."

Skulduggery's head tilted. Valkyrie heard a faint tapping of metal against metal.

Dragonclaw grabbed a knife and strode over to Valkyrie. "Stop that," he ordered. "Stop it right now or she dies."

"You're not going to kill her," Skulduggery said. "If you kill her, in thirty seconds I will kill you. You don't want to die, not when you're this close to the Passage."

Dragonclaw pressed the blade to Valkyrie's throat. It was cold against her skin. "Stop. Stop it."

"Twenty seconds, Dragonclaw. And what a ridiculous name that is. Almost as ridiculous as your beard."

The blade bit deeper, and then stopped, and all at once Dragonclaw was pushing her aside and storming towards Skulduggery. Valkyrie stepped behind him and kicked low, sweeping his feet at the ankles. Dragonclaw yelped and Skulduggery moved, smacking his knee into the Necromancer's face as he fell. Dragonclaw bounced off Skulduggery's knee and crumpled to the ground.

Skulduggery squatted beside him, managing to get his hands into the folds of the robe.

"You don't have his pen," Valkyrie said.

"No," Skulduggery admitted. "He never had one. Well done, by the way."

She nodded, didn't answer.

He found the keys, and by the time he stood up, the shackles were already off. He uncuffed her and she felt magic flood her body. It was a nice feeling.

He opened the door, looked out, then gestured to her to stay put before going on ahead. She looked at him, her friend, as he sneaked to the corner, and she tried equating that with all the horror stories she'd heard about Vile. He'd saved her life and she'd

weird

313

saved his, and she had felt closer to him than she had to anyone else. If there was one person who would understand her, she had known it would always be him. But now… *What?*

Two Necromancers came round the corner and Skulduggery took them out. It was vicious and it was ugly, and neither Necromancer had time to even cry out. Valkyrie joined him, stepping over their unconscious bodies, and they moved on. He was in a bad mood. She knew the feeling.

The doors opened ahead of them before they could react, and six Necromancers came striding through. They didn't seem particularly surprised to see a teenage girl and a skeleton walking around unsupervised. They stood in a straight line, side by side, the blackness of their robes flowing together so that they looked like a single creature with six heads.

"You think we were going to let you walk out of here?" one of them asked.

Valkyrie and Skulduggery stayed where they were, waiting for them to make a move. The ring on her hand was ready to throw up a wall of shadows to block the strikes she knew were coming.

And then the Necromancers reached into their robes and pulled out sub-machine guns.

"Hell," was all Skulduggery had time to say before they opened fire.

Valkyrie crossed her arms over her head as bullets slammed

into her. She staggered back, winded, her clothes dissipating the impacts. More bullets hit her arms, but she kept them where they were, kept them tight together, not letting any through. Skulduggery was saying something, but she couldn't hear him over the gunfire, and then she felt him grab her from behind and pull her back round the corner. Out of the firing line, he pushed her against the wall.

"Are you OK?" he asked quickly, his hands checking her for bullet hits. "Are you hurt?"

Valkyrie shook her head, unable to speak until there was breath in her lungs again. Something flew round the corner, bouncing on the floor beside them. She hadn't even registered what it was before Skulduggery reached out his hand. The grenade went off, but Skulduggery kept the explosion contained in a tight bubble of air. He released his grip and the smoke curled through the corridor.

They ran back the way they had come.

Dragonclaw was in the corridor, using the wall to support himself. He saw them coming and his eyes managed to widen. He dug a hand into his robes.

Valkyrie sprinted for him. Two Necromancers emerged from an adjoining corridor just as she passed. They raised their weapons, but she left them to Skulduggery. She heard their grunts and cries of pain and kept going towards Dragonclaw. He pulled a gun from his robe, Skulduggery's gun, raised it with a trembling hand and fired. The bullet missed Valkyrie completely and she swiped at the air, yanking the weapon away from him. The gun fell and she collided with him, her elbow crunching into his face. He reeled back, squawking, but she was latched on to him now and she didn't stop hitting until he was on the floor, his arms flopping uselessly at his sides.

Skulduggery hauled her up with one hand, his gun flying into the other, and he kept her moving as he fired behind them. Sub-machine guns peppered the corridor with bullets, the walls spitting chunks of plaster and plumes of dust. They got behind the next corner and ran on, straight into a dead end. They turned, but it was too late, the Necromancers were already there.

And then the Necromancer furthest away stiffened, his gun falling. Valkyrie frowned as the next one did the same, and the next one, and finally the Necromancer closest to them exhaled, and his face went blank. All six of them stood there, suddenly very pale. Then they fell, one at a time, the closest Necromancer first, the effect rippling backwards.

Skulduggery walked forward warily, and checked for a pulse. "He's dead," he said, a hint of surprise in his voice.

He picked up a sub-machine gun, stepped over the dead Necromancer and continued on, back the way they had come. Valkyrie's ring was like ice.

The Temple was quiet. Every corner they turned revealed more dead people in black robes. Bison Dragonclaw lay sprawled across the floor, eyes open, seeing nothing.

Doors opened ahead of them and Melancholia stepped through. She was smiling. "Wasn't that fun?"

Skulduggery raised the sub-machine gun to his shoulder, finger hovering over the trigger. "You did this?"

"I needed a boost," Melancholia said with a shrug. "A little pick-me-up. Valkyrie knows what I'm talking about, don't you, Valkyrie? That little ring is burning so cold now, isn't it? My whole body is burning like that. It's intoxicating. But don't worry – I didn't kill all of them. There are still plenty left to fawn over me."

"You're under arrest," Skulduggery said.

"Don't be stupid. I'm going to kill you and then I'm going to save the world."

"By killing half of it."

"Omelettes and eggs, skeleton."

"Give up. This will be your only warning."

Melancholia laughed, shook her head, and as she opened her mouth to speak, Skulduggery pulled the trigger. Melancholia jerked back into a sudden cloud of darkness as gunfire filled the air and bullet casings rattled on to the floor. When the gun was empty, he dropped it and clicked his fingers, summoning flames into his hands. Valkyrie readied shadows of her own.

The cloud faded. Melancholia was still standing. "You're sneaky," she said. "I like you."

Skulduggery threw a fireball but Melancholia sent the darkness to extinguish it. He pushed at the air and she staggered, sent a spear of shadows his way in return. He twisted, the spear missing him by inches. Valkyrie whipped the darkness at her but Melancholia rose on to a wave of pitch-black. Columns of dark shot out, too fast to dodge. One column struck Valkyrie, taking her off her feet. Skulduggery was hit square in the chest, and twice more as he tried to recover. *wow!*

The wave lowered Melancholia to the ground, and at a gesture it turned towards Skulduggery. It crashed down on top of him, dispersing into tendrils that threw him down the corridor.

Valkyrie swept the air in around her and hurtled towards Melancholia. She almost reached her, too, but a wall of darkness appeared between them. Valkyrie hit the wall and it drank her in. She struggled, tried to pull away, but it was like quicksand. Her arms and legs were already in and she turned her head away, arching her spine. The corridor lit up with flame and suddenly she was free. She dropped to the ground while Melancholia dodged another of Skulduggery's attacks. He had run in close, trying to get his hands on her.

Melancholia kept throwing shadows between them, but the shadows were flimsy. She was panicking, trying to give herself some room to manoeuvre. Given the space, she could send out an attack that was impossible to defend against. Skulduggery was making sure that didn't happen, and he was using skill, determination and luck to do it. But while his skill wasn't going to fade and his determination wasn't going to falter, his luck was an element he had no control over.

Another panicked move by Melancholia sent a tentacle of shadow whipping for him. He saw it coming and ducked, weaving under it, but the tentacle flexed at the last moment before it dissipated, and it caught him in the side of the head. He stumbled, and Melancholia struck, sending him spinning backwards.

Something heavy landed on Valkyrie's back as she tried to get up. A mass of shadows, keeping her pinned to the floor. She cursed and strained, but couldn't move.

Skulduggery groaned. Melancholia was doing something to him. Shadows curled out from the cuffs of his jacket, out around his collar, through the buttons on his shirt. But then Valkyrie saw the expression on Melancholia's face. She was frowning – not with intent, but with curiosity. Whatever was going on with Skulduggery, Melancholia wasn't the one doing it.

Skulduggery arched his back and darkness burst from his chest in a steady stream, writhing and twisting in the air, collecting on the far side of the room. A shape formed, the stream broke from Skulduggery, and the shape became solid. A tall man, encased head to foot in black armour that shifted and moved on his body. Valkyrie stared.

Lord Vile hadn't been hiding in a cave or an old base somewhere – he'd been hiding within Skulduggery himself.

Melancholia stepped back, her eyes wide with fear. Lord Vile held out his arm and his hand lengthened to a sharp point that flew at her. She cried out, barely managing to deflect the strike. He went at her again, and again, and she stumbled from each attack, her hair in her eyes. The darkness that had been holding Valkyrie down was gone, and she got up, watching Melancholia being stalked like a deer.

"Help me!" Melancholia cried. "You can't let him kill me! Please!"

The Death Bringer, begging for help. The only person who had the power and the intention to kill three billion people, begging for someone to step in and save her. Valkyrie wasn't going to do it. She couldn't do it. She had to let Vile kill her. It was the only way to save all those lives.

"Valkyrie!" Melancholia called. "Please help me!"

And suddenly Valkyrie was running, and she was running straight at Lord Vile, while every part of her mind screamed at her to stop. But her body kept going, it wouldn't listen, and Vile waved his hand and she went flying back through the air. As she spun, she saw shadows grow from beneath Melancholia's robes, and then she felt the air shift around her. Her trajectory changed and she fell against Skulduggery, who staggered slightly as he caught her.

Melancholia's shadows sprang at Lord Vile, whose armour grew tendrils that intercepted each one of them. Melancholia was rising to her feet now, standing just beyond arm's reach of Vile. Their shadows, sharp and jagged, pressed and darted and defended. More grew, and still more, pushing out of their arms and legs and torsos. They started to resemble a pair of weird insects, or crabs maybe, snapping at each other with an ever-increasing array of weapons.

Melancholia was smiling. Her blonde hair was obscuring most of her face, but she was definitely smiling, and now Valkyrie could see why. Her shadows were thickening, getting bigger, and Vile was being pushed back. He wasn't whole, after all. He was merely the *armour* of Lord Vile, Skulduggery's old Necromancer power given sentience. If Skulduggery had been in that armour, the Death Bringer would have met her match. But the armour was empty, and the Death Bringer was realising just how powerful she really was.

The shadows behind Melancholia swooped in through her body and erupted from her chest, slamming into Vile and taking him to the far end of the room. He was thrown with such force he hit the double doors and burst through, splintering the wood and ripping them from their hinges. The shadows retracted, back inside Melancholia, and she turned to Valkyrie and Skulduggery, and smiled.

"You saved my life," she said, laughing. The darkness moved in around her, and she disappeared just as Vile lunged at her from the shadows. He grabbed nothing but air.

Skulduggery stepped in front of Valkyrie. "Stop right there," he said.

Lord Vile, the armour, turned towards him.

"I want you gone," Skulduggery said. "You're a part of me, and I want you gone. I left you behind a long time ago and I have no intention of letting this continue. Your time is up."

Vile sent a shadow crashing into him.

"Hey!" Valkyrie shouted. "Hey! What the hell are you doing?"

Four spears of shadow rose up over Vile's head, and Valkyrie turned and ran. They shot towards her as she jumped sideways. All but one of the spears missed her. The last one glanced off the back of her jacket and spun her round as she fell.

There were shouts. The barricades had been breached. Sanctuary operatives were storming the Temple. Vile tilted his head, the same way Skulduggery did. Then the shadows swirled and he was gone.

32

A BAD NIGHT IN HAGGARD

Valkyrie sat hunched over on a fallen headstone, her hands in her pockets and her eyes on the ground. Around her, Cleavers and sorcerers filed in and out of the Temple. They hadn't started bringing the bodies out yet. She didn't want to be here when they did.

She watched Skulduggery talk to them, nodding and pointing, issuing commands. She didn't even understand how any of this was possible. She wanted to travel back in time, back to before she knew the truth. If only she hadn't followed Wreath, left herself open to attack, then Tenebrae would never have had the chance to spoil everything. Skulduggery turned, walked over, and Valkyrie suddenly felt sick, like her insides were rotting away.

"Are you OK?" he asked her.

She nodded.

"Wreath and Craven are unaccounted for – we don't know how many others. We have teams out searching, but I don't like our chances. We'll head back to the Sanctuary, brief the Council."

"Not me," Valkyrie said.

"What?"

"Not me, all right? I'm tired, and I'm bruised, and I just want to go home. I don't care about any of this any more. I'm going to let other people save the world this time."

"Listen, I know you've been through a lot, but—"

"Enough," she corrected, standing up. "I've been through *enough*. In the last few days, I was slashed half to death, I was healed by a monster who once dissected me, I was betrayed and attacked by Solomon Wreath, who I thought was my friend, and then… you."

"Valkyrie…"

"There is absolutely nothing you can say to make this better, so don't even try."

"You've got to understand—"

"I don't want to talk to you," she said, and walked away.

She could have called Fletcher, but she really didn't want to come up with a lie to tell him that would explain her mood. She got a lift into the centre of town from one of the sorcerers she knew, and hopped on a bus. She sat with her arms folded, leaning her head against the cool window. The bus would go over a bump and she'd rock slightly. She didn't think of anything. She just looked at the seat in front and let the bus take her to Haggard.

She got off and cut through the small park, walked through darkness instead of the brightly lit Main Street. She didn't want to talk to anyone. All she wanted to do was pick up her baby sister and hug her.

The lights were off in her house, and there were no cars in the driveway, so Valkyrie let herself in the front door. Her family wasn't in. She went up to her room, but her reflection wasn't there. Frowning, she took out her phone, dialled a number and waited.

The call was answered, and she heard her own voice say, "Hello?"

"It's me," Valkyrie said. "Where are you? Where is everyone?"

"We're at the hospital," the reflection said.

Alarm pulsed through Valkyrie like electricity and she gripped the phone tighter. "What? What happened? Is it Alice? Is something wrong?"

"It's not Alice," the reflection said calmly. "It's your mother. She was mugged this afternoon."

Valkyrie went cold. "Mugged? By who? By a mortal?"

"Yes. It happened on Main Street. Everyone's saying it was a stupid place to mug someone. No one ever gets mugged in Haggard. It's too small. He hit her. She's fine, but she was brought to hospital to make sure. So we're all in here."

"Is she hurt?"

"She has a bruise on her cheek."

Valkyrie stood in the middle of her room, trying to make sense of this. "Who did it?" she asked. She was surprised at how soft her voice sounded.

"I only heard his last name. Moore. He's not from Haggard. His car broke down, the Guards said. Dad was in the pharmacy paying, and Mum was standing outside with Alice in the pram and Moore ran up, grabbed her handbag. She pulled it back, he hit her in the face, took the bag and ran right into Dad. Dad threw him through the pharmacy window. The ambulance people put on a few bandages and handed him over to the Guards."

"He's still here, then? In Haggard?"

"As far as I know. They rang Dad—"

"Stop calling him that."

"Sorry. They rang your father and told him they were charging Moore with assault and battery. They still have him in the police station."

Valkyrie stood very still, the phone to her ear. Her body was numb.

"Are you still there?" the reflection asked. "I have to go. Your father's waiting."

"You should have called me."

"They tell you to turn your phone off when you're in the hospital building."

"The moment you heard about it, you should have called me."

"I was never given those instructions."

"You should have assumed."

"It's not for me to assume anything. As you keep reminding me, I'm not real. I have no thoughts of my own. I only do what I'm told."

"Then *do* what you're told. From this moment on, tell me *immediately* if anything bad ever happens to my family."

"Very well. What are you going to do?"

"What do you mean?"

"Now. What are you going to do now?"

"What do you think I'm going to do?"

"I think you're very, very angry. I think you're going to break into the police station and hurt the man who hurt your mother."

Valkyrie didn't say anything. She hung up the phone, and left the house.

Running was an odd sensation. It was like she was hovering above, watching her body move of its own accord. She watched herself run through the narrow lanes of Haggard, keeping away from the bigger streets and roads, keeping away from people. She passed in and out of shadows, in and out of sight, a wraith in black with murder in mind.

The police station was well lit. Valkyrie approached it from the side, dropping from the high wall into the car park. No one around. Not many cars. She avoided the security camera and ran to the nearest window. Suddenly she was no longer floating above – she was sucked back into her own head, and she felt how cold she was, how the rage burned like ice in her belly. Tendrils of darkness slithered between the window and its frame, and she twisted her hand and the tendrils snapped the lock and the window popped open. She used the air to boost herself up, then climbed into a bright bathroom that smelled of disinfectant.

She went to the door, listened for a moment. Somewhere, phones rang. Somewhere, people talked.

She stepped into the corridor. It wasn't a big building, and Valkyrie figured the cells would be as far away from the main entrance as possible, so she turned right. She rounded the corner and ducked into a room, an interview room by the look of it, to avoid a passing cop. She waited until his footsteps receded before she emerged and continued on. She came to three cream-coloured steel doors with glass partitions. The first two cells were empty. There was a man lying on a bed in the third.

Shadows crept into the lock and smashed it from within, and Valkyrie was walking into the cell before Moore had even lifted his head from the thin pillow. The door closed behind her.

He looked at her. He was in his early twenties, skinny, with a bad haircut and a cleft in his chin. A plaster covered a thin cut along his cheek. His left forearm was bandaged. He stood up, still looking at her, frowning now. She reached a hand towards the camera, up high in the corner of the cell, and sent a dart of shadow into the lens. Moore stepped back.

"What was that? What the hell *was* that? Who are you?"

She stepped closer, hands by her sides, shoulders relaxed. Inside she was cold. There was a block of ice inside her. The voice spoke to her.

Kill him.

When she was close enough, she swung her right hand up, fingers splayed and palm open, twisting into the strike. She caught him on the hinge of the jaw and he crashed back against the wall. A power-slap, Skulduggery called it. As powerful as a punch, without the risk of broken knuckles. One of the new weapons in her arsenal, ever since Tanith went bad. Valkyrie watched Moore try to stand up straight. His legs gave out and he fell back. His mouth was hanging open and his eyes were clouded. She waited while he shook his head and his eyes refocused. He looked at her and she watched his anger build.

Moore sprang from the wall. She let him grab her, let him pull her in, and she fired an elbow into his face two, three times. He let go, but she didn't, she latched on, kept firing those elbows, driving him back, never letting go of him. He tried to shout, but she hit him in the neck and he gagged. She didn't give him a chance to throw a punch of his own, didn't give him a chance to push her away. She was all over him, elbows and headbutts. In between his sudden yelps of pain she heard someone snarling, realised it was coming from her. She didn't stop. She had blood on her face and it wasn't her blood and she didn't stop. This man had attacked her mother. This man had attacked her *mother*.

Kill him.

He was on the floor now and she was on top of him, her hands tightening round his throat. His strength was gone. His efforts to dislodge her, to break the stranglehold, were useless. He was weak and she was strong. The coldness inside her was burning. She was talking to him, her words scraping through gritted teeth, but she couldn't hear what she was saying.

His hands fluttered uselessly around her arms. His eyes were rolling back. Blood and spittle flew from his mouth. He was turning purple.

Kill him, the voice in her head whispered.

She dug her fingertips in even tighter. This must have been how Melancholia felt when she held Valkyrie's life in her hands. It was power, pure power, pure and beautiful. It filled her, energised her, mixed with her rage and made her smile, just like Melancholia had smiled.

Valkyrie frowned, saw her hands around his throat, saw Moore's life about to leave him. Her hands sprang open and she staggered to her feet. He turned on to his side, coughing and sucking in great gasps of air.

The voice was gone now. Banished from her mind. She suddenly felt queasy, like she was going to vomit.

Moore dragged himself away from her, towards the far wall. Valkyrie's hands were shaking. Her legs were trembling. Her head pounded.

"If I ever see you in this town again," she said to him, "I'll come back for you and I won't stop. Stay away from this town. Stay away from my mother. Or I swear to God, I will kill you."

He curled up and she left the cell. She retraced her steps, squirmed out through the window, barely getting outside before she threw up. Her legs were liquid, wouldn't support her weight. The cops were going to find her out here. She realised she was crying.

A shadow fell over her, blocking the moonlight. Caelan reached down, took her into his arms like she weighed nothing, and carried her into the darkness.

In her back garden, she watched him and he watched her. The night was warm. The sounds of the waves drifted over the wall.

"You've been following me," she said.

The shadows draped themselves over his sharp features. He didn't say anything. Didn't deny it.

"You've been doing that a lot, haven't you? Following me. Watching me."

"Looking out for you," he said. "But only at night. Only when you're vulnerable."

Valkyrie shook her head. "That isn't right," she said. "You shouldn't do that to people. You shouldn't watch them. I don't want you to do it any more."

"I need to make sure you're safe."

"I don't need your protection."

He didn't respond to that. Instead, he asked, "Did you kill him?"

She hesitated. "No."

"Did you want to?"

"Yes."

"You sound ashamed. You shouldn't be. You have darkness in your heart, as do I."

"That's not true."

"Of course it is. It's a part of who you are. You can't fight it."

She heard a car. "They're back," she said. "You have to go."

"I'm not leaving you."

"I don't want you watching me or my family."

"You better hurry, they're almost in the house."

She gave him one last look, then hurried through the back door and ran up the stairs, and she heard the front door open and her mother's voice. She went to the window, looked out. She couldn't see Caelan out there, but Valkyrie knew that he was.

33

WILLOW HILL

When Willow Hill Retirement Home had closed down twenty years earlier, nobody had wept. It had been a cold place, of long halls and strong smells, that seemed to infect its staff and its citizens with a dangerous level of indifference. Bodies, once young and strong, wasted away with barely a whisper of protest, following dutifully after minds that were in no condition to lead them. People gave up in Willow Hill. In Willow Hill, nobody seemed to bother.

The Necromancer Order had purchased the Home ten years previously, and had done nothing to prevent the slow decay that seeped through the walls. They let it crumble. They let the local kids throw rocks through the windows and spray-paint the outside. The only thing they didn't allow was anyone to break in, to spend the night. There was no telling when the Order might be in need of refuge, and they didn't want to deal with an infestation of mortals when this need arose.

Craven, in particular, liked retirement homes. He liked the peace and the quiet, the still quality of stale air. Most of all he liked the death that lingered like a faint memory.

His fellow Necromancers, thirty-four in all, were gathered in what had once been the dining hall. Craven waited at the door, judging the pitch of a dozen conversations, and then he walked slowly into the room and waited for everyone else to stop talking. When there was silence, he cleared his throat, closed his eyes, and shook his head sadly. "It is with deepest sorrow," he said, "that I tell you today that High Priest Auron Tenebrae has rejoined the stream of life." Shocked mutterings reverberated through the assembled Necromancers, and Craven continued. "Lord Vile killed him before turning his sights on our saviour, the Death Bringer. She was strong enough to survive. The High Priest, unfortunately, was not."

"Where's the body?"

Craven frowned, seeking the one who had interrupted his solemnity. It was Wreath. Of course it was Wreath.

"We were unable to retrieve it, Cleric Wreath," Craven said.

"But I saw it happen myself. High Priest Tenebrae is no more. This is a day of great sadness."

"It is indeed," Wreath said, "because we didn't just lose Tenebrae, did we? We lost over three dozen others."

"A terrible tragedy."

"Tragedy, you call it? Melancholia killed them. I call it murder."

Craven looked shocked, and glanced back at Melancholia. She was sitting with her head down and her hood up. For a moment there seemed to be a slight smile on her face. Craven turned back to the crowd. "Murder? How can it be murder? This is the Death Bringer. She released our fellow Necromancers to the great stream because she needed their strength and their courage to defeat Lord Vile and those Sanctuary dogs. I assure you, every single one of them was prepared to make the ultimate sacrifice, and I'm sure they did so gladly."

"She didn't exactly give them a choice," Wreath said.

"I didn't have time." All eyes turned to Melancholia, who kept her head down. "I'm sorry I killed those people. I knew all of them. I'll miss them, but I know I'll see them soon, just as I know I'll see the High Priest again. I have a... a responsibility, Cleric Wreath, to bring about the Passage. That's the only thing that means anything any more. Surely you, of all people, know that we must do whatever we can to ensure that the world is saved."

"And you think you're really the one to do that?"

"I don't know. In all honesty, I don't know. I have doubts. Beneath this power I am still me, I am still Melancholia St Clair. I have my fears, Cleric. I'm afraid I'm not going to be strong enough, or brave enough, and I'm afraid I'm going to falter just when you need me the most. I don't want to let you down, Cleric."

Craven didn't smile, even though his lips wanted to. He watched Wreath glower, while all around him the Necromancers were looking at Melancholia with a new level of understanding. It was a masterful speech.

"The Sanctuary will be getting desperate," he said, drawing their attention back to him. "As long as we remain here, we should be safe. Another four days. That's all we need. Let the Sanctuary agents tire themselves out searching for us. They won't find us. They won't find anyone who knows where we are. As long as we remain here, as long as we remain together, they will not defeat us, and we will save this world."

He clasped his hands and closed his eyes, and they began applauding. They were *applauding*.

He turned, left the room. The White Cleaver trailed after him as per his new assignment – Personal Bodyguard to Vandameer Craven. Craven was sure that the Cleaver was deeply honoured by such a position, even if he didn't show it.

Shadows collected ahead, and when they dissipated, Solomon

Wreath was standing there with his arms folded. "You saw it, did you?"

Craven slowed as he neared. "I'm sorry?"

"Tenebrae. You saw Vile kill him?"

"Yes. Yes, I did. It was quick, though, and from that we must take comfort."

Craven turned to one of the grimy windows that lined the corridor. "It's all changed, isn't it? There's no going back – not now. I… I need someone I can trust by my side, Solomon. Are you that man?"

Wreath grunted. "I wouldn't have thought so."

Craven turned, smiled. "Nor would I, my friend. Between us, there has been nothing but animosity and distrust. Years, foolishly wasted on childish games – for what purpose? Pride? Vanity? I know not. But we are here. Now. Thrown together. You, the last Cleric of our Temple. And me, suddenly looked upon as prophet, as leader, as High Priest."

Wreath unfolded his arms. "I'm sorry, what? Exactly *who* is looking at you that way?"

"Why, *they* are. Our fellow Necromancers. They look to me for answers I cannot give."

"Because you're not the High Priest."

"But if I am not," Craven said, as gently as he could, "then who is?"

Wreath frowned. "Craven, you're a Cleric. We lost a High Priest, another will be assigned. It's how these things work."

"Would you wait for someone new to come in and take over? If we stand united, we need no one else."

"If we stand united under *you*, you mean."

"Then I won't be the High Priest," Craven said impatiently. "It's just a title, after all. A name. It's all meaningless, the petty rivalries, the power plays. Oh, how I lost myself to it, back when my eyes were shut and my mind was closed. But now, I see. The way is clear. The Death Bringer will unite us, my friend. If you cannot believe in me, at least believe in her."

"She killed thirty-eight of us."

"For which she has just apologised."

"She's unstable."

"She's adjusting."

"She's a mental case. And what about her power? One moment she can barely lift her head, the next she's flinging people around like they're leaves in the wind. How can she be expected to usher in the Passage if she can't control how long she'll be able to stand upright?"

"I have faith."

"I don't."

"That is... troubling."

"No, it's reasonable."

"Melancholia is the Death Bringer. Yes, it's not like we thought it would be. It's not as clean. But it's real, and it's happening. She has the power to do this."

"She had better. If she doesn't, if she fails, we'll never get another chance. They know what we want now – they know what we're after. If we continue with this, and she fails, we'll be hunted down across the world. They'll destroy our Temples, our teachings, everything. She'd better be the one, Craven."

"She is."

"Because if she isn't, we should kill her now and see what we can salvage."

Craven's eyes widened. "What?"

"If we stop, now, immediately, we can take care of this. We can take the blame – me, you, Melancholia, the others. We can take the punishment. But our brothers and sisters around the world will be left alone, left to find the one true Death Bringer."

"Melancholia *is* the one true Death Bringer!"

"No, she's the one *you* made."

Craven fell silent.

"This is our last chance. If there is any doubt about her, we should sacrifice ourselves for the greater good."

"There is no doubt in my mind that she can do it."

"Well, there's plenty of doubt in mine."

"Our enemies are closing in," Craven said angrily. "We need

to stop them. We need to strike back. Instead, we are at each other's throats once again, when we can least afford it." He sighed, and turned to the window. "Leave me now. I am tired."

Wreath didn't speak for a moment. "Craven, I'm going to be very nice to you, and not break your jaw for what you just said to me. I'm just going to forget you ever said it, and backtrack a little. You think we should strike at our enemies, do you? With what, exactly? We have just over thirty Necromancers, and practically none of them have combat experience. And even if they did, who should we strike against, do you think? The Sanctuary? Its agents? Pleasant and Cain, maybe? Or how about Lord Vile? Should we strike against him?"

Craven turned. "You mock me, Cleric Wreath."

"Oh I do, Cleric Craven, for you are easily mocked. You have no idea what it is you're saying at any given moment, do you? You think just as long as you're issuing orders, you're a leader. Well, here's a newsflash for you, sunshine. That's not how it works."

"You are most insolent."

"You're not the High Priest, Vandameer. If our enemies *are* closing in, then this would appear to be the perfect time for Melancholia to initiate the Passage. If she proves unable to carry out her duties, she must be put down."

"Those are dangerous words you speak."

"Well then," Wreath said, "it's a good thing you're not in charge, or I'd really be in trouble, wouldn't I?"

He walked away, robbing Craven of the chance to do that himself. Craven stayed where he was, at a dirty window he could barely see out of, and seethed with anger.

what?

34

VALKYRIE AND FLETCHER

Morning came, and Valkyrie woke. She pulled on a dressing gown and went downstairs. She left her phone by her bed. She didn't want anyone calling her. Her mum was eating breakfast. Alice lay in her basket on the table.

"How are you feeling?" Valkyrie asked.

Her mum smiled. "I'm fine. You can all stop worrying about me. I had to literally push your father out the door a few minutes ago. He can be really sweet when he wants to be." The smile faded. "What happened to you?"

Valkyrie blinked at her. "Sorry?"

"Is that a bruise?"

Valkyrie ducked back into the hall and checked herself in the mirror. A nice round bruise had appeared where her forehead had met Moore's face. She glared at herself, then returned to the kitchen. "I banged my head last night," she said.

"How?"

Valkyrie shrugged. "Just one of those things. Woke up suddenly, turned the wrong way, banged my head on the wall."

"Nightmare?"

"Can't remember. How did you sleep?"

"Not the best," her mother admitted. "But I'm used to only getting a few hours' sleep with the Little Miss here." She put down her toast and picked up Alice. "You were great yesterday," she said. "Des was just talking about it. You were so calm and collected, and the way you took care of Alice while we were running around like headless chickens... Thank you, sweetheart."

Valkyrie's smile was brittle. It had been the reflection who had been there to help. Valkyrie had been too busy with her other life, where her best friend used to be a mass murderer.

She went upstairs, selected a small healing rock from the collection Kenspeckle had once given her, stripped off and took a shower. She soaked a sponge around the porous rock and gently dabbed the sponge against her forehead. The bruise would disappear soon enough, just like almost every other injury she'd ever suffered. She looked at the palm of her right hand, where Billy-Ray Sanguine had cut her with his straight razor. She still had the scar. It would never go away. She thought about Tanith, and wondered how she was. She missed her. She missed having someone to talk to.

The water was hot, and felt good. Valkyrie held her face against the spray, eyes closed, standing there for the longest time. When she was done, she stepped out, grabbed a towel, walked barefoot across the landing. She dried off in her room, pulled on a pair of loose jeans and a T-shirt. Her phone rang. It was Fletcher. Again. She ignored it.

He appeared in front of her.

Valkyrie jumped back, then lunged past him, shutting her door. "What the hell are you doing?" she whispered. "Anyone could have been in here!"

"You haven't been answering my calls," Fletcher said.

"I was in the shower!"

"I've been calling for days. Val, the last time I saw you, you were in the Sanctuary covered in blood. I've been worried sick."

"You knew I was OK," she shot back.

"Don't I deserve a little *more* than that? Don't I deserve to see you?"

"Fletcher, seriously, this is not a good time, all right?"

"Ghastly told me Melancholia got away. They'll get her, you

know they will. They have every sorcerer out there right now, hunting them down."

"This isn't about that."

"Then what's wrong?"

Valkyrie laughed. "Everything's wrong. Nothing's wrong. I just want to be left alone."

He looked at her, then turned to her desk, started playing music. He turned up the volume. "Now we can talk," he said.

"Turn that down," she snapped. "Mum's been through enough without you giving her a bloody headache."

"What do you mean?"

"She was mugged yesterday. She's fine, she's fine, everyone's fine. She was mugged and the Guards grabbed him, a guy called Moore. I paid him a visit in his cell last night."

Fletcher stared at her. "You what?"

"He attacked my mother. What was I supposed to do? Let him get away with it?"

"He didn't get away with it, Valkyrie. He got caught. He was arrested. He was in a cell. What did you do?"

She met his eyes and didn't answer.

"What did you do?" he asked again, stepping forward.

"I hurt him," she said. "I could have killed him, too. He's lucky I didn't."

Fletcher shook his head. "You don't mean that."

"Again, I'll say it because you may have missed it the first time. He attacked my mother."

"You nearly killed him?"

"He deserved it."

"What? What did you say? He deserved it? Are you serious? You went in there with your magic and your training, you almost *killed* him, and you're OK with that? You'd do it again?"

"Nobody hurts my family."

"You're spending way too much time with Skulduggery. I'd expect this from him, wading in, leaving a trail of bodies behind. But you? This isn't you. This isn't who you are."

"You don't know me well enough to say that."

"No, obviously I don't. The Valkyrie I thought I knew would argue with me every time I even *implied* that she was violent. She certainly wouldn't do what you did."

"If you're going to give me another lecture, save your breath."

"Oh, I wouldn't dream of it. I wouldn't dream of telling you what to do. You know it all, don't you? You know exactly what you're doing, and everyone around you is so very happy to let it continue."

"What are you on about now?"

"Did Skulduggery scold you for breaking into that police station? Did he caution you against beating up a prisoner? No? I'm not surprised. That's exactly the kind of thing *he'd* do."

"Oh I see," said Valkyrie. "Now that Kenspeckle's gone, you've taken it upon yourself to tell everyone when they've crossed a line, have you?"

"Someone has to. It's not going to be Skulduggery. Ghastly's too busy. I *was* relying on Tanith, but I can't do *that* any more. You need someone to rein you in."

"And that's you?" she laughed. "*You* are my moral compass? My God, things are worse than I thought. And I haven't told Skulduggery yet. I don't want to talk to him. I don't want to talk to *anyone*."

"Well, I'm not going to just stand around while you go down a path you're going to regret."

"Do yourself a favour, OK? Stay out of it. You think we're in this together? We're not. I'm in this. That's all."

"I'm your boyfriend, Valkyrie. It's not as simple as that."

"Well, we can make it that simple."

He looked at her. "You want to break up?"

"I don't know," she said, defiance rising in her voice. "If you don't stop complaining all the damn time, maybe I do."

"Be careful."

"Of what? Of hurting your feelings? Because you're so delicate?"

"Be careful of saying something you won't be able to take back. You're angry. You're not thinking right."

"I'm thinking fine, Fletcher. Maybe we *should* break up. Maybe we need a change. We've been together for too long as it is. We should have broken up ages ago."

He shook his head. "You're angry. You don't mean it."

"Yes I do."

"No you don't. Stop being so bloody silly."

"*Silly?*" she snapped. "*Silly?* You don't say that to me. You don't *get* to say that to me. We're breaking up, Fletcher. We're through."

"Wait a second, OK? Calm down. Think about it. This is heat of the moment stuff. You don't mean any of it."

"Heat of the moment? This isn't heat of the moment, this has been building for a while. I've wanted to break up with you for a long time, I just didn't realise it. You think we're good together, do you? You think we're a happy little boyfriend and a good little girlfriend? Well, I'm not a good little girlfriend."

"Val, just take a breath, count to ten—"

"I've been seeing Caelan behind your back."

Fletcher froze, and Valkyrie instantly regretted it. More than regretted it. She hated it. She hated the words she'd just said. She hated the look on Fletcher's face. She hated herself. She wanted to claw it all back, to scrub it all away, but it was out, it was in the open, and she was talking again, saying something, she didn't know what, but she shut up when he looked at her.

He said, "What?" in a dull, dull voice.

There was something in her chest that stopped her from

speaking. She had tears in her eyes. She was crying. When was the last time she'd cried? He looked at her and all his questions were answered. His face changed.

"I thought you loved me," he said.

"Fletcher, I'm sorry."

"Why?"

"I don't know... I'm not sure..."

"You must know. You must. You always know what you're doing. You always know why you do things. It's how you're able to be right all the time. It's where you get all this confidence from, the fact that you are the one who is always right. So why did you do it?"

"I don't know."

"You're lying. You know exactly why you did it."

"Fletcher, it's not important."

He laughed horribly. "Not important to you, Val, but it's plenty important to me. Do you even care? I mean, I know you're crying, I can see the tears, but they're not tears for me. You're crying because you feel bad. Those tears are about you, because everything is about you. It always is, isn't it? The world revolves around you, because you're just that selfish."

"I didn't want to hurt you."

"I don't think it even occurred to you that I would be hurt. It never even entered your head. You're obsessed with yourself, you know that? You always have been, but I've been OK with it, because I was obsessed with you too. How stupid am I, huh? Boom, just like that, I'm cut off and now I can see the whole thing. You've never done anything for anyone else. You've never inconvenienced yourself purely for someone else's benefit. The rest of us have. It's what makes us good people. You? You've saved the world, but you're not a good person. I don't know what you are."

"Fletch, please—"

"Please what? Please stop making you feel bad? Oh, wow, I'm sorry. I'm so sorry. I didn't realise I was ruining your day. Maybe you should run back to Caelan… maybe he can comfort you."

Valkyrie shook her head. "It's not like that."

"Oh, so you're not dumping me for him?"

"I'm not dumping you for anyone."

"Does he know this?"

"I couldn't care less what he knows."

"That doesn't surprise me."

"Listen, you can stand there and insult me all you want, but the fact is, this has been coming for a while."

"And yet it's the first I've heard about it."

"Of course it is, because you haven't wanted to hear about it."

"Ah, right. OK. I get it now. Basically, I should have seen this coming, yeah? I should have seen the signs, and realised what was about to happen?"

"Yes," she said.

"So in a way, when you think about it, all this is my fault."

Valkyrie looked away and sighed.

"Which makes perfect sense," he continued. "Because you can do nothing wrong. Because you can never be selfish or self-centred because the fault always has to lie with someone else. I am really stupid, Valkyrie, and I apologise."

"Don't be like this."

"Don't be like what?"

"Don't be so bloody childish. Don't sulk. Don't feel sorry for yourself. Your girlfriend broke up with you. Fine. It happens all the time. Grow up and move on."

"Like you, you mean. Because you're so mature, taking everything in your stride, accepting any and all responsibility that comes your way. That's you, isn't it? Little Miss Perfect?"

"I never said I was perfect."

"But my God, do you think it."

"Don't be ridiculous."

"But why wouldn't you think you're perfect? Haven't I spent the last two years telling you how beautiful you are, how smart, how exceptional? Hasn't Skulduggery been telling you how great you are, and powerful, and amazing? Everyone you meet is instantly impressed with you, because you're so confident and capable. You can do anything you put your mind to. You go from schoolgirl to sorcerer overnight. You're descended from the Last of the Ancients. The Necromancers meet you and you're immediately one of the nominees to be their impossibly powerful saviour. With all these people going crazy over you, Val, I'm actually surprised you stuck with a nobody like me for so long."

"Right now," she said angrily, "I'd have to agree with you."

There were tears in Fletcher's eyes, but he didn't cry. "Well? If you're expecting me to teleport away, you can forget about it. You're the one doing the dumping, so it's up to you to walk out first. So go on, Val. Walk."

There was a silence, and in that silence she thought of all the other things she wanted to say. Instead she nodded, turned, placed one foot in front of the other, and all too soon she was at the door. But she had to say something. She couldn't let it end like this, in anger, with his eyes drilling holes in her back. She turned again.

"I still care for you," she said.

"Wouldn't worry about it," he replied, back to acting cool, "it won't last long. You look at Skulduggery and that's who you model yourself on. He's brave, you're brave. He's cold, you're cold. He's ruthless, you're ruthless. Well done, Val, you share the emotional range of a dead man."

He folded his arms and did that cocky smirk of his, only now it looked mean, and Valkyrie left her bedroom. When she looked back in, he was gone.

35

TEACHING THE TWINS

Valkyrie ate a lunch she didn't feel like, then took Alice for a walk. She headed up Main Street, sunglasses on, ignoring the smiles and the looks from the people she passed. Everyone wanted to tickle Alice's chin and waste Valkyrie's time. They'd all heard about the mugging, of course. Big news travels fast in small towns.

Carol and Crystal came round the corner and it was too late to hide – they'd already seen her.

"We heard about your mum," Crystal said. "Is she OK?"

Valkyrie nodded. "She's fine. She was more shaken up than anything else."

"Who did it?" whispered Carol. "Was it a sorcerer?"

"Nope, just a regular kind of scumbag."

"You wouldn't think anything like that would happen here," Crystal said. "You hear about fights outside pubs and the chipper and that, but not people being mugged. It makes you realise that nowhere's safe, doesn't it?"

"You should probably take up self-defence," Valkyrie said, turning the pram round and heading for home.

"Or you could just teach us magic," Carol suggested.

Valkyrie shook her head. "We've been over this…"

"Are you going to teach Alice magic?" Carol asked.

"Uh, no. I don't think so."

"You don't think so? So you might?"

"Well, no, I mean, I don't want to. I want her to be normal."

"But there's still the possibility that you might?"

"I… I suppose…"

"Then we think it's unfair that you won't teach us."

Valkyrie sighed. "Yeah, I know, but—"

"Teach us for, like, just a few hours this afternoon. If we can't do any tricks by the end, then at least we'll know that we tried."

"They're not called tricks, Carol."

"Illusions, sorry."

Crystal nudged her sister. "That's on stage. When Valkyrie does it, it's called magic. So? Will you teach us? A few hours?"

Ordinarily, Valkyrie would have said no, but she needed something to fill in the time that had suddenly expanded all around her. She sighed again. "Fine. A few hours."

The twins broke into the biggest smiles she'd ever seen them wear.

"Can Fletcher come?" Carol asked.

"Uh, Fletcher and I broke up."

"Oh that's awful. Did he dump you?"

"No, we just broke up."

"Is he seeing anyone else?"

"I wouldn't expect so."

"Can I have his number?"

"I think he wants to be left alone."

"Why did he dump you?"

"He didn't—"

"Did he think you were too immature?"

"He never mentioned—"

"How long did it take you to get over it?"

"Um, I'm not sure what..."

"When did it happen?"

"Three hours ago."

They stared at her.

"You're so brave," Carol said.

"Did you cry?" asked Crystal. "If you want to cry in front of us, you can."

"Thanks," Valkyrie said, "but I think I'm fine now. I'll meet you down on the beach in half an hour, OK?"

"Will we need anything?" Carol asked.

"Just your wits."

They looked confused.

Half an hour later, Alice was back home and Valkyrie was standing with her cousins at the far end of the beach, where the sand gave way to hard pebbles. They were alone here, tucked away in the corner. Carol and Crystal looked at her eagerly.

"Elemental magic is influence over air, fire, water and earth," Valkyrie said. "The first one we're going to look at is air, and with this, the main thing to keep in mind is that everything is connected. It all interlocks. There's a, a kind of fault line between spaces, and once you find the pressure point, you push."

"I don't get it," said Crystal.

"You don't have to get it," Carol said. "You just have to do it."

"Uh, actually, you do have to get it," Valkyrie said. "Magic is all around us, but the only way we can really use it is if we understand how it works. It's like science."

"I hate science," said Carol.

"I preferred drama," Crystal nodded. She snapped her palm, again and again, and nothing happened. "Isn't there any magic where you don't have to learn so much? That's a magic ring you're wearing, isn't it? Could we use that?"

Valkyrie smiled. "Afraid not. This is Necromancy."

"Do you need to study stuff to use it?" Carol asked.

Valkyrie hesitated. "Not really…"

"So it's easier than pushing air?"

"Just because it's easier doesn't mean it's better. There is a downside to power that comes without effort."

"It sounds perfect for us, though," Crystal said. "Can I try?"

"I'd… I'd have to give you my permission to use it."

"So? Give your permission. Please, Stephanie?"

Her cousins opened their eyes as wide as they could go, a trick that worked on their parents, Valkyrie knew, but which had the unfortunate side-effect of making them look like startled goldfish. She shrugged.

"Crystal," she said, "I give you my permission to use this ring." She pulled the ring from her finger and handed it over.

Mouth open in awe, Crystal examined the ring for a few moments before slipping it on. Immediately she frowned. "Oh," she said. "It's cold."

"Necromancy is death magic," Valkyrie said. "Believe me, when that ring is around death, it gets even colder."

"That's disgusting."

Carol reached out. "Let me try."

Crystal pulled her hand away. "Wait your turn. So what do I do, Stephanie? Is there a magic spell I have to say, or something?"

Valkyrie scanned the area, making sure there was no one about. "No spell. Can you feel anything, apart from how cold the ring is? You should feel it in your fingertips."

Crystal narrowed her eyes and waggled her fingers. "I don't know," she said. "I think so. I might."

"See our shadows? Try and grab them."

"Really?"

"Just try it."

Crystal bit her lip, then hunkered down and clutched at the sand their shadows covered. "Am I doing it right?"

"Not really," Valkyrie admitted.

"My turn," said Carol.

"Just wait a minute," Crystal responded, grabbing at sand, her annoyance increasing.

"Stephanie, she's had her go," Carol whined.

"Just give her another few seconds," Valkyrie said. "You keep pushing at the air."

"Pushing at the air is stupid," Carol muttered, but she did it anyway.

Valkyrie watched them both – Carol trying to shove the breeze and Crystal trying to pick up her own shadow – and she did her best not to laugh.

"Girls," said a voice behind them.

They turned quickly. Fergus stood there, hands on his hips and looking displeased.

"Hi, Dad," Carol said.

Crystal stood up, hiding the ring behind her back. "Hi, Dad. We were just…"

"We were doing t'ai chi," Valkyrie said. "It's very relaxing."

Carol nodded quickly. "We've been very tense lately."

"Girls," Fergus said, "your mother wants you back at the house. Go on, now."

The twins glanced at each other, then Crystal stepped in front of Valkyrie in the most unconvincing attempt at nonchalance ever witnessed. Valkyrie took her ring back, and Crystal turned to her.

"Thanks for trying to teach us," she said.

"No problem."

The twins walked off, leaving Valkyrie and Fergus alone on the sand. His eyes never left her.

"How's your mother?" he asked.

"She's OK. It was more the shock than—"

"How's your dad?"

"Uh, he's OK."

"The baby?"

"Alice's fine too."

Fergus nodded. "And how are you, Stephanie? Are you keeping out of trouble?"

"So far."

"And what's that you were showing the girls? T'ai chi, was it?"

"Yep. It's a martial art, but it's very gentle and—"

"I know what t'ai chi is, Stephanie. I've seen people do it in the park. And that wasn't what you were teaching them."

"Well, I, I might have been doing it wrong…"

His next words were angry. "What gives you the right?"

She blinked. "Uh… I'm sorry?"

"You heard me. What gives you the right?"

"I'm not entirely sure what you mean."

He stepped forward quickly, closing the gap between them. His fists were clenched and his face was red. For a moment, Valkyrie even thought he was going to hit her.

He snarled, "What gives you the right to teach my daughters that filthy magic?"

She stared. "*What?*"

"They're my daughters!" he snapped. "They're good girls! I've kept them out of the kind of trouble you get into and I will be *damned* if I'm going to let you drag them down with you."

She took a step back. "Fergus, what the hell are you talking about?"

"Don't play stupid!" he roared, then immediately looked around, making sure no one else had heard. When he spoke again, his voice was quieter but no less intense. "You're not stupid, Stephanie. You're not a stupid girl. We all know it. We all know how smart you are. My girls aren't like that. My girls need someone to look out for them. That's *my* job."

"I'm not getting them into anything," said Valkyrie.

"This is a sickness, you know that?" he said, so angry he was almost laughing. "My grandfather had it. This magic thing. He told us all about it when we were kids, me and Gordon and your dad. He tried to pass on what he knew to us. He didn't have much magic. He couldn't do a whole lot. Some people can't, he said. He was hoping that we'd be different, that we'd be proper sorcerers. We loved the idea, but our dad, he hated it. He didn't want us growing up and getting into wars that had nothing to do with us. He wanted us to be normal. He wanted us to be safe."

Valkyrie just stared at him, unable to speak.

"When our grandfather died, our dad asked me to cut it out – cut out all the nonsense and the games and the stories. He asked me, and he cried as he was asking me. The only time I'd ever seen my old man cry. Of course I said yes. I started telling Des that it was all just pretend. After a while, he believed me. But

Gordon wouldn't play along. He was the eldest, and he refused to do what our dad wanted. Maybe it was because he was the eldest that he felt he needed to rebel, I don't know. They barely spoke after that."

"So you've known all along," Valkyrie said.

Fergus nodded. He seemed suddenly drained, like this had been building inside him for years and now that it was out, he had nothing to hold him up. "I knew that Gordon always wanted to be a sorcerer, but he just didn't have it in him. So he wrote about it instead, and he travelled that world, surrounded himself with all these strange people. I don't know why he did it, to be honest. It must have been hell, to be surrounded by the kind of person that you wanted to be with all your heart, but knew you never could.

"We had so many arguments about it. I was focusing so much on keeping all of this away from your dad. I was terrified that Gordon would do or say something that'd make Des realise that it was all true. And then what would he do? Would he change his life, now that he knew magic was out there? Would he take Melissa with him? Would he take you with him? Would he ruin your lives as well as his own?" Fergus shook his head. "I saw some of Gordon's friends, over the years. I met this beautiful woman. My God, she was beautiful. The first time I saw her, I actually fell in love with her. Can you imagine that? I actually fell in love. I was ready to leave Beryl for her, for this woman who barely even noticed me. That's magic for you, isn't it? It can ruin your life with one little glance. I saw others, too. That tall man, the one who was at the reading of Gordon's will, you remember him?"

"Skulduggery Pleasant," Valkyrie said softly.

"Oh," said Fergus. "So you *do* remember him."

"Yeah."

"Magic ruined our family. My grandfather and my father argued about it constantly. Gordon and my father barely spoke because of it. And Gordon and me... When he died, we hadn't spoken in four years. Four whole years, I didn't speak to my own brother. I cry about that at night, you know. Some nights, I just can't help it. Don't let this ruin your family, Stephanie. Your parents love you. Your dad loves you. Do you know what he'd do if anything bad ever happened to you?"

"Nothing bad is going to happen."

"Don't insult my intelligence," he said, glaring. "I was never as smart as either of my brothers, but I'm not stupid, either. If you're involved in that world, your life is in danger."

Valkyrie said nothing.

"I don't want you teaching my daughters anything," he said.

"I don't want to either, I swear I don't. They saw me do something last year, and they've been at me ever since. I think I can convince them that they don't have any magic, and then hopefully they'll stop trying."

"Do I have your word on that?"

"Yes. Of course."

"I'm holding you responsible if anything… *magical* ever happens to them."

"OK," she said.

He nodded, looked out to sea, and then back to her. "I'm sorry I shouted at you."

"It's fine. Really."

"Are you going to be teaching Alice any of this? When she's old enough?"

"I… don't know. I'd prefer not to."

"Then you understand why I don't want my girls taught?"

"Yes."

He nodded again, then looked down at his feet. "Give our best to your mother," he said.

"Sure."

He turned, started to walk away.

"Gordon couldn't do magic," she called after him, "but what about you?"

He didn't stop walking, and he didn't answer. He just held up his left hand, and clicked his fingers. Even in the bright sunlight, Valkyrie saw the spark between his fingertips.

36

CONFIDING IN UNCLE GORDON

he taxi driver peered out through the windscreen. "I know this place," he said. "This is where that writer lived. What's his name? Edgley."

Valkyrie gave a murmur of affirmation from the back seat.

"I read his books, you know. Some of them. He wasn't the best, was he? I mean, he was OK. He was readable. He was no Stephen King, but he was fine. Didn't like the way he'd kill off his characters, though. That was never nice."

"Suppose not," Valkyrie muttered.

"He wrote those books about the army deserter, didn't he?

Corporal Fleece, getting into all those mad adventures with the ghosts of dead wizards and whatever."

"Dead sorcerers," she corrected automatically.

"Same thing, isn't it? Did you read any of them? In the first book you meet him, you think he's the brave hero. But he's not. He's a selfish little coward. Didn't like that. It was funny enough, in its own way, but I didn't like it. I like my heroes to be, you know, good guys."

Valkyrie sat forward. "You can let me out here," she said. "I'll walk the rest of the way."

She paid the man and got out, then walked up the long driveway. She missed being able to call Fletcher, have him teleport her wherever she needed to go. He could be annoying, he could be *very* annoying, but he always smiled when he saw her, and it was like he'd been saving up that smile all day until they were together. She liked that feeling, as much as she hated to admit it. She liked being around someone who was genuinely happy to be around her.

It wasn't the same feeling she got when she was with Caelan. There was too much pressure there, too much expectation. He looked at her like she belonged to him, like they belonged together. He was handsome – he was *so* handsome – and he was smooth and dark and dangerous. But beyond that, there wasn't much to him. Valkyrie really didn't see that lasting. She needed someone fun, someone who could make her laugh, who could take her places she'd never been. If she didn't have anyone like that, then what was the point of being with anyone less?

Valkyrie let herself into Gordon's house, deactivating the alarm. She went through, passing the rooms she normally visited, noting how clean everything looked and how fresh everything smelled. She pushed open the double doors into the ballroom, turned on the light. Brand-new chandeliers hung from the ceiling, sparkling like diamonds. The floor was polished, with tables and chairs stacked up on one side, ready to be set out. It was quiet right now, her every footstep echoing around the empty space, and she tried imagining what it would look like filled with people. The last time the house had been full was at Gordon's funeral.

She climbed the stairs to Gordon's study where he'd done all his writing when he was alive. In here Valkyrie flicked the switch and the bookcase opened. She walked through into the hidden room. Gordon Edgley looked round, smiled, and held up a hand while he finished speaking.

"… it lunged, this thing of claws and fangs and muscle, and with a swipe, it opened the belly of the prison guard, spilling his entrails across the rough stone floor. Recording end." The electronic device on the table beeped, and Gordon grinned. "The new book is going really well."

She nodded appreciatively. "It sounds it."

"I dare say it's better than anything I wrote when I was alive. It has pathos. It has emotion. It has entrails. It has everything you could want in a posthumous bestseller, recently uncovered in a hidden archive. This is going to make you a lot of money, my dear niece. But then, what do *you* care about money? When have you *ever* cared about money?"

Valkyrie shrugged. "I'm sure it'll come in useful. Probably more for Mum and Dad than for me, though."

"And little sister," Gordon said. "Don't forget the new addition. I was thinking, I might write a book for younger readers when I'm finished with this one – give her something to read when she's a little older. Oh, the possibilities. To think, if it wasn't for you *insisting* that I reveal my existence to Skulduggery and the others, I'd be spending my days in the Echo Stone, waiting for you to drop by for a visit."

The stone lay in its cradle on the desk, the cradle itself standing on a symbol that China Sorrows had carved into the wood. It fooled the stone into thinking there was a living person in the room at all times, meaning Gordon's image could stay active. In this room he had voice-activated televisions and computers, gadgets of all kinds. He was loving this second chance at life.

"I like the chandeliers," said Valkyrie.

"You don't think they're too over the top? I was worried they might be. This is going to be a big night for me. This is the first time I get to meet most of these amazing people, and I don't want anyone to think I'm showing off."

"They're lovely."

"I'm glad you think so. There have been cleaning crews in here for the last few days, getting everything ready for Sunday. Do you have your dress picked out?"

"I don't know if I'm going."

Gordon frowned. "What? But you have to go. This is your house."

"It's *your* house, and you don't need me."

He looked at her. "Tell me what the matter is."

"I just had an interesting conversation with Fergus."

"Oh?"

"Why didn't you tell me that he knew about magic?"

Gordon blinked. "Excuse me?"

"I was giving the twins a lesson on the beach. He saw us, sent them away, started on a whole tirade about refusing to let me drag them into magic because magic had torn his family apart."

"Really?"

"Very really."

"That... that surprises me."

"It caught me a little off guard too. He gave me the whole family history on the subject."

"That must have been nice."

"It was a bonding moment."

"To be honest," Gordon said, "I thought he'd convinced himself that none of it was real. He did such a good job with your dad, I thought he genuinely believed it himself. Once we got into our twenties, you see, we never argued about actual *magic*. We argued about the weirdos and the freaks I associated with, we argued about my lifestyle and my attitude, but by then he had stopped using words like *sorcerers*. I didn't realise he was still... aware of it all."

"Well, he was, and he still is. He even has some himself."

"Fergus? Fergus has *magic*?"

"There's definitely something there," she said. "Without proper instruction he wouldn't be able to do anything more than generate a spark, but even so..."

"Even so," Gordon finished, "it shows he has magic. How I would have envied him if I had known while I lived."

"You don't envy him now?"

Gordon smiled. "I have so many other things to envy him for, my dear, such as living, that magic becomes insignificant. How did you leave it?"

"He told me not to teach the twins anything, and I agreed."

"That's it?"

"Pretty much."

Gordon shook his head. "That brother of mine is a riddle wrapped in a mystery wrapped in a cardigan."

"Oh, there is something else. He said he regrets not speaking to you for four years."

Gordon smiled sadly. "Mm. Well. Yes. Regrets. I've had a few. That's all very interesting, I have to say. All very interesting indeed. Do you have any other bombshells to drop on me today? You may as well get it over with while I'm still partly in shock."

There was a single chair in the room, and Valkyrie slouched into it, crossing her legs. "I've got one or two. The least of which is that I've broken up with Fletcher."

"Oh, dear. Oh, dear me. Well, we knew this would eventually happen. Um… The important thing is to remember the good times, but not dwell on them… Dwelling leads to miserable thoughts and the playing of bad music. It is to be avoided at all costs. Fletcher… There will be another Fletcher, and another one after him, and another… It's not the end of the world, Valkyrie. You *know* what the end of the world looks like – by all accounts you're the cause of it."

He chuckled. She didn't. He stopped chuckling.

"He didn't dump me," she said. "*I* broke up with *him*."

"Oh," said Gordon, much brighter now. "Well, that is completely different! Excellent. Bravo. Well, not excellent. I liked the boy. He seemed nice. But obviously, you had a good reason for ending it."

"It just felt like the time. I was getting… bored."

"The death knell for many a mediocre relationship. I can't tell you how many beautiful women have broken up with me because they were bored. I can't tell you because it never happened. They all adored me."

"It was your humility, wasn't it?"

"I'm sure that had something to do with it. You're like me, Valkyrie. You're never going to be content until you find that one person, that one single person, who fills you with delight every time you hear their name."

"Did you ever find that person?"

He hesitated. "Yes. I did."

"And what happened?"

"Does it matter? What matters is you. You can't let this get you down."

"I wasn't. I'm upset about it, I suppose, but… There's other stuff happening too."

"There always is."

"Skulduggery kept a secret from me."

"I see. You think that was wrong of him?"

"No, not *wrong*, but it's a pretty big secret, and it's… it's bad."

"Is he still your friend?"

Valkyrie sighed.

"Has he moved against you in any way? Has he hurt you?"

"No."

"Then is he still your friend?"

"I suppose."

"This secret, how long has he had it?"

"Hundreds of years."

"Then it has nothing to do with you. It's quite simple, isn't it? He kept something from you, something about his past, and now you know it, and now you deal with it and move on."

She filled her cheeks with air, then blew it out. "It sounds really easy when you say it. It doesn't *feel* easy."

"Everyone has secrets, Valkyrie. I don't need to tell you that. So long as he hasn't used this secret to intentionally hurt you, however, I don't see the problem. Friends stick by each other. That's what they do."

She looked at him. "You are a wise and noble man, Uncle Gordon."

"And good-looking. You forgot good-looking."

"That's taken for granted."

"As well it should be. Now then, do you have any other problems I can help you with?"

"There's a vampire who's in love with me."

"Dump him. Any other problems?"

Valkyrie laughed. "Nothing I can't handle."

"In that case, be off with you. I have a book to write, characters to kill, and a party to plan."

37

THE WISDOM OF
LEONARD COHEN

Ghastly checked his watch as he walked the corridors of the Sanctuary, resigning himself to the fact that, once again, it looked like he'd be spending the night in his office instead of going home. He yawned heavily as he rounded the corner, and saw Fletcher Renn sitting outside his door.

"Fletcher," Ghastly said.

The kid looked up. His jeans were tattered, his boots were scuffed, and his T-shirt was a faded advertisement for a band Ghastly had never heard of. It was the eyes, though, that marked him out as truly tired. The eyes, and the hair. Usually so meticulously untamed, tonight it hung long and flat and swept back off his forehead.

"Hi," Fletcher said. "I know it's late, but… And I'm sorry if you're busy."

Ghastly was always busy these days. He had closed his shop and embraced the duties of an Elder, letting his new responsibilities wash over his old life and consume him completely. "I have some free time," he lied. "What can I do for you?"

Fletcher got up slowly, stiffly, like he'd been sitting there for hours. When he didn't say anything, Ghastly spoke again.

"Where have you been?" he asked.

"Around," Fletcher said.

Ghastly nodded, but the floodgates of conversation didn't burst open. This in itself was unusual. For as long as Ghastly had known him, Fletcher had never known when to shut up. To see him standing there in the corridor, hands in his pockets, eyes cast to the floor and giving one-word answers, was more than a little unsettling.

"Come inside," Ghastly said, unlocking the office door and walking in. He removed his robe, hung it on a hook on the wall and loosened his tie. He went to the side table and plugged in the kettle. "Cup of tea?" he asked.

"Sure."

"Fletcher," he said, "I'm not one of life's great conversationalists, so you're really going to have to help me out here. Start talking about something."

Fletcher looked at him. "Have you found a cure for Tanith yet?"

"Start talking about something else."

"Why?"

"Because I said so."

"You're mad that you don't know how to help her," Fletcher said, "and you're mad that you haven't found her yet, aren't you?"

"Is that what you wanted to talk about? Because I don't see what this conversation will lead to, other than annoying me."

"You asked her out."

"Fletcher, I have things to do."

"You asked her out, finally, and she said yes. She kissed you, then went away. And that's the last you saw of her before the Remnant got into her. And now she's out there somewhere, no one knows where, but she's out there with Billy-Ray Sanguine."

Ghastly looked at the kid and said nothing while he waited for the flash of anger to fade. He saw the hurt in Fletcher's eyes. "This is about Valkyrie?" he asked.

The boy looked at the floor again. "We broke up. She broke up with me. I'm sorry. I know it's different. I know Valkyrie hasn't been possessed and she's not gone, not like Tanith is. But... you loved Tanith, and then all that happened. You had her, you finally had her, and you lost her. How do you deal with that?"

"I drink a lot of tea. Fletcher, I've been around for a long time. I've been in love too many times to count. I'd like to say it gets easier, but it doesn't. The pain you're feeling now is the pain you're going to feel again and again. The advantage of having lived through this is that I do know I'll come out the other side. The pain lessens. You manage to distract yourself until the distractions become more important than the thing you're distracting yourself *from*."

"Do you think she loved you?"

"I don't know. I don't know if I want to know. If she did love me, then I wasted a lot of time thinking about it instead of doing something."

"I don't think Valkyrie loved me," Fletcher said, and suddenly laughed. "I'm sorry, this is so stupid. You probably think I'm just a stupid kid. I don't know anything about love or any of that."

"You know enough for it hurt."

The smile faded. "Yeah. She said she loved me. She made a joke, said something and then said 'and that's why I love you' and I latched on to it. Like an idiot. I decided to believe that this was her way of telling me how she felt. But she was making a joke. And I knew she was making a joke. But I wanted to believe it so much."

The kettle boiled. Ghastly made two mugs of tea while Fletcher talked on.

"It's pathetic," Fletcher said. "I went from thinking I was top geezer, the last Teleporter in the world, to someone who followed her around like a puppy. All she had to do was call, and I'd be there. The last two years of my life, of my *life*, have revolved round her. That's two years of me living for someone else. How sad is that? Nothing was more important than her. I offered her everything because I could *give* her everything. I could take her *anywhere*. There was nothing I wouldn't do for her and she knew that. She accepted it. I'd become, like, a part of her life, but not in a good way. Not in a healthy, happy, boyfriend kind of way. She knew she had me, faithful old Fletcher, and she knew that all she had to do was click her fingers and she'd get whatever it was she needed. I made her life easier.

"And whenever she or Skulduggery, or even Tanith, was in danger of taking something too seriously, they turned to the easy target. They turned to me and made a joke. I was OK with it, actually. It meant something, at the time. It meant I was part of the group, I was one of the gang."

"And it meant you could spend more time around her," Ghastly said, sitting on the edge of his desk, "which is all you really wanted."

"Yeah," Fletcher murmured. He looked at the mug of tea in

his hand, but didn't drink from it. "But all that's gone now. She's with Caelan. Did you know that? She was seeing him behind my back."

Ghastly hid his surprise. "That… doesn't sound like Valkyrie."

"Well, there you go. She cheated on me with a bloody vampire. A *vampire*. Are… are you smiling?"

"Yes," Ghastly said sadly. "I am. I never thought we'd have so much in common, to be honest. The girl you love is in the arms of another, and that other happens to be a murderous monster. And the woman I love is in the arms of a psychopathic hitman. What a pair we make."

"I can't help it," said Fletcher. "Images of Valkyrie and that… thing, of the two of them together, keep coming into my head."

"I've been living with something like that for the past few months. It makes your insides go cold, doesn't it? It makes you want to kill someone."

"I want to kill the vampire," Fletcher said softly.

"The feeling is natural. I don't blame you for that at all. And while I know you're a good kid, and you're not a killer, I am going to say this – that's a road you don't want to go down."

Fletcher put the mug on the worktable, spilling some of his tea. "I just need to show Valkyrie that she's wrong," he said. "I just need to show her that she's made a mistake. I need to prove myself."

"You want to make her beg to take you back."

"No. No, of course not."

"You want to punish her."

"Fine," Fletcher snapped. "Yes. Is that wrong? She's the one who cheated on me."

"It's never going to happen," Ghastly said. "This is Valkyrie we're talking about. She doesn't beg. If she changes her mind, she'll come at you with a very practical reason why you're getting back together. If you put her in a position where she'd have to beg, she's going to walk away out of sheer principle."

"So... how do I get her to take me back?"

"I don't know. But my first suggestion is to take some time."

Fletcher frowned. "What? No. The longer I leave it, the more Caelan will sink his fangs into her."

"Caelan doesn't matter. He's never mattered. That's not going to last. Guys like that never do. But you'll do yourself no favours if you run up to her with tears in your eyes."

"I never mentioned tears," he said defensively.

"A friend of mine once said that a man never got a woman back by begging on his knees. Give yourself some time. Get over the pain. Man up. Then go back to her. Let her see what she's missing. I'm not saying it's going to work, but I'll be honest, it's your best shot."

Fletcher nodded. "Thanks, Ghastly. I didn't have anyone else to talk to. I'm pretty sure I don't even have any friends. Valkyrie was my only friend."

"Then you need to get yourself a life, kid."

"Yeah," said Fletcher. "Yeah, I do."

38

BACK AT THE WINDOW AGAIN

A tapping woke her.

Valkyrie groaned, turned over in bed, cracking her eyes open to look over at the window. The morning sunlight framed the curtains, and through a sliver of an opening she saw Skulduggery's gloved hand. Her parents were gone but she still lay where she was, unsure if she even wanted to talk to him. Then she got up, wrapped the sheet around herself, and walked over. She pulled the curtains apart and undid the latch, then returned to her bed. She was snuggling down again as the window opened and Skulduggery climbed in. Valkyrie turned so she was facing the wall.

"I'm in bed," she told him. "I'm having a lie-in."

"I can see that. Do you plan on rising any time soon?"

She shrugged.

"Oh," he said. "So that's it."

She waited for him to continue.

"I was wondering how you were going to punish me for not confiding in you. Punishment, actually, is something I've been thinking about for a long time. What form of punishment is enough for what I did? Imprisonment? Death? Something else? Something scarier? I could only think of so many horrible tortures before they stopped having meaning. But you, you've come up with a punishment I never considered. You're going to sulk me to death."

"I'm glad you find this amusing."

"I've had years to see the funny side."

"What do you expect me to do? It's not the... This isn't about the Vile thing. Yes, it's awful, yes, it's insane, but OK, it happened, it's in the past."

"Not as in the past as we'd like."

"Shut up."

"Of course. You were saying?"

"This is about you and me, and you not telling me the truth. It's about—"

"May I interject?"

"No."

"I'm going to interject anyway, simply to point out that you only told me about the 'Darquesse thing' *after* you had Nye seal your true name. You may continue."

She turned over, and glared at him. "That was different."

"Yes, it was. It was you."

"I kept it from you because I was scared and confused and I didn't know how you'd react…" She faltered. "Shut up."

"I didn't say anything."

"You didn't have to. I know what you're thinking. You're thinking the things we didn't tell each other cancel each other out. You're thinking if I keep on being angry with you, I'll eventually realise that I don't have a leg to stand on, and start to feel stupid. Well, you're wrong. I do have a leg to stand on. And I never feel stupid."

"That's good to hear."

"You should have told me about Vile."

"And you should have told me about Darquesse. And please remember that when you did, eventually, get around to telling me, I accepted it with grace and understanding."

Valkyrie narrowed her eyes. "Because you knew what it was like. *That's* why you took it so well! I thought you were just being really nice!"

"I'm often nice, but rarely really. I couldn't be angry with you, Valkyrie. I am many things, but I am not a hypocrite. Are you?"

"That isn't fair."

"Are you?"

She sighed, and sat up, holding the sheet against her. "OK. Fine. I forgive you. And now that we're confessing, is there anything else you'd like to tell me? Any other huge big massive secrets you've been hiding?"

"Virtually none."

"Virtually?"

"Practically. And you?"

"Being the psycho who kills the world is the only one worth mentioning."

"Excellent. Then our consciences are clear."

"Is that it? Do we go back to being friends now?"

"I certainly hope so. Unless you were enjoying sulking?"

"I hate sulking."

"You're very good at it."

"Thank you. I didn't think it'd be this easy – going back to being friends, I mean. It's a pretty big thing that just happened, isn't it? There's a part of you that's... evil."

"Yes."

"Just like there's a part of me that's evil."

He tilted his head. "You think we're different from everyone else?"

"Aren't we?"

"Every human being who has ever lived has the same potential in them for good and evil. Mortal or sorcerer, it doesn't matter. Power has a way of bringing out the worst in people. Mevolent. Serpine. Hitler. Lord Vile. Darquesse. We're all the same."

"You just put me on a list with *Hitler*."

"You're going to start sulking again, aren't you?"

"*Hitler*, for God's sake."

"Power corrupts, Valkyrie. You're better off learning that now, so you can prepare for later."

"But *Hitler*."

"We may need to focus here."

"Right. Yes. OK. Turn round."

"Are you going to throw something at me?"

"What? No, I'm getting out of bed."

"Ah," he said, and turned.

She swung her feet to the floor, stood up and adjusted the sheet, then walked out of the room. "So what are we dealing with? Is Lord Vile your subconscious, or is it your old Necromancer power with a mind of its own?"

Skulduggery followed her on to the landing. "I think it's both, to be honest."

"Was he hiding inside you this whole time?"

"It certainly looks that way. I didn't see him, of course. When you can turn to shadow, it's easy enough to find places to hide, even in a skeleton. It's all very unsettling, to be honest."

She went into the bathroom while Skulduggery waited outside.

"And did you notice that he's terribly unruly?" he asked through the door. "He completely ignored my commands."

Valkyrie dropped the sheet and got in the shower, talking loudly over the water. "So how do we stop him? Do we just send you to a psychiatrist or something?"

"Excuse me?"

"Hey, it's *your* subconscious that's attacking people."

"I don't need therapy."

She turned her face up to the showerhead. "Have you ever tried it?"

"Talking about one's feelings defeats the purpose of having those feelings," she heard him say. "Once you try to put the human experience into words, it becomes little more than a spectator sport. Everything must have a cause, and a name. Every random thought must have a root in something else. This is all missing the point."

"But if you can confront your inner demons—"

"I did confront my inner demon. I punched him in the face and he exploded."

Valkyrie had to laugh. "But now he's back."

"Of course he's back. He's resourceful. He is *my* inner demon, after all."

"But he ignored your commands. He, it, whatever, ignored you. He doesn't need you. He's become a… a being, a person."

"Completely independent," Skulduggery said. "An individual. I'd be proud, if I wasn't so disturbed. Does this mean I don't have a subconscious any more? If my subconscious is up and walking around and calling itself Lord Vile, then what do I have left?"

"Skulduggery, now *you* need to focus."

"Yes. Of course. Besides, that's more of a conversation to have with Gordon. Conversations I have with you, Valkyrie, revolve around finding solutions and saving the day."

"That's what I want to hear," she said as she turned off the water. She got out of the shower, grabbed a towel and wrapped it around herself. "So how do we stop Vile?"

She opened the bathroom door and Skulduggery tilted his head at her. "Very simple," he said. "We don't."

Valkyrie frowned. "That *is* very simple. In fact, it's a little *too* simple." She walked back to her room.

"The Sanctuary is going to say the same thing," he said, following behind. "Vile is after Melancholia, so we should leave him alone, see how far he gets. He might get lucky."

"He might kill her."

"That's what I mean."

Valkyrie got back inside her room, turned and held up a hand to stop Skulduggery from coming in after her.

"Ah," he said, and nodded as she closed the door.

"Skulduggery, it's Melancholia. I know I hate her, and I know she tried to kill me, and I'm well aware that she plans to kill billions of people, but we can't just let her *die*."

There was a pause before Skulduggery responded. "I have to admit," he said, "I did not think that sentence was going to end where it ended."

"I'm just sick of everyone killing everyone else. When I heard that Mum had been hurt, I went to Moore's cell with the intention of killing him. I wanted to actually *kill* him. I don't like that. I don't like that I wanted that. There's too much killing, I think." Valkyrie scrubbed herself half dry, then had a better idea and straightened up, went back to the door and opened it. "Hat in front of your eyes," she said. "No peeking."

He did as he was told and raised his free hand. She held the towel away from her as the moisture drifted from her body.

"You should be able to do this yourself by now," Skulduggery said from behind his hat.

"I can do it," she said. "But I always leave my skin too dry." She stepped back inside her room and closed the door again, then she went to the mirror and tapped the glass. Her reflection blinked, and stepped out.

"Why can't we arrest Melancholia?" Valkyrie asked, taking her black clothes from the wardrobe. "Put some shackles on her, send her to prison for a few years, then let her out and tell her to be good?"

"Because she's the Death Bringer," said Skulduggery.

"She's Melancholia. She's the annoying girl I used to laugh at. I don't want her dead."

The reflection shrugged. "Melancholia doesn't share that compunction," it said.

Valkyrie frowned at her mirror image.

"Either you're arguing with yourself," Skulduggery said from the landing, "or your reflection makes more sense than you do."

"Shut up," Valkyrie said to the door, and then looked back at the reflection. "And you, nobody asked for your opinion. And stop standing there all naked and stuff. You're distracting."

The reflection shrugged again, went to the dresser and started picking out clothes.

Valkyrie pulled on her underwear and trousers. "We can't just let Vile kill her," she said loudly. "We have to try and arrest her."

"We will," Skulduggery answered.

"But it's a race, is that what you're saying? If we get to her, we arrest her. If he gets to her, he kills her."

"If she resists arrest, we might have to kill her too. Don't forget that."

"So no one is going after Vile."

"That's correct."

She grabbed her boots, started putting them on. "And what about when all this is done?"

"If the Death Bringer, for whatever reason, ceases to remain alive, there's a good chance that the thing that is Lord Vile will simply... disappear. Whatever aspect of my subconscious that is walking around will come back to me, the armour will return to its inert form, and everyone will be happy."

"Except Melancholia."

"Except Melancholia, who will be dead."

Valkyrie stood up. "And me?"

"Hopefully, you won't be."

"But if Melancholia dies," the reflection said, still picking out clothes, "then won't the title of Death Bringer switch over to Valkyrie?"

"Stop contributing to this conversation," Valkyrie said crossly.

The reflection gave another shrug.

"Well?" Valkyrie said loudly. "Will it switch over to me?"

Skulduggery hesitated. "That is a possibility, I grant you."

"And if it does, then Vile will want to kill me too, won't he?"

Another hesitation. "Perhaps."

"So we're going to have to figure out a way to stop him, no matter what happens," she said, her voice muffled slightly by the T-shirt she was dragging over her head.

"Not quite," Skulduggery answered. "There is the possibility that he will go up against Melancholia and she will destroy him utterly, which will take care of the Lord Vile problem quite nicely but, obviously, add to the Melancholia problem. And it might also pose a problem for me, if someone manages to kill my subconscious."

"This is getting very complicated."

"Not if you pay attention."

"Do you think he can do it?" Valkyrie said, running a brush through her hair. "Do you think he has a chance?"

"I don't know. From what we've seen, her power ebbs and flows. If he manages to catch her when she's at her weakest, yes, he will kill her in an instant. But if he gets to her when she's strong…"

"And we have the same problem, which means we have to arrest her when she's ebbing, not flowing. How do we do that?"

"First, we have to find out where they're hiding her."

Valkyrie put the brush down, went to the door and opened it. "Can I ask you a question? And I don't mean this in a bad way, but *are* you insane?"

Skulduggery looked at her. "Would it make any difference if I was?"

"Probably not."

"Then why put labels on ourselves? That's a job for a psychiatrist. We punch people, Valkyrie. That's who we are. Embrace your inner lunatic. Fun times guaranteed."

She smiled. "You're a bad influence."

"I never claimed otherwise. Your reflection is still naked, by the way."

Valkyrie shrieked, shoved him back and slammed her bedroom door closed.

39

KILLING CRAVEN

Wreath never had a problem with killing people, but he always preferred it when he had right on his side, when they deserved it, and when he was sure he could get away with it. Today he planned to kill Craven, and while he was sure that right was on his side and that Craven thoroughly deserved what was coming to him, he wasn't overly confident he could get away with it. Still, he figured, sometimes you've got to do what you've got to do, and then sometimes you've just got to run like hell after it's done.

Getting Craven alone was proving to be a problem, however. He had everyone convinced that he had all the answers, so now they flocked around him like he was the High Priest. It was a most disheartening sight. Necromancers were feared the world over. Nobody trusted them, nobody liked them and everyone had a scary Necromancer story to tell around the campfire. Necromancers were supposed to be cold and weird, pale-faced and disturbing. It was an image that had been carefully cultivated over generations. And now, here they were, sycophantic and scared, gushing praise and mindless worship over a man who could very well be leading them towards a most inglorious end.

"I have just spoken with the Death Bringer," Craven announced solemnly. Wreath watched as an expectant hush spread through the crowd. "Last night, the souls of our dead brothers and sisters spoke to her in a dream. They thanked her for her actions, told her they had never felt more powerful." A woman appeared beside Wreath, her hood up to cover her face. She said nothing, just watched as Craven continued. "They explained that they were now a part of her, adding to her strength, adding to her wisdom, and that once the Passage happens, they will return to us and guide us towards our destiny. They asked her to tell you all not to worry, not to fear. Cast your doubts aside, they said. Embrace what is to come."

He closed his eyes and bowed his head, allowing the murmurs to ripple.

"I dreamed of no such thing," said the woman beside Wreath, her voice low enough so that only he could hear.

He looked at her. The hood was still up but he could see the point of her chin, and the raised scars that crossed it.

"This is what he wanted all along," Melancholia whispered. "He wanted everyone listening to him, paying attention to what he has to say. That's why he did it."

"That's why he did what?" Wreath asked.

Melancholia moved slightly, and he saw a thin smile. "That's why he made me who I am. That's why he had Tenebrae killed."

Wreath glanced around, making sure no one could overhear. "Craven had Tenebrae killed?"

"As good as," said Melancholia. "He brought him to see me. What was I supposed to do?"

"And why are you telling me all this?"

"Why do you think?" Melancholia murmured, just as the crowd started to quieten down again. "Because he plans to kill you next."

"Brothers and sisters," Craven said, drawing everyone's eyes back to him, "we are preparing to bid farewell to the world we know. This existence is a flawed thing. It needs to be improved. It needs us to do it. Because of us, because of you, the Death Bringer will usher in the Passage… tonight."

The congregation of easily led idiots gasped. Someone at the back actually started sobbing with joy. Wreath turned to Melancholia, but she was gone. He spied her on the far side of the room, slipping out the door. Nobody noticed her. They were all watching Craven.

"Tonight, my friends, our destiny is at hand. No longer shall we grovel at the whim of forces beyond our control. Tonight, we seize control. Tonight, we become the masters of existence!"

There were cheers, and chanting, which would probably have been impressive if there had been more than thirty people in the crowd. But as it was, it sounded weak and a little silly.

"Prepare!" Craven roared, as if he were addressing an amphitheatre. "The day of reckoning is upon us!"

Thirty morons cheered, and Wreath started to look forward to the moment he used the knife.

"Rousing speech," Wreath said.

Craven looked up, startled, as Wreath stepped out of the shadows. "Cleric," he said, his hand patting his chest, "you shouldn't do that. For a second there, I thought you were Lord Vile."

"Lord Vile probably wouldn't have cared how rousing the speech was," Wreath pointed out.

"True, I suppose," Craven said. "So, are you excited?"

"About?"

"Why, the Passage, of course. Weren't you the one who said the sooner the better?"

"I suppose I was. And she's ready, is she? Melancholia?"

"She fully expects to be."

Wreath nodded, searching his peripheral vision for the White Cleaver. When he didn't see him, he stepped a bit closer. "I expect that dream she had was a comforting one," he said.

"Indeed it was," Craven nodded. "It allayed a lot of her fears. One tends to forget her young age. In many ways she is still a child, and like any child, she needs an encouraging word every now and then. She has been comforted."

Wreath was close now, close enough to take the knife from his coat and plunge it into Craven's soft belly. He glanced over his shoulder, making sure everyone else was walking the other way. "Do you think our brothers and sisters are ready?" he asked.

"I think so," Craven said. "Don't you?"

Wreath smiled at him. "I think they're dumb enough to do whatever they're told. How about you, Cleric Craven? Are you ready?"

"I am, Cleric Wreath. This is what we have been living our lives for, is it not?"

"True enough, I suppose."

"Forgive me, but you don't look like a man whose dreams are about to come true."

Wreath looked him right in the eyes, right in those soft, wet eyes that looked like drops of blue ink swimming in milk, and he let himself smile. "How about now, Craven? Now do I look like a man whose dreams are about to come true?"

He took the knife from his pocket and Craven saw it, stepped back, mouth open to scream, then there was a blur of white and Wreath ducked, barely avoiding the scythe that swooped towards his head. He raised his cane, blocking the scythe handle as the Cleaver spun, tried to stab with the knife but a boot came from nowhere, sent him pinwheeling back.

Craven had found his voice and he used it to scream for help. The Cleaver darted towards Wreath and he darted back, cursing himself for his impatience. He brought the shadows in around him and stepped through them to the next room, moving quickly, shadow-walking again to the other side of the walls, emerging into the morning sun. He ran, took off before they could follow him. He'd left a car out there for a quick escape, but even as he jumped in and gunned the engine, he realised he had only one place left to go – and it wasn't going to be pretty. Roarhaven never was.

He parked off Roarhaven's main street, if it really could be called that, and waited for the Bentley to show up. The town was small and withered and nasty, and the Sanctuary was big and grey and ugly. He was hungry, but he didn't dare step into the squalid café that jutted from the street beside him like an uneven tooth. Apart from all the obvious concerns regarding his personal safety, the place just didn't look *sanitary*.

An hour or so after his stomach first started rumbling, the Bentley swept by, and parked outside the Sanctuary. Wreath got out, wondered about the likelihood of Skulduggery Pleasant shooting him before he got halfway across the road, and then decided to shadow-walk over to them. The shadows curled around him, and when they dissipated, he was standing by the rear wheel as Valkyrie closed the passenger door.

"Now, before you do anything rash—" Wreath started, and she spun and hit him, cracked her knuckles painfully along his jaw. He went back a step, one hand to his face, nodding. "OK, that's fair, but before this gets out of control—"

Skulduggery jumped and slid across the roof of the Bentley, the heel of his shoe slamming into the side of Wreath's head. Valkyrie snapped her palm at the air and his cane flew from his grip. Wreath staggered, waving his hands.

"Please," he gasped, "stop hitting me for five seconds."

Valkyrie glanced at Skulduggery, who paused. Wreath spat blood and straightened up. "Thank you," he said. "I've come to discuss—"

Skulduggery punched him and Wreath's head rocked back, and he dropped.

"There," Skulduggery said as his consciousness left him. "That's five seconds."

When Wreath opened his eyes, he was lying on the floor of a room in the Sanctuary with his hands shackled behind his back. Skulduggery sat on a chair with his legs crossed, looking down at him. Valkyrie stood beside him.

"Interesting," Wreath said. "You haven't killed me."

Skulduggery took off his hat, flicked something from the brim, and put it on his knee. "There's still time," he said.

Wreath grunted slightly as he sat up without the use of his arms. Valkyrie waited till he was sitting straight, then stepped over and put her boot to his shoulder. "Very mature," Wreath sighed as she tipped him over again. He lay with his face squashed against the floor. "But if this is how you want to conduct this conversation, it's fine. I am hardly in a position to argue."

"You're damn right," Valkyrie said. "You attacked me."

"I did, I'm sorry. I didn't want to, but I did it. I hope I didn't hurt you too badly."

"If I were you," Skulduggery said, "I'd be more worried about your own state of discomfort."

"Oh, I am, Skulduggery, believe me. My overriding concern right now is my own well-being. Which is why I'm here. I've come to make a deal. I can tell you where Melancholia is."

Skulduggery's voice betrayed no hint of surprise. "Why would you want to?"

"Because she's going to ruin everything. Her and Craven. They're going to bring the Necromancer Order to its knees. They need to be stopped, and you're the only ones who can do it. Well, you and the rest of the Sanctuary agents, obviously."

"So you suddenly want to stop the Passage?" Skulduggery asked.

"Stop it? Good God, no. The Passage is the only thing that will save the world. But Melancholia is not the one to bring it about. She's too unstable. She's too unpredictable. Does she have the potential to kill millions? Yes, probably. But billions? I doubt it. And unless three billion are killed in the same instant, it's not going to work. The only thing she'll accomplish is the pointless death of millions of innocent people."

Valkyrie shook her head. "You've got some warped ideas of right and wrong, you know that? So you come running to us to clean up the mess you made? Why don't you guys handle it?"

"Because I'm the only one who can see the truth. The others, there aren't many but there are enough, have been blinded by Craven's words. I tried to take care of it without you, but my little assassination attempt didn't work out too well."

"Then where is she?" Skulduggery asked.

Wreath smiled. "Not yet. First, you get the Council to agree to my terms."

"There are no terms, Solomon. Tell us where she is."

"I want my attack on Valkyrie and my involvement in events so far forgiven and forgotten."

Skulduggery took his hat from his knee and uncrossed his legs as he sat forward. "You were planning the murder of three billion people."

Wreath nodded. "And I'd like that to be forgotten about, please."

"What do you think will come of this? We know what the Passage is now. Everyone does. You think it's going to go back to normal, with Necromancers left alone to scheme and plot? Temples are going to be torn down all over the world. It's over for all of you."

"Not necessarily. I think it's still possible to blame this whole thing on one man."

Skulduggery tilted his head. "Craven."

"His mad ramblings have led to this," Wreath said, displaying an impressive air of sadness. "He wilfully misinterpreted our sacred teachings. He warped what the Passage is truly about. Can we be held responsible for the actions of a madman? A fanatic?"

"You really think that act is going to work?" Valkyrie asked, frowning.

Wreath smiled up at her. "Why not? Everything that man has done reinforces what I've just said. He experimented on poor Melancholia. Brainwashed the poor girl. His insane ambition drove him to murder our kind and gentle High Priest, Auron Tenebrae. Tenebrae would never have condoned the actions he's taken. But Vandameer Craven is unlike anyone I've ever met before. He is magnetic. He makes you want to follow him into destruction and madness. I am ashamed to say that I, too, was under the spell of his fervour, his faith, and his charisma."

Valkyrie blinked. "Charisma?"

"Yes."

"Don't you think that's stretching it a little too far?"

"Do you think so?"

"Some people will have met him."

"Hmm. You have a point. OK, then maybe not charisma. I'll think of some other lie. It'll be fine. The point is, yes, the Temple here in Ireland will be tarnished. It will probably be torn down, and Necromancy banned. But it will survive in the rest of the world, so long as Melancholia isn't allowed to start killing people. Get the Council to agree to my terms, and I'll tell you where they are. I'll even *take* you there."

40

THE END OF THE DEATH BRINGER

nce Erskine Ravel, with great reluctance, granted him amnesty, Wreath took Skulduggery and Valkyrie into the grounds of an abandoned Retirement Home, then nodded across to the main building. "In there," he said. "I hope you still have your Teleporter, because the only way you're going to catch them by surprise is if you manage to skip all the defences they've built up around them."

Valkyrie frowned. "They're *here?*"

"Next to graveyards and hospitals, Old Folks' Homes are great places to absorb a whole lot of death. This one, however, hasn't seen any activity in over twenty years. It's kind of flat, as these things go. But beggars can't be choosers, and Craven is most definitely a beggar right now."

"How many are in there?" Skulduggery asked.

"Not counting Craven, Melancholia and the White Cleaver, thirty-three. But they aren't experienced. They've spent most of their adult lives in one Temple or another. They'll put up a fight, but it won't be a good one, so I'd consider it a personal favour if you don't kill every last one of them."

Skulduggery turned to him. "What makes you think we're inclined to do you any favours?"

"I don't know. Naivety?"

"Why don't you want them dead?" Valkyrie asked.

Wreath shrugged. "They're scared and confused and they're a little dim, to be honest. But they don't all deserve to die, not if they don't have to. Craven absolutely deserves it. Melancholia, it'd be safer for everyone if she stopped breathing. But the others…"

"They're harmless?"

"Well," Wreath said, managing a smile, "maybe not harmless, but certainly misguided. They're my brothers and sisters. Granted, not the type of brothers or sisters that you actually *like*, but even so, I'd hate to see them die for nothing."

"We'll keep that in mind," Skulduggery said. "How long can we expect them to stay here?"

"Oh, they're not going anywhere. Apart from the fact that they have no other back-up available to them, this is where Melancholia will try to usher in the Passage."

Skulduggery's voice turned sharp. "Tonight?"

"Yes indeed. I don't know what Craven is thinking, because Melancholia will be much more powerful tomorrow night. Maybe he anticipates your interference, and he wants to get it all out of the way as soon as possible."

Valkyrie ducked back. "I saw someone at the window. They're in there, all right."

"Then my work here is done," Wreath said. "I wish you both the best of luck, and I have faith that you will foil their evil plans and save the day. Skulduggery, it's been a pleasure as always. Valkyrie, once Melancholia falls, there's going to be an opening in the Death Bringer department, so if you ever want to continue your training with me…"

"Don't hold your breath," she said sourly.

Wreath smiled, the shadows curled around him, and he was gone.

Valkyrie looked at Skulduggery. "Another raid on a Necromancer stronghold?"

"It would appear so," he said. "Although this is less a stronghold than a Retirement Home, but your point is well made. Still, I have a feeling this one is going to go much quicker than the raid on the Temple, so long as…"

"So long as we have Fletcher with us."

"Yes. I am sorry, Valkyrie, but we do need his help."

"Don't apologise," she said. "Just don't ask me to call him. I doubt he'd pick up."

An hour later, Valkyrie was in a closed-down old factory ten miles from the Retirement Home. She nodded to two young women she knew, Kallista Pendragon and Rosella Ember. They were new to the Sanctuary, brought in as part of the effort to refill the ranks. There were a lot of new faces around, now that Valkyrie looked. The turnover rate for Sanctuary operatives had been getting pretty high in the past few years.

She saw Fletcher talking to Skulduggery. He glanced up, their eyes locked and her heart lurched, then he looked away again and she felt terrible. She stayed well away, letting Skulduggery brief him on what they needed to do. It was to be a two-man incursion – Skulduggery and Fletcher – sneaking into the Home in order to check out the layout and the opposition. Once Melancholia was located, Fletcher would teleport them both out, everyone else would link up and they'd all teleport back in – hopefully, for a surprise attack.

When Skulduggery had told her that it was to be only Fletcher and himself, Valkyrie hadn't argued. Her insides wrenched every time she remembered the look on Fletcher's face, and the last thing she wanted to do was make her ex-boyfriend hurt even more.

When they were ready, Skulduggery and Fletcher vanished, and Valkyrie waited with all the others. She didn't like waiting. It annoyed her. Irritation added to the butterflies in her stomach. Ghastly came over, nodded to her, let a few moments slide by before speaking.

"So," he said, "I heard you two broke up."

"I suppose we did."

Ghastly nodded. He had a look on his face like he wanted to ask something, but didn't want to actually utter the words.

She frowned. "Fletcher talked to you, didn't he?"

"He didn't have anyone else he could go to," Ghastly confessed. "He's upset."

"I know."

"He cares for you a great deal."

"And I care for him," she said, surprising herself with how defensive she suddenly sounded. "Why does nobody understand that you can still care for someone and not want to see them at the same time? It's not like I suddenly can't stand him or anything."

"Then why did you break up?"

"I just didn't want that kind of relationship any more. It's hard to explain."

"He thinks it's something to do with the vampire."

Valkyrie hesitated. "How much did he tell you?"

"He said you're with a vampire now."

She groaned. "OK, first of all, he shouldn't have said that. Second, it's not even true, not really. Third, you and me? We're not talking about it."

"Vampires are dangerous, Valkyrie. They're monsters, pure and simple. I'm surprised Skulduggery is allowing it to continue."

She arched an eyebrow. "Skulduggery doesn't have a say in it, and neither do you, and neither does Fletcher. It's no one's business but my own."

"I'm just looking out for you."

"I know. It's appreciated. Up to a point."

Ghastly nodded. "Can I ask a question, though? The last one, I promise."

"Sure."

"Did you take Fletcher for granted?"

Valkyrie was quiet for a moment. "I suppose I did. I knew he'd always be there for me so, like… where was the challenge?"

Ghastly nodded. "That's what he figured."

"Do you think he'll be OK?"

"Of course he will. Just give him time."

"How much time? I want us to be friends. You can't spend all that time together and then all of a sudden not care if you never see that person again. I miss him already, you know? I don't want to get back with him, but I miss him."

"All you can do is wait, Valkyrie."

"I hate waiting."

"I've noticed."

Ten minutes later, Fletcher and Skulduggery were back.

"OK," Skulduggery said. "Most of the Necromancers are in a large, open room, so that's where we'll be teleporting. Very little furniture, very little cover. We'll be dealing with thirty-five Necromancers, plus Melancholia, who will be on a raised stage directly in front of us when we arrive. You leave Melancholia to us. You stay away from the White Cleaver. Your job is to keep the rest of the Necromancers off our backs. Our aim here is to subdue Melancholia and teleport her out."

"Subdue?" asked Kallista.

"We're trying to take her alive."

The collected sorcerers frowned.

"Not to be a pain," said Rosella, "but wouldn't it be easier to just kill her?"

Kallista nodded. "More fun, too."

"It might come to that," Skulduggery said, "but we're not a death squad. We've issued a warrant for her arrest, and so we want to arrest her. It's really that simple. Everyone clear? Then link up."

They formed three rows and linked arms, Skulduggery standing between Valkyrie and Fletcher. At Skulduggery's command, the factory became the Retirement Home. Big windows, lots of sunshine and open space, floors that may have once been used for ballroom dancing. One Necromancer saw them and the others turned, shouting, cursing, throwing shadows. Valkyrie saw Craven with his eyes wide, grabbing the White Cleaver and holding him as a shield. Behind Craven, Melancholia stood on the stage in a black cloak, the hood up and covering her scars.

Skulduggery's arm encircled Valkyrie's waist and they lifted into the air while the invading force engaged the Necromancers. Three of the Necromancers sent shadows up to intercept their flight, like missiles speeding towards a jet fighter. Skulduggery cursed, throwing Valkyrie forward a millisecond before the shadows hit him. She used the air to spur her on, over the heads of the others. Melancholia looked up, snarled at her, and then they crashed together and went down.

Valkyrie was the first to her feet, and she hauled Melancholia up and threw her against the wall. Melancholia whipped her hand at her but Valkyrie knocked it away, stepped in and crunched an elbow into her chin. Melancholia staggered, her eyes wide but unfocused. Valkyrie pressed the attack. To hesitate would be to allow her enemy to stir the shadows into a storm and rip her apart, just like she had done on the cliff top in Haggard. Valkyrie hit her again and Melancholia howled in pain.

"Leave her alone!"

Valkyrie turned, saw the fighting behind her, saw Skulduggery and the White Cleaver go at it, saw Craven staggering towards her with a bloody nose. "Leave her alone!" he screeched again, hurling sharpened shadows.

Valkyrie threw herself down and the shadows missed and continued past her. Melancholia wasn't fast enough to dodge them. They cut through her flesh, shearing her from left shoulder to right hip.

She gave a small gasp as her body came apart.

Valkyrie stared as the two halves of Melancholia collapsed on to the stage. She was aware of the sounds of battle, of grunts and yells and cries, and she was aware of Craven's screaming. Melancholia's face was turned towards her. All those small scars on that pale face, the lips that used to sneer at her now parted slightly, the eyes that used to glare at her now blank and staring sightlessly.

Craven rushed by, completely forgetting Valkyrie was even there. He fell to his knees, ranting and raving, screeching obscenities, howling like a wounded animal.

The sounds of fighting died. The Necromancers stood there, horrified looks on their faces.

The White Cleaver leaped on to the stage, and shadows curled from the amulet around Craven's neck, wrapped them both in darkness with the remains of Melancholia, and then they were gone. Up and down the room, Necromancers were suddenly shadow-walking away, only the unconscious and those restrained by Valkyrie's colleagues remaining.

Bony hands picked her up, and Skulduggery led her off the stage. No one spoke.

Valkyrie sat on the concrete step of the Retirement Home, watching the sorcerers and the Cleavers depart. Skulduggery sat beside her. "Are you OK?"

She exhaled. "I don't know. I suppose so. I'm not the one who got chopped in half. And she would have killed me if she'd had the chance, so that stops me from actually, you know, feeling sad about it."

"But you still didn't want her to die."

"No. Of course not. She wasn't like Vengeous or Serpine. She was…"

"Like you."

She scowled at him. "She wasn't a *bit* like me. She was an idiot. And smug. God, she was always so smug and condescending. But still… she was only a few years older. She never even got the chance to realise what an annoying little twerp she was being."

"Life isn't fair," said Skulduggery. "In my experience, death isn't so different."

"What do you think Craven will do now?"

"Panic, presumably. This was his one power play. This was his big moment. I doubt he even had a back-up plan. He got away with seventeen Necromancers. Maybe they're scattered, maybe they're together, I don't know. It doesn't matter. We're going to round them all up before they slip out of the country."

Valkyrie sighed. "Can't we leave that to someone else? What's the point of being part of the Sanctuary if we can't assign some of the rubbish jobs to other people?"

"My thoughts exactly."

"So that's it? We're done?"

"The Death Bringer is dead, the crisis is averted… It would seem like we have triumphed once again."

"Yay us," Valkyrie said, and stretched. "I'm tired."

"Fletcher's hanging around inside. He could take you home."

"I'd prefer the drive, actually."

"Is it because of the scintillating conversation?"

"That must be it."

"This wasn't the ending we wanted," Skulduggery said.

"No it wasn't," replied Valkyrie. "It was the ending we got, though."

"Yes it was."

41

HOME SWEET HOME

Saturday morning came and went, and Valkyrie slept through most of it. When she woke, she just lay there, looking up at the ceiling. She thought about Melancholia, and Wreath, and Moore, and about Fletcher and Caelan. All of it jumbled together this past week, becoming mixed up and messed up, one thing after another. She hadn't had time to really dwell on recent events. That might have been a good thing.

She crawled out of bed, showered and dressed, went downstairs. Her parents were heading out that afternoon, but when she walked into the living room, her father was leaning over the basket, prodding Alice with his finger. "Hello, small person," he said.

"Desmond," her mum said from the couch, "don't poke the baby."

Her dad stopped, looked guilty, then leaned closer. "You may have won this round," he whispered, "but I *will* have my—"

"And don't threaten the baby, either."

"I wasn't," he said, straightening up immediately.

"Just leave her alone. You're annoying her."

"I'm not annoying her. She doesn't even know enough to *be* annoyed. She's, what, a week old?"

"She's three months."

"She's three months in *our* years, but how old is she in baby years?"

"Come away from her. Steph, could you pick her up? It's time for her feed."

Valkyrie went to the baby while her dad frowned.

"Why didn't you ask me to pick her up? I was standing right there. Don't you trust me? That's it, isn't it? You don't trust me."

"I do trust you," her mum said. "I just don't trust you a *lot*. Stephanie has safe hands."

"You want to see safe hands?" her dad asked. He went to the fruit bowl on the side table, took two apples and proceeded to juggle them. "See? Safe as anything."

Her mum frowned at him. "Are you proposing you juggle our new-born child?"

"Of course not," he said. "I'd only be able to juggle her if you'd had twins. Otherwise it's just throwing."

"Steph," her mum said, "give me my baby and never let your father near her."

"Deal," Valkyrie said, handing her sister over.

Her dad put the apples back in the bowl. "Everyone seems to forget that I'm not a complete novice at this. Don't I already have one beautiful daughter, and she turned out OK, didn't she? I didn't drop her once."

"You dropped her when we were at the zoo," Valkyrie's mum said.

Valkyrie spun her head to him. "You dropped me?"

"Ah," he said, "I'd forgotten about that. In my defence, though, you were a very wriggly child. One moment you were there, the next you were, you know, on the ground in the penguin enclosure."

She blinked. "You dropped me in the *penguin enclosure*?"

"I was leaning over the railing and you just plopped out of my grip. You weren't hurt, or anything. And even if you had been, I'm sure the penguins would have taken you in, raised you as one of their own. It would have been a different life for you, but still a good one."

"I can't believe you dropped me."

"Neither could the people around us. Some crazy woman stormed up and roared at me for five minutes about how I shouldn't be putting my child in danger."

"That was me," Valkyrie's mum muttered.

"Now it makes sense," Valkyrie said, collapsing on to the couch. "My fear of zoos. My fear of penguins. My fear of being dropped in a zoo with the penguins. It's all Dad's fault."

"Most things are," he admitted sadly, and wandered over to his wife. "But I won't make the same mistakes again, I promise. From this moment on, I will be the best father the world has ever seen. Wifey, may I please hold my child?"

"I'm feeding her."

"Give me the child and the bottle. I'll feed her."

Valkyrie's mum looked at him suspiciously. "When you hold a baby, what is the most important thing to remember?"

"Not to drop it," he said proudly.

"Well, yes, well done, dear, but I was thinking more about *how* you hold the baby."

"Ah," he said, "of course. The secret to holding a baby is to pick it up by the scruff of the neck."

"You're thinking of kittens."

"Pick it up by its ears, then."

"You're thinking of nothing."

"Can I please just hold her?"

"I don't think that's wise."

"A lot of things aren't wise, Melissa. Is crossing the road with your eyes closed wise? No, but I do it anyway."

His wife nodded. "Stephanie, you're in charge of teaching Alice how to cross the road."

"Gotcha."

Her dad held his hands out, and finally her mum sighed. "Be careful," she warned.

"Trust me," he said.

She handed the baby over. Valkyrie's dad held Alice out straight, looked at her and smiled. "Aren't you so cute?" he asked. "Aren't you? Aren't you the cutest?" He brought her in close, held her against his face and staggered around the room. "Help me!" he cried. "A facehugger has me!" Valkyrie and her mother observed him as he lifted her off, chuckling. "You know," he said, "from *Alien*. The facehugger." He held the baby against his face again. "Help me, Sigourney Weaver! Help me!" Alice, for her part, seemed bemused by the whole thing.

They left half an hour later, when Alice was in her basket and sleeping. Valkyrie dialled Skulduggery's number and he picked up.

"Hey," she said softly. "It's me."

Skulduggery paused. "No, it's not. If it were me, then I'd be talking to myself, and I don't do that any more. I certainly don't ring myself. That's one of the first signs of madness, and if it isn't, it should be."

She sighed. "Are you finished talking nonsense?"

"I haven't talked nonsense all morning. I miss it. Why are you speaking so quietly?"

"Because the baby's asleep."

"Can she walk yet?"

"No."

"I could walk from a very young age, you know. I was a very advanced child."

"You must be so proud."

"I am."

"It's funny, actually. I've never thought about what you'd have been like as a child. What *were* you like?"

"I was shorter."

"I bet you never shut up."

"Actually, I found it very difficult to speak. I had a stutter, you see."

"You?"

"It's hard to believe, isn't it? It didn't stop me from developing a razor-sharp wit, though, even if the townspeople *did* suspect that I was possessed by the devil. Four hundred years ago, no one really understood why people stuttered. They were simpler times."

"So why *do* people stutter?"

"I don't know. They're probably possessed by the devil."

"You are so annoying. Any word on Craven?"

"Three of his Necromancers have been arrested trying to flee the country – that leaves us with fourteen more, not counting the White Cleaver or Craven himself."

"So he's still at large."

"Yes, but that won't last long. If it were Wreath we were talking about, he'd vanish and we'd never see him again. But Craven has spent most of his adult life in one Temple or another. Only rarely did he venture out into the real world. We'll catch him soon enough."

There was a knock on the door.

"Hey," she said, "I have to go. Call me if there's, you know, anything to talk about."

He sounded amused. "You're bored, aren't you?"

"No," she said, walking into the hall. "This is my day off and I'm enjoying being normal."

"You're bored."

"You're the one who's bored. Without me around, you're lost, aren't you? Just admit that you miss me."

"You are an amusing oddity."

She grinned. "That'll do for now."

She hung up, and opened the door. She put her phone in her pocket as she stepped out and looked around. No one. Shrugging, she went back inside, walked into the kitchen.

God, she was bored.

When Alice was awake, time flitted by. But when she was asleep, Valkyrie had nothing to do. She needed a hobby, something that didn't include hitting people. Or maybe some friends that she could invite over on a Saturday morning to keep her company while she babysat. She felt a pang when Fletcher flashed into her head, and fought it down hard. She refused to feel lonely, not on her day off.

Valkyrie walked to the back door, which hadn't been closed properly, shut it and locked it. There was now a baby in the house, after all. She couldn't take the chance that a wild animal might wander in and make off with Alice, like those dingoes in Australia. She was probably being unfair to both dingoes and Australia, but she couldn't risk it. Locked doors kept the dingoes out, and that's all there was to it, even if she didn't know what a dingo actually was. She took out her phone, searched the Internet, found a picture of a baby dingo and now she really wanted a baby dingo for a pet.

Valkyrie sighed, putting the phone away. She really needed a hobby. She walked out of the kitchen and someone grabbed her, smashed her head against the wall. White light exploded behind her eyes. She wanted to drop to the ground, but there were hands on her, someone speaking, and then the hallway blurred as she was thrown the length of it. She hit the ground, banging her chin and biting her tongue. Blood in her mouth, thunder in her head. She felt fingers in her hair, heard herself cry out as she was wrenched back. More talking, but the words slipped by. Her ears were buzzing. Her head snapped. Someone had hit her. She was on the floor again, on her back this time. Someone sitting on her, straddling her. A hand at her throat. She tried to push at the air but she couldn't focus. She clicked her fingers but couldn't find the spark. Her head was splitting.

She blinked, the man on top of her becoming less hazy. For a moment she didn't recognise him. All she saw was the snarling mouth with the cut lip and the spittle that flew as he spoke. She saw the eyes, wide and bruised and burning with anger. A name drifted to her. Moore.

"You thought I wouldn't come back at you?" he sneered. "You thought you could do that and get away with it?"

His hand at her throat was cutting off her air. She realised she already had her hands up, trying to release the pressure. She brought her knees in so they were pressed against him from behind, and then she hooked her left foot to the outside of his right. He didn't notice.

"They had to let me go," he said. "Cops can't have someone beaten up in their own cells, not without a lawsuit."

He pulled his right hand back, cracked it against her cheek. Her head swam but she fought through it.

"I saw your mother's address on one of their files. I thought to myself, the moment I get out of here, I'm paying that girl a visit. I'm going to give her some of what she gave me." He leaned down, his face mere inches from hers. "I don't know how you did all that crazy stuff, but I can do some crazy stuff of my own. I can beat that pretty face of yours right off you."

She waited until he started to lean away, then she trapped his right hand at her throat and smacked her own right hand up into his chin. She didn't even give him time to feel it. Her hand went to his shoulder, fingers closing around his jacket, and she snapped her body off the ground, bridging him up and over and now she was on top, smashing her elbow down into his face, again and again while he attempted to cover up.

He tried to push her off but she kept bringing the elbow down. He started shouting, cursing at her. Somewhere in the distance she heard a baby crying. Alice had woken up.

Her head felt light and for a moment she thought she was going to faint. Moore seized his chance, started to push her off. Her head cleared as he turned over, tried to crawl out from under her. She fell on to him, right arm wrapping around his throat, the other searching for a sleeper hold. He gagged, raised up to his hands and knees, but she stayed on his back, hooking her feet into his legs. He launched himself sideways. She tucked her head against him, clung on like a limpet. He rolled, gasping and gagging, doing everything he could to throw her off. Her left arm snaked closer to that sleeper hold. They crashed into the hall table. The vase toppled, smashed on the ground. Flowers and water went everywhere.

She found the sleeper hold, started to tighten, then she felt something slice into her left arm. She cried out, but only let go when Moore twisted the shard of broken vase. She fell back, clutching her arm, blood dripping through her fingers. Moore got to his feet, staggered slightly, his face bright red, bleeding and sweating, the shard in his hand. She tried to push at the air but her focus was gone. Her head buzzed too loudly, every movement sending pain ricocheting against the inside of her skull.

She backed off to the front door and he closed in, teeth bloodied and gritted. If she had been wearing her black clothes, a shard of vase wouldn't have worried her too much. But she was wearing jeans and a T-shirt. Her black clothes were upstairs, in her room, with her Necromancer ring.

Moore came in, stabbing towards her gut. Valkyrie jerked her hips back as she tried to grab his wrist with both hands. She missed, had no choice but to commit, so she grabbed his arm where she could and launched herself at him, slamming her forehead into his face. She felt the shard slice across her hip. Her momentum took her forward as he stumbled, and she had a good grip of his arm now. She slid in, clasping his arm across her body tightly while her free hand sent palm shot after palm shot towards his face, trying to get his chin. *Hit the chin, shake the brain*, that's what Skulduggery said.

The vase shard dropped and Moore lost his footing, went down, dragging Valkyrie off balance. She tumbled over him and he grabbed at her, but she kicked him away, got up, ran for the stairs. She took them three at a time, but he was after her, lunged and caught her ankle. She fell against the stairs painfully. He was gripping her leg with one hand, the other reaching up, hooking into the waistband of her jeans, dragging her down towards him. She twisted, crunching his fingers between her back and the wooden step, and he roared and released. She scrambled up, got to the landing, burst into her room, flung open the wardrobe and grabbed the black clothes, searching the pockets for the ring.

Moore collided with her from behind. He was roaring now, a constant roar of anger and murderous hatred. He threw her back. She fell on to her bed and he was on top of her. She crossed her arms over her head and his knuckles cracked against her elbows. He hissed in pain, grabbed her arms, tried to pull them away from her face but she resisted, her muscles burning. She waited until he gave an almighty heave and then she shoved him, adding to his own strength, and he fell backwards off the bed. She tried to spring past him but he flailed, caught her leg. She hit the ground and he was on her. The Necromancer ring was on the floor of the wardrobe. She didn't need to focus to use it. She reached out but it was too far. She could see herself in the mirror, see Moore on top of her. He caught her eye and grinned. She stopped reaching for the ring, and instead her fingers tapped the mirror. Her reflection, bloody and bruised, blinked, and stood up.

Moore froze. "What the hell...?"

The reflection's foot came out of the mirror and lashed into Moore's face.

He went backwards. Valkyrie heard him crash into her desk. She turned over, and the reflection pulled her to her feet.

"This isn't right," Moore gasped, sucking in air through broken teeth. "How did you do that? What the hell is that?"

The reflection left Valkyrie standing there and closed in. For a moment Moore looked like he might shrink back, but fear mixed with his anger and he snarled again. He threw a punch and the reflection lunged, its arms crossed in front of its face, taking the punch on its forearms. It grabbed Moore's head and started slamming in headbutts. Moore's legs gave out and he slipped from the reflection's grasp, his face a mess, already unconscious as he hit the floor.

The reflection looked back at Valkyrie. "We should kill him," it said.

Valkyrie frowned. "Don't be ridiculous."

"It's not ridiculous, it's practical. I'll do it if you don't want to. You can call Skulduggery. We'll need to hide the body."

Valkyrie fought to get her breath back. "We're not killing him, OK? We're not killers. Or *I'm* not a killer, and that means you're not a killer, either."

The reflection looked at her. "He's the one who broke in and attacked you. If your parents were here, he would have attacked them, too. For all we know, he might even have hurt Alice. We should kill him."

"No, all right? We're going to do this like normal people. I'm calling the Guards."

"He'll identify you as the person who attacked him in his cell."

"And I'll say he's lying."

"And what will you say when he mentions me?"

"I'll say I hit him so hard he was seeing double. Nobody's going to believe a word he says, especially when he starts talking about anything magical."

"If you call the Guards, they'll arrest him, put him on trial, throw him in jail. And what are you going to do when he gets out again? He'll come back, you know he will, and you're not going to be here."

"No," Valkyrie said, "but you are. And you're going to protect my family."

The reflection looked down at Moore. "If he comes back," it said, "I'm going to kill him."

Valkyrie kept her eyes on the reflection, and didn't say anything. That sounded fair to her.

42

A NEW MISSION

Scapegrace threw open the doors to the pub, and nobody came in. The people of Roarhaven wrinkled their noses at his disfigured appearance as they passed. Not one of them said hello. Not one of them stepped inside. He turned, went back into the cool interior, away from the glare of the sun and the glares of the people.

Years ago, when he had first run the place, the bar had been split into two. There was a section for the regular people, and a section for the special guests, the VIPs. Now there weren't any VIPs, but neither were there regular people. There was just Scapegrace, the owner and bartender, and Thrasher, the idiot who wiped the tables.

"Stop wiping the tables," Scapegrace said. "There's no one here. You keep wiping the damn tables. You do a loop of the room, humming away to yourself, wiping the tables one after another... It's insane. You look like an insane person doing that."

"Sorry," Thrasher said, his head drooping.

"Go clean the toilets."

"But they're disgusting."

"So are you. Clean them."

Thrasher's head dipped even lower, and he trudged away to do his duty.

Sometime around mid-afternoon, two men walked in. They wore black, and Scapegrace had never seen them before. They certainly weren't Roarhaven natives. One of them held the door open and two more men walked in. The first was dressed in a black robe, and the second was dressed all in white. Scapegrace's eyes would have widened if they'd been able, but having half his face burned off severely limited his expressions of surprise. He stared at the White Cleaver until the man in the black robe cleared his throat.

"You're a zombie," said the man.

Scapegrace nodded. No point in denying it.

"Do you know what that means?" the man continued. "It means that you, like the White Cleaver here, are a product of Necromancer magic. As such, you are bound to Necromancer will."

"I am?" asked Scapegrace. It was news to him, and yet he did feel an odd urge to bow.

"Oh, you are," said the man. "And that means you are bound to *my* will. I am High Priest Vandameer Craven. I am your master."

Thrasher popped his head out of the toilets. "Are you my master too?"

High Priest Craven glanced at him distastefully, then looked back at Scapegrace. "This is one you turned? Why is it still with you?"

"I've tried getting rid of him," Scapegrace offered. "But he keeps coming back."

High Priest Craven sighed. "No matter. I have a task for you, zombie. You will obey without question."

Scapegrace nodded eagerly. He had only just met his Master, but already he could tell that the Necromancer was a very important man.

Thrasher hurried forward. "Can I obey too?" he begged. "All I do here is clean the toilets. I long to serve!"

The Master's lip curled. "If you shut up and move away from me, yes, you can obey."

Thrasher squealed with delight and ran back beside Scapegrace.

"I need you to steal something for me," the Master said. "It looks exactly like this." He showed them a gold disc, the size of his palm. "There is undoubtedly one to be found in the offices of the Elder Mages. All I need is one. When you have located said disc, substitute it with this forgery." The Master threw the disc to Scapegrace. He snatched it from the air and held it close to his heart. "Do not, under any circumstances, arouse suspicion. It is to be a straight swap. Do you understand?"

"Yes Master," Scapegrace said.

"Yes Master," Thrasher said, and started bowing like the pitiful fool he was. It was an utterly pathetic display. Scapegrace got to his knees, showing everyone what *real* bowing was.

The Master looked at them both, and then shifted his eyes to the man who had held the door open. "These are the only zombies in town? We're absolutely sure there are no others?"

The man shook his head sadly.

The Master looked annoyed. "Very well," he said. "They'll have to do."

Scapegrace was so happy he could have cried, had his tear ducts not long since dried up.

43

A & E

Alice's eyes were wide open, watching the activity in the Accident and Emergency Room with interest as Valkyrie rocked her with her free hand. Her other arm was flat on the table as a cute doctor stitched her up.

"You sure you're OK?" he asked again.

"I'm grand," she said. The leaves she'd chewed while she waited for the cops to show up were still working to dull the pain. She winced every time the needle went through her skin, but that was more for show than anything else. He'd already stitched the cut on her hip, assuring her as he did so that there probably wouldn't be a scar. She'd shrugged. A scar on her hip was the least of her worries.

She heard her mother's voice, looked over as a nurse led her parents into the A&E.

"There," the doctor said. "Finished. I'll have a nurse bandage this up. I swear, I wish all my patients were as calm as you, you know that?"

"Thanks. I wish all my doctors were as hot as you."

He laughed, then stood aside as Valkyrie's mum barged through, arms out to hug. She stopped abruptly, backed off, looked at the doctor.

"Is it OK to hug her?" she asked.

"We actually encourage it," he said, smiling, and walked off as the hug came on.

"My baby," her mum said. "My poor baby."

"I'm fine," Valkyrie said, her voice muffled. Her eyes flickered to her dad, who was checking on Alice. He looked grim. She wasn't used to him looking grim. Her mum started crying. Automatically, Valkyrie stiffened, blinking back the tears that had sprung up without warning and now threatened to spill over.

"Mum," she said, laughing as she pulled away. "Mum, I'm grand. Look. Not a bother on me."

"Your face," her mother said.

"Cuts and bruises, already fading."

"Your poor arm."

"Stitched up and healing. Honestly, I'm fine."

"He beat himself up in his cell," her dad said. He was still looking at Alice. "That's why they let him out. They should have been outside. The moment they let that scumbag walk free, they should have parked a squad car outside the house."

"Dad, they didn't know he knew where we lived, and they certainly didn't know he'd want some kind of stupid revenge for getting thrown in jail in the first place. You can't blame them."

"They let him go."

"This isn't their fault."

He looked at her for the first time. "He could have…"

"Des, don't," her mum said, her hand covering her mouth. "Please. Don't say it."

Valkyrie made herself smile. "Hey, the pair of you, snap out of it. Alice slept through the whole thing and I'm fine."

A nurse came over. "Excuse me? I just have to bandage up your arm."

"Bandage away," Valkyrie said.

The nurse smiled, started working. "I heard what happened," she said. "They're all talking about it. I thought you might like to know that the man who attacked you is being treated in a secure room, surrounded by three very angry-looking Guards. You broke four of his ribs, his nose, his jaw, cracked three fingers, knocked out three teeth, and gave him a concussion. He was seeing two of you, do you know that?"

Valkyrie's mother blinked. "Stephanie did all that?"

"She sure did," said the nurse. She secured the bandage in place. "I'll be right back with the paperwork."

The nurse walked off. Valkyrie's parents stared at her.

"What?" Valkyrie asked as innocently as she could. "I've been taking self-defence lessons at the gym. Hard Target Krav Maga type stuff. Combatives, things like that. It's really not a big deal."

"But he was a grown man," her mother said.

"There's not really a lot of point to self-defence if you can't use it against just that type of person. Oh, Mum, your vase got broken. The one in the hall. Sorry."

Her mum blinked. "That's... quite all right. It was an ugly vase and I never liked it anyway."

"See?" Valkyrie beamed. "It's worked out well for everybody."

"Are you sure you're not in shock?"

"Honestly, I'm good. I'm just glad Dad wasn't there or he'd have thrown him through another window."

Her mum smiled, and hugged her husband. "I have a family of fighters," she said. "Alice, it looks like it's up to you and me to be the reasonable ones."

Alice gurgled.

*

439

Her parents drove her home. It was weird, sitting in the back seat of a car. She almost felt like a kid. Music was playing and she started singing softly to Alison. Alison smiled, and Valkyrie laughed.

They got home and spent the evening cleaning up the mess. There was a knock on the door and her dad went to answer it. He came back in, paused, then spoke. "Fletcher's here," he said. "I told him if he's here to argue with you, he should just walk away. But he said he's not. Maybe you should talk to him."

Her mum nodded. "He's a nice boy. He deserves it."

"Yeah," Valkyrie said. "I know." She took a breath, then walked into the hall. Fletcher stood in the doorway. She stuffed her hands in her jeans. "Hi," she said.

He looked at her. "Go for a walk?"

"Sure."

He turned, started walking down the path. She followed him out, closing the door behind her. They walked towards the park.

"Are you talking to me again?" she asked.

"I suppose I am," he said. "You look like you've been in the wars."

"You know me, always running into trouble."

"And coming out the other side. That's the important bit." He kicked a pebble and it skittered away. "I don't forgive you," he said. "I'd like to. I'd like it if we could just forget about it all, get back together, carry on like before. But that's not going to happen."

"I know," said Valkyrie quietly. "But I don't want you to hate me, Fletch."

"That's a little out of your hands, though, isn't it?"

"I suppose."

"It's kind of hard to stay angry at you. You probably don't feel you did anything wrong, do you?"

"Of course I do. I cheated on you."

"But why?"

"Because I was stupid, and I didn't think about it, and—"

"No," Fletcher said. He looked at her. "At the time, what was going through your head? Why did you do it?"

"How is this going to help anything?"

"It'll help prove my point."

Valkyrie sighed. "I thought, at the time, that you were being too... boyfriendy."

"Is that the technical term for it?"

"You were being too protective. You were..."

"Go on."

They were in the park now, sticking to the well-lit areas. There was nobody else around. "You were lecturing me. You were disapproving of the things I did. I thought it was all just too safe, you know?"

"And you turned to Caelan. Who is anything but safe."

"I suppose."

"So when you cheated on me, you knew why you were doing it. You could justify it."

"To a degree."

"So in your head, it was all my fault."

"What? No, that's not what I meant."

"Val, you did what you did, you made those decisions, because you were doing what you thought was the right thing for you at the time. I try to be angry but I just… can't. You did what you thought was best for you. That's how you live. You never set about to be mean or cruel. These are just things that happen, kind of like a side-effect."

"Because I'm selfish."

"Yeah. Because you're selfish. Maybe you'll grow out of it in a few years. I don't know. I hope you do."

"That'd be nice," she murmured.

"I don't hate you," said Fletcher. "I may not like you all that much right now, but I don't hate you. And I really don't think it'd be a good idea to be around you any more. I'm moving."

Something yanked at Valkyrie's heart. "Where to?"

"Australia. I like it there. It's warm, and they talk funny."

"But what about your training?"

"Australia's a Cradle of Magic, just like Ireland. There'll be plenty of boring old people over there who can offer me useless advice, same as here. What's wrong?"

"I just… I don't want you to go. We weren't *just* boyfriend and girlfriend. We were *friends*, too. I don't… I don't have many friends. I don't want to lose another one."

"Well, you break a heart, that's what happens."

"Yeah," she muttered.

"Besides," he said, "I'm a Teleporter. We're never really that far away, wherever we are. Take care, Valkyrie."

She went to speak but he vanished mid-step.

She turned round, walked home.

44

MISSION ACCOMPLISHED

For once, Scapegrace didn't mind the midday sun, or how harsh it was on his skin. He would gladly let the seasons rot him away if that was the Master's wish – although he sincerely hoped it wasn't. He climbed down from the Penguin-Mobile to the dirt track, and hurried over to where High Priest Craven and the White Cleaver were waiting. Secret meetings were exciting.

"Sire," Scapegrace said, dropping to one knee and holding the gold disc up to him with both hands. "I have returned." Thrasher fell to both knees beside him, hands clasped in prayer.

"I see that," High Priest Craven said, snatching up the disc. "You did as I instructed?"

"Oh yes, Sire."

"Exactly as I instructed?"

"I located Ghastly Bespoke's quarters, let myself in—"

"Let *ourselves* in," Thrasher corrected.

"– and then I located the disc. I substituted—"

"*We* substituted," Thrasher corrected.

"– the fake disc you had given me, and returned here to you, now, with the real disc. So now he has the fake disc and you have the real disc. I live only to serve."

"*We* live only to serve," Thrasher corrected.

"You don't live," the Master said, examining his prize. "And nobody saw you?"

"Nobody, Sire. I was like the wind."

"*We* were like the wind," said Thrasher.

"But I was like the wind more."

"I was more breeze-like," Thrasher said, and bowed forward until his forehead was touching the ground. It was, once again, an unsurprisingly pathetic display, and one that Scapegrace would have no problem surpassing.

He laid himself flat on the ground, face stuck into the dirt, and waved his arms in the air. "Give me another order, Master, I beg of you."

"Me too," Thrasher said, lying beside Scapegrace, doing his best to wriggle deeper into the dirt. Furious, Scapegrace started wriggling alongside him.

"If you were not already dead," the Master said, pinching the bridge of his nose, "I would gladly kill you both. Stop wriggling, and listen very closely. I want you to gather more like you."

"More zombies?" Thrasher asked, spitting out a small stone.

"I said *listen*, not *talk*. I want twenty by this time tomorrow. If you fail me…"

"I won't," said Scapegrace.

"I won't," said Thrasher.

"He might," said Scapegrace.

"Shut," the Master said, "up."

Scapegrace stayed where he was until the Master and the White Cleaver were gone, and then he got up. Thrasher stood beside him, brushing the dirt from his clothes. "You're pathetic," Scapegrace sneered.

"I know," Thrasher said meekly. "But whenever the Master is around, nothing else matters but him. It's like he said, zombies are made to serve Necromancers. That… that doesn't mean I still don't value your leadership, sir."

"Yeah, well," Scapegrace said, curling what was left of his lip, "just don't you forget it."

45

THE NICEST TOWN IN IRELAND

Geoffrey had been the key.

It was a good trick, all right, getting people to believe whatever he told them. He hadn't reckoned on Kenny's journalism training being able to renew his interest in the story, but that wasn't Geoffrey's fault. It was a fluke, nothing more. Kenny had no trouble believing that Geoffrey's power would work on anyone. And that had got him thinking.

He had spent the last few days digging out all the reports he'd found that had later been retracted. He read over them again with fresh eyes, with a new perspective. What if these reports hadn't been hoaxes or mistakes? What if they were genuine, and had only been retracted after someone like Geoffrey had convinced the poor, frightened people that they hadn't seen what they'd thought they'd seen?

Kenny had laid all these reports out on his floor, and he'd spent hours going through them. One of them caught his eye. Only a few lines long. A few years ago, a man in north County Dublin had called the cops after witnessing a dark-haired girl fleeing from a pack of white-skinned "animals" who ran on two legs. The girl – he hadn't seen her face – led them towards the pier.

His statement was taken by the local cops. The next day he denied ever seeing such a thing. The day after that, the cops who had taken his statement denied ever doing so. It would have been completely forgotten about if Kenny hadn't been such a keen collector of oddness.

It was a long shot, Kenny knew. There were plenty of dark-haired girls in Ireland. There was absolutely no reason to think that it was the same girl who Geoffrey had called Valkyrie Cain. But the name of the town in which this had happened was Haggard, which was only a kilometre or two from the town in which there had been all that Insanity Virus trouble at that nightclub. And so Kenny got the bus to Haggard. He stayed in a B&B and talked to the couple who owned it about any odd occurrences they might have heard about. *Odd?* they said. *Sure nothing odd ever happens in Haggard.*

By the end of his second day, he was believing that. Haggard was rapidly becoming the nicest town in Ireland, where nothing weird ever happened.

The oddest thing, according to a small old man in a farmer's cap who didn't appear to have any teeth, was a car that had been showing up regularly for the last five years or so. Kenny didn't know much about cars, but he knew what a Bentley was when the old man mentioned it. A real beauty too, apparently. A few times a week, usually at night, the Bentley could be seen driving through town. Nobody knew who owned it. Sometimes there'd be a passenger, a dark-haired girl. She always kept her head down.

Kenny felt the flutter of excitement building inside him. It was them. He knew it was. It had to be.

His attention caught by this mysterious Bentley, Kenny didn't pay much attention to the news that a local woman had been mugged on Main Street. Everyone was talking about it. Melissa Edgley had had her handbag snatched by a thug called Ian Moore. Melissa's husband had thrown Moore through a window, and the cops had come and Moore had been escorted into a cell. No magic or super powers involved.

But then, the next day, they were all talking about Moore again. The Guards had been forced to let him go, the nice people of

Haggard said, and he'd gone straight to Melissa Edgley's house looking for revenge. Melissa's daughter, Stephanie, had been home with her new-born sister, and Stephanie had managed to overpower the thug and call the police. *The poor girl*, the good people of Haggard said. *She must have been terrified. It must have been awful. Isn't it great how she overpowered him, though? Isn't that amazing? Wonder how she did it?*

And then the good people of Haggard would shrug. *But then, she's always been an odd one, has that Stephanie.*

And Kenny's interest was piqued.

46

THE REQUIEM BALL

There was a box on the table when they walked into Skulduggery's house. It was done up with a ribbon tied into a bow. Valkyrie opened it, took out a beautiful black dress.

"Wow," she said.

"Normally, Ghastly would have been happy to make you a dress," Skulduggery said, "but all his spare time is invested in tracking down Tanith. So I thought I'd spoil you."

"This is… wow."

"I'm glad you like it. We leave for the Ball in twenty minutes."

She glared at him. "I have to wash my hair."

"Then you had better hurry."

She showered in the bathroom that had been specially installed for her. As she did her make-up, she checked herself for scars and bruises. Apart from the bandage on her forearm there was nothing much to report. She would have liked to have gone to one of the Sanctuary doctors instead of making do with stitches and a bandage, but mortal problems meant mortal solutions. A physical injury that could be photographed and documented would help the Guards in their prosecution, whereas an injury that disappeared overnight would only help Valkyrie look better in her dress.

Not that she needed any help as far as that was concerned. The dress was long and slinky, strapless, silk and chiffon. Her shoes were gorgeous.

She stepped into the living room and Skulduggery, wearing the sharpest tuxedo she had ever seen, complete with black gloves and a white scarf, tilted his head to her.

"You're late," he said.

"I'm beautiful."

"You're always beautiful."

"I'm always late, too."

He put on his hat, black to match the tux, and they walked out of the house. He opened the car door and she slipped in.

They left Dublin City, heading north, passed the turn-off for Haggard and continued on to Gordon's house. There was no one guarding the gate, but even so, Skulduggery slowed to a stop. He took their passkey from his pocket, a gold disc no bigger than his palm, and pressed it between his thumb and forefinger. Once it started to glow they drove on, and Valkyrie saw the symbols pulse on either side of the gate, nullifying the security measures. Gleaming cars were parked on both sides of the long driveway, and Valkyrie glimpsed figures standing in the darkness. Men and women, dressed similarly to Cleavers but in black, with twin sickles in sheaths on their backs.

"They're Rippers," Skulduggery said. "Cleaver-trained private security. Only the richest can afford them."

They got out of the Bentley. Skulduggery had a stern word of warning with the valet, and they walked into the house.

Valkyrie imagined that this was what a high society party looked like – people in expensive clothes sipping champagne and laughing politely. The only difference was that, here and there, there were examples of the extraordinary – an otherwise sombre gentleman with green hair, a woman in a shimmering dress with shimmering skin, a man with claws, and of course the walking skeleton beside her. The richest and the most influential sorcerers in the world. Valkyrie could feel the power the moment she stepped in the door, and it made her insides tingle.

A waiter with dirty fingernails offered her a glass of wine on a silver tray. She politely declined, and as the waiter disappeared in the crowd she frowned after him. Dirty fingernails, at a function like this? She shrugged, letting it go. In one of the rooms there was a small orchestra, whose music drifted throughout the house at a perfect pitch. No one had to raise their voice to be heard.

Everything in here positively glowed. Valkyrie was glad the dress Skulduggery had bought her was so beautiful – it was a match for the others she saw.

Skulduggery handed his hat and scarf to a woman who smiled and took them away. Valkyrie stayed by his side. They passed through to the next room, and Skulduggery did his best to tell her who everyone was. She recognised a lot of the names.

Everyone, it seemed, knew Skulduggery, but not all of them liked him. For every smile they got, there was at least one scowl.

"As you can see," Skulduggery said quietly, "I'm very, very popular."

"I can tell."

Gordon stood by his Echo Stone, chatting to a group of people who laughed at whatever story he was telling. He saw Valkyrie and waved, his eyes sparkling, then returned to his story. She grinned.

Ravel came over, shook Skulduggery's hand and kissed Valkyrie's cheek. "You look stunning," he told her.

She smiled back at him. "Not so bad yourself, Grand Mage."

He laughed, then caught sight of a group of foreign sorcerers standing nearby, and sighed unhappily. "I must go," he said. "The curse of this job is that I have to mingle. Just when you meet someone interesting, you're called away by someone mundane."

Ravel moved off, and Ghastly arrived to take his place. "Sorry I'm late," he said. "I'd trouble getting in. My disc wasn't working right, and I'd barely passed the gates before I was surrounded by Rippers."

"Oh Elder Bespoke, that's dreadful," Valkyrie teased. "Didn't they know who you were?"

He looked at her. "You're making fun of me, aren't you?"

"Not Valkyrie, Your Lordship," Skulduggery protested. "She wouldn't dream of it."

"I hate you," Ghastly muttered. "I hate you both. Oh, we have a surprise guest."

Skulduggery's head tilted. "We do?"

Ghastly nodded ahead of them, and the crowd parted to reveal a man with short blond hair, his face lighting up when he saw them. He looked young and fit and healthy – no more than thirty years old, wearing his tuxedo with the bow tie undone and the top buttons of his shirt open.

Skulduggery stepped forward to clasp this man's hand in his, as if they were old friends.

"It's been too long," Skulduggery said.

"It has at that," the newcomer replied. His eyes left Skulduggery and found Valkyrie.

"Hi," she said. "I'm—"

"Val!" he exclaimed, and enveloped her in a hug. "Any friend of Skulduggery's, providing she's pretty enough, is a friend of mine!" He let go of her and stepped back. "You are now my friend."

"Valkyrie," Skulduggery said, "allow me to introduce the one and only Dexter Vex, obviously taking a short break from his life of adventuring and derring-do."

"A very short break," Vex said, stepping back and flashing her a grin. Oh, she liked *him*.

"I've heard a lot about you," she said. "You were one of the Dead Men."

"Indeed I was," Vex nodded, "cursed to follow this bumbling fool from misadventure to misadventure in the days of our youth. Is he treating you well? He doesn't boast too much, does he?"

"Sometimes it's like that's all he ever does."

He held her hand in both of his. "I feel your pain," he said sadly.

Skulduggery pulled their hands apart. "Yes, well, quite enough of that. If you feel the need to gang up on me, at least have the decency to wait until my back is turned. When did you get into town?"

"This morning," Vex said. "Ghastly sent me an invitation a few weeks ago, and even though I was kind of busy, when someone like His Holy Eminence sends you an invite, you really can't say no."

"Oh, great," Ghastly said, "now you've got him at it."

Valkyrie laughed, hooking her arm through Ghastly's. "We're only messing," she said. "And by the way, you look *amazing* in that tuxedo."

Ghastly smiled. "Why thank you, Valkyrie."

Vex chuckled. "See that? He hasn't changed a bit. No matter how bad a mood he pretends to be in, all it takes is a nice word from a pretty girl and he's putty in her hands. Skulduggery, remember that French girl we met in Saipan? What was her name?"

"Oh," Skulduggery said. "Françoise."

"That's it," said Vex. "Françoise. Remember her, Ghastly? Remember that weekend we couldn't find you? We thought Mevolent had snatched you away and was torturing you to within an inch of your life. Valkyrie, would you like to know what he was *really* doing that weekend?"

"Yes I would," said Valkyrie.

"No she wouldn't," said Ghastly.

"I think she would," Skulduggery said.

"If you tell her," said Ghastly, "I will have the both of you arrested. And possibly flogged."

Vex sighed. "Sorry, Val. What *happens* in wartime, apparently *stays* in wartime."

"Aw," Valkyrie said, her shoulders drooping.

A woman stopped beside Ghastly, whispered something into his ear. He nodded.

"If you'll excuse me," he said, "I have people to talk to. Important people, people of influence and stature, and hopefully people who won't laugh at me."

He walked away, and immediately Vex leaned in.

"Don't worry," he said, "we have plenty of other stories to tell you. And I have plenty of stories to tell you about Skulduggery too. Good stories. Scandalous stories. Stories to use against him no matter what the situation."

"Suddenly this entire night seems like a bad idea," Skulduggery said.

The conversation died as a man appeared beside them, luxurious blond hair swept back off his fleshy face, wet lips curled in a smile. Behind him stood a boy of Valkyrie's age.

"My my," the man said, his chins quivering with his words, "if it isn't the Skeleton Detective himself, come down off his mountain to grace us lowly sorcerers with his presence. I am so honoured and awestruck that I fear I am at a loss. Should I bow? Kneel? Curtsey?"

"Leave?" Skulduggery suggested, and the man laughed uproariously.

His small eyes turned to Valkyrie. "And you, my dear, this vision in black, must be Valkyrie Cain herself." She didn't like the way he looked at her – he was taking far too long. "Skulduggery, my sincerest congratulations – you've picked a good one here. Pretty, too. I can see why you take her wherever you go. Not too smart, though, am I right?"

Valkyrie glanced at Skulduggery. "It's not just me, is it? He is begging for a box, isn't he?"

"Indeed he is," Skulduggery said.

"I think so too," nodded Vex.

"You can go ahead and hit him if you like," said Skulduggery.

The man laughed, held up his hands. They were pale and soft, like they'd never seen a day's work. "I surrender!" he mock-cried. "I yield! Please don't let the girl strike me!"

Valkyrie was going to hit him out of pure principle, but the boy in the tuxedo took hold of the fat man's arm and tugged it sharply.

"Father," he said, "I think you've had too much wine. Perhaps you would like some air?"

"There's plenty of air in here," the man said, "although it seems to be primarily *hot* air." He laughed at his own joke, and disentangled himself. "Miss Cain, this is my son, who has taken the grand and noble name of Hansard Kray, and I am his embarrassing father, the scurrilous and drunken Arthur Dagan. See how he blushes for me? Is that not the sign of a loyal and loving child?"

"I'm very sorry," Hansard said. He was taller than his father, and lean. The only trait they seemed to share was the colour of their hair.

"Don't apologise for me!" Arthur snapped. "And especially not to her!"

Skulduggery was right by Valkyrie's elbow, but remained quiet. She appreciated that. Any other man would have leaped in to defend her honour. Valkyrie was quite capable of doing that herself.

"Do you have a problem with me?" she asked Arthur.

"A problem?" he echoed. "No! My word, no! Not at all! I'm sure, given time, we could be the best of friends, were it not for your unfortunate habit of murdering my gods."

"Oh," she said, understanding at last. "You're a disciple of the Faceless Ones."

"Indeed I am," Arthur said, bowing before her. "In the spirit of openness and togetherness that the new Council of Elders wants to project, I have been invited, for the first time, to the Requiem Ball, where all you people laugh and chortle and pat each other's backs for defeating the evil Mevolent and his evil followers – of which I was one."

"You didn't have to come," Valkyrie pointed out.

"And *you* don't tell *me* what to do," Arthur sneered. "You'll get your come-uppance, you know. You'll pay for all the things you've done."

"It was a pleasure to meet you," Hansard Kray said, trying to pull his father away.

"I should put you over my knee," Arthur said loudly, keeping his eyes on Valkyrie, "and spank you here in front of everyone."

A waiter appeared, tried to help Hansard's efforts, but Arthur shoved him back. He waved a fat finger at Valkyrie. "You watch yourself, girl. You watch yourself. Your time is coming."

Finally, Hansard managed to turn his father, and they plunged through the gathered crowd until it swallowed them up. A moment passed, and slowly the conversations picked up again.

Valkyrie turned to Skulduggery. "He was *lovely!*" she beamed.

"Arthur Dagan's family was once royalty," Skulduggery told her, "or something close to it. Mevolent served under his grandfather for a time, before he came to power himself. Arthur hasn't handled their fall from grace with as much dignity as one might wish for. Hopefully, his son fares better."

There was a shout, and then a door burst open and men in ski masks poured into the room, waving guns.

"Nobody move!" one of them screamed, firing into the air. "We're here for your jewellery and wallets! Anyone tries being a hero, they'll be shot *dead!*"

47

THIS EVENING'S
ENTERTAINMENT

The gunshot stopped the music. Everybody stopped talking, and just stared in absolute astonishment. Valkyrie couldn't quite believe it.

The guest with the claws spoke up. "You're… you're here to *rob* us?"

"Yeah!" the leader of the gang said. Then he faltered. "What's up with your hands?"

One of his friends, a man in a red ski mask, was already panicking. He held his gun in a tight grip, and even from where she was standing, Valkyrie recognised the dirty fingernails of the waiter who had offered her champagne. "I told you, Larry, this isn't right. Look at these people. They're not *right*."

Someone in the crowd started laughing. Someone else joined in. Within moments, practically every one of the assembled guests was doubled over with laughter. Larry and his ski-masked friends did not appreciate the joke.

"Shut up!" Larry screamed. "Shut up!"

Valkyrie was barely able to keep track of what happened next. The air rippled, taking one of the ski-masked men off his feet. A ball of yellow light sped towards Larry and exploded. He was flung backwards. Streams of different colours criss-crossed around the other members of the gang, slamming into them and spinning them around. The man with the dirty fingernails was the last one standing. Ghastly stepped out of the crowd beside him and took his gun away. China Sorrows, dressed in an exquisite silk gown, tapped her arm. An ornate symbol glowed on her skin for a moment, and when she touched the man he screamed and toppled over.

Everyone cheered, the music started up again and the guests got back to chatting.

China approached. "Valkyrie," she said, "you look beautiful. I always knew there was a pretty girl underneath all those bruises." She saw Vex and raised an eyebrow. "Dexter Vex is back in the country. All we need is Anton Shudder and Saracen Rue to show up and we'd have a Dead Men reunion right here."

"Hello China," Vex said, leaning forward to kiss her cheek. "Have you got over your love for me yet?"

"I take each day as it comes," she replied, and he laughed.

The orchestra started into a waltz. China held her hand out towards Skulduggery. "They're playing our song."

Skulduggery looked at Valkyrie. "If you'll excuse me…?"

She smiled. "Go right ahead."

Skulduggery took China's hand, and led her to the only open space in the room. Valkyrie watched him look into China's eyes, and they began to dance, moving over and around the unconscious forms of the ski-mask gang like they weren't even there. They danced like two people were meant to dance – with strength, grace, and passion.

"He sure can dance, can't he?" Vex said.

Valkyrie took her eyes away from the dancing, and smiled. "He told me he could. I was a fool to doubt him."

She looked back. She could see China's lips move as they danced, and she wondered what they were talking about.

"I taught him everything he knows, of course," said Vex with a nod. "Before he came to me, he had all the co-ordination of a turnip. I turned him into the dancer you see before you."

Skulduggery dipped China, and then swung her up and she pressed against him.

"But do I get any thanks?" Vex continued. "Do I get even a

nod of appreciation? No I do not. It's quite fortunate that I don't need other people's approval to feel good about myself. But it would help."

Ghastly appeared between them. "Are you still complaining about that?"

"I'm not complaining," Vex corrected. "I am merely voicing my displeasure." He frowned. "By the way, all joking aside, do I call you Ghastly or Elder Bespoke?"

"You can call me whatever you want."

Vex nodded. "Thank you Gladys. Where's Shudder tonight, anyway? Don't tell me that miserable sod's staying in that Hotel while there's a party on."

"I'm afraid he is," Ghastly said. "You know very well that Anton isn't one for small talk."

"The years were meant to mellow the man, didn't you tell me that once?"

"I was evidently wrong," Ghastly conceded.

Vex suddenly smiled. "Remember how Larrikin used to wind him up? We'd be sitting around, waiting in a ditch or something for the order to strike, all of us tense and humourless, the enemy a mere stone's throw away... and then Larrikin would whisper something to Shudder. Remember that?"

A grin formed on Ghastly's face. "I remember Shudder's birthday."

Vex laughed and Valkyrie had to join in, it was so infectious.

"We were huddled down in a field in France," Ghastly told her, while Vex snorted at the memory. "This was, I don't know, 1850 or so. We were all there, all seven Dead Men – Skulduggery, Larrikin, Dexter, Hopeless, Saracen, Shudder and me. We hadn't moved from that spot in three days. Apart from Skulduggery, we were all cold, wet and starving. Anyway, Larrikin decided on the third day that it was Shudder's birthday, and there was nothing Shudder could do to convince him that it wasn't."

"The problem," Vex said, picking up the story, "was that it was getting close to Go Time. There was a squad of Mevolent's men we'd been tracking for days, and we had to take them out without raising the alarm. But now, suddenly, Larrikin was insisting on a birthday cake and a sing-song. The rest of us were focusing on not cracking up, but Shudder was taking it seriously, and couldn't understand why Larrikin would want to do something so dangerous."

"We were sitting in a hole we'd dug," Ghastly said, "with the wind howling and the rain falling, and Larrikin squirmed up beside Shudder and kept trying to hug him."

"And Shudder's not a hugger," Vex said.

"It developed into an extraordinarily quiet wrestling match," said Ghastly, grinning. "They rolled over and over in the mud, Larrikin with this enormous smile on his face and Shudder silently furious."

"Shudder got him in a choke hold," Vex said. "Larrikin started digging around inside his clothes for something. He was going purple by this stage, though still smiling. And then he brought out a bun."

Valkyrie laughed. "A bun?"

"A very crushed bun," Ghastly said. "Crumbs now, mostly. Barely held together. He'd kept it hidden for days. And with his other hand he stuck a candle in it."

"Only time I've ever seen Anton Shudder smile while on a Dead Men mission," Vex said, eyes sparkling with approval. "That was a good day."

"That's why we won," Ghastly said, a little quieter.

Valkyrie looked at him. "That mission?"

"Hmm? No, no. The mission was just a mission, the latest in a long line. No, the reason we won was friendships like that. They called us the Dead Men because they said we weren't afraid of dying. Mevolent's lot? They wanted to bring the Faceless Ones back, but the main thing was that they wanted to *be* there when it happened. After all, what's the point of going to all that trouble if they weren't around to enjoy the results? So there were no sacrifices to save their friends, none of that. And that's one of the main reasons they lost. It got to the point where they couldn't trust each other, because it was all about personal survival. Whereas with us… we were fighting, and dying, for each other."

"Larrikin saved my life," Vex said. "We were in Wales, and Serpine had sneaked right up behind me, about to use that red right hand of his. Larrikin pushed me away, shielded me. He died screaming." Vex shook his head sadly. "Never forget those screams. You were there when Skulduggery killed Serpine, weren't you?"

"Yes," Valkyrie answered.

"I would have liked to have seen that."

"Larrikin was a good man," Skulduggery said, and they turned as he led China off the dance floor towards them. "As was Hopeless. They died for what they believed in."

"Hopeless tried to kill me once," China said, almost wistfully. "This was back when I was fighting for the other side, of course. We had some good, good times."

"Hopeless and Larrikin," Ghastly said, raising his glass.

"Hopeless and Larrikin," they echoed.

48

GOING UNDERGROUND

own deep in the caves below Gordon Edgley's house, the zombie horde moved in silence. Twenty recruits to Scapegrace's undead army, all with bite marks and blood splatters, all waiting for the order to charge into battle. Holding flashlights to penetrate the darkness, they looked slightly bewildered, but Scapegrace didn't mind that. In his experience, zombie hordes always looked bewildered. This was his second horde, so he reckoned himself to be something of an expert.

Shards of moonlight somehow found their way through cracks and fissures in the cave ceiling to bathe parts of the tunnels in a hazy silver blue. Master Craven had been so kind as to provide him with a map. If this map were by anyone else's hand, Scapegrace would have dismissed it as crudely drawn – but the Master's work was a deceptively childlike scrawl that implied more than it showed. As such, even though Scapegrace was having trouble working out where exactly they were going, he had a much deeper cultural understanding of where he had been.

Thrasher hurried up, looking anxious. "Master Scapegrace," he whispered. "I think we have a problem."

Scapegrace scowled and shone his flashlight straight into Thrasher's face.

"It's one of the zombies," Thrasher said, blinking quickly. "Reggie. You remember him, don't you, sir? He has a little beard? I… I think he's been eaten."

Scapegrace froze. "Eaten? Someone's eaten him?" He turned to the horde. "What did I tell you? What did I tell you about eating human flesh?" The horde looked at him dumbly. "Only I can do that and keep my thoughts intact! If any of you try it, you become a mindless, shambling zombie right out of a movie. How many times did I warn you? Eh? Well, come on. Own up. Who did it? Who ate Reggie?"

"Uh," said Thrasher. "It wasn't one of *them*, sir."

"What? What do you mean?"

Thrasher led him back down the tunnel. The horde followed.

"Reggie was walking behind us," Thrasher said. "He was lagging a bit and I told him to hurry up, and he ignored me. I kept walking, and he was lagging even more, and I heard something, something chattering, and I looked around and…"

"Chattering, huh?"

"Very distinct chattering," Thrasher said, shaking his head at the memory. "So I walked over, searched around a little, about to call his name, and then… I came here. I believe this to be the scene of the crime."

"You don't say."

"Judging from the signs of disturbance, sir, I think he's been eaten."

"The signs of disturbance?"

"Yes."

"And what would these signs of disturbance be, I wonder?"

Thrasher pointed with his flashlight. "Well, I mean… the *foot.*"

In the middle of the tunnel before them, illuminated by the flashlight, a single foot, still in its shoe, was sitting quietly.

"You worked that out all on your own?" Scapegrace said. "I'm very impressed."

Thrasher didn't seem capable of appreciating sarcasm, so he smiled gratefully. "Just doing my job, sir."

Scapegrace hunkered down beside the upright foot, examined it more closely. It was severed just above the ankle, with what looked an awful lot like a big bite mark. Scapegrace couldn't tell for sure. That stupid skeleton was the detective, not him.

Thrasher suddenly screamed and Scapegrace leaped up and whirled in circles until he was sure there was nothing creeping up behind him.

"There!" Thrasher gasped, pointing off into the darkness.

Scapegrace looked into the gloom. "There what?"

"I saw it!" Thrasher said. "The thing that ate Reggie! I saw it! It was right there!"

Anxious mutterings spread through the horde like a bad smell. Scapegrace needed to take control of the situation, and fast.

"What did it look like?" he asked. "For God's sake, calm the hell down and tell me what it looked like."

Thrasher took a deep breath, even though zombies didn't need to breathe. "It looked like, it looked like a cross between a monster and an alien."

Scapegrace stared at him. "Yeah, OK, that is absolutely no help at all. Did it have arms?"

"Oh yes."

"Two arms?"

"At least," Thrasher nodded. "Maybe less."

"What about legs?"

"It had a few of those."

"What was its body like?"

Thrasher concentrated. "It was, it was either really hairy, with thick black hair all over it, or it didn't have *any* hair, and it was just the way the light fell."

"Its head, then. Did you get a good look at its head?"

"What, like, would I be able to pick it out in a line-up?"

"I'm just looking for basics here."

"OK, well, let's see. It had... I'm not too sure if it had any eyes, and I didn't see a nose, as such. But it had a mouth. A very big mouth, with teeth, teeth as sharp as needles. But I may have imagined that bit."

"The teeth bit?"

"No, I may have imagined the mouth. I'm not sure if it had a mouth. It probably did. Everything has a mouth, right?"

"Unfortunately," Scapegrace muttered.

"It would need a mouth if it was going to eat Reggie. That only makes sense, doesn't it? Yes. It had a mouth. I'm sure of it now."

One of the zombies held up his hand.

"What?" said Scapegrace irritably.

"Hi," the zombie said. "Uh, I'm Keith? From the...? You bit me?"

"I can't remember every single person I bite," Scapegrace said, even though he could, because it really wasn't very many, all things considered. "What do you want, Keith? Why is your hand up?"

"I was just wondering," Keith said, "if there really are monsters down here?"

"There are a few, yes," Scapegrace said. "No one knows how many, or what they're called. All anyone knows is that they're pretty impervious to magic, so… so don't use magic. Not that you could, because you're mortal. Or, you used to be. Anyway, magic attracts them."

"Um," said Keith.

"What now?"

"When you… remember when you bit me? And I woke up, and I was all, oh, what's happening? And your friend explained it?"

"He's not my friend," said Scapegrace.

"I'm his second-in-command," explained Thrasher.

"Oh, OK, sorry," said Keith. "Anyway, he told me I was a zombie now, and that magic was now sustaining me and everything, and all that's fine, but does that mean that now *we* will attract all the monsters because we have magic inside us, or am I just talking complete nonsense?"

Scapegrace looked at him. *Oh, hell.*

"Right," Scapegrace said loudly. "Everyone fall in, and pay attention."

Thrasher joined the horde, and Scapegrace looked at them like a general might survey his troops.

"We have been charged with a mission. We are deep in enemy territory. In order to achieve our objective, we must pass through hostile terrain. Keith is absolutely right. Our very presence here will attract the monsters."

The horde gaped at him, suddenly terrified. Scapegrace pressed on.

"So we will move! Like lightning! And we will arrive at our destination and we will engage the enemy! In years to come, they will speak of this battle and they will speak of the sacrifice we made here! They will speak of the brave Army of the Undead, the horde that turned back the tide, who fought with everything that is in them to make this world *our* world! I have seen the faces of our enemies! I have looked into the eyes of our foes! Do you know what I have seen?" Scapegrace snarled, making them wait for the revelation. "Faces and eyes, gentlemen. Faces... and eyes."

The horde frowned at him, and Scapegrace realised he had lost track of his speech. Panicked, he continued. "We do what we must. We do what we can. We do what we will. We do what we... we don't do what we won't."

"Uh..." someone said.

"What will you give?" Scapegrace roared. "What will you give for one chance, *just one chance*, to say to your enemies *this far, and no further*?"

"Who are our enemies again?" someone asked.

"Are you *with* me?" Scapegrace screeched.

"Not really."

"*Are you with me?*"

"I'm with you!" Thrasher squeaked excitedly.

"*Is anyone apart from Thrasher with me?*" Scapegrace hollered. He decided it was best not to wait for an answer. "Then let's go! Let's fight! Let's show them what it means to die!"

Roaring, Scapegrace charged for the tunnel, Thrasher at his heels. After a moment, the horde started jogging after them. They ran through the darkness and the swaying light, and now some of the horde were joining in with the roars, and by the time they reached the end of the tunnel they were a charging mass of fury and violence, waiting to be loosed upon their enemies. Their feet thundered on the rocky ground, fists pumped the air, their cries turning animalistic, inhuman, a wave of death about to crash down on whoever they found in their way.

They came to a dead end and there was some jostling, and Scapegrace led them back a bit, took the first turn they came to, and the roars started up again and the thunder echoed in the caverns and Scapegrace waved his hand in the air. "Back," he said, "back. It must be the next turn," and they turned round again and charged back the way they had come.

49

THE PRE-EMPTIVE STRIKE

e crouched in the bushes with the others, all fourteen of them, black-robed and scared, watching the people come and go from the Requiem Ball. Craven refused to allow his own fear to show through. Great leaders did not get scared, after all. Plus, he had an advantage that none of the others did – he had the White Cleaver to protect him should anything go wrong.

"This is highly dangerous," Cleric Solus whispered. "We must leave now. If they find us—"

"We are done discussing this," Craven snapped. "I have made my decision, Solus. You will obey."

"You are not the High Priest," Solus said.

"Do you wish to test me? Do you wish to test my resolve? You say we are surrounded by the enemy. I say we have the enemy right where we want them."

"And how do you plan to get us inside the house?" Solus asked. "Did you happen to have the zombies steal another disc that would make the Rippers abandon their posts?"

"Of course not," Craven answered. "I have something much more rudimentary planned."

There was a gunshot from inside the house. They watched the Rippers run towards the sound. Once the path was clear, the White Cleaver led the way from the bushes to the side door of the house. Craven darted back through the trees, found her waiting there with her back to him.

"It's time," he said softly.

She turned slowly, and took down her hood, releasing her blonde hair, letting the moonlight fall across her scars. Melancholia allowed him to take her hand, and he guided her into the house behind the other Necromancers.

Once they were inside, and the music started up again in a far-away room, the White Cleaver killed two Rippers and four guests, and the only sound was the soft splatter of blood on walls. The bodies were hidden and they continued on, Craven keeping Melancholia close to him as they moved.

They found the cellar empty. Craven led them down the steps, three Necromancers remaining behind, dressed in ill-fitting tuxedos. They were Temple-born and got nervous easily, but all they had to do was stop anyone from entering. Even *they* couldn't mess that up.

The cellar was filled with glorious darkness. The caves were beneath them, and provided a last-resort exit in the unlikely event of things going disastrously wrong. There was a secret door somewhere in here, he knew, but it was so well disguised it would take a less intelligent man weeks to find. But Craven had all the angles covered. He took a stone from his robes, gave it to Adrienna Shade.

"Walk with this held close to the ground," he instructed her. "When it glows blue, tell me."

"Yes, Your Eminence," she said, and did as she was told.

Amid the junk that had been collected in the cellar, there was an old table upon which Melancholia sat. She closed her eyes and breathed, preparing herself for what was to come. Craven considered it best to leave her alone. He turned to find Solus looking at him.

"*Your Eminence?*" Solus said, mocking. "Is that how we address you now? You're a Cleric, Vandameer. The same as me."

"Be careful, Cleric Solus," Craven said. "The last man to question me like you do was Solomon Wreath, who then tried to assassinate me. If you continue to act like him, I might start to fear for my life. And then the White Cleaver would be forced into action."

At the mention of the Cleaver, Solus's face went slack. To cover his fear, he nodded to Shade. "And what do you have her doing? Walking around with a stone?"

"Below us," Craven said patiently, "the zombies are standing at the secret door, having made their way through the caves. Once the stone comes into close proximity with its twin, in the possession of the zombies, it will glow. In the case of an emergency, therefore, we know where to blast through in order to make our escape."

"It's still reckless," Solus said, but speaking without gusto. "If they find us here, all our plans will be for nought."

"No matter where the Death Bringer is when she initiates the Passage," said Craven, "the Sanctuary forces will converge on her. They may even stop her before the Passage is complete. We can't risk that. All my plans have been born out of necessity. We needed someone to tip them off as to our whereabouts, so Melancholia told Wreath he was in danger. We needed to make them think Melancholia was dead, so I killed her reflection before any seasoned sorcerer could get a good look at her. We need to take out our enemies before the Passage begins, so we come to *them*, and allow the Death Bringer to use her wonderful new talents to snatch their lives away. No fighting. No violence. No chance of defeat. I have thought of

everything, Cleric Solus. All you need to do is trust me. So I ask –
do you trust me?"

The White Cleaver stepped beside Craven, and Solus swallowed
thickly.

"I trust you," he said.

"You trust me...?"

Solus cleared his throat. "I trust you, Your Eminence."

Craven smiled. "I thought you might."

50

CHINA'S ALLY

China hated mingling, but it was a necessary evil to which she had grown both accustomed and excessively proficient in. Even without her ability to make people fall in love with her, she could charm a room as easily as shrugging. A little light laugh, a touch on the arm, a lingering look, the right words at the right time, they could all get her what she wanted, providing she had an agenda she wished to fulfil.

And tonight, she had such an agenda.

The drawback of being notorious, as China could well attest, was the ripple effect. When she had been at the peak of her notoriety, she could walk into any room and every head would turn and every conversation would grow quiet. Hushed whispers would spread outwards from the epicentre, ensuring that everyone would know where she was and who she was talking with.

Even as little as ten years ago, China would have had that effect on this room. But thanks to a growing, and somewhat puzzling, aura of respectability that had surrounded her lately, this year the Most Notorious honour went to Eliza Scorn.

China drifted from conversation to dance to anecdote, always with Eliza in sight, keeping note of who she spoke to and, just as importantly, who she ignored. Gallow had promised to furnish China with the list of benefactors, but he was running late.

"China," a deep voice rumbled behind her. Frightening Jones was a large man with ebony skin who fitted into his tuxedo exceedingly well. "Always a pleasure," he said, bowing slightly.

"Frightening," China replied, "how good to see you again. The last time I saw you, you were trying to kill me."

"I doubt I would have posed much of a threat to one such as you, China, even with a Remnant inside me."

"You flatterer," China said, manoeuvring slightly so that she kept Eliza in view. "But you're quite right. I almost killed you, in fact. It was only your ex-girlfriend who stopped me."

He raised an eyebrow. "Tanith? How is she? Have you heard anything?"

"Nothing at all," China said, doing her best to sound as if she was sad about that. "She's on the run with that dreadful Texan. You should talk to Ghastly about it – he'd know much more than I."

"Ah," Frightening said, looking uncomfortable, "maybe later. Elder Bespoke is a busy man."

China smiled, amused. "And you're sure it has nothing to do with you being in love with the same woman?"

"In love, perhaps, but at different times, and that's the important part. My love for Tanith has faded somewhat since we parted, so I now only have a deep, deep affection for her. Ghastly, however, is neck deep in love."

"I will never understand the taste of certain otherwise intelligent men."

"You don't approve of Tanith, I take it?"

"I never have. She's always been too... brash for my liking."

"Some people like brash."

"And they are welcome to it."

"Of course," Frightening said with a smile, "some people like other things as well."

China laughed. "I admire your audacity, Frightening. It is completely wasted on me, but I admire it nonetheless."

A pale, fleshy hand clamped on to Frightening's shoulder – not an easy task, as the owner of that hand had to reach up to do it. "Frightening!" boomed Quintin Strom, lurching slightly into him, "aren't you going to introduce me to your beautiful friend?"

Frightening sighed. "Elder Strom, you already know China Sorrows."

"I know I do," the British Elder grinned, "but it never hurts to make a second first impression. Hello, Miss Sorrows, you are looking ravishing tonight." He was, quite clearly, drunk.

"Elder Strom," China said, nodding politely. "How have you been? I have heard no scandal about you at all in the past few years."

"Because I've been behaving myself!" Strom laughed. "It hasn't been easy, but I've been keeping out of trouble. Unlike yourself, my dear. For someone who is apparently neutral, you find yourself fighting by the Skeleton Detective's side an awful lot. Is there something I should know? Should every man in this room be jealous?"

Frightening sighed, smiled at China and backed away, leaving her to cope with Strom alone.

"There's no need for friends to ever be jealous," she told him.

He clasped her hand in his. "And what of those who could be more than friends?"

"My darling Quintin," China said, "you will always be very special to me. A very special friend, with a very special wife. Where is she, by the way?"

Strom shrugged. "Somewhere over there. We have an understanding."

"That must be wonderful for you both," China said, realising she'd lost sight of Scorn. Her phone rang, and she disentangled herself from Strom's hand. "Excuse me for just a moment."

"It's me," Gallow said when she answered. "I have her list. Twelve people, most of whom should be with you right now."

China smiled tightly at Strom and walked away from him, speaking quietly. "Where are you?"

"Parked in the woods to the north-east of the house. I can't get any nearer without setting off the alarms."

"Stay there," China ordered. "I'll be with you in a few minutes."

She paused to check around her, making sure Scorn wasn't anywhere about. Then she slipped by the Rippers at the door and walked quickly between the rows of cars, sticking to the shadows as much as possible. Her shoes, magnificently elegant though they were, had not been designed for walking across gravel, and were totally unsuited to walking across grass or, indeed, through woodland. But China had grace, and poise, and where a lesser woman would already have toppled, China remained upright. The real trick, of course, was to make it look effortless, even when there was no one around to appreciate it.

She cracked twigs and speared leaves with virtually every step, and there were certain kinds of branches that only wanted to snag her dress as she passed. She stepped from the treeline into a clearing. Gallow's car sat quiet and dark, and China was already scowling as she approached. She banged her fist on the passenger side window. She doubted it would give Gallow a scare, but she had to at least make the effort after walking all this way. She opened the door and stooped to get in, froze when she realised Gallow wasn't moving. She took a breath, bent lower. Gallow's chin was resting on his chest. The upper half of his head was sitting on his lap.

There was a note on the dashboard, illuminated by a strip of moonlight. *Too late, sweetie.*

China stayed where she was. If anyone was sneaking up behind her, they weren't making a sound. If anyone was watching from the trees, they weren't making a move. She straightened up slowly. If this was a trap, then she was already at a disadvantage, and she wasn't going to make things any better by losing her composure.

Her heart was beating so fast and so loud she swore it was audible. Resisting the urge to spin round, she smoothed down her dress and turned. No one jumped out at her. Back through the trees, back the way she had come, she could see the lights of the house. A house filled with sorcerers who didn't exactly trust her, perhaps, but it was still a refuge. Skulduggery and Valkyrie were there, and Ghastly and Ravel. She would be safe there. At least she'd be able to see who was going to attack.

But if the roles had been reversed and it had been China who had planned this trap, then she would be lying in wait somewhere along that trail. Lure the prey in, scare the prey, and attack when the prey tries to run to safety. An ambush as simple as it was effective. Her options were clear. Take the quickest route out of the woods and probably run right into the attack, or turn and go the other way. Deeper into the woods.

Neither option appealed to her, but as much as she despised the idea of walking for an hour in these shoes to get away from an attacker who may not even be there, she despised the idea of having her head cut off even more.

So she quelled her pride, turned, and stalked away through the trees.

51

FLIRTING DISASTROUSLY

eople were dancing and chatting, talking business and politics and history, drinking wine and champagne and toasting fallen comrades. The house had been transformed from the quiet, safe place that Valkyrie came to when she needed respite to a glamorous ballroom of extravagance. As much as she appreciated the change, there was a part of her that couldn't wait for the people to clear out and normality to return.

She waited until Gordon's latest audience had moved away, and then she approached him before anyone else had a chance. "Enjoying yourself?" she asked.

"Immensely," Gordon said, beaming when he saw her. "I'd never met most of these people when I was alive, but I'd heard about them. I'd heard all the stories, all the legends. Some of these people, quite literally, saved the world."

"Pretty impressive."

He arched an eyebrow at her. "Don't be sarcastic."

"I'm not," she laughed.

"For someone like you, who actually *has* saved the world, such a feat might lose some of its romance. But for me, a dead writer who just *wrote* about these things? It is still quite remarkable."

"And humbling?"

"Well, maybe not humbling. I'd like to see any of these people write a best-selling novel. *Then* I'd be impressed."

"Are you getting any ideas for more books?"

"My head is filled with ideas. If I weren't hosting this shindig, I'd be composing words right this second. I swear, I haven't talked to this many fascinating people since I made a surprise appearance at my fan club meeting. Do you think they're enjoying it? Is there enough wine?"

"There's plenty of wine, and those little canopies are lovely."

"Canapés, my dear."

"They're a bit small, though."

"They're meant to be small."

"They'd be more satisfying if they were bigger."

"I think you're slightly missing the point of canapés."

"But all in all, yeah, everyone seems to be enjoying themselves."

"I thought I'd find you here," Skulduggery said, walking over. "I assume your detective instincts kicked in and you were going to ask your uncle about those men with the guns...?"

"Of course," Valkyrie nodded. "Gordon. The morons in the masks. How did they get in?"

"Ah," Gordon said, his face clouding, "now that I do not know. As you can imagine, there aren't many catering companies who specialise in events like this, but I was assured every person working tonight was discreet and had experience. I've had someone trying to get through to the planner, but no luck so far."

Valkyrie shrugged at Skulduggery. "I have been unable to find a clue."

"You're a wonderful detective," he sighed. "Are you ready for Round Two? There are still plenty of people who want to meet you."

"There's more?" she whined. "But my face is tired from smiling."

"I never said you had to smile. I never smile."

"You're a skeleton. You're always smiling."

"Not inside. Inside it's a scowl. I think there are also one or two young men who would like to ask you to dance. And now that you're not with Fletcher any more..."

She narrowed her eyes. "What young men?"

"You were talking to both of them a few minutes ago. Hidalgo Bolt and Geraint Mizzle."

"Really? Hidalgo? He's kind of cute, I suppose. And when you say young men... what ages are they?"

"Hidalgo is, I don't know... He might be in his fifties."

She stepped back. "Oh gross!"

Skulduggery's head tilted. "Charming. Geraint's younger, if that's any use to you. He's in his twenties."

"That the lanky guy with the frizzy hair? He didn't exactly come across as overly confident, did he? Or co-ordinated. How'd he get an invitation?"

"He didn't. His mother brought him. She wants me to help set you up with him."

Valkyrie glared. "Don't you dare."

"I happen to think that you'd get on very well with Geraint. I doubt he'd speak much, which would suit you down to the ground because then you can just talk without fear of interruption."

"Oh, I'm not denying that, on paper, he sounds like my perfect man, but there is no way in hell that's going to happen. Tell his mummy no."

"She'll be heartbroken."

"I don't care."

"She had such high hopes for you two."

"Stop joking about this, I swear to God."

"Gordon, what do you think? You think she should at least dance with Geraint?"

"What harm could it do?" Gordon asked.

"Great harm," Valkyrie said. "Huge harm. Let's face it, if he dances with me when I'm wearing this dress and looking like this, he's going to fall in love with me."

Gordon laughed, and clapped his hands. "Yes, he is, my dear."

"I don't mean to be cocky," she said, "but it's inevitable, right?"

Skulduggery nodded. "Can't argue with you there."

"And the fact is, I don't need another guy telling me how great I am. I know how great I am. I'm me. And, to be honest, I'm finding it fairly weird that you're suggesting this so casually when the guy is, like, ten years older than I am. Aren't you supposed to be advising me *against* older men?"

"This is very true," Gordon said. "And you're absolutely right. This Geraint is far too old. You're to stay away from that boy."

Valkyrie frowned. "And now suddenly he seems so much hotter."

"Typical teenage girl," Skulduggery said, "wanting what she can't have."

"So now *you're* saying I can't have him? My God, Geraint Mizzle is the hottest guy I've ever known."

Skulduggery swept his hand towards the crowd. "Then go to him. Dance and fall in love."

"Ah," she said, shrugging, "maybe later."

Hansard Kray came over, nodding to all of them. Valkyrie found herself standing a little straighter. "Pardon the interruption," he said.

"Not at all," Gordon replied, grinning. "Having a good night, are we? Do you like the music? It's certainly music made to be danced to, isn't it?"

Valkyrie glared at Gordon, but he ignored her.

"It is," Hansard said, "and the night has been wonderful, thank you very much for inviting us. I was wondering, though, if any of you had seen my father."

Gordon looked more disappointed than Valkyrie actually felt. "Oh," he said. "No, I'm sorry, I haven't."

"He's had too much to drink," Hansard said, blushing slightly. "I'm afraid he might be wandering the house, insulting anyone he meets." He looked at Valkyrie. "I do apologise for the things he said. Please know that if you *had* hit him, I would have understood."

She smiled. "That's good to know. I could help you look for him, if you want."

"You would?" he said, relieved. "Oh, thank you very much. If you could search those rooms over there, I'll search these rooms over here, and between us we should find him."

He smiled again, and hurried off. Valkyrie frowned.

"I never thought I'd see the day," Skulduggery said. "A boy who can resist the charms of Valkyrie Cain."

"Shut up," she growled, walking off. He followed.

"He's seventeen, you know," he said. "From what I can gather, a thoroughly nice lad."

"I don't care."

"I don't know much about him, not really. His family keeps to themselves."

"That's nice." They walked from room to room.

"From what little I do know, however, he *does* like girls, if that's what you're worried about."

"I'm not worried about it. Why should I be worried about it? I don't even care. I don't even know the guy. Why are you so intent on setting me up with someone all of a sudden? Haven't I made enough of a mess of this kind of thing already?"

"You have," Skulduggery conceded. "But everyone needs a hobby."

They moved towards raised voices, sliding through the gathered onlookers to see Arthur Dagan pinned to the ground by a small man with glasses.

"Caste," Skulduggery said, "let him up."

The small man shook his head. "Every time I let him up he flings himself at someone else."

"I'll kill you!" Arthur warbled, his face smushed into the floor. "I'll kill you all!"

"I'll take responsibility for him," Skulduggery said. "Let him up, if you would."

Caste sighed, and stood away. Arthur struggled to his hands and knees.

"Before you stand," Skulduggery said, "know this. If you attack anyone, I'll call in the Rippers. They'll lock you up for the night and they won't be gentle about it. When you stand, we will escort you to your car, and then your son can drive you home. If you agree to this, stand. If you don't, you may as well lie back down."

Arthur glared, then stood. "Very well," he said. "But I can walk to my car without your assistance." He swayed dangerously, and Skulduggery took his arm before he fell. "Unhand me!"

"Don't be stupid," Skulduggery said. Valkyrie walked on Arthur's other side as they moved to the front of the house, but didn't help. She didn't think he'd appreciate it.

"The Requiem Ball," Arthur said, spitting out the words. "Just another excuse to meet up and be smug and superior. If we had won, we wouldn't hold a gloating party."

"If you had won," said Skulduggery, "we'd all be dead, yourself included."

"You don't know what you're talking about. You're a heathen."

"I was closer to the Faceless Ones than you could ever hope to be, Arthur. I was trapped with them for almost a year, and do you know what I learned in that year? That your gods are just as petty and spiteful and small as anyone I've ever met."

"Your bones will burn for your insolence!" Arthur said, outraged. He tugged his arm free, would have toppled were it not for Valkyrie. He recoiled from her touch, and sneered. "And you, the god-killer. How do you think you'd fare against the Faceless Ones without the Sceptre of the Ancients, eh? Do you think it would be quite so easy to murder them now that your weapon has been destroyed?"

"No," she said, frowning at him. "Obviously not."

"The Dark Gods shall rise again," Arthur promised loudly, and vomited. Both Valkyrie and Skulduggery pulled away instantly.

"Aw," Arthur said, looking down at himself.

"You're disgusting," Valkyrie told him.

"I don't feel well," Arthur said, and burped.

Skulduggery's hand closed around Arthur's upper arm, and he shepherded him out into the night air.

"You found him!" Hansard said, running up behind.

The valet brought the car round, and Skulduggery and Hansard managed to bundle Arthur in. "We will have our revenge," Arthur vowed from the back seat.

"Not tonight you won't," Skulduggery said, slamming the door.

Hansard stood and shook his head. "I knew it would be a mistake coming here," he said. "But my father said it was important. He said we had to attend. It's probably an honour thing or something. Although he doesn't *look* very honourable right now."

Valkyrie peered at Arthur through the window, and winced. "I think he threw up again."

"Typical," Hansard said. "Well, thank you both for your help." He shook Skulduggery's hand, then Valkyrie's. "I hope to see you again."

"I'd like that," Valkyrie smiled.

"Until next time," Hansard said, "when hopefully, you won't have my father's vomit in your hair."

Valkyrie's eyes widened and she dropped her head forward, saw a strand of hair with something dripping off it, and shrieked. Skulduggery quickly passed her a handkerchief. She wrapped it around the strand and scrubbed, then she flung the handkerchief to the ground and flicked her hair away from her face. When she looked up, Hansard was already driving away.

She glared at Skulduggery. "You could have told me!"

"I was waiting for a good time."

"There is never a good time to tell a girl she has sick in her hair!"

"And that is what I learned tonight," he said, nodding.

Valkyrie looked at the departing tail lights. "Whenever he thinks of me," she moaned, "this is what he'll think of. He won't think of me totally owning this dress. He'll think of me with sick in my hair."

"What does it matter to you?" Skulduggery asked. "You don't care, do you? You don't even know him."

"Don't use my words against me," she grumbled. "I hate when you do that."

52

ALL FALL DOWN

Melancholia opened her eyes. "I'm ready," she said.

Craven took a moment to appear serene, and nodded. "Kill them without pain," he said gently. "They are not our enemies, not really. They are merely ignorant. Kill them, take their lives, grow ever stronger. Then the Passage can begin."

She lowered her head. Craven made sure that when he stepped behind another Necromancer, he did so very discreetly. If the others thought that he was even the slightest bit wary of Melancholia's new ability, they could lose faith in his leadership.

"I can feel them above us," Melancholia murmured. "Almost three hundred lives. So, so bright."

Craven managed to get to the far side of the cellar, and stayed by the steps. If he saw any Necromancer in this room fall, he was ready to bolt.

"There are others outside," Melancholia continued, "but I'm leaving them for now."

"Focus on taking the lives of the people in the house," Craven called over. "And try not to kill our own people upstairs." He said that with a smile, but his insides were fluttering.

Melancholia took a deep breath.

Ghastly saw someone in the crowd and frowned. He moved to her, took hold of her arm, turned her so he could see her face. "What are you doing here?"

"Mingling," Eliza Scorn replied, smiling. "I'm not allowed to mingle?"

"I wasn't aware you were on the guest list."

"I'm owed favours," she said. "And I have friends. I have so many friends. I even have friends that you think are *your* friends. Are you having a good night?"

"You should leave."

"But the party's just getting…"

She stopped talking, frowned and swayed, and Ghastly's vision dimmed. All around him people were dropping. Scorn fell and Ghastly's strength left him, the ground came up to meet him and then everything went dark.

Melancholia sighed. She kept her eyes closed and didn't say anything. She didn't have to. Craven and everyone else in the room could feel the death seeping down towards them.

"Magnificent," somebody breathed, and Craven had to agree. To experience the sudden death of that many people in the same instant was a rare treat — but one that would soon be dwarfed into insignificance by the death of half of the world's population.

"Now," Craven said, "we're ready for the Passage."

Broad smiles broke out, and laughter. Hands were shaken and backs were slapped. A joyous occasion, indeed. The culmination of everything they had worked for their entire lives. Craven barged through them, back to Melancholia. It was important to be seen close to her at a time like this. Such things are remembered, after all. Who was standing next to whom. Who gave the orders. Who took the credit.

Before he got to her, he heard running footsteps, then one of the Necromancers he had posted outside the door appeared at the top of the stairs. "Rippers!" he cried. "They're coming!"

"Hold them off!" Craven shouted, chopping an invisible line

across the basement with his hand, then sweeping it forward. "Go! Hold them off!"

The Necromancers on the losing side of the invisible line stared at him, wide-eyed.

"I command it!" he roared.

They looked at each other, and then one of them moved, and then another, and then they were rushing up the stairs to their deaths.

Once they were out, he slammed the door after them, catching a glimpse of his brethren, their shadows hesitant and wavering, stumbling towards the sickle-waving Rippers. He locked the door to their screams, and half-stumbled down the steps.

Six Necromancers remained down here, plus the White Cleaver and Craven himself, all looking towards Melancholia, who sat with her head down, the hood covering her face, making it impossible for Craven to judge her mood. If any kind of a pattern had emerged, her mental instability would have grown along with her power, and he didn't want to be on the receiving end the next time she lashed out. He motioned to the Necromancer nearest him.

"Solus," he said. "Make sure the Death Bringer is able to stand."

Solus stared at him. "Me?"

"Do not make me repeat my instructions," Craven said tartly, making sure he stood beside the White Cleaver.

Solus hesitated, then took a step, and another, until he stood before Melancholia.

"Um," he said. "Death Bringer? Are you, uh… Are you OK? Do you need anything?"

Melancholia didn't look up. Outside the door, there were more screams and howls of pain.

"Only," Solus continued, "we don't have an awful lot of time, and… and we really need you to initiate the Passage at your earliest convenience."

"Are you telling me what to do?" came Melancholia's soft voice from beneath the hood.

Craven watched Solus go pale. "No," he whispered. "I'd never presume to…" His words failed him, and he stood there, and a tear actually rolled down his cheek.

Melancholia's shoulders rose and fell in a weary sigh. "Oh, Solus," she said.

"Please don't kill me," Solus said.

Melancholia stood up slowly. "But your death will add to my strength."

"Please, I want to stay alive."

"You're a Necromancer. You're meant to embrace death."

"I… I don't embrace it… I'm scared of it…"

"I know you are. I know you all are. Which tells me that none of you truly understands." She took her hood down, and when

504

she opened her eyes to look at the gathered Necromancers, they were glowing red. "You're hypocrites. All of you. You talk of the stream of life and death, you talk of the beauty of it. But the true beauty is to become part of it, to flow from this existence into the next. Yet the Passage is meant to block the stream. Why?"

Craven forced himself to step forward and inject some authority into his voice. "Melancholia," he said, hoping no one noticed how high-pitched he sounded, "these are philosophical discussions best left to the scholars in the classrooms. You have fulfilled your potential at such a young age that you have not yet had the opportunity to see these arguments resolved. Therefore, you must trust in our judgement and wisdom that this course of action is best for everyone."

Melancholia smiled at him. "And yet, Cleric Craven, I do not trust in your judgement *or* your wisdom."

The strength flowed from Craven's legs, but by some miracle he remained upright.

"The Passage is an idea concocted by the small-minded," Melancholia continued. "The great irony is that the sorcerers who fear death the most are the sorcerers who claim to understand it the fullest. The Necromancer Order is an Order of hypocrisy and fear and ignorance. You have no right to speak of death the way you do, because you so obviously cling to stale ideas of immortality. Truly, I feel sad for you."

Craven felt the eyes of every Necromancer on him, but he couldn't speak. His mouth was dry and his tongue was far too thick to form words.

"Which leaves me with a problem," Melancholia said. "I have all this power, but nothing to do with it."

"You must initiate the Passage," Solus said. A shadow snaked up behind him and skewered him through the neck. He fell, gurgling blood. Melancholia didn't even look round.

"The Passage will destroy the stream," she said, "and I have no wish to banish death. All I want to do is share it with as many people as I can."

Craven frowned. "What?"

"Once you experience it, you will understand. This is not something you can learn about in old books. It's not something you can comprehend through philosophical debate. You need to become part of the stream. All of you."

Craven backed away. "Us?"

"You. Everyone for miles around. Maybe even the whole country. And when this country is dead, I'll move to the next. I'll bring death to everyone. Then you'll see how beautiful it really is."

Craven was so scared that he was actually relieved when the door burst open and the Rippers stormed in.

Three Necromancers panicked so much they found themselves charging towards the sickle-wielding maniacs. Swift swishes of those long blades cut them down mid-step, with only one of them having the time to make a sound. Craven grabbed the White Cleaver, pushed him towards them.

"Save me!" he screeched. "Protect me!"

The White Cleaver needed no further instruction. He dived into their midst, his scythe flashing.

Craven stumbled back with Adrienna Shade, doing his best to keep her in front of him. Melancholia strode across the floor to them, smiling.

"Shall we depart?" she asked, her hands on their arms, and the shadows swirled around them and then they were in darkness and gloom, away from the sounds of fighting. They were down below, in the caves. Shade tore herself from Melancholia's touch, turned and ran. Melancholia laughed and sent a shadow to slice through her back. Shade collapsed and Melancholia smiled at Craven. "You're not going to run from me, are you?"

"No," Craven managed to say.

"I need somewhere quiet if I want to kill a country, and I need someone to look out for me while I do it."

"I'd... I'd be honoured. But we need to keep moving. There are creatures down here who feed on magic, and if the Rippers find us..."

"I wouldn't worry about the Rippers or the monsters," she laughed. "If I were you, I'd worry about Skulduggery Pleasant."

Craven stared at her. "He isn't dead?"

"Oh, he's dead, but it's the same dead as always. He and Valkyrie weren't in the crowd when I took all those lives. I'd say they're looking for us as we speak. Come."

She turned, led the way through the tunnel.

She was going to kill him. There was no way round it – Melancholia was going to kill him, and she wasn't trying to hide it. Craven knew what his options were. He could run, but he doubted he'd get very far, or he could fight, but that option scared him even more than running. He knew what Solomon Wreath would do in his place. He would bide his time, wait until Melancholia was distracted, and then he'd attack. It would be short, sharp and brutal. She'd be dead before she knew what had happened. That's what Wreath would do, and he wouldn't hesitate, either. He'd have that assurance he was always so good at wielding.

Craven didn't have that level of assurance, though. He was afraid he'd panic, misjudge the attack, or miss the moment. And then what would happen? She'd turn to him, laugh at his pathetic attempt, and with a casual flick of the wrist, she'd tear him apart.

His eyes came to rest on the back of Melancholia's head as she walked. If Wreath was with him, it would have been over by now. Melancholia would be lying dead on the ground, and they'd go back to looking for a Death Bringer they could control. But Craven was alone, and it was up to him to save himself. He raised his hands, feeling the power in his amulet ready to burst forth. His tongue slid over his dry lips. The ground levelled off and Melancholia walked in a straight line, like she was inviting him to try it.

What if she *was* inviting him? And what if he missed?

Head pounding in his chest, Craven lowered his trembling hands. He couldn't risk it. He couldn't risk making the attempt and failing. He couldn't risk angering her. For all he knew, maybe she'd decided that she needed him around to look out for her. Maybe she wasn't going to kill him after all.

Melancholia looked at him over her shoulder, and he saw the smile on her lips and in her eyes, which were still glowing with that deep, deep red.

53

THE DEATH BRINGER RISES

They had come when they'd heard Gordon shouting for help. Skulduggery had leaped over fallen bodies, Valkyrie right behind him. They burst into the ballroom. All around them, the guests lay on the floor, silent and unmoving.

The ring was so cold on Valkyrie's finger that it almost burned. "They're dead," she whispered.

"They just fell," Gordon said, from the far side of the room. His eyes were wide, his voice hollow. "They were standing and talking and laughing and then they... they stiffened, and breathed out, and fell."

Valkyrie frowned. "Melancholia?"

"She's not dead," Skulduggery murmured, and then his head tilted to the people around them. "Which means neither are they."

"What?"

"She sucked their lives from them, drank those lives in, used them to make her stronger. If we can get to her before she wastes that strength, we can force her to return those lives to their owners."

"That'll work?"

Skulduggery raised his hands, fingers flexing. "In theory."

Valkyrie's breath became a cloud in the air. "What are you doing?"

"Cooling things down," Skulduggery said. "Their life forces won't do them a whole lot of good if we allow their brains to die. You have a change of clothes, I expect?"

She hugged herself as the temperature plummeted. Particles of frost began to glisten on the faces around her. "In the Bentley."

He threw her the keys. "You might want to hurry."

She nodded, backed off, turned and ran.

There was a commotion. Rippers had run in from outside, congregating at the door to the basement. Valkyrie ran past, out of the house, kicking off her shoes and unlocking the Bentley with a beep. The boot opened and she grabbed her trousers from her bag, pulled them on under her dress, buckled them, pulled on her socks and boots. She searched for the zip on her dress, cursing, yanking the whole thing round her body till she found it. She whipped the dress off, stuffed it into the trunk, couldn't find her T-shirt so she just grabbed her jacket, put it on as she ran back to the house. It was freezing in there, so cold it actually made her hesitate. She zipped up her jacket as Skulduggery walked from the room beside her, and he joined her as she ran for the basement.

They passed three bloodied bodies, and Skulduggery went first down the steps. Dead Necromancers and Rippers covered the floor like a carpet. The White Cleaver stood half-crouched, his back to the wall, his scythe swinging. The remaining Rippers had him surrounded.

"A girl," Skulduggery said, ignoring the Cleaver situation as he started turning over bodies, "blonde, scars on her face. Is she here?"

The Rippers didn't answer.

"She's not here," Valkyrie said, running her eyes over the upturned faces. "Neither is Craven. If she shadow-walked, she could be anywhere up to two kilometres in any direction."

Skulduggery picked a stone up off the floor. He was quiet for a moment. "They're in the caves," he said, dropping it. "They had someone down there already, searching for the other side of the entrance. If they shadow-walked anywhere, they'd have shadow-walked down there." He went to the wall, removed the brick and twisted the key behind it. A section of the floor rumbled and opened. Valkyrie followed him to the stone steps, looked back at the Rippers.

"Any of you coming?" she asked, but they didn't move.

"They're not Cleavers," Skulduggery said, already halfway down the steps. "They're mercenaries. They were paid to provide security, not chase after people. Their job is everything above ground – which means the White Cleaver."

The Rippers paid her no attention. They started to close in on the White Cleaver, and Valkyrie left them to it. She hurried down the steps as the floor closed above. "They didn't do a very good job at providing security," she pointed out to the back of Skulduggery's head. "Everyone's *dead*."

"True enough," he said.

They emerged into the caves. A Necromancer woman lay dead before them – proof, if any was needed, that they were on the right track. They summoned flames into their hands and ran.

Valkyrie had been down here before, and each time she'd been lucky to escape with her life. The tunnels twisted into each other, opened out into vast, empty spaces and closed down into the narrowest of gaps. Travellers needed to respect the caves as much as any adversary – a wrong turn could lead to a step off a precipice and a long fall into cold darkness. And that was before the creatures down here were taken into account.

Skulduggery slowed, and she did the same. They extinguished

their flames, letting their way be lit by the shafts of silver light that worked their way down from the surface.

"We're waiting," called a voice, echoing playfully towards them.

Skulduggery grunted, and they stood up straight and walked forward. They emerged from the tunnel to stand atop a gentle slope that led ten feet down to the cavern floor. On the other side of the cavern stood Melancholia and Vandameer Craven.

"Now this is funny," Melancholia continued. Her eyes were red. "We were hurrying along, Vandameer and I, and a thought struck me. Why am I doing this? Why am I running? I can understand why Vandameer runs – he's a weakling who's afraid of practically everything you'd care to mention. But me? Who do I have to run from? So I stopped running, and turned, and look who appears…"

"Melancholia," Skulduggery said, "we don't want to hurt you."

Melancholia laughed. Her laugh echoed. "You actually believe you can stop me? The two of you? I killed three hundred of the world's most powerful sorcerers in the blink of an uncaring eye. What makes you think, even for a moment, that I won't snuff out your weak, flickering flames just as quickly?"

"Because," Skulduggery said, "to do that, you need a moment or two of concentration. And we don't plan on giving you that."

Melancholia laughed again. "You seem to know a lot about my powers, skeleton."

"Well, I should. I was the Death Bringer before you were even born."

"I'm not sure I get the joke."

"No joke," Skulduggery said. "I was Lord Vile."

Valkyrie could see Craven's frown from where she stood. "What are you talking about? We saw you and Vile in the same room!"

"That wasn't Vile," Valkyrie told them. "That was Vile's armour."

"I'm the real thing," Skulduggery said. "So I know exactly what I'm talking about, Melancholia, because my powers were just like yours – except I came by mine naturally."

"You're lying."

"You can reach out with your mind, can't you? You can sense the life around you, and you can reach for it. It's like a bubble that keeps expanding and then, when you release, the bubble withdraws and drags all that life back to you, leaving the bodies to fall behind."

"It's a death bubble," Valkyrie said.

"Don't call it that," said Skulduggery.

She frowned at him. "Well, what *do* you call it?"

Skulduggery hesitated.

"See?" Valkyrie said. "Death bubble."

"Shut up," Melancholia said. She narrowed her red eyes at Skulduggery. "You were Vile? But you're an Elemental."

"As it turned out, I was what some people call magically ambidextrous. It's rare. It's exceedingly rare, in fact, and I didn't even know it myself until after it happened. But during the war I got… lost. I was consumed by the endless battles and bloodshed, the terrible things I saw and the terrible things I did. I waded in blood and I emerged as… something different. Some*one* different. I put on the armour and found I had a real flair for Necromancy.

"I shouldn't have been surprised, I suppose. I had always been good with death. Pretty soon, they were proclaiming me to be the Death Bringer – and yet they wouldn't tell me what the Passage actually entailed, other than it would save the world. They were talking about immortality. But I had no interest in saving the world. I had no interest in helping weak men and women live for ever. I wanted sudden and violent death for everyone. That's why I joined Mevolent. Finally, I thought, someone who shares my appetite for destruction. I didn't believe that the Faceless Ones were real, and even if they were I certainly didn't believe he'd be able to bring them back, but a part of me hoped that he would. Because then I'd be able to kill an entire race of gods, after I was finished with people."

"You," Melancholia said, "are a dark, dark man."

"Aren't I just?"

"So why didn't you kill us all?" Craven asked.

"I simply came to my senses. Do you know, do you have any *idea*, how many people I killed when I called myself Lord Vile? I don't. But it was a lot. I killed whole battlefields. All that violent death, so tinged with fear and panic… it made me so, so strong. I could have cracked this world wide open. But I didn't. One day, I just stopped. I walked deep inside a mountain, took off the armour, and I've been trying to make up for it ever since. I never will, of course. Such redemption is well beyond me at this stage. But I try. And stopping people like you, Melancholia, is how I try."

"So you *do* think you can stop me."

"I don't want to fight you. I want you to give the people above us back their lives."

"I'm the Death Bringer, not the Life Giver."

"You're neither, actually. You're not even close to being as strong as I was. But you can still release the energy you stole from them."

Melancholia smirked. "And they'll just return to life as if nothing happened?"

"Their energy will seek them out, yes."

"You're sure of this?"

"Relatively sure."

"And why would I ever want to release this energy?"

"Because if you don't, we will fight you and we will kill you, and then the energy will return to them anyway."

Melancholia shrugged. "Then let's fight and see what happens."

"You can still do the right thing."

"Do you want to attack first, or will I?"

Skulduggery held up a finger. "Do you mind if I confer with my colleague for a moment?"

"By all means."

Skulduggery leaned in towards Valkyrie. "Damn," he whispered. "She's not going to do the right thing."

"Did you really think she would?"

"I was really hoping."

"Can we beat her?" Valkyrie asked.

"I don't like our chances."

"What *are* our chances?"

"We don't have any," Skulduggery admitted. "Do you think you can take Craven on your own?"

"No."

"Me neither. Do you want to leave him to me, then, and you can take her?"

"I like that idea even less."

"I don't blame you."

She sighed. "We're going to get killed, aren't we?"

"It looks likely. Our only hope is a surprise attack."

"They're looking right at us."

"Dammit."

Skulduggery straightened up. "We have discussed the situation," he said to them, "and decided that it would be in everyone's best interests for me to fight you, Melancholia, and for both Cleric Craven and Valkyrie to stand back and cheer or boo as they see fit."

Valkyrie grabbed his arm. "What are you doing?"

"We can't win this," he said softly. "And I would rather not watch you getting killed alongside me."

"Well, I'm not going to watch *you* getting killed, either!"

"And yet I'm the one who said it first, so there's precious little you can do about it."

"Who made up *that* rule?"

"I did, just now."

"We accept your proposal," Melancholia called across to them. "But after I kill you, I reserve the right to kill *her*."

"By which time I shall be past caring," Skulduggery said. He slipped off his jacket. His gun hung heavy in the shoulder holster, but he didn't reach for it. He folded the jacket, pressed it into Valkyrie's arms. "Keep this as something to remember me by."

"I'm not going to just stand by and do nothing," she said through gritted teeth.

"You can, as I said, cheer my name, if you want."

"You must have *some* kind of plan, even a really bad one."

"Plans are like buses," he said. "Sometimes they just don't turn up when you need one."

He started down towards the cavern floor. "I've enjoyed our

time together, Valkyrie," he said over his shoulder. "You are quite a remarkable girl."

There were a hundred things she needed to say to him, needed to tell him, needed him to know. There were a thousand words she needed to speak, needed to whisper, needed him to hear. But she stayed quiet, and watched him descend. She'd tell him afterwards. When all this was done, when they'd saved the day and were joking about it on the drive home, that's when she'd tell him. They had time. No matter how scared she was for him right now, they always had time.

He reached the cavern floor, and Melancholia floated down on a gentle wave of shadows. They faced each other.

"I'm going to enjoy this," she said.

"I dare say I'm not," Skulduggery responded.

He strode towards her and she smiled, and her eyes glowed brighter, and he stiffened. His gloved hands fell from his wrists, and the bones of his arms slipped through his shirtsleeves to clatter to the rock floor. His knees buckled, his legs parting from his shoes as his body collapsed on to itself. His ribcage bulged against his shirt and his head hit the ground and rolled, the jawbone spinning away.

Valkyrie breathed out, the air emptying from her lungs. She was still and quiet and cold. She was calm. Melancholia had taken Skulduggery's soul. Without his soul, there was no magic to keep his body together. Now it was just a skeleton, just a heap of old bones. He was gone. He was gone and Melancholia had taken him from her.

Melancholia smiled. "That was easy," she said.

Valkyrie breathed in, breathed in all her pain and anger and fury. She breathed in all those things she wanted to tell him, but now never could, all those words she wanted to say, but now never would. She breathed in her strength and her horror and her loss, let it fill her, let it fill every inch of her, and then she screamed, threw Skulduggery's jacket to one side and jumped, using the air to propel her down towards Melancholia like a bullet. Melancholia laughed and flicked a hand, and the shadows rose to slam Valkyrie into the cavern ceiling. They vanished and she fell, trying to use the air to cushion her landing, but another shadow wrapped itself around her waist and yanked her sideways. A second flick of Melancholia's wrist and Valkyrie was hurled into the wall. The impact forced the breath out of her, and she dropped and lay there, gasping.

A shadow tightened around her ankle, and she groaned as she was lifted off the ground. She dangled, swaying, trying to breathe, upside down and at eye level with Melancholia.

"Such an anti-climax," Melancholia said. "Isn't it? Can't you feel it? With all the animosity between us, all those jibes, all that history… And here, right at the end, we have our final showdown and you… you are found wanting, as they say." Melancholia leaned in. "Goodnight, Valkyrie. It's been irrelevant."

The shadows rose around them, turned sharp, and Valkyrie snarled, grabbed Melancholia's hair and slammed her forehead into that smirking face. White light exploded behind her eyes, the shadows vanished and Valkyrie fell as Melancholia stumbled back, howling in pain. Valkyrie blinked, struggling to get her bearings. She managed to get to her feet, but she was so dazed she fell to one knee again. Melancholia cursed and staggered around, blood pumping from her nose. She stumbled right in front of Valkyrie and Valkyrie lunged, smashed into her, taking her to the ground. She dropped elbows and palm shots, barely able to focus, only knowing that she couldn't let up, not even to catch her breath.

"Craven!" Melancholia cried. "Get her off me!"

And still Valkyrie hit her, trying to get through the arms that Melancholia held up to protect her head. Not one thought was given to Craven. Craven wasn't important. The only important thing was to smash Melancholia into unconsciousness.

"Craven!" Melancholia screamed.

A fist of shadows collided with Valkyrie, shunting her off, sending her sprawling. Melancholia clambered to her feet as Craven hurried over.

"Are you OK?" he asked. "Is there anything I can—"

Melancholia reached out, and a tendril of darkness coiled

around Craven's neck and tightened. "You were going to leave me," she snarled, spitting blood. "You were going to let her kill me."

"No," Craven gasped.

"You wanted her to kill me, so that you wouldn't have to try and do it yourself, didn't you?"

Craven dropped to his knees, his face red, his eyes bulging.

Melancholia stood over him. "But you're too much of a coward even for that, aren't you? You couldn't take the risk that she wouldn't be able to finish me. You were terrified of what I'd do to you."

Craven was unable to speak. The only thing he could do was nod. The tendril released him and he fell forward, sucking in air.

"You'd do well to remember that fear," Melancholia said, as she turned back to Valkyrie. Blood covered her face. Her lips were split and her nose appeared to be broken.

Valkyrie got up slowly, fists clenched. She suddenly flicked her hand, grabbing shadows of her own, but Melancholia brushed them aside. Darkness curled around Valkyrie's arm and yanked the ring from her finger. It dropped to the ground and bounced, and Melancholia slammed her heel down on to it. The ring shattered, blackness flowing back into Valkyrie.

"And that," Melancholia said, "is the main flaw with Necromancy. Destroy the object and you have all that magic, but nothing to focus it with. Look at me. Do you see any reliance on an object for me? No. I am beyond all that. My body is all I need to focus my power."

"Congratulations," Valkyrie said. "But you're still going to die."

"And how do you think that's going to happen? Are you going to try hitting me, like a barbarian? That won't happen again, little girl. I underestimated your savagery, and you spoiled my good mood."

Valkyrie smiled. "You think I've spoiled your good mood? Then you're *really* going to hate him."

Melancholia frowned and turned, and saw Lord Vile striding towards her.

54

MONSTER, MURDERER

ile fired off sharpened shadows and Melancholia stumbled back, eyes wide in terror. "Help me!" she screamed.

Craven stood with his mouth open, his feet stuck to the floor.

Melancholia fell to her knees while Vile pummelled her. "Craven! Help me! Or I'll kill you!"

Craven raised his hands and Valkyrie pushed at the air, flinging him back. He went rolling across the floor and she ran in, aiming a kick at his head. He saw her coming at the last moment, covered up, taking the boot along his arms. He howled in pain and lashed out, a shard of darkness sliding uselessly across her jacket. Flame flared in her hand and she flicked it on to him. He shrieked as his robes caught fire. He tore the robes off and hurled them away, turning to face her wearing faded thermal long johns, his amulet bouncing on his chest.

"I never liked you," he sneered. "And now finally I get to—"

She flicked her hand and his amulet flew from around his neck. He cried out and reached up for it as she stepped in and rammed her elbow into his chin. His head rocked back and he was unconscious even as he was falling.

Valkyrie let the amulet drop and looked back as Vile stumbled. The shadows coiled and lashed around Melancholia's feet. She wiped the blood from her face.

"I'm not scared of you," Melancholia said. "You're only his armour, after all. You're not the *real* Lord Vile. I *killed* the real Lord Vile."

Vile sprang, but a wave caught him, sent him spinning into the wall. That little victory boosted Melancholia's confidence.

"I'm curious as to how you're still functioning without the skeleton, though," Melancholia said. "I thought he was controlling you with his mind or something. No? That's not it? You're a little more independent than that?"

Vile flung his shadows at her but she batted them down.

"Oh well," she continued, actually starting to smile now. "I suppose we'll never know. You will remain a mystery."

Shadows detached themselves from the cavern ceiling and fell like javelins. Vile didn't even see them coming. The first missed, but the second one caught him in his shoulder and kept going through his armour, impaling him to the floor. The third caught the calf of his leg. He stood there, trying to move away, trying to free himself, but the shadows were solid.

Instead of gloating, as Valkyrie fully expected her to do, Melancholia doubled over, like she was trying to catch her breath. The shadows flexed suddenly and she grimaced.

Valkyrie narrowed her eyes. "You feeling OK, Mel? You don't look too good. Do you want to lie down?"

"Stop," Melancholia hissed, "talking."

Darkness sprang from Melancholia and Valkyrie flinched, but it retracted before it hit her – retracted so violently that Melancholia stumbled.

"It's all a bit much, isn't it?" Valkyrie said. "All those powerful sorcerers you killed, their energy speeding around inside you. I bet you can feel Skulduggery, can't you? I bet you can feel him whirling around in there."

"He's gone," Melancholia said. "They're all gone."

"I think you're lying. You can feel him, can't you? Buzzing in your ear? He wants to be let out."

Darkness rammed into Valkyrie and she went backwards, barely avoiding the slashes that followed, and then the shadows snapped back to Melancholia. The Death Bringer's hands went to her head.

"Let him out," Valkyrie said.

"You don't know what you're talking about."

"Sure I do. You have his energy inside you. It's hurting you. So let it out."

Despite her obvious pain, Melancholia laughed. "What do you expect will happen if I do that? You expect the skeleton to sit up?"

"Yes, as a matter of fact I do."

Melancholia straightened, her jaw clenching. She swayed for a moment. "And what," she said tightly, "is to stop that energy from just floating away?"

"I haven't a clue," Valkyrie told her. "This is Skulduggery's idea, not mine. Once you release the energy, it all flows back to its source. He should know, right? He was Death Bringer before you, after all."

She shook her head. "You're not getting him back."

"Sure I am."

"*You're not!*" Melancholia screeched, and the shadows went wild, thrashing so hard they cracked the rocks around them.

Valkyrie smiled. "He's about to break free."

"Don't be stupid."

"You lose control one more time and he's gone."

"Don't be…"

"Skulduggery," she called. "Be right with you."

Melancholia charged forward and Valkyrie stepped back, allowing her eyes to widen, allowing fear to show. She stumbled over Skulduggery's leg, falling to the ground as Melancholia swept her arms wide, gathering shadows, and then the shadows swooped down and Valkyrie used the air to shoot sideways. The shadows hit Skulduggery's ribcage and Melancholia shrieked, ripped them away and fell back. The darkness contorted around her as she staggered.

And Skulduggery's body sat up.

Valkyrie ran over, grabbed his skull and his jawbone, tried to fix them back together. "How do I do this? How does it work?" The skull didn't answer. "Here, you do it."

She held it out, then realised his arms weren't attached. Cursing, she dropped to her knees, found his right humerus bone through his shirt and lifted it until it clicked into his shoulder. Working quickly, she attached the rest of his arm, then carefully added his gloved hand to the wrist. Two fingers and his thumb suddenly flexed. The other two fingers hung crooked. She picked up his skull and he guided her hands to the top of his spine. It cracked as it attached.

"Ow," Skulduggery moaned. "How on earth did you do that?"

"I just got her thinking about you," Valkyrie said, helping him attach his other arm. "Put the idea in her head that you were waiting to pop out. I figured she's that unstable, all she has to do is think something will happen, and it'll happen. Then I got her to touch you. Easy, really."

"You are magnificent," he said.

"Yeah," she grinned. "I know."

"I'm astonished that worked."

"Yeah," she grinned. "I know. Do you need help with your legs?"

He suddenly shoved her to one side and rolled to the other as a great blade of darkness sliced through the space between them. She saw Craven, his face a frozen mask of desperation, about to send another blade towards them. Skulduggery propped himself up into a sitting position, his gun in his hand. His forefinger was bent backwards so he pulled the trigger with his middle finger.

The shot rang out and Craven flipped backwards, a bullet between the eyes.

Skulduggery swivelled, emptied his gun at Melancholia, but the shadows looked like they were obeying her again. They caught the bullets and she stood there, twenty paces away, seething with anger. "You tricked me."

"That's what the smart do to the stupid," Valkyrie said, getting up while Skulduggery dropped the gun and worked at reattaching his legs.

"So now what are you going to do? Team up? I'm going to kill you from here the *moment* you do something to annoy me."

"Well, then," Valkyrie smirked, "I guess we won't do anything to annoy you, you moron."

Melancholia immediately raised her arms.

"Wait!" Skulduggery said from the ground. "Now, just wait a moment. Melancholia, Valkyrie is very sorry that she annoyed you."

"No I'm not."

Skulduggery got up, swaying a little. "Valkyrie, please, let me handle this. Melancholia, I know you're very confused right now."

"I'm not confused at all," Melancholia answered.

He clicked his bent fingers back into place, hissing slightly with each one. "Are you sure? Not even the slightest bit? You still want to kill everyone?"

"More than ever. And I want to thank you, by the way, for the opportunity to kill you in front of Valkyrie for a second time. That's just... delicious."

"I'm afraid that's not going to happen," Skulduggery said, and waved a hand. His tuxedo jacket floated over to him. He put it on, and straightened his bow tie. "If I get lost," he said to Valkyrie, "you need to find a way to stop me."

She frowned at him, but he was already looking back at Melancholia.

"You think you can beat me?" Melancholia said with a laugh. "I killed you with a *thought*, you ridiculous thing. I killed you, I defeated Lord Vile… what else do you have to throw at me?"

"That wasn't Lord Vile."

"It certainly looks like him," Melancholia said, glancing behind her to the spot where Vile had been impaled. Her smile faded. He wasn't there any more.

Skulduggery fixed his cuffs. "As I said, that wasn't Lord Vile." He raised his head. "*This* is Lord Vile."

Darkness leaked from Skulduggery's shirt. It wrapped around his body like a bandage, growing thicker, forming armour, covering him from head to foot. Valkyrie stepped back, found herself retreating as fast as she could.

And then Skulduggery was gone, and in his place stood Lord Vile.

Melancholia didn't move for a few seconds, then she shook her head, as if to wake herself up. "You don't scare me," she said before whipping up the shadows and lashing them at Vile. A wall arose in front of him, absorbed the shadows and then melted away.

Melancholia snarled. The shadows behind her grew and writhed, then swooped in through her back and burst from her chest. The stream of darkness slammed into Vile, drove him backwards a single step. Melancholia started to curse him as more shadows poured through her. At Vile's nod, a sliver of darkness severed the stream and Vile absorbed the rest of it into his armour.

He swept his arm wide, firing a salvo of black arrows, three of which got through Melancholia's shield as she stumbled away.

"Stop!" she shouted, like a child who didn't like how the game was being played.

Vile shadow-walked the space between them, appearing behind her. Instinctively, the darkness around her swelled, keeping him at bay, and Melancholia tried to use this as her chance to escape. But Vile sent his shadows after her. One shard nicked the back of her leg and she cried out, and the next slashed across her forearm. Blood sprayed and she shrieked, clutched her arm to her and fell to the ground. She curled up, moaning and sobbing and howling in pain while the shadows around her went nuts. Vile strolled up, stood over her. So absorbed was she in her own distress that she didn't even notice him.

Valkyrie ran forward. "Skulduggery! Don't do it!"

Vile ignored her, reached down to take hold of Melancholia's head. A shadow rippled across her skin, exploding in a dark burst above her that sent Vile flying. Melancholia started crawling away, and Valkyrie grabbed her, hauled her to her feet.

"I'll kill you," Melancholia snarled.

"I'm helping you, you moron. Run!"

55

TUNNEL VISION

hey got to the tunnel and Valkyrie dragged Melancholia after her. "Hurry!"

"Shut up!" Melancholia snapped, shoving Valkyrie away. "I don't need your help! I killed him once, I can do it again."

She turned back the way they had come, and took a deep breath. "He's up," she said. "On his feet. I can feel him. I can feel his energy. It's not like the others. But it's strong. I... there's something... there's something blocking me..."

"What are you trying to do?"

"I'm trying to take his soul."

Valkyrie punched her, right across the jaw. "I'm not going to let you kill him, you nutcase. You think I'd ever choose you over him?"

"Doesn't matter," Melancholia said, her voice quiet. "I can't do it. He's cocooned himself away, I can't... I can't kill him."

"Good."

Melancholia glared up at her. "If I can't kill him, how are we going to stop him?"

"We're not," Valkyrie said. "We're going to run and hide, that's what we're going to do. What the hell is wrong with you, anyway?"

"I'm covered in blood and you're still going to ask me that?"

"No, I mean what did he do to you? That isn't just a cut he gave you."

"These symbols," Melancholia said reluctantly. "They're designed to take the power of my Surge and loop it around my body continuously."

"I know," Valkyrie said. "Craven turned you into a self-charging battery. So what?"

Grimacing, Melancholia held her wounded arm up. The gash cut diagonally across her flesh, splitting symbols. "Vile's damaged me. The power isn't looping like it should. I'm not recharging like I should. It's going wrong."

Valkyrie knelt by her. "Release the energy you stole."

"Get us out of here."

"Release the energy, then I'll help you."

"He's after us!" Melancholia snapped. "If he catches us, I'll need all the strength I can find! And you want me to just release *half* of it?"

"Yes."

"That doesn't make sense."

"Release it now, at once, immediately, or I walk away and leave you here."

"You wouldn't do that."

"It's you or my friends, and I'm always going to pick my friends."

"Help me up before he comes. We can argue about this later."

Valkyrie stood back. *Leave her here*, said the voice in her head. *Vile will kill her, the energy will return on its own. Leave her. She's not worth it.*

Valkyrie gave Melancholia another few moments, then she turned and started to walk away.

"You can't be serious," Melancholia said. "You're really going to abandon me?"

Keep walking.

"You're really going to let him murder me?"

Don't look back.

"Fine!" Melancholia shouted. "Fine! I'll release it!"

Valkyrie turned, and waited.

Melancholia glared at her then shut her eyes. Her breathing became strained and she winced. Something like steam rose from her, drifting up and disappearing into the tunnel wall. She opened her eyes. They were no longer red. She was sweating. "There," she said, panting. "Happy?"

"That was it?" Valkyrie asked dubiously. "That was the energy of three hundred people? A little bit of steam?"

"What were you expecting? Sparkling lights? A ray of sunshine? It is what it is. Now help me up."

Valkyrie took out her phone, dialled Ghastly's number. Even though her phone was magically enhanced, she barely had a single bar down here in the caves. Even so, it was enough for the call to go through, and enough for her to hear Ghastly's tired voice, like he had just woken from a deep sleep.

"Ghastly?" she said. "Can you hear me? Can you—?"

She lost the signal, and put the phone away.

"Satisfied?" Melancholia asked.

"Very."

"I hope you're this smug when Vile catches up with us and I can't do a thing to stop him."

"Me too."

They moved on, struggling to maintain a decent pace. More and more of Melancholia's weight pressed down on to Valkyrie, and with every step her injured leg took, the Necromancer's face would screw up in pain. She wasn't going to last long in here, that much was obvious.

The ground dipped ahead of them and Valkyrie stopped, looked back, looked around.

"What are you waiting for?" Melancholia said. "Come on. Keep going."

Valkyrie ignored her, looked up, saw a ledge. "There," she said. "Climb."

"What? Why? We'll be faster going downhill."

"We can't go deeper. We have to stay as close to the surface as we can." She tried pulling Melancholia to the ledge, but Melancholia yanked her arm from Valkyrie's grip.

"I'm injured, you silly little girl. I can't go around climbing everything for no reason at all. I say we vote on it."

"We're not voting. You're going to do what I tell you."

"And why would I do that?"

"Because I've been down here before. If we go deeper, we're going to get lost. If we do manage to avoid Vile, we'll either die of thirst or get killed by one of the things that live here. Either way, we end up dead."

"I'd rather take my chances with rats and creepy-crawlies than with Lord Vile."

"There are monsters down here, Melancholia, and they're immune to magic."

"Rubbish," Melancholia said. "Nothing is immune to magic."

"Well *they* are, and they're a *lot* bigger than rats, believe me."

Melancholia looked up at the ledge, and scowled. "Give me a leg-up."

Valkyrie interlaced her fingers and crouched. Melancholia steadied herself on her wounded leg, placed one foot in Valkyrie's hands, and straightened as Valkyrie heaved. Melancholia grunted and cursed, but eventually hauled herself over. Valkyrie used the air to give herself a little boost, and she joined Melancholia.

"There," she said, nodding to a gap in the rocks ahead of them. She led the way, and Melancholia followed.

"Why?" Melancholia asked as they moved.

"Why what?"

"You know what. Why didn't you let him kill me? Why are you doing all this for me?"

Valkyrie frowned back at her. "I don't… I don't really know. I'm sick of people dying, I suppose."

"Even your enemies?" Melancholia said. Her eyebrow rose. "That's ridiculous. The only point in having enemies is so you can defeat them, kill them, brush them aside."

"Or give them a chance to redeem themselves."

Melancholia smiled. "You honestly think I'm going to change my ways? I want to kill you. I want to kill everyone. I finally understand what death is. I understand its beauty, but I'm not stupid. I know very few people will share this view. You want to stop me from spreading the beauty of death. You think I'm the villain, don't you?"

Valkyrie shrugged as she walked. "One of them."

"And I think *you're* the villain for trying to stop me. I have nothing to redeem myself for, because I've done nothing wrong."

"You're something of a sociopath, then."

"No, I've just moved beyond what living people think of as important. Living is not important. It's just not. Neither is dying, for that matter. But the two of them together, this wonderful stream of existence… Wait till you see it. You'll wonder why you ever tried to stop me."

Valkyrie stopped, and turned. "See, you're talking, and in theory your words are linking up and making sense, but I still haven't a clue what you're on about. And even if you do have a deeper understanding of life and death than the rest of us, which I doubt, that's still no reason to start killing millions of people."

"I'm going to kill them because I *can* kill them, that's all. Lives are meaningless."

"I don't think you believe that."

Melancholia laughed. "Oh really?"

Valkyrie resumed walking. "I think, OK, for a moment, you glimpsed a great truth about life and death. Maybe your power surged in such a way that it pushed you a little further, opened your mind a little wider. OK, I can accept that. But that's not how you feel now."

"How would you know what I feel now?"

"Because you are running from Lord Vile, just like I am."

She heard Melancholia's smile fade from her voice. "I don't *fear* death," she said. "I just don't want the inconvenience of it right now."

"You can look at it like this, if it helps. For a few moments, your power drove you insane, made you a sociopath with glowing red eyes who wanted to kill millions of people. But you got better."

"I wasn't insane."

"You were a little."

"I think I'd feel OK about killing *you*."

"Don't worry," Valkyrie said, looking back, "that'll pass."

"My eyes were really glowing red?"

"Yep."

Melancholia nodded to herself. "Cool."

They walked on for another ten minutes, until Melancholia's leg buckled under her and she fell against the wall of the tunnel.

"I can't go on," she said. "I just can't."

"You're sure?" Valkyrie frowned.

"Of course I'm bloody sure."

Melancholia was pale and sweating, and her hands were shaking. Valkyrie took a leaf from her jacket pocket, and handed it over. "Chew this. It'll numb the pain."

Melancholia stared at it. "You had this? You had this in your pocket the whole time and you waited until now to give it to me?"

"It's the only one I have, and it wouldn't have lasted for the whole journey."

"I've been in agony!"

"So get chewing."

Melancholia stuffed the leaf into her mouth, and staggered back against the wall. Valkyrie sat on a pile of small rocks.

"I hate you," Melancholia said, still chewing.

"I know."

"I've never hated anyone so much."

"Is it working yet?"

"Yes," Melancholia snapped. "But I still hate you."

"You're allowed," said Valkyrie. The pile of rocks shifted beneath her, and when she put her hand down to steady herself, they scattered and she slid to the ground. Her first instinct was to laugh, but the rocks swarmed her, a chattering mass of legs and teeth, dozens of them. She swiped three of them off her chest, realised she was moving, they were carrying her, and she tried to gain some purchase, tried to get up, but there was nothing to hold on to.

"Help!" she shouted to Melancholia, who stood there, open-mouthed. "Help me!"

Valkyrie twisted, glanced at where the things were taking her, saw nothing but the tunnel wall with another pile of rocks at its base. That pile came alive too, and parted, revealing a dark hole, and they carried her through. She clicked her fingers, summoned a flame, saw smooth rock passing above. The creatures, whatever they were, remained unaffected by the light. All she saw were legs and teeth beneath those rock-like shells, no eyes. They didn't need eyes down here.

The tunnel got narrower and her claustrophobia kicked in. She kept her arms bent, hands at her chest. Her shoulders scraped the tunnel walls. A sudden fear flashed through her, that she'd get jammed in here, unable to move. She let the fire go out and covered her face with her hands. She was sweating. Breathing fast. Close to panic. Her progress slowed, the creatures working to get her through. The tunnel walls were tight against her shoulders. Her arms were forced down by her sides. It was too small. The space was too small. Too narrow and too low. She wanted to scream and lash out, flail and kick, but there was no room for that. She had to keep it together. She had to. She had to remain calm. She had to keep control.

The creatures were all over her. All she could hear were their scuttling legs and her own breathing. Another sound escaped her. A sob. Was she crying? No, not yet. But close. Very close.

"Please," she whispered. "Please please please please."

The creatures gave another determined shunt, and her head banged painfully off the tunnel ceiling and her shoulders jammed and she came to a sudden, jarring halt.

She was stuck.

Her arms were trapped by her sides. She could open and close her hands, and she could kick her feet a few inches, but that was all.

Valkyrie opened her eyes to complete blackness. She heard the creatures scuttling away to either side, which meant the tunnel had opened to something wider. She just had to get her shoulders through this last narrow bit, and she'd have room.

She started wriggling. She couldn't bend her knees much, but she tried her best, tried to gain a foothold and push off from it. Her fingers scraped the rock. Her hips squirmed as much as they could.

Her shoulders wouldn't budge, though. Nothing she was doing was moving her further on.

Closing her eyes, she forced herself to take deep breaths. Her hands were slick with sweat, and the air felt cold against her skin. She could feel the air against her feet, too, even through the boots. It was faint, very faint, but it was there, that space where it all connected. All she had to do was push off from it, then fly like a torpedo from a launch tube. Easy. It was going to be easy.

Her heartbeat slowed. She took another breath. Let it out. In control again. In control.

She pushed off hard, felt the air rushing around her body, felt it shoot up through the gaps and blow her hair off her face. But she didn't move. She didn't move, not one inch.

She tried to kick, banged her knee. She clawed at the rock, felt a fingernail break. The fear and panic and fury built up inside her, rose from her belly and swelled in her chest and burst from her mouth in a long, raw scream tinged with terror.

A shaft of light appeared overhead.

"Help!" she shouted. "Help! I'm down here! I'm stuck!"

She got no shout in return, save for her own echo. Another shaft of light hit the rounded wall of the small chamber. It was like a chimney, leading up, and she was at the bottom.

"Hey!" she shouted. "I need help!"

Another shaft of light, and another. Another patch of light, and another. Salvation, slowly being revealed. But it wasn't like an escape route being uncovered, with rocks and debris being cleared away from the other side. Instead, it was like there was something on this side of the escape route, slowly uncurling. Something that had been blocking it, maybe sleeping beneath it. Something that she had woken up with her screams.

Something that those rock creatures had maybe been feeding.

56

PANIC

She could move her right shoulder slightly. She tried forcing it down, but it was just too tight. She scraped her left hand across her belly, fingers scrabbling for the sleeve of her right arm. She grabbed it, tugged as hard as she could. A few flecks of rock fell on to her neck as a reward. She tried again, snarling as she did so. Her shoulder popped free. She could move it now. Not much, but she could move it. She squirmed into the newfound space until she could move her left shoulder. Both hands pressed against the top of the tunnel and her heels dug in. More shafts of light were revealed, and others were momentarily blocked off as whatever it was made its way down towards her. Valkyrie gritted her teeth, fingers and legs straining, and heaved herself a few inches back inside the tunnel.

Her fingers flattened, her heels dug in and she heaved. Another few inches, this time. And then another few more. Her chin was almost inside the tunnel now. Her feet kicked around until she found a good place of purchase. Heaved again.

Inch by inch, with agonising slowness, Valkyrie got her whole body back inside the tunnel. Sweat stung her eyes and she couldn't wipe it away. She kept going. She had to. She didn't know if the thing behind her had arms or tentacles, but she couldn't stop.

She had more space now. She could heave herself a greater distance.

There was a sound above her. She cracked open an eye against the sweat, saw a blurry shape filling the tunnel behind her head.

She didn't waste her breath cursing. She just went faster, splintering another nail, banging her head. More space above. She squeezed one hand past her face, wiping her eyes as she did so, grunting in exertion. Finally, it broke through, and then she did the other. It got stuck halfway and Valkyrie suddenly started crying. She twisted and squirmed, felt the rock rip the skin on the back of her hand as it burst through to join the other. Now both hands were over her head, and she felt the air, felt the creature closing in, and she pushed.

She shot away from the creature, yelling in pain. Her jacket rode up over her chest, leaving her back bare against the sharp rocks beneath. She stopped and screamed, but didn't let herself pause. She pushed again, cracking her head against the wall, feeling the skin rip all the way up her back.

She had space now, space to hug herself, space to bend her legs and raise her head. The exit was in sight.

"Melancholia!" she shouted. "Hey!"

There was no movement out there in the larger tunnel, and Valkyrie screamed her curses. She brought her legs in towards her, twisted sideways, cursing and grunting and sobbing, and managed to turn her body so that she could crawl the rest of the way.

She got out, got to her hands and knees, tried to stand, but she was trembling so much she collapsed. All she wanted to do was stay curled up like this. But she couldn't stop. She couldn't even rest. She opened her eyes, looked around. Melancholia wasn't even there to help her up.

Her hands were cut raw, fingernails on both hands cracked and broken. The back of her jacket was soaked with blood. Every movement made her whimper.

She got up. At least her legs were OK. She could still run.

Holding her hands close to her chest, her fingers curled protectively, Valkyrie hurried on. Melancholia wouldn't have been able to get that far, not with how badly she was limping. Valkyrie didn't know what she was going to do when she caught up with her. Melancholia hadn't even helped. She'd just stood there while Valkyrie was carried away. Valkyrie had half a mind to throw her to Vile and run on without her.

Valkyrie faltered when she heard a roar up ahead. Grimacing, she sneaked to the end of the tunnel, peeked round.

Melancholia was trying to climb to a higher ledge while three rat-monkeys attacked Lord Vile.

Valkyrie looked closer, trying to come up with a better description than rat-monkey. But no, rat-monkey was exactly what they were. They were humanoid, as tall as she was, covered in patches of dirty brown fur. Their faces were long and their mouths were small but packed with sharp teeth. Vile threw shadows, but they dissipated on impact. The rat-monkeys leaped on him, shrieking, bringing him down.

Above it all, Melancholia was halfway to the ledge.

Vile kicked the first rat-monkey away, slammed an elbow into the second. The third fell on him and they rolled. The rat-monkey was up first, dancing and chattering. Vile got to his feet, lunging, his hands closing around the creature's throat. The rat-monkey squawked, its hands and feet flailing as Vile's arms straightened and he lifted. They may have been immune to magic, but Vile had hundreds of ways to take a life. Even from where she stood, Valkyrie heard the snap of the creature's neck, and then

Vile threw it to one side and turned to face the other two.

They snarled and shrieked their rage. Vile sent a shadow up to the ceiling. It wrapped around a stalactite and snapped it off, then swooped down and drove it through the smaller rat-monkey's chest.

The remaining creature howled in anguish and went straight for Vile. It leaped for him but he moved, got behind it, wrapped an arm around its neck. He held it struggling against him while he strangled it, then let it fall.

Vile nudged the creature with his foot, while a shadow rose through the air after Melancholia. It lazily wrapped around her ankle and tugged, and she fell to the cavern floor, cursing. Vile lost interest in the rat-monkey, strode over to Melancholia as she did her best to stand.

"Stay away from me!" she roared.

Valkyrie took a breath, and sprinted from cover.

Melancholia tried to sweep Vile away in a wave of shadows, but something went wrong and she cried out, fell to her knees. Darkness pulsed through her skin.

Vile shadow-walked to her side, but just as he reappeared, the darkness pulsed again and he was gone.

Valkyrie skidded to a halt. "Where'd he go?"

"Thought you were dead," Melancholia murmured.

"Where's Vile? What did you do?"

Melancholia grimaced, and got up. "I don't know. I think I redirected his shadow-walk."

"Where?"

"Not sure. I don't know how this works."

"Is he far away? Are we safe?"

Melancholia hesitated, then shook her head. "I can feel him. He's still down here. Still after us."

Valkyrie looked up to the ledge. "You were going to climb up there? Let's go."

Melancholia scowled, and they started climbing. Valkyrie's bloody fingers made climbing difficult, but she hissed through the pain, letting it make her angry, letting it reinforce her strength. She got to the top, turned and helped Melancholia up. They straightened just as someone stepped from the darkness beside them, and the White Cleaver swung his scythe at Valkyrie's neck.

"Stop!" Melancholia yelled.

The blade halted, a hair's breadth from Valkyrie's skin.

"We need her to get out of here," Melancholia said, wincing. "We can throw her to Vile as a decoy, or something. We have to keep going. You understand?"

The Cleaver nodded, slid the scythe into its fixture on his back, and scooped Melancholia into his arms. Then he took off running, and Valkyrie did her best to keep up.

57

BEHEADED

The echo of their footsteps changed, and they emerged from the tunnel into a cavern with a still lake in the middle. It was vast and black.

Valkyrie heard footsteps and turned as Vaurien Scapegrace charged out of the darkness, yelling a war cry. The White Cleaver suddenly thrust Melancholia into Valkyrie's arms. His scythe glinted, and Scapegrace's head popped off. Valkyrie stared as his body kept running and toppled into the water.

The White Cleaver swished his scythe into its fixture, then took Melancholia back from Valkyrie. There was another cry, this time a long, mournful wail, as Thrasher staggered towards them.

"What have you done?" he cried. "What have you done?"

"Don't kill him," Valkyrie told the White Cleaver. Melancholia nodded her agreement, and so when Thrasher was close enough, the White Cleaver merely kicked him. Thrasher went hurtling back into the shadows.

Valkyrie hesitated, then picked up Scapegrace's head. She'd never liked him. The first time she'd met him, he'd tried to throw her off a building. Time and time again, he'd tried to kill her, until his failures actually started to endear him to her. She realised she had begun to view him as a dumb little puppy who would always turn up, sooner or later, to chew on her sock or poo in her shoe. She was going to miss him.

He swivelled his eyes to her and she yelped and dropped his head. He bounced, and landed on his ear.

"I'll get you," he wheezed. "All of you. You're dead!"

Valkyrie didn't know what to do. She glanced back. Even Melancholia's eyes widened in surprise.

Valkyrie picked up the head again. "Sorry," she said.

Scapegrace tried to bite her hand, and she slapped him lightly. "Behave."

"When my Master hears about this—"

"Scapegrace, what the hell are you doing down here?"

He sneered. "I'll never tell!"

"Who's your Master?"

"I'll never tell you that, either!"

"How did you even *get* here?"

"Let me bite you. Just let me bite you."

She slapped him again. "Scapegrace, listen to me. You've got a choice. Either tell me what I want to know, or I throw you into the lake."

"I'm not afraid!" Scapegrace said defiantly.

"Are you sure about that? On the lake bed, all alone. Who knows how long it'll take for you to rot away?"

"Go to hell!"

"I wonder what strange mutant monster fish they have down here. I bet they'll start to nibble at you."

"You can't scare me!"

"You'll go mad first, of course. Mad with despair. Mad with hopelessness. It could take years."

"Shut up," Scapegrace said feebly.

"Is your Master a man called Vandameer Craven?" Valkyrie asked.

"Yes!" Scapegrace wheezed proudly.

"He showed you another way into these caves?"

"Yes!"

"You need to tell us where you came in."

"My Master will kill you all."

"Craven's dead," Melancholia said.

His eyes swivelled to her. "What?"

"He's dead, killed by Skulduggery Pleasant. But you'll take orders from *any* Necromancer, won't you? My name is Melancholia St Clair. I'm a Necromancer."

"Mistress," Scapegrace wheezed adoringly.

Valkyrie turned him back towards her. "You take your orders from us now, all right?"

Scapegrace looked at her for a long moment, then his face crumpled. "I can't even nod! You took away my body, now I can't even nod!"

"Were you trying to nod?"

"Yes!"

"Maybe you should tell us if you're doing something like that."

"Fine, I'm nodding, OK?"

"Good. Melancholia needs to find another way out of here."

"Turn me round." She did so. "See that tunnel up there? See the light? That's a flashlight. Thrasher dropped it, like an idiot. There were a lot of us when we came in. Now there's only two of us left."

"Well," Valkyrie said, "there's one and a bit of you left."

"Turn me round again." She did so. He tried to bite her.

She held him by the few strands of hair that still clung to his burnt, rotten scalp. "When we get to that tunnel, where do we go?"

"Follow the flashlights the others dropped," he snarled. "But there are monsters up there. Horrible, chattering monsters, and they'll eat you. I hope they eat you. Not *you*, Mistress. But I hope they eat *her*."

"I understand," Melancholia said. "Can we get rid of him now?"

Valkyrie looked at Scapegrace. "I was actually going to miss you, you know that?"

"I hate you and I hope you die."

"Right," Valkyrie said, and drop-kicked the head as hard as she could. It shot past Melancholia and the Cleaver and was gaining height when Thrasher suddenly appeared from nowhere and leaped up, his hands closing around it. He landed and ran off, head under his arm, and they watched him go.

"I'll get you!" they heard Scapegrace wheeze, as the two zombies vanished into the shadows. "I'll get you, Valkyrie Cain!"

A couple of moments passed. "Well," Valkyrie said eventually. "That's something you don't see every day."

"He's coming," Melancholia said.

Valkyrie turned. The darkness writhed in the tunnel behind them.

"If we can ambush him—" Valkyrie began, but Melancholia shook her head.

"Are you insane? We can't ambush him. And even if we could,

then what? Are you going to talk to him? Try to get through to him? Your friend is gone, you stupid little girl. We have to run. We have to get out of here." She turned to the Cleaver. "Delay. You understand? Do whatever it takes to delay him."

The White Cleaver nodded, and took out his scythe.

Valkyrie wrapped Melancholia's arm around her neck and they hurried to the base of the tunnel.

"Hold on to me," Valkyrie muttered, sweeping the air in. It lifted them, but for a moment Valkyrie didn't think it would be enough, so she reached out desperately for more. The air buffeted them up and over, and Melancholia cried out as they landed heavily.

Valkyrie pulled her to her feet, ignoring the curses, and they hobbled for the tunnel. Before they reached it, Valkyrie looked back and saw Lord Vile emerge. The White Cleaver stood in his way, blocking his path. Two dozen shadows surged from Vile's armour and speared the Cleaver's body. The Cleaver managed to remain upright for a few seconds before a spasm rippled through those shadows and tore him apart.

Valkyrie dragged Melancholia onwards.

58

THE MAIN EVENT

It came from above, scuttling from the tunnel ceiling to the curve of the wall, moving so fast it was hard to keep track. Before it slipped into darkness, Valkyrie saw its pale skin glisten wetly.

"I don't think we should go this way," she said softly.

"You heard the zombie," Melancholia responded. "This is the way out. What do you want to do? You want to go *back*?"

"There's something up ahead."

"There's something behind us too. Throw a ball of fire at whatever it is and it'll run off. Do I have to think of everything?"

"So far you haven't thought of *anything*," Valkyrie said, but resumed walking. "The creatures down here are not friendly, and they're not easily stopped."

"Maybe not by you, but I'm the Death Bringer."

"You still believe that?"

"You saw what I can do."

"You said it yourself, you're a rechargeable battery."

"You have no *idea* how powerful I am. I can take lives by reaching out with my mind."

"And how's that going for you?"

Melancholia glared. "This is your fault. You tricked me into giving the skeleton his life back. Without the skeleton, Vile would still only be an empty suit of armour, which I'd have destroyed by now."

"And if you had destroyed it, then you'd have killed me, and then millions of others. Sorry Mel, you don't get to paint yourself as the innocent victim here."

"There's something wrong with you, you know," Melancholia said. "Twenty minutes ago I tried to kill you, and now you're helping me run from your friend who is now trying to kill us both. That's a very healthy relationship you have there, by the way."

"At least Vile isn't going to try to kill the world after this. All he wants to do is kill you and whoever might replace you."

"Why do you keep calling him Vile? What happened to calling him Skulduggery?"

"When he wears that armour, he's Lord Vile. That's how I've got to think of him. It's the only way we're going to survive."

Melancholia snapped her head around. "Did you hear that?"

Valkyrie disentangled herself from Melancholia, left her leaning against the tunnel wall. There was something up ahead. She could see it in the gloom. It leaped up, and charged.

Valkyrie pushed at the air and it came right through, barged into her and Valkyrie went down, getting tangled in its limbs, in its clutching hands. Its knee dropped to her belly and the breath rushed from her lungs. She latched on to it, wrapped her arms around its skinny frame and didn't let go, burying her head into its shoulder. It snarled and bucked and she strained to hold on, even when it started rolling. She tucked her legs around its waist. If she lost her grip, her stomach muscles would cramp up, leaving her defenceless. Holding on was all she could do. Holding on was the only thing keeping her alive.

The creature, whatever it was, was shrieking now. They rolled to the edge and dropped a few feet. Valkyrie landed on her shoulder and her arms almost sprang apart. It pulled her hair and scraped her face. She kept her head down and her eyes tightly shut. She pulled in a sliver of air. When she was sure she wasn't going to curl up the moment she released her grip, she raised her head and opened her mouth, snarled and sank her teeth into the creature's neck.

It screamed, a sound of pure panic, and it struggled but Valkyrie didn't let go. Blood washed into her mouth and she gagged and did her best not to swallow. They rolled sideways. Valkyrie used her hips to heave herself forward, and now she was on top, with the creature wriggling and squirming beneath her. Valkyrie's jaw was aching, but she held on. Her mouth was filling with warm blood. It spilled over her face, down her neck, beneath her clothes. It spilled on to the ground, splashing into the dirt.

Gradually, the struggling weakened.

When enough feeling had returned to her, Valkyrie rolled away and immediately threw up. The creature lay still, mouth open and eyes closed. There was blood everywhere. Valkyrie spat and crawled further away, then collapsed.

The inside of her mouth tasted like blood and sick. She had meat between her teeth.

"Are you… OK?"

She looked back. Melancholia was staring at her. All Valkyrie wanted to do was curl up and cry.

Melancholia held out her hand, and helped her up on to the upper ledge.

"We have to keep going," Valkyrie murmured.

"We can rest if you—"

"No," Valkyrie said, and got to her feet. "We have to keep going."

They walked on, Melancholia getting weaker and weaker. By the time the gloom began to brighten, she was practically unconscious. Valkyrie dragged her the last few hundred metres, finally emerging from the cave mouth into the moonlight. She laid Melancholia on the ground and stumbled to her knees. The cool breeze brushed the sweat on her face. Her back was on fire, the blood sticky on her skin. She didn't even notice her cut hands or her broken fingernails any more.

There were a few vehicles parked nearby – two cars and a jeep and, for some reason, an ice-cream van. She didn't wonder why there was an ice-cream van. Wondering was the luxury of the curious, and curiosity was a luxury she just didn't have time for.

Groaning with the effort, Valkyrie stood on legs that were made of lead. Her muscles were thick, heavy things that couldn't be trusted. She hobbled to the nearest car. The keys were still in it. She collapsed against the bonnet, eyes closed in relief. She really didn't want to hobble back and drag Melancholia over.

"Hey," she called to her, her voice croaky. She needed water. "Hey, Mel. Get up."

Melancholia stayed passed out.

Valkyrie tried using the air to pull Melancholia closer, but her hand waved uselessly. She was too tired. She needed to rest, just for ten minutes, just to regain a little of her strength. That wasn't too much to ask, not after coming all this way, not after going through all that. Just a little rest.

"You look dreadful."

Valkyrie opened her eyes. Melancholia was looking at her from where she was lying. Valkyrie gave a short laugh. "Yeah," she said, "because you look so good down there."

Melancholia smiled weakly, and shuddered as a pulse of darkness passed through her. "I don't know what's happening..."

"We'll get you to the Sanctuary," Valkyrie told her. "There's a doctor there. Its name is Nye. You're going to love it."

Melancholia tried to rise, then laid her head back on the ground. "You know," she murmured, "I don't think I want to kill millions of people any more."

"That's good."

"Now I only want to kill *you.*"

Valkyrie grinned. "Well... it's progress, I suppose."

"Help me up, you lazy cow."

Valkyrie laughed again, then she saw the shadows shifting in the tunnel and her heart plummeted. She pushed herself away from the car, forced her legs to run to Melancholia, but it was too late. The darkness reared up and held her back, and Lord Vile emerged into the night.

"Skulduggery!" she cried. "Please listen to me! She's hurt! She's damaged! She's not the Death Bringer any more!"

Lord Vile ignored her. Melancholia started to crawl away, and a black claw grew from Vile's fist.

Valkyrie pushed through the darkness, went stumbling, managed to fall beside Melancholia. She grabbed her. "Kill me," she whispered. Melancholia tried to push her away, but Valkyrie gripped her tighter. "Kill me. It's our only chance."

"What are you—"

With the last ounce of her strength, Valkyrie punched. It wasn't a good punch, and it wasn't a strong punch, but it did the job, and Melancholia's anger flared.

"I hope you know what you're doing," she growled. Her eyes narrowed.

Valkyrie took a breath, immediately felt cold. She could sense Melancholia reaching out with her mind, using her last reserves to expand the death bubble around them both. Then the bubble retracted, and Valkyrie started to go with it, started to leave her body. As she was pulled gently closer to Melancholia, she paused a while to examine what was happening. Her body's heartbeat slowed. Her brainwaves began to flatten. The bio-electricity in her body dampened. She was leaving her shell behind, and her thoughts were becoming clouded. She was about to lose who she was. Her identity was in her personality, and her personality rested in her body. Fascinating. The whole process was so very fascinating.

She couldn't allow it to happen, of course. She pulled back, felt her synapses firing again, felt her heart quicken, felt her body around her. Melancholia's eyes were closed. It was all too much for her, the poor thing. Still, she'd done her job. She'd endangered Valkyrie's life, and awoken the beast within.

Darquesse stood up, and looked at Lord Vile. "Be honest," she said. "You've been looking forward to this, haven't you?"

Vile opened both hands, pulling shadows from the mouth of the cave. They curled and thrashed behind him, then rose in a giant wave that rolled towards her. Darquesse fell to one knee under the onslaught. It was a test. He was testing her, seeing how strong she was. When the wave was gone, she lunged. He ducked under the punch and grabbed her low, lifting her off her feet, taking her to the grass. His fists came down, battering her face. She tried to wrap her legs around his waist but his armour expanded, keeping her from locking her ankles together. His fists were hammers, driving her down into the ground, the earth giving way beneath her. An extraordinary sensation.

She reached up with one hand, her fingers gripping his armour, and she pulled him down to her as she rose up, slamming her forehead into his armour-plated face with enough force to break boulders. Vile swayed slightly and she heaved herself out of the depression she had made, flipping them both over, just like Skulduggery had taught her. Had taught Valkyrie. Whatever.

She pushed herself to her feet and kicked, her boot finding a perfect spot on Vile's ribs. She kicked again, and again, shunting him along the ground. He tried to get up and she grabbed his head, started twisting, aiming to pull the whole thing right off. Shadows flew at her, covered her face, cutting off her oxygen. She felt Vile slip from her grip and lashed out blindly. Her left hand connected with him and the shadows went away as Vile stumbled back.

They observed each other, and Darquesse smiled, then quickly lifted off the ground. Vile followed her. It was as if the night reached down and raised him up. Darquesse laughed.

She flew high, and fast, and he gave chase. The sky was cloudless, the moon half-full, the stars out over the countryside that flashed beneath her. He was gaining and so she flew faster. She glanced back in time to see him give a burst of speed, and they collided, went spinning through the air, grappling. Everywhere Vile was in contact with her spikes would grow. They couldn't get through her clothes but they cut her hands, her neck, her face. She hit him but his mask had turned sharp and jagged and it punctured her fist, breaking the knuckles.

She kicked away, swooped under his grab and veered towards the lights of the city, to where the sky turned orange and hid the stars. As she flew, she examined the pain she was feeling, then dampened it and healed herself. Healed her back and her fingernails too, all the little cuts and scratches and bruises. It was freezing up here, but she didn't care about the cold. The wind in her face, her hair blown back, the trouble she was having taking a breath… It was all just a part of being alive. And Darquesse liked being alive.

She looked back. Vile flew like a bullet, arms down at his sides, streamlined and efficient. She laughed, holding her own arms out like Superman. All she needed now was a cape.

The night snatched Vile away. One moment he was behind her, the next he was gone. She looked round and he emerged from the dark ahead of her but she didn't alter her course. She curled her hands into fists and flew straight into him, catching him in the gut, speeding on with him folded over her. His left hand grabbed her wrist, squeezed it so tightly her bones broke. She healed them instantly. He reached to her with his right hand, his armoured glove finding her face, his thumb seeking her eye. She turned her head but he had a good grip. If he burst her eyeball, how quickly would she be able to repair it?

She didn't know, so she let him do it, and as an experiment she allowed the pain in. His thumb burst her eye and she shrieked. Her body convulsed and she twisted in mid-air. Vile's momentum carried him onwards, but Darquesse didn't care about him – all she cared about was the extraordinary pain she was experiencing. Her hands were covering her face, feeling the blood and the jelly leak down her cheek. She realised she was still screaming, screaming and roaring and crying, turning in circles in the air. When the pain was too much, she shut it off, and calmly pressed the remains of her eye back into its socket. An interesting experiment.

She opened her good eye, saw Vile coming for her. His shoulder slammed into her belly, his arm encircled her, and they hurtled downwards. She blinked. The vision in her bad eye turned from nothing to blurry to perfect. Better than her right eye, in fact. To compensate, she sharpened that eye as well, and then returned her attention to her current predicament. She tried to look down at what they were flying towards but the wind was blowing her hair in the way. She wrapped her legs around Vile's waist, grabbed him where she could, and flipped, so that now she was the pilot forcing *him* down. And now that her hair was out of the way, she could see what they were heading towards. O'Connell Street, in the middle of Dublin.

"Oh," she said, and then they crashed.

59

HERO AND VILLAIN

Darquesse lay there in the broken road, looking up at the suddenly starless sky in the last few moments of life, and she managed a shaky laugh. Her body was smashed. Her lungs were burst and her heart wasn't beating. Her limbs were twisted, her spine was pulverised, her head was cracked open. She could feel her brain starting to swell, so that was the first thing she healed. She wouldn't be able to do much thinking without her brain.

It was somewhere between four and five on a Monday morning. She healed her spine and raised her head, looked around. No civilians were standing there, staring with open mouths. Pity. She'd have liked to have seen their faces when she stood up after a fall like that.

Lord Vile lay a few feet away. He wasn't moving.

Darquesse repaired her internal organs, restarted her heart and drew air into her newly re-formed lungs. Next came her limbs. Her bones made cracking sounds as they realigned and knitted back together. She reached behind her head, made sure her hair didn't get trapped in the fissure that healed in her skull. Her ruptured skin closed over. A lot of her blood covered the ground, so she made more, and stood up.

Headlights swept in and she turned. A taxi slowed to a stop, and the driver got out. He looked at her, looked at Vile, looked at the churned-up road. He didn't ask any questions, he just stood there like he was waiting for an explanation. She didn't like that. She didn't like him. She stepped forward to tear him in two and then Vile grabbed her jacket from behind, lifted her off her feet and slammed her through the bonnet of the car.

Her face crunched into the engine block, and he hauled her out before she even knew what was happening, and hurled her through the window of a Burger King. She hit a table and flipped sideways to the floor, coming to a stop in the dark as an alarm started up, so loud that it pierced the world. She got to her hands and knees, spitting blood, and the shadows snaked out, seized her wrists, and she flew back out through the broken window, hitting the ruined taxi, denting the passenger-side door. Above the alarm, she heard the driver screaming as he ran away, and then Vile reached down, closed his fingers around her throat.

Her held her off the ground with his left hand and hit her with his right. His fist was a block of stone, showing her explosions of bright light every time it connected. She needed to stop him before he punched her brain out through her skull. She'd done that once. It was funnier when it happened to other people.

She took hold of his left wrist with both her hands, and squeezed. Vile's head tilted. He reinforced the armour on his forearm, but Darquesse just squeezed harder. Finally, he had to release his grip, and she smacked him under the chin. He hurtled backwards off his feet and she launched herself into the air, smashed into him, flying low. The street whipped by underneath. She got a hand around his throat and dipped, smashed the back of his head into the steps that led up to Eason's bookshop. The steps cracked under the impact and Darquesse smashed his head down again, and again. A pillar of darkness erupted from his chest like a piston, throwing her to the pavement. He stood and she waved an arm.

The energy that enveloped him would have turned rock to dust, but all it did to Vile was send him staggering to the metal shutter covering the shop window. The shutter melted, the glass shattered and another alarm rang out. Darquesse leaped to the top of the steps and barged into him, taking them both through the window into the shop.

The shadows converged, tried to wrap around her hands and feet. Darquesse snarled, cutting through them with her fingernails. She gagged suddenly, saw blood, took a moment to work out that her throat had been slashed. She healed it and saw Vile, conducting the shadows like an orchestra. She blurred to him, threw him back against the wall, spilling books and breaking shelves. She was on him again, holding him above her as she launched upwards. She smashed him through the ceiling into the floor above, smashed through into the floor above that, and the floor above that. There he broke free, elbowed her, impaled her cheek with the spike that grew from that elbow, and wrenched it out. She spat blood on to the eye-slit in his mask and he tried to push her away, but she grabbed him, spun, and hurled him to the line of windows overlooking the street. He smashed through and she saw the night swoop down and catch him.

She was breathing hard, covered in dust and blood and plaster. She was sweating, too, and starving. All this energy, all this magic, being used on someone who seemed to be just as tough as she was. Maybe even tougher. She healed her face and walked to the windows. Vile hovered in mid-air, looking at her. His armour was spiked, ready for round two.

Below, sirens wailed and blue lights flashed. Above, a police helicopter sped towards them, searchlight probing the streets. Darquesse smiled.

She ran for the window, jumped and took flight, the wind in her hair again. She flew up, away from Vile, towards the helicopter. She ducked the searchlight, coming around low, but before she could punch through the underside, Vile had his arms around her and was pulling her away. They tumbled out of the sky. For a moment it looked like they might smash into the fire engine speeding across O'Connell Bridge, but Vile changed their trajectory and they hit the water, went deep into the Liffey, and Vile lost his grip.

Darquesse powered through the dark river, Vile right behind, reaching out. He snagged her foot and she veered up, broke the surface, trying to shake him. He twisted in mid-air, threw her like a baseball. It was almost fun, the speed at which she was thrown. Another window smashed to smithereens around her. She hit a railing, tumbled down some stairs, came to rest against a shelf, comics falling on top of her. She saw a sign that said Forbidden Planet. A comic shop. How fitting.

She looked up. Vile stood at the top of the stairs.

"We should really stop throwing each other through windows," she told him. She reached up to the counter, pulled herself to her feet. "You know what the funny thing is? I actually don't care any more if you kill Melancholia. Isn't that funny? In fact, if you'd be agreeable, maybe we could pop back for a moment and I'll kill her myself. What do you say?"

He stood there, a dark shape, unmoving.

A shard of glass had managed to sneak into her belly, between her trousers and jacket. She gripped it with two fingers and pulled it out slowly. It was much longer than she'd expected. When it was out, she dropped it and pulled another shard from her forehead. "So that's a no, then, is it? Pity."

He walked down the steps.

"Does that mean you've changed your mind?" she asked. "Don't you *want* to kill the Death Bringer? What about me? Do you want to kill me? I'm going to kill the world, after all. This might be your only chance to stop me."

He reached the bottom and just stood there, looking at her.

"I'm only going to get stronger," she said, "and you know it. This is your only chance. No? You're not going to take it?" She laughed. "I'm disappointed. I've heard so much about the great Lord Vile, and now look at him. He's not even going to kill his enemy when she's right in front of him. What do I have to do? How do I provoke such a scary, scary man like you into doing what needs to be done? Do I go out there and kill someone? What about those cops? Do you need me to kill those cops? I'd like another go at that helicopter, actually. I'd like to see it crash and burn. Or maybe something else. What else could I do, I wonder?"

"Valkyrie," Lord Vile said. His voice was a whisper.

Darquesse smiled. "*I'm* Valkyrie. Whatever you've got to say to her, you can say to me. What was it Skulduggery said earlier? I'm her bad mood."

That whisper again. "Let her out."

"But I'm not repressing her. I know you understand this. I *am* Valkyrie. I'm just embracing my potential. If my conscience never reasserted itself, I'd stay like this for ever. Just like you'd stay like *that*, Skulduggery."

Vile tilted his head. Then his hands went to his mask and she heard the clasps open, one by one. Shadows leaked, dissipating in the air. He pulled the mask away, revealing the gleaming skull beneath.

"I wouldn't stay like this," Skulduggery said. "I like being me."

Darquesse smiled. "Do you really? Do you really like carrying around all that shame and guilt? I doubt it. I bet you *anything* that being Lord Vile was the most fun you've had in years."

"You'd be wrong."

"I think you're fibbing."

He let the chest plate fall. Beneath it, his shirt was rumpled, and his bow tie was askew. "The most fun I've had recently was St Patrick's Day last year. You remember it?"

Darquesse frowned. "Did we *do* anything on St Patrick's Day?"

He continued to strip the armour away. "We were on a stake-out.

It was you, me and Fletcher. For the first hour, he wouldn't shut up. Then you started insulting him."

"Oh," Darquesse said. "I remember."

"It was five hours with the three of us stuck in a room, and then another four hours with just the two of us, after Fletcher couldn't take it any more."

Darquesse laughed. "I've never seen him sulk so *hard*."

"That was a good day for me," Skulduggery said. "I didn't have to hit anyone. I didn't have to shoot anyone. I just sat around and talked to my good friend and partner, Valkyrie Cain."

"And insulted her boyfriend," Darquesse grinned.

"Indeed."

Valkyrie shrugged. "Ex-boyfriend now, of course."

"Fletcher was always going to be your ex-boyfriend, from the moment you met him. He's just finally caught up with where he's supposed to be."

"What a nice way of looking at it."

The last bit of Skulduggery's armour joined the pile. "Maybe you should share that with him the next time you see him."

"Maybe." She looked round at the shattered glass and the mess. "I'm tired."

"I don't blame you."

"People saw us. That taxi driver. He saw me."

"That's what people like Scrutinous are for."

"I'm me again, by the way."

"I know."

Valkyrie let out a deep breath. "Did you see what I did? I was practically dead and I healed myself. How did I do that? I don't even know what kind of magic it was. It certainly wasn't Elemental, and it was like no Adept discipline I've ever heard of. It didn't follow any of the rules."

"I don't know, Valkyrie."

"I wonder what else I can do?" she said, and heat rose in her face. "I mean… I don't *want* to know. I don't want anything like that to happen again, I just…"

"I know," Skulduggery said. "You're just wondering."

"Yeah," she said. "Exactly. It was… amazing. I was flying, for God's sake. Me. On my own. I was doing all these incredible things…"

Skulduggery held his hand over the armour, and the various sections melted into each other. He picked up what was left. "Power is intoxicating."

"That's a good word for it."

"And like any intoxicant, it's also addictive."

She fell silent.

They climbed the stairs and stepped out through the window. Dawn was on its way. Valkyrie took out her phone to check the time. It fell to pieces the moment it left her pocket.

"Huh," she said. "I think I need a more impact-resistant phone."

Skulduggery took out his. "Three missed calls, all from Ghastly."

"At least he's alive."

Skulduggery wrapped one arm around her waist, and they rose up off the pavement. "Thanks to you," he said.

They flew over the city, the wind gently boosting them. The flashing lights and the sirens faded and Valkyrie looked to the approaching horizon, fighting the voice in her head. She used to love it when Skulduggery would take her into the air. The pure sensation of flying used to make her smile so, so wide. But now she wanted to pull away, to flatten out and go like a rocket. She wanted to do it herself. She wanted to feel that level of power again.

Soon, the voice in her head told her. *Soon.*

60

TATTLETALE

Warmth and sunshine never really seemed to reach Roarhaven. It was as if it had its own extra layer of atmosphere that kept out anything that could possibly lighten the mood of its citizens. The same dour faces peered at the Bentley as they passed, unimpressed with the activity that was making the Sanctuary hum.

The Bentley stopped right at the end of the main street, and Skulduggery and Valkyrie looked at all the sorcerers streaming in through the Sanctuary doors. Today, they were to be honoured by the guests and the Council of Elders for their work to prevent the Passage, and for their efforts to save the lives of the people who were gathering. Ravel had assured them it would be a quiet ceremony.

"It doesn't *look* quiet," Valkyrie said.

"Indeed it does not," Skulduggery murmured.

"Are they going to give us medals, or something? Maybe vouchers? I could use some vouchers."

"There's going to be speeches. Everyone of importance will want to stand up and give a speech. I hate speeches. They're only good when I give them."

Valkyrie sighed. "How long before it starts?"

"Ten minutes."

She opened the car door. "I'm going for a walk."

"You better not be late."

She grinned. "Would I do that to you?"

She got out, and the Bentley moved on. She crossed the street. There would be enough hand-shaking and polite smiles as it was – she didn't need to turn up early and subject herself to more.

"Here she is," said a voice from behind her, "the hero of the hour."

She turned, watching warily as Solomon Wreath approached, his cane tapping the pavement. "Are we going to start fighting?"

"Why ever would we do that?" he asked, smiling.

"I'd say I'm not the Necromancers' favourite person right now."

"Oh," he said, "*that*. That'll pass, Valkyrie. You've got nothing to worry about – the Order poses no threat to you. Especially here in Ireland. The Temple is empty. The Elders say they're going to tear it down, or convert it into something that could be used by the Sanctuary. I'd say such a move would be sacrilegious, but no one would care."

"I certainly wouldn't."

"There you go." He sighed, and looked at her. "How is our little Death Bringer, anyway?"

"Unconscious," Valkyrie said, "and she'll remain that way for a long time. Doctor Nye induced a coma. It was the safest thing to do, apparently. Her power was surging and looping and going nuts. She could have gone off at any time."

"Gone off?"

"Like a bomb, Nye said. Like a small nuke, in fact. All that uncontrolled magic just… exploding. Scary stuff. And all because of you and your friends."

"Craven was not a friend."

"I meant Necromancers in general."

"Oh. Then yes, it was all our fault. But look on the bright side. Nobody died."

Valkyrie frowned. "Lots of people died."

"But nobody you *like*. Everyone at the Ball got up and walked away, didn't they?"

"I suppose. Scapegrace got his head chopped off, though."

"I don't know who that is."

"You don't have to. I don't really like him, anyway."

"See? Happy endings all round. Any word on Vile?"

Valkyrie shook her head. "He disappeared. Hasn't been seen since."

"Melancholia must have really thrown him about the place. O'Connell Street is in ruins."

"Yeah," Valkyrie said, "she must have."

"Your friend Scrutinous has undoubtedly been working overtime to keep the truth of what happened out of the news reports."

"Ruptured gas mains are terrible things."

"Makes you wonder, though, with all that damage, why Vile didn't just kill her."

"He didn't have to. He'd sabotaged her power. He didn't need to do anything else."

"But this is Lord Vile we're talking about. He's not the kind to leave jobs half done."

Valkyrie shrugged. "Well, the next time I see him, I'll ask him, OK? And what are you going to do now? Join a Temple in England? America?"

Wreath hesitated. "The Order isn't too keen on taking me back, actually. Even though I've been exonerated of all wrongdoing, they feel my presence might tarnish their good standing in the rest of the world, or what there is of it. They'd rather everyone just forgot about the Passage for a few years. I don't really see that happening, but Necromancers have a proud history of sticking their heads in the sand. No, Valkyrie, I'm basically going to walk the earth. Walk from place to place, meet people, get in adventures."

"Like Jules, in *Pulp Fiction*."

"Something like that, yes."

"Cool."

"Or I could stay here, and you could continue your lessons in Necromancy…?"

"I'll keep practising on my own, thank you very much."

"You might need this," he said, and tossed her a black ring, identical to the one Melancholia had destroyed. "It's empty, and waiting for you to pour your magic into."

"Thank you."

He smiled. "It's hard, isn't it? Giving up power like that?"

She looked away. "You have no idea."

The Bentley pulled up beside them. Skulduggery got out.

"Detective Pleasant," Wreath said. "All's well that ends well, eh?"

"I don't want to see you around for a while," Skulduggery said. "Nothing personal, you understand."

"I do, of course," Wreath said, and bowed slightly. He looked at Valkyrie. "I'm expecting great things from you, my dear."

She nodded, didn't answer. The shadows swirled, and he was gone. She walked over to the Bentley. "Is it time?"

"Yes it is," Skulduggery said. They got in the car, and slowly pulled away from the kerb.

Valkyrie frowned. "We're going the wrong way."

"Are we?"

"The Sanctuary's behind us."

"Oh dear."

They kept going. Valkyrie smiled. "Are they going to be upset?"

"Probably," he admitted. "But I just couldn't subject you to an entire afternoon of people telling us how great we are. We don't *need* people to tell us that. We *know*. If I were you, though, I'd turn off your phone."

"Good idea," she said. As she dug her new phone out of her pocket, she asked, "Where are we off to?"

"China's library. She left me a message to come and see her as soon as we can. I think that takes priority over a needless ego boost, don't you?"

"Absolutely."

They left Roarhaven by the dusty road that linked it to the outside world.

They were lying, of course, and they both knew it. It wasn't the speeches that kept them from the ceremony, or the hand-shaking or the polite smiles. It was the fact that they were being celebrated for actions they couldn't be proud of. The only way to beat Melancholia had been for Skulduggery to become Lord Vile, and the only way to beat Lord Vile had been for Valkyrie to become Darquesse.

"There's something wrong with us," Valkyrie murmured as they drove.

"Yes, there is."

"What are you going to do with the armour?"

"Seal it away. It's the only thing I *can* do."

"You might need it again."

"Hopefully not."

She turned her head to him. "If Darquesse comes out again and I can't regain control, you're going to need some way to stop me. You can't let me kill my family, Skulduggery."

He looked at her. "That's not going to happen."

"We *saw* it happen."

"We saw a vision of one possible future."

"You have to stop me," she said, switching her gaze to the road ahead.

He was silent for a moment. "I will," he promised, his voice soft.

They drove the rest of the way in silence.

China and Eliza Scorn were fighting in the street when they reached the tenement building. The Bentley screeched to a halt and Skulduggery and Valkyrie leaped out.

"Hey!" Valkyrie roared. "Get away from her!"

Scorn rammed China into the side of the car. China staggered, caught a punch right on the hinge of the jaw that dropped her to her knees. Scorn kicked her full force in the belly and China folded.

Skulduggery's gun was in his hand. Scorn crouched low, using China as a shield.

"Don't shoot," Scorn called.

"Stand up and move away," Skulduggery ordered.

"So you have a clear shot? I don't think so."

China moaned as she sucked in air. "Kill her," she managed. "She's... got a... bomb."

"I have a bomb*shell*," Scorn corrected, "of information."

"What's that in your hand?" Skulduggery asked.

Scorn smiled. She was holding a small black cylinder with a red button on top. "OK, fine, I do have an *actual* bomb too. A few bombs, in fact. Small ones, but you work with what you've got. They're spread around the library, and there are a few in China's apartment, too. Don't worry, there's nobody up there. No one's going to get hurt."

Skulduggery thumbed back the hammer of his gun. "Drop the switch."

"I'm not going to do that."

"If you press that button, you'll end up in a cell."

"I don't think I will. I think, when I do press this button, you're going to let me walk away."

"And why would I do that?"

"Because I have information you're going to find very interesting. I've been researching this over the last few months, actually. Do you remember the day your family died?"

"It's always amusing," Skulduggery said, "when someone tries to use that to goad me into doing something."

"Oh, I'm not goading you. I'm genuinely asking." Ever so slowly, Scorn stood up straight. "I wasn't even in the country at the time. I think I was in Spain, doing a thing. Anyway, Nefarian Serpine – great guy, by the way – needed to throw you off balance, needed you distracted, needed you to get angry and stop thinking straight. So obviously, killing your wife and kid in front of you was the only reasonable way to do that. He wasn't well, that man. He had issues, you know what I mean? He needed to distract you and the only thing he could come up with was to murder your family? Not have someone wave to you, or something? But that was him all over, wasn't it? He went to extremes, and this was one of them."

China suddenly moved, grabbing Scorn's leg, but Scorn just leaned down and punched her. Skulduggery took a step forward, but Scorn held up the switch. "The thing is," she continued, "Serpine was so busy organising a whole range of assassinations and murders that week that he just didn't have the time to go out and round up your family himself. So he sent a group of people he knew he could count on. He sent the Diablerie."

Valkyrie went cold, and saw China sag. Skulduggery's gun didn't waver.

"I'm sure you remember who was in the Diablerie back in those days," Scorn said. "There was Vengeous – before he became one of Mevolent's Generals, of course – Gruesome, Murder Rose – delightful lady – Jaron Gallow, may he rest in peace – a few others... and China. The leader of the pack, as it were. If I'm right, and I think I am, Rose went after your child. That wasn't much of a problem. To be honest, from what I've read, the biggest danger there was whether Rose would go too far and kill the kid. But for once, she obeyed orders.

"China, because she enjoyed that kind of thing, went after your wife. By all accounts, it was a knock-down, drag-out fight. There was blood, sweat, tears, hair-pulling, even some name-calling. Things got pretty heated, but eventually China emerged triumphant, and she shackled your pretty little wife and hauled her all the way back to Serpine's castle. Then she stood in the shadows, and watched you run in, saw you scream when they died. She was there while Serpine was torturing you. Apparently, different members of the Diablerie liked to stop by every now and then to watch. That's pretty dark, isn't it?"

Skulduggery lowered his gun.

"Of course," Scorn said, "this probably makes no difference to you in the slightest, does it? I mean, you're already friends with her. You've already forgiven her for the things she did during the war. This is just one more thing, am I right? Just one more thing to forgive her for."

She held up the switch. Skulduggery didn't move. Scorn smiled, and thumbed the little red button. The windows on the top floor of the tenement building exploded, spraying glass all the way across the street. Flames licked the air. Black smoke billowed. Burning pages rained down. China shook her head slowly and Valkyrie stared, but Scorn just smiled and Skulduggery still didn't move.

China tried to get up and Scorn drove a knee into her face. She started kicking her, lashing her boot in. China gagged and curled up.

Skulduggery turned round, started walking back to the Bentley.

People were stumbling out on to the street, staring at the fire and calling the fire brigade, looking at Scorn beating China and calling the cops. Valkyrie ran over, shoved Scorn back. China lay gasping between them.

"You want to take her place?" Scorn asked, eyes narrowed.

"If you make one move towards me," Valkyrie said, "Skulduggery will kill you. Leave. Now."

Scorn observed her for another few moments, and then that

smile returned. "Of course, Detective Cain. Whatever you say."

She cast another glance down at China and her smile widened. Then she moved off, disappearing into the crowd.

China turned over on to her back. Her face was a mess. Swollen and cut and bloody. She held her arm against her ribs, and every breath seemed to hurt. She grimaced, forced herself to sit up. She didn't raise her eyes. "I won't blame you," she said, her voice tight with pain, "if you walk away."

"Good," Valkyrie said, and she did just that.

61

MY TWILIGHT

The first time she'd met China, Skulduggery had warned Valkyrie not to trust her. She could only be relied upon to serve her own best interests, he had said, and people like that were the most dangerous kind.

But since then, even Skulduggery's attitude towards China had softened. They'd all been through so much together. They'd fought side by side. They'd faced death and overcome certain destruction. China had been shifting, ever so slightly, from her throne of neutrality to being an ally who could be depended upon. And ever since Valkyrie had lost Tanith, China had become something even more – she'd become a friend.

But now all that was over. Because of his own past, Skulduggery could forgive a great many sins. But this? Being directly involved in the murder of his wife and child? Valkyrie feared that it would be asking too much of him to forgive a crime of that magnitude.

She hadn't heard from him in two days. She kept expecting a call from Ghastly, informing her that Skulduggery was in custody, charged with the unlawful killing of China Sorrows. But as the darkness drew in on another day her phone, thankfully, remained silent.

She was in no mood for Caelan that night. He tapped on her window and she stared at him for the longest time, then pointed behind him, at the pier, and he nodded, and vanished. She got dressed, sneaked out.

"I'm sorry," he said when she neared.

"For what?"

"For not being there when you needed me. You went through all of that without me."

"It's grand, OK? Forget about it."

"But I failed you, Valkyrie."

She sighed. "I can't do this any more."

"You can't do what?"

"Caelan, whatever we have, it's over, all right? We never went out, but we're breaking up, even so."

His beautiful eyes widened. "What are you talking about?"

"You're way too intense for me. I mean, for God's sake, every word out of your mouth is how much you love me and how we're meant to be together. I don't look forward to seeing you any more because I know exactly what I'll be getting."

"You don't mean that."

"Yes, Caelan, I do. We're not Buffy and Angel, or Romeo and Juliet, or those two from *West Side Story*. We're not even Edward and Bella, OK? You're far too freaky for me."

He looked at her. "We're meant to be together…"

"And this is exactly what I mean."

"Our love is written in the stars."

"And there you go again."

"I love you."

"You bore me."

He faltered. "What?"

"Seriously. You do. I hate to be so mean, but you're just not hearing this. You bore the hell out of me. At first, you were cool. But my God, you got boring really fast. There's only so much of this brooding loner thing a girl can take before she really just needs someone to make her laugh. You're not a funny guy, Caelan."

"I don't understand."

"You can't tell jokes."

"No, I mean I don't understand why you're saying these things."

"And you just missed another joke. See?"

"It's Fletcher, isn't it?"

"Fletcher has nothing to do with this, other than I can't believe I've had to break up with two guys in the space of a week."

He grabbed her arm. "I can change," he said.

"That's not going to do it."

"Then *you* can change."

"Excuse me?"

"You can do what *I* say for once. Have you never thought that the reason you are unhappy is because you never obey me?"

"Seriously? No, that thought never entered my head."

"I only want what's best for you."

"Let go of my arm."

"Why? Do you think I'd break it? I would never hurt you, Valkyrie. This? This isn't pain." He squeezed, and she grimaced. "This is nothing compared to the agony I feel in my heart. A bruise, a broken bone is paltry."

"Caelan, let go of me right now."

"Why?" he asked, a sneer on his lips. "So you can run away from me? So you can leave me, and fall into the arms of another? Who is he, Valkyrie?"

"There's no one else, you psycho."

"Stop lying to me!"

Valkyrie twisted her arm and yanked it from his grip and Caelan caught her across the jaw with his fist. She was halfway to the ground when his hand closed around her throat and suddenly he was slamming her against the wall on the far side of the road.

"Who is he?" he snarled. "Who are you with? Give me his name!"

She clutched at his hand, but couldn't prise it off, and her head was pounding and lights danced before her eyes.

Suddenly the grip was released, and Valkyrie slumped to a sitting position. A moment passed, and then a hand stroked her face tenderly.

"I'm sorry," Caelan said. "I'm sorry, Valkyrie. I didn't mean to strike you. I would never hurt you, you know that. But sometimes... sometimes you just have to listen to me, and do what I say. Now, if you tell me there is no one else, then I believe you. Of course I do. Because I love you. Do you understand me?"

She nodded. He smiled, took her hands, and raised her slowly to her feet.

"Are you all right?" he asked gently.

"I'm OK," she said.

"I love you," he smiled.

She snapped her palms and the space between them rippled and Caelan flew backwards. He managed to land in a crouch, and leaped at her, but she sent the shadows to intercept, pulling him from the air and driving him head first into the ground. He got to his hands and knees, dazed, and Valkyrie ran up, went to kick, but he batted her foot away and his fist crunched into her belly. She doubled over with a cry of pain that turned into a strangled wheeze.

"Why do you do this?" he raged. "Why do you defy me? I love you, Valkyrie! Do you know what that means?"

She dropped to her knees.

"I love you," he said in her ear. "We're meant for each other. Can't you understand that? I've tried to be patient. I've tried so hard. But you just don't get it. You continue to fight."

His hand closed around her jaw, and lifted her face to him.

"You think it's easy for me?" he asked, tears in his eyes. "You think it's easy to give my love? I've tried, in the past. Girls, women, so many, they each stole my heart. But each time it ended I lost a piece of myself."

Her hand went to her pocket, fumbled with the phone.

"But you," Caelan said, "you're different. The others, they couldn't keep the monster away. As much as I loved them, our love just wasn't strong enough to keep them alive. Sooner or later, the monster would emerge. That's when Dusk found me." He sneered. "He said I was endangering everyone with the things I did. He tried to stop me, but he couldn't kill me. He was living by the code. We don't kill our own kind. The vampire he had with him, he was even worse than Dusk. He talked about living in darkness, in solitude, keeping away from the mortals.

One day I'd had enough of his lectures, and I slit his throat and took his head. And because of that, I was exiled, cast out to an existence of loneliness. Until I found you. We're meant for each other. And if you can't understand that, I'll have to make you."

Moonlight made the sweat on his brow glisten. He opened his mouth, his fangs growing.

"Caelan."

Caelan snarled, and turned. Fletcher stood there.

"Get away from my ex-girlfriend, you moany little whinge-bag."

Caelan took a breath, like he was in pain, and straightened up. His voice was low, guttural. "I was hoping I'd get the chance to kill you."

"You won't be killing anyone, you sad little emo git."

"You've stood in the way of our love for long enough."

"Just listening to you makes me want to top myself, you self-pitying Paranormal Romance reject."

Caelan glared. "Stop insulting me."

"Why? If you cry, will your mascara run?"

"You're just making me angrier. And I really should have taken my serum tonight."

Caelan's fingers dug into his shirt, into his flesh, and he ripped it off, revealing the bone-white skin beneath. A suddenly clawed hand went to his face, tore it from his head, taking the hair with it. The vampire shook off the ragged remains of its human form, its black eyes gleaming as it advanced.

Fletcher licked his lips nervously and backed off. Valkyrie did her best to sit up, watching the muscles move beneath the vampire's pale skin. A creature made for killing. She wanted to shout out, to warn Fletcher, to tell him to go and get Skulduggery, but all she managed was a moan.

Fletcher teleported, reappearing a moment later with a baseball bat in his hands. He teleported behind the vampire, swung, but the vampire was too quick, and twisted out of the way. Fletcher barely had time to vanish before a claw lashed through him.

Fletcher appeared, regarding the vampire warily. The vampire snarled. They circled each other. Fletcher teleported again, appearing behind his foe, then teleported to the other side as those claws came for him again. He swung for the head, but the bat was knocked from his hands. Fletcher stumbled, the vampire lunged, found nothing but empty space.

It wasn't working. The vampire was just too fast.

Fletcher picked up the fallen bat. He held it in a tight grip, brought it up over his shoulder, settled into his stance, like he was expecting the vampire to oblige him by charging across the ten metres that separated them. Then he swung, solid and vicious, and for a heartbeat he was beside the vampire, the bat crashing into that snarling face, and then he was back out of range, the bat recoiling after the impact. The vampire roared, and Fletcher smiled.

He swung again, teleported behind the vampire just at the point of impact and then teleported away. Again and again he did it, and the vampire twisted and slashed and snapped, but Fletcher was only in range for the length of an eyeblink before he was gone again. The vampire stumbled to one knee. The bat *cracked* against the vampire's ribs. The bat *cracked* against the vampire's back. The bat *cracked* against the vampire's head, and it splintered.

Fletcher was gone for a moment, and returned with an axe. He swung, teleported, and the axe blade dug into the vampire's shoulder. But when Fletcher teleported away he took the vampire with him. He cursed when he realised what he'd done, tried to release the axe but the vampire's hand closed around Fletcher's arm and Fletcher screamed as nails perforated his flesh. Fletcher was sent rolling across the ground, clutching his arm and screaming. The vampire reached up, dislodged the axe and threw it away.

Fletcher scrambled up, fell, scrambled up again, running on to the pier to get some distance between them, to get some time to focus and teleport. It wasn't going to happen. Valkyrie could see that. The pain was too intense. The panic had set in. The vampire moved after him.

Fletcher tripped and fell, tried to crawl on, leaving a trail of blood. The vampire hissed and snarled, but followed slowly, the way a cat would follow an injured mouse. It kicked Fletcher over on to his back, looked down at him, claws flexing. It dropped to its knees, straddling him. It wasn't going to bite him. It wasn't going to give him the chance of living as a monster. It was going to rip him open, from chest to throat. Its claws lifted.

Valkyrie dived at it, hooked her arm around its neck, hauling it off Fletcher and bringing it to the ground. They rolled and it struggled, but she held on, still rolling, and suddenly there was nothing beneath them and they were falling.

They hit the water. Valkyrie's leg banged against the rocks and she screamed through gritted teeth. The vampire thrashed but she held it down in the darkness beneath the surface. It managed to shake her off and she swam backwards against the current. The waves brought the vampire in towards the rocks and it grabbed them, started to haul itself out. For one terrifying moment, Valkyrie thought the salt water hadn't worked. But then the vampire's movements grew weaker, and its hands went to its throat. It turned its head to her, black eyes open wide, mouth gagging gently. Then it stopped.

Valkyrie swam over, pulled herself on to the rocks, moaning in pain. She reached the rusted ladder set into the side of the pier and climbed slowly. Fletcher lay on his back, his breathing shallow and quick. He looked at her as she crawled over.

"With one exception," he managed to say, "you've got terrible taste in men."

She lay beside him, too tired and sore to answer.

"You're going to have to take me off speed dial," he said. "I don't want to waste time being mad with you, but you're still not my favourite person in the world right now. I'm not going to be jumping back here every time you get yourself in trouble."

"I know," she said. "Fletch? Thank you."

He nodded, and grimaced. "I am *really* bleeding a lot here. You might want to hang on. I think we're in need of some medical assistance."

Valkyrie moved her hand till she found his. "I was an idiot for the way I treated you," she said.

"At last," he said, "something we can both agree on."

And they vanished.

62

THEY WALK AMONG US

Kenny lowered his camera as Valkyrie Cain disappeared into thin air. His hands were shaking. He didn't know who the kid with the stupid hair was, but he'd find out. And that *monster*...

This was bigger than he'd ever dared imagine. He stood up on shaking legs, and decided, then and there, that Valkyrie was the name he was going to use for her in the article. It was a good name. Certainly a name that deserved to be spoken aloud alongside Skulduggery Pleasant. But as far as the book was concerned...

He could see it now. A story like this was too big for a mere newspaper article. Much too big. He'd use the article to alert the world, but the full story needed something grander to contain it. It needed a book and an accompanying TV special. He already had a provisional title picked out: "They Walk Among Us: The Sorcerers In Our Midst". A world-changing exposé on the secret magical subculture that exists in every country around the planet.

He decided now that it would be in the book where he would focus on Valkyrie Cain. She was the perfect figure for the audience to identify with, to root for. A normal girl, thrust into a life of danger and excitement, taken under the wing of an honest-to-goodness living skeleton. It was like Peter Parker being bitten by that radioactive spider – a normal kid given extraordinary powers. It was beautiful. It was perfect. It would make him a household name and a billionaire, all in one go.

But it would be in the TV special, not the book and not the article, where Kenny would reveal to the world that badass sorcerer Valkyrie Cain had really been mild-mannered teenager Stephanie Edgley all along.

Because if there was one thing the public was going to love more than a superhero, it was a superhero unmasked – live on air.

Watch out for

Derek's

World Book Day story:

A Skulduggery novelette set after the events of *Death Bringer*,
and coming to bookshops in March 2012...